HUNTER KILLER

Patrick Robinson is the author of eight previous international bestselling thrillers: *Nimitz Class, Kilo Class, H. M. S. Unseen, Seawolf, The Shark Mutiny, Barracuda 945* and *Scimitar SL-2* and, most recently, *Ghost Force*. He is also the author of several non-fiction bestsellers including *True Blue* (with Dan Topolski) and *Born to Win*. He is the co-author with Admiral Sir Sandy Woodward of *One Hundred Days*.

Praise for Patrick Robinson

'An absolutely marvellous thriller writer' Jack Higgins

'The new Frederick Forsyth' *Guardian*

'Rivals the best of Tom Clancy and Dale Brown' *Courier-Times*

'Patrick Robinson is quickly replacing Tom Clancy as the pre-eminent writer of modern naval fiction' *Florida Times-Union*

'Britain's answer to Tom Clancy' Sarah Broadhurst, *Bookseller*

'Watch out for Robinson. He is in the same league as Clancy' *Birmingham Post*

'An edge-of-your-seat terror ride. Patrick Robinson has tapped into our fear to create a spellbinding novel' *Herald Express*

'A gripping tale rich with excitement and suspense' *Tampa Tribune*

'A ripping yarn . . . like a big-screen disaster movie in the making' *Peterborough Evening Telegraph*

'Fast-paced, hi-tech, high thrill action with a nightmare scenario' *Northern Echo*

PATRICK ROBINSON
HUNTER KILLER

arrow books

Published in the United Kingdom by Arrow Books in 2006

3 5 7 9 10 8 6 4 2

Copyright © Patrick Robinson 2005

First published in the United Kingdom in 2005 by William Heinemann

Arrow Books
The Random House Group Limited
20 Vauxhall Bridge Road, London SW1V 2SA

Random House Australia (Pty) Limited
20 Alfred Street, Milsons Point, Sydney
New South Wales 2061, Australia

Random House New Zealand Limited
18 Poland Road, Glenfield
Auckland 10, New Zealand

Random House (Pty) Limited
Isle of Houghton, Corner of Boundary Road & Carse O'Gowrie
Houghton 2198, South Africa

Random House Group Limited Reg. No. 954009

www.randomhouse.co.uk

A CIP catalogue record for this book
is available from the British Library

Papers used by Random House
are natural, recyclable products made from wood grown in
sustainable forests. The manufacturing processes conform to
the environmental regulations of the country of origin

ISBN 9780099474340 (from Jan 2007)
ISBN 0 09 9474344

Typeset by Palimpsest Book Production Limited,
Polmont, Stirlingshire

Printed and bound in Great Britain by
Bookmarque Ltd, Croydon, Surrey

CAST OF PRINCIPAL CHARACTERS

United States Senior Command
Paul Bedford (President of the United States)
Admiral Arnold Morgan (Supreme Commander Operation Tanker)
General Tim Scannell (Chairman of the Joint Chiefs)
Admiral Alan Dickson (Chief of Naval Operations)
Admiral Frank Doran (C-in-C Atlantic Fleet)
Admiral George Morris (Director National Security Agency)
Lt. Commander Jimmy Ramshawe (Personal Assistant Director NSA)
Admiral John Bergstrom (SPECWARCOM)

United States Foreign Services
Charlie Brooks (Envoy US Embassy, Riyadh)
Agent Tom Kelly (CIA Field Officer, Marseilles)
Agent Ray Sharpe (CIA Brazzaville, Congo)
Agent Andy Campese (CIA Chief, Toulouse)
Agent Guy Roland (CIA, Toulouse)
Agent Jack Mitchell (CIA Field Officer North Africa, Rabat, Morocco)

United States Navy

Captain Bat Stimpson (Submarine Commanding Officer, USS *North Carolina*)

Captain David Schnider (Submarine Commanding Officer, USS *Hawaii*)

Captain Tony Pickard (Commanding Officer, USS *Shiloh*)

Lt. Billy Fallon (Helicopter aircrew, USS *Shiloh*)

Lt. Commander Brad Taylor (SEAL Team Leader)

French Senior Command

The President of France

Pierre St Martin (Foreign Minister)

Gaston Savary (Head of the Secret Service, DGSE)

General Michel Jobert (C-in-C Special Operations)

French Navy

Admiral Georges Pires (Commandement des Fusiliers Marine Commandos COMFUSCO)

Admiral Marc Romanet (Flag Officer Submarines)

Captain Alain Roudy (CO hunter killer submarine *Perle*)

Commander Louis Dreyfus (CO hunter killer submarine *Améthyste*)

Lt. Garth Dupont (Commander Frogmen *Améthyste*)

Commander Jules Ventura (Commander Special Forces in Gulf, *Perle*)

Lt. Remé Doumen (Leader Assault Team Two, Saudi Loading Docks)

Seaman Vincent Lefèvre (Assistant to Commander Ventura)

French Special Force Commanders Saudi Arabia
Major Etienne Marot (2/IC Troop Three, Khamis Mushayt)
Major Paul Spanier (CO Troop One, Airbase Assault)
Major Henri Gilbert (Troop Two, Airbase Assault)

French-Appointed Military Commanders Saudi Arabia
Colonel Jacques Gamoudi (Ex-Foreign Legion. C-in-C Saudi Revolutionary Army in Riyadh)
Major Ray Kerman (aka General Ravi Rashood, C-in-C HAMAS, C-in-C Southern Assault Force, Saudi Arabia)

French Foreign Services
Agent Yves Zilber (DGSE, Toulouse)
Michel Phillippes (DGSE, Field Chief, Riyadh)
Major Raul Foy (DGSE, Riyadh)
Envoy Claude Chopin (French Embassy, Brazzaville, Congo)

Members of the Kingdom's Royal Family
Prince Khalid bin Mohammed al-Saud (Playboy)
The King of Saudi Arabia
Prince Nasir Ibn Mohammed al-Saud (Crown Prince)

Saudi Military Personnel
Colonel Sa'ad Kabeer (Commander 8th Armored Brigade, Diversionary Assault Airbase)

Captain Faisal Rahman (al-Qaeda batallion, Riyadh)
Major Abdul Majeed (Tank Commander Airport Assault)
Colonel Bandar (Tank Commander Revolutionary Army, Riyadh)

The Israeli Connection
Ambassador David Gavron (Washington)
Agent David Schwab (Mossad, Marseilles)
Agent Robert Jazy (Mossad, Marseilles)
Daniel Mostel (*Sayanim*, Air Traffic Control, Damascus)

Key International Personnel
Corporal Shane Collins (British Army electronic intercept operator, JSSU, Cyprus)
Sir David Norris (Chairman International Petroleum Exchange, London)
Abdul Gamoudi (Father of Colonel Jacques Gamoudi)

Wives
Mrs Kathy Morgan
Mrs Shakira Rashood

European 'Royalty'
Princess Adele (South London) (deceased).

PROLOGUE

Prince Khalid bin Mohammed al-Saud, aged twenty-six, was enduring a night of fluctuating fortunes. On the credit side, he had just befriended a spectacular looking Gucci-clad blonde named Adele who claimed she was a European princess and was just now clinging on to his left arm. On the debit side, he had just dropped $247,000 playing blackjack in one of the private gaming rooms.

The Casino in Monte Carlo was currently costing Khalid's great-great uncle, the King, around the same amount every month as the first-line combat air strength of the Royal Saudi Air Force. There were currently almost 35,000 Saudi royal princes giving new meaning to the word hedonism.

Like young Prince Khalid, many of them loved Monte Carlo, especially the Casino. And blackjack. And baccarat. And craps. And roulette. And expensive women. And champagne. And caviar. And high-speed motor yachts. Oh, boy; did those princes ever love motor yachts?

Prince Khalid pushed another $10,000-worth of chips towards his new princess and contemplated the sexual pleasures which most certainly awaited him. Plus the fact that, like him, Adele was of royal birth. The King would approve of that. Khalid was so inflamed by her beauty he never even considered the fact that European royalty did not usually come with what sounded suspiciously like a south London accent.

Adele played on, laughing gleefully, fuelled by vintage Krug champagne. She played blackjack with all the subtlety of a train crash. It took her precisely nine minutes and 43 seconds to lose the $10,000, and even Prince Khalid, a young man with no financial brakes whatsoever, found himself groping as much for the anchors as for Adele's superbly turned backside.

'I think we shall seek further pleasures elsewhere,' he smiled. He caught the eye of a champagne waitress and requested a floor manager to settle his evening's account.

Adele's laughter carried across the room but no one turned a hair as the young Saudi prince blithely signed a gambling chit for something in excess of $260,000. It was a bill he would never see. It would simply be added to the losses he had already accumulated that month, totalling more than a million dollars. And then it would be forwarded directly to the King of Saudi Arabia, whose office would send a cheque, sooner or later. These days it was later rather than sooner.

Prince Khalid was a direct descendant of the mighty Bedouin warrior Abdul Aziz, 'Ibn Saud', founder of modern Saudi Arabia, progenitor of more than 40 sons and God knows how many daughters before his death in 1953. The young Prince Khalid was of the ruling line of the House of Saud, but there were thousands of cousins, uncles, brothers and close relatives. The King treated them all with unquestioning generosity.

With such generosity, in fact, that now, towards the end of the first decade of the twenty-first century the great oil kingdom of the Arabian Peninsula now stood teetering on the brink of a financial precipice, because millions and millions of barrels of oil needed to be pumped out of the desert every day purely to feed the colossal financial requirements of young spendthrifts like Khalid bin Mohammed al-Saud.

He was one of dozens who owned huge motor yachts moored in the harbours the length of the French Riviera. His boat, *Shades of Arabia*, a growling 107-foot long, sleek white Godzilla of a powerboat, could not make up its mind whether to remain on the water or to become a guided missile. Built in Florida by the renowned West Bay SonShip Corporation, it boasted five staterooms and for its size was just about the last word in luxury yachts.

The captain of *Shades of Arabia*, Hank Reynolds, out of Seattle, Washington, nearly had a heart attack every time Prince Khalid insisted on taking the helm. It made no difference if the yacht was on a calm open sea, either. Prince Khalid had two speeds. Flat out or stopped.

He had been arrested five times for speeding in various French harbours along the Riviera. Each time he had been fined heavily, twice he had ended up in jail for a few hours, and each time the King's lawyers had bailed him out, on the last occasion stumping up a fine of $100,000. By any standards, Prince Khalid was an expensive luxury for any family, but he could not have cared less. And he was certainly no different from all the other young scions of the House of Saud.

Slipping his hand deftly around Adele's waist, he nodded to the other 10 members of his entourage who were crowded around the roulette wheel, playing for rather smaller stakes. They included his two minders Rashid and Ahmed, both Saudis, three friends from Riyadh, and five young women, two of them Arabian from Dubai and wearing Western dress, three of them of European royal lineage similar to that of Adele.

Outside the imposing white portals of the Casino, three automobiles – two Rolls-Royces and a Bentley – slid into the forecourt attended by a uniformed doorman from the world's most venerable gaming house. Prince Khalid handed him a $100 bill – the equivalent of more than two barrels of oil on the world market – and slipped into the back seat of the lead car with Adele. Rashid and Ahmed, each of them highly paid servants of the King himself, also boarded the gleaming dark-blue Silver Cloud, both of them in the wide front seat.

The other eight were spread evenly between the

other two cars and Prince Khalid instructed his driver. 'Sultan, we will not be returning to the Hermitage for a while – please take us down to the boat.'

'Of course, Your Highness,' replied Sultan, and moved off towards the harbour, followed, line astern, by the other two cars. Three minutes later they pulled alongside *Shades of Arabia*, which rode gently on her lines in a flat calm harbour.

'Good evening, Your Highness,' called the watchman, turning on the gangway light. 'Will we be sailing tonight?'

'Just a short trip, two or three miles offshore, to see the lights of Monaco, then back in by 1 a.m,' replied the Prince.

'Very good, sir,' said the watchman, a young Saudi naval officer who had navigated one of the King's Corvettes in the Gulf Fleet headquarters in Al Jubayl. His name was Bandar and he had been specifically selected by the C-in-C to serve as first officer on *Shades of Arabia* with special responsibilities for the wellbeing of Prince Khalid.

Captain Reynolds liked Bandar and they worked well together, which was just as well for Captain Hank because one word of criticism from young Bandar would have ended his career. The Saudis paid exorbitantly for top personnel from the West, but tolerated no insubordination directed at the royal presence.

Gathered in the magnificent stateroom which contained a bar and a dining area for at least 12, Prince Khalid's party drank more vintage Krug from dewy magnums which cost around $250 each. On the dining-room table there were two large crystal bowls, one containing prime Beluga caviar from Iran, about three pounds of it, never mind $100 an ounce.

The other contained white powder in a similar quantity and was placed next to a polished teak stand upon which were set a dozen small, hand-blown crystal tubes, four and a half inches long, each one exquisitely turned. The content of the second bowl was approximately twice as expensive as the Beluga. It was also in equal demand among the party.

Including the cost of the two stewards in attendance, the refreshments in the stateroom represented the sale of around 600 barrels of Saudi crude on the International Petroleum Exchange in London. That's 6,600 gallons. Prince Khalid's lifestyle swallowed up gas faster than the late lamented Concorde had in its day.

Right now he was blasting the white powder up his nostrils with his regular abandon. He really liked cocaine. It made him feel that he was the right-hand man of the King of Saudi Arabia, the only country in the world that bore the name of the family which ruled it. His name.

Prince Khalid did his best not to confront the undeniable truth that he was as close to useless as made no difference. His Bachelor of Arts degree from a vastly expensive California university was, so far, his only true achievement. But in order for that degree to be awarded his father had had to persuade the King to build a huge new library for the university *and* stock it with thousands of books.

These days, as he wandered the glorious seaports of the Mediterranean all summer, reclining in the opulence of *Shades of Arabia*, it was only when he took his nightly snort of cocaine that he felt he could face the world on equal terms. Indeed, on some evenings, with exactly the right combination of Krug and coke, Prince Khalid felt he could do anything. Tonight was one of those evenings.

The moment his head cleared from the initial rush he ordered Bandar to the bridge to inform Captain Hank that he, Khalid, would be taking the helm as soon as the great motor yacht had cast her lines and was facing more or less in the right direction. 'Have the Captain call me as soon as we're ready,' he added, making absolutely certain that Adele could hear his stern words of command.

Ten minutes later he took Adele up to the enclosed bridge area with its panoramic views of the harbour and assumed command of the yacht. Captain Hank, a burly north-westerner who had spent most of his life on freighters on Puget Sound, moved over to the raised chair of First Officer Bandar, who stood directly behind him. Adele slipped into the navigator's spot next to Prince Khalid.

'She's ready, sir,' said Hank, a worried frown already on his face. 'Steer zero-eight-five, straight past the harbour wall up ahead, then come right to one-three-five for the run offshore . . . and watch your speed, *please*, Your Highness . . . that's a harbourmaster's patrol boat right off your starboard bow . . .'

'No problem, Hank,' replied the prince. 'I feel good tonight; we'll have a nice run.'

And with that he rammed open both throttles, driving the twin 1800hp DDC-MTU 16V2000s to maximum revs, and thundered off the starting blocks. Adele, whose only previous experience of ocean transport was a cheap day trip on the ferry from Gravesend to Tilbury in south-east London, squealed with delight. Hank Reynolds, as usual, nearly went into cardiac arrest.

Shades of Arabia, now with a great white bow wave nearly five feet above the calm surface, charged through Monte Carlo harbour at a speed building to 25 knots. Her powerful surge shot both crystal bowls clean off the dining-room table, and the white dust from the billowing cloud of cocaine caused even the ship's pure-bred Persian cat to believe that at that moment he could probably achieve anything. His purring could be heard in the galley, 50 feet away, like a third diesel engine.

Meanwhile, ships and yachts moored in the harbour rocked violently as the heavy wake from *Shades of Arabia* rolled into them, caused glasses and crockery to crash to the floor, and even people to lose their footing and bounce into walls. For a brief moment the whole point of the Draconian French laws about speeding, which are enforced in every Riviera harbour, became clear to everyone.

Prince Khalid never gave them a thought. He

hurtled past the harbour walls, missing the flashing light on his port side by about 10 feet, and roared out into the open sea. With all care cast aside by the Krug–coke combination, he hammered those big diesels straight towards the deep water, less than a mile offshore.

And out here, with more than 60 fathoms beneath his keel, the prince began a long swerving course through the light swell, to the delight of his guests, all of whom were by now on the top-deck aft viewing area, marvelling at the speed and smoothness of this fabulous ocean-going masterpiece.

No one took the slightest notice of the big search-light a mile astern which belonged to the coastguard patrol launch, summoned by the harbourmaster and now in hot pursuit, making almost 40 knots through the water.

The night was warm but there was heavy rain cloud overhead and it was extremely dark. Too dark to see the massive shape of the ocean liner which rode her gigantic anchor one mile up ahead. In fact, there was a light sea mist, not quite fog, lying in waxen banks over the surface of the sea.

One way and another the 150,000-ton Cunarder, the *Queen Mary 2*, was extremely difficult to see tonight, even with all her night lights blazing. Any approaching vessel might not lock on to her, even 500 yards out, unless the afterguard was watching the radar sweeps very carefully, which Prince Khalid was most certainly not doing. Captain Hank was so busy staring at the blackness ahead that he too was neglecting the screen. But at least he had an excuse, mainly that he was frozen in fear for his life.

At length he snapped to the prince, 'Steady, sir. Come off 15 knots. We just can't see well enough out here . . . this is too fast . . .'

'Don't worry, Hank,' replied Prince Khalid. 'I'm feeling very good. This is fun . . . just for a few minutes I can cast aside the cares of my country and my responsibilities.'

Captain Hank's eyes rolled heavenwards as his boss tried to coax every last ounce of speed out of the yacht, despite the fact they were in another fog bank and visibility at sea level was very poor.

The watchmen on the largest, longest, tallest and widest passenger ship ever built did, however, spot the fast-approaching *Shades of Arabia* from a height close to that of a 21-storey building. They sounded a deafening blast on the horn which could be heard for 10 miles and at the last minute ordered a starboard side reverse thrust in order to swing around and present their sharp bow to the oncoming motor yacht rather than the 1,132-foot hull. But it was too late. Much too late.

Shades of Arabia came knifing through the mist, throttles wide open, everyone laughing and drinking up on the aft deck, Prince Khalid tenderly kissing Adele, one hand on the controls, the other caressing her. Hank Reynolds, who had heard the *Queen Mary*'s horn echo across the water, yelled at the last moment, 'JESUS CHRIST!!' He dived for the throttles but not in time.

10

The 107-foot motor yacht smashed into the great ocean liner, fine on her port bow. The pointed bow of *Shades of Arabia* buried itself 20 feet into the steel plating. The colossal impact caused a huge explosion in the engine room of the prince's pride and joy and the entire ship burst into flames. No one got out but bodyguard Rashid, who had seen the oncoming steel cliff and hurled himself off the top deck 20 feet into the water. Like Ishmael in *Moby Dick*, he alone lived to tell the tale.

Two days later in a palatial private residence in the northern suburbs of the city of Riyadh, Prince Nasir Ibn Mohammed al-Saud, a devout fifty-six-year-old Sunni Muslim, and the heir apparent to the King, was sipping Turkish coffee and staring with horror at the front page of the London *Daily Telegraph*.

Beneath a picture of the badly listing *Queen Mary 2*, spanning six columns was the headline:

DRUNKEN SAUDI PRINCE ALMOST SINKS
THE WORLD'S LARGEST OCEAN LINER
*High-speed motor yacht rams the QM 2
causing mass evacuation in
100 fathoms off Monaco*

The picture showed what was left of *Shades of Arabia* jutting out from the bow of the ship. It clearly showed the heavy list to port on the for'ard half of the mighty ship. But more alarming were the French coastguard helicopters swarming above the stricken

11

liner, evacuating some of the 2,620 passengers and 1,250 crew.

The lifeboats were also being lowered, even though there was no immediate danger of the great ship sinking. But it could not propel itself and would have to be towed into port to be pumped out and temporarily repaired, in preparation for the 2,000-mile journey to the mouth of the Loire, to the shipyards of Alstom Chantiers de l'Atlantique in St-Nazaire where she had been built.

Prince Nasir was appalled. An inset picture of young Prince Khalid was captioned:

> *He died in a fireball precisely as he lived – reckless to the end*

The story named the prince's dead companions, chronicled the consumption of champagne in the Casino. It told of Prince Khalid's losses at the tables, his womanising, his love of cocaine, his incredible wealth. It quoted Lloyd's insurance brokers ranting and raving about their losses, bracing themselves for a huge payout to the Cunard shipping line for collision damage to the $800 million ship, loss of income, law suits from passengers, compensation to the French Government for the costs of the evacuation.

Prince Nasir knew perfectly well this was the biggest story in the world, one which would sweep the television and radio stations of the United States and Europe, as well as every newspaper in the world. And it would go on doing so for several days yet.

The prince loathed everything about it. He hated the humiliation it brought upon his country. He detested the flagrant defiance of the Koran. And he abhorred the sheer self-indulgence of Prince Khalid and the irreparable damage to Saudi Arabia's image caused by this lunatic spending of petro-dollars by young men in their twenties.

Prince Nasir would one day be king. And the only obstruction standing between him and the throne of Saudi Arabia was his well-publicised and vehement disapproval of the lifestyles of the royal family. For the moment, however, he was the nominated Crown Prince, a wise and devout Muslim who had made it quite clear that when he ascended the throne it was all going to end.

Nasir was the outstanding political and business mind in the Kingdom, at home in the corridors of power in London, Paris, Brussels and the Middle East. The King valued his counsel in a wary and cautious way, but, of course, Prince Nasir had countless enemies: sons, brothers and grandsons of the King.

There had been three attempts to assassinate him. But the Saudi populace loved him. He alone stood up for them, gave interviews revealing the real reason for the drop in their state incomes from $30,000 to $7,000 over 15 years: the astronomical cost of the royal family.

Nasir was a tall, bearded man, descended like most of the royal family from the great Ibn Saud. For him the call of the desert was never far away. Most evenings he would be driven out to the cooling, lonely sands north of the city, and there he would rendezvous with friends, and his servants could spread upon the desert floor a vast near-priceless rug from Iran. A three-sided tent would be erected, and there they would dine and talk of the great revolution to come, a revolution which would surely one day topple the ruling branch of the House of Saud.

Today the prince rose to his feet muttering, as he had done many times before, 'This country is like France before the Revolution. One family bleeding the state to death. In eighteenth-century Paris, it was the Bourbon kings. In twenty-first-century Riyadh, it's the al-Saud family.'

And then, louder now, as he hurled the newspaper aside, '*THIS HAS TO STOP!*'

CHAPTER ONE

King Khalid International Airport
Tuesday 6 May 2009

The black Cadillac stretch limousine moved swiftly around the public drop-off point to a wide double gate, already opened by the two armed guards. On each wing of the big American automobile fluttered two pennants, the green and blue ensigns of the Royal Saudi Naval Forces.

Both guards saluted as the instantly recognisable limo swept past and out towards the wide runway of Terminal Three, the exclusive enclave of Saudia, the national airline.

Inside the limousine was a solitary passenger in Arab dress: Crown Prince Nasir Ibn Mohammed, Deputy Minister of the Armed Forces. Both sentries saluted as Prince Nasir went by, heading straight for the runway where one of the King's newest Boeing 747s was awaiting him, engines idling preparatory to take off. Every other flight was on hold until the meticulously punctual Prince Nasir was in the air.

The prince was escorted to the steps of the aircraft by both the chief steward and a senior naval officer. Prince Nasir's own son, the twenty-six-year-old Commodore Fahad Ibn Nasir, served in a Red Sea frigate, and his father was always treated like an admiral wherever he travelled in the Kingdom.

He was also the only passenger on board, and the moment he was seated in the upstairs first-class section the door was tightly secured and the pilot opened the throttles. The royal passenger jet, revelling in its light load, roared off down the runway and screamed into the clear blue skies, directly into the hot south wind off the desert, before banking left towards the Gulf, and then north-west across Iraq, towards Syria.

It was almost unheard of for a senior member of the royal family to travel alone, without even a bodyguard, but this was different. The 747 was not going even halfway to Prince Nasir's final destination. He used it only to get out of Saudi Arabia, to another Arab country. His real destination was entirely another matter.

A suitcase at the rear of the upstairs area contained his Western clothes and, as soon as the flight was airborne, Prince Nasir changed into a dark grey suit, blue shirt and a maroon-patterned silk Hermès tie, completed with a solid gold clip in the shape of a desert scimitar. He wore plain black loafers, hand-made in London, with dark grey socks.

The suitcase also contained a briefcase, containing several documents, which the Prince removed, and he then packed away his white Arabian *thobe*, red and white *ghutra* headdress with its double cord, the *aghal*. He had left King Khalid International Airport, named for his late great-uncle, as an Arab. He would arrive in Damascus every inch the international businessman.

When they touched down two hours later, a limousine from the Saudi Embassy met him and drove him directly to the regular midday Air France flight to Paris. The aircraft sat with its passengers in their seats; although none of them knew it, they were awaiting the arrival of the Arabian prince.

The aircraft had in fact pulled back from the jetway and a special flight of stairs had been placed against the forward entrance. Prince Nasir's car halted precisely at those stairs, where an Air France official waited to escort him to his seat. Four rows, eight seats that is, had been booked in the name of the Saudi Embassy on Al-Jala's Avenue. Prince Nasir sat in seat 1A. The rest of the seats in the row would remain empty all the way to Roissy-Charles de Gaulle Airport, 19 miles north of Paris.

The cabin crew served a special luncheon, prepared by the cooks at the embassy, of curried chicken with rice, cooked Indian-style, followed by fruit juice and sweet pastries. Prince Nasir, the most devout of Muslims, had never touched alcohol in his life and disapproved fiercely of those of his countrymen who did. The late Prince Khalid of Monte Carlo had had many failings. The great man knew, beyond any doubt, of the antics of that particular deceased member of his family.

They flew on across Turkey and the Balkan States,

finally crossing the Alps and dropping down above the lush French farmland lying south of the forest of Ardenne, over the Seine, and into north-west Paris.

Once more, Prince Nasir endured no formalities or checks. He disembarked before anyone else, down a private flight of stairs, where a jet-black, unmarked French government car waited to drive him directly to the heavily guarded Elysée Palace on rue St-Honoré, the official residence of the Presidents of France since 1873.

It was a little after 4 p.m. in Paris, the flight from Damascus having taken five hours, with a two-hour time gain. Two officials were waiting at the President's private entrance and Prince Nasir was escorted immediately to the President's private apartment on the first floor overlooking rue de l'Elysée.

The President was awaiting him in a large modern drawing room, hung with a selection of six breathtaking Impressionist paintings – two by Renoir, two by Claude Monet and one each by Degas and Pissarro. One hundred million dollars would not have bought them.

The President greeted Prince Nasir in impeccable English, the language agreed for the forthcoming conversation. By previous arrangement, no one would listen in. No ministers. No private secretaries. No translators. The following two hours before dinner would bring a meaning to the word 'privacy' rarely, if ever, attained in international politics.

'Good afternoon, Your Highness,' said the President

in greeting. 'I trust my country's travel arrangements have been satisfactory?'

'Quite perfect,' replied the prince, smiling. 'No one could have asked for more.' The two men knew each other vaguely, but could not be called friends, let alone blood brothers. Yet.

The door to the drawing room was closed and two uniformed military guards, summoned from the exterior security force, stood sentry in the outside corridor. The President of France himself poured coffee for his guest from a silver service laid out on a magnificent Napoleonic sideboard. Prince Nasir complimented the President on the beauty of the piece and was amused when the President replied, 'It probably belonged to Bonaparte himself – the Palais de l'Elysée was occupied by Napoleon's sister Caroline for much of the nineteenth century.'

Prince Nasir loved the traditions of France. A highly educated man, he not only had a Bachelor of Arts degree in English Literature from Harvard, but also a *maîtrise* (Master's degree) in European History from the University of Paris. The knowledge that Bonaparte himself might have been served from this very sideboard somehow made the coffee taste all the richer.

'Now, Your Highness,' said the President, 'you must tell me your story, and why you wished to have a talk with me in this most private manner, at such very short notice.' He was keenly aware of the way most high-born Arabs operated: talk about almost anything else for half an hour before tackling the main subject.

19

Prince Nasir knew time was precious at this level. The balding, burly politician who stood before him had, after all, an entire country to run. He decided to speak carefully, weighing his words appropriately.

'Sir,' he said. 'My country is in terminal decline. In the past 20 years the ruling family – my own – has managed to spend over $100 billion of our cash reserves. We are probably down to our last $15 billion. And soon that will be $10 billion and then $5 billion. Twenty years ago my people received a generous share of the oil wealth that Allah has bestowed upon us. Around $30,000 per capita. Today that figure is close to $7,000. Because we can afford no more.'

'But, of course,' replied the President of France, 'you do own 25 per cent of all the world's oil . . .'

Prince Nasir smiled. 'Our problem, sir, is not the creation of wealth,' he said. 'I suppose we could close down modern Saudi Arabia and all go back to the desert and sit there allowing our vast oil revenues to accrue, and make us once more one of the richest nations on earth. However, that would plainly be impracticable.

'Our problem is the reckless spending of money by a ruling family which is now irredeemably corrupt. And a huge percentage of that expenditure goes on the family itself. Thousands and thousands of royal princes are being kept in a style probably not seen on this planet since . . . well, since the Bourbon royal family's domination of your own country. I have stated it often enough. Saudi Arabia is like France before the Revolution. Monsieur Le

President, I intend to emulate your brave class warriors of the late eighteenth century. In my own country, I intend to re-enact that renunciation of the rights of the nobility.'

The President's early left-wing leanings were well documented. Indeed, he had risen to power from a base as the communist mayor of a small town in Brittany. In a previous incarnation, this particular French President would have stormed the gates of Paris in the vanguard of Revolution. Prince Nasir was aware that use of the word 'Bourbon' would elicit instant sympathy.

The President shrugged, a deep Gallic heave. Then he held out both hands, palms upwards. 'I knew of course some of the difficulties in Saudi Arabia . . . but I put it down mostly to your closeness to the Americans.'

'That too is a grave problem, sir,' replied Prince Nasir. 'My people long for freedom from the Great Satan. But this King is a vigorous globally ambitious man, aged only forty-eight, and under him it would be impossible. We are bound up with the the infidels so tightly . . . even though the majority of Saudis wish devoutly that they could be once more a God-fearing nation of pure Muslims. Not terrorists, just a religious people in tune with the words of the Prophet, rather than the grasping material creeds of the United States.

'I tell you this, sir. If Osama bin Laden suddenly materialised in Riyadh and ran for President, or even King, he would win in a landslide.'

The President of France smiled uneasily. 'I imagine there are many Saudi princes who would not agree *exactement* with your views,' he said. 'I don't imagine that young man who almost sunk the *Queen Mary* last week would have been . . . er . . . too *sympathétique*.'

'He most certainly would not,' said Prince Nasir, frowning. 'He was a prime example of the endless corruption in my country. His type are wastrels, bleeding the country dry with their excesses. If they continue in this way, we will be in danger of becoming a godless Third World country. To stand in one of our royal palaces today is to watch something close to the fall of the Roman Empire!'

'Or the British,' countered the President, smiling more comfortably. 'May I offer you more coffee from Napoleon Bonaparte's sideboard?'

Although he barely knew him, Prince Nasir had always liked the French President, and he was extremely glad to have the opportunity to get to know him better.

'Thank you,' he said. And the two men walked across the room towards the silver coffee pot. They were already in step.

'Well, Your Highness, you are outlining to me a very regrettable state of affairs. And I agree; if I were the Crown Prince of such a nation I too would be extremely exercised by the situation. But, to the outside world, Saudi Arabia looks very much like the one constant in a turbulent Middle East.'

'That may have been the case 20 years ago, but it

is most certainly not so today. It is my belief that this corrupt ruling family must be overthrown, its excesses removed, the lifestyles of the princes terminated. And the colossal spending on military hardware from the United States ceased forthwith. Everything has to change, if we are to survive as the prosperous nation we once were.'

The prince rose to his feet and paced the room. 'Remember, sir, as a nation we are not yet 80 years old. The active members of this family are just a generation, maybe two, from men who grew up in goat-hair tents and followed the rhythms of the desert, from oasis to oasis, subsisting on dates and camel's milk . . .'

'You are surely not advocating a return to those days?' asked the President.

'No, sir, I am not. But I know we must return part of the way to our Bedouin roots in the desert, to the written creeds of the Prophet Mohammed. I do not wish to see our sons spending millions of dollars on Western luxuries. '*Wallahi!*' he exclaimed – *By God* – 'What could that boy Khalid possibly have been doing with those cheap women on a yacht fit for a President, out of his mind on drugs and alcohol?'

'Very probably having the most wonderful time,' smiled the French President, his mind slipping briefly away from matters of state. 'But I do of course understand. It plainly is not right that there should be thousands of these young men ransacking the Saudi Treasury every month, at the expense of the people.

23

I think you are very probably correct. Something will soon need to be done. Otherwise the people will rise up against the King and you might be looking at a bloodbath . . . as we had in Paris in the eighteenth century. And, by the sound of it, equally as justified.'

Prince Nasir sipped his coffee. 'The problem is,' he said, 'our King is quite extraordinarily powerful. Not only does he pay all of the family's bills – none of the young princes ever sees a bill, for anything. Every charge they incur goes directly to the King, from all over the world.

'But he also controls the Army, the Air Force and the Navy, plus all of the security forces. Only he can pay them. And they are loyal to him alone.'

'How large is the Saudi Army these days?'

'Almost 90,000 – nine brigades, three armoured, five mechanised and one airborne. They're supported by five artillery battalions, and a separate Royal Guard Regiment of three light-infantry battalions. The armoured brigades have almost 300 highly advanced tanks, the M1A2 Abrams from the United States. Of course, one of our armoured brigades is entirely French-equipped.'

Though well out of his depth, the President nodded sagely. 'And the Navy?'

'It's the smallest of our services. Just a few corvettes in the Red Sea, and a few guided missile frigates, purchased, as you will be aware, from France. But the Navy is not our greatest strength.'

'And the Air Force?'

24

'This is our strongest force. We have more than 200 combat aircraft in the Royal Saudi Air Force, with 18,000 personnel. They are deployed at four key airfields. And their mission is very simply to keep the Kingdom safe, in particular to keep our oil installations safe.'

'Well, Your Highness, I would assess that is a *magnifique* amount of firepower to put down a revolution. If our Bourbon kings and princes had possessed half of that, they'd still be here, raping and pillaging the land.'

Prince Nasir laughed, despite himself. He sipped his coffee, and then said, 'Sir, the Achilles heel of the Saudi King is not the ability of the military to fight. It's his ability to pay them.'

'But he has all the money in the world, flowing in every month, to achieve that,' replied the President.

'But what if he didn't?' asked Prince Nasir Ibn Mohammed. 'What if he didn't have that money?'

'You mean, if someone took all the oil away from him?' said the President. 'That sounds most unlikely given all those armoured brigades and fighter jets.'

'No, sir. What if the oil was taken out of the equation? What if it simply no longer flowed, and the King had no income to pay the armed services? What then?'

'You mean, supposing someone destroyed the Saudi oil industry?'

'Only for a little while,' replied the Prince. 'Only for a little while. Let me elaborate.'

Momentarily stunned by the enormous implications of what he was hearing, the President briefly stopped listening to the prince. When he heard his voice again, it was that of a man speaking a long way off.

'. . . the Red Sea terminals should be hit and destroyed. Another prime target is Safaniya, the largest offshore oilfield in the world, 160 miles north of Dhahran. The reserves out there number 30 billion barrels − that's around 500,000 barrels a day for about 165 years.

'The biggest terminal on the Gulf is Ra's Tannurah which has capacity for 4.3 million barrels of oil a day. The loading dock is offshore at the Sea Island terminal where Platform No. 4 pumps over two million barrels a day into the world's waiting tankers. A direct hit on that platform would effectively close down Ra's Tannurah, especially if the pipeline from Abqaiq were taken care of.

'The final, critical hit should be slightly north, at Ra's al Ju'aymah, which has the capacity for 4.2 million barrels a day. It is the principal loading bay for liquid petroleum, propane.' If that happened, the prince added wryly, the whole of Japan would find itself eating a great deal of sushi, accompanied by stone-cold sake.

He continued. 'The terminals of Ra's Tannurah and Ra's al Ju'aymah, plus the Red Sea ports, load Saudi Arabian oil products into 4,000 tankers a year. You will not be surprised to know that ARAMCO − the Arabian American Oil Company − owned

100 per cent by the Saudi Government since 1976, is the largest oil company on earth. Its headquarters are in the eastern province city of Dhahran, and its capability is approximately 10 million barrels a day, though since the year 2000 it has pumped considerably less.

'Twenty-six per cent of all the oil on the planet lies beneath the Saudi desert – that's around 262 billion barrels, which, at 5.5 million a day, ought to last for some 130 years. The Saudi royal family are the sole proprieters of ARAMCO, which owns every last drop . . .'

The President listened to Prince Nasir with a growing sense of excitement. What the prince was suggesting was enormously risky and startlingly audacious, but the payoff seemed worth it. All he needed now was someone to kickstart the operation and take care of the practicalities. And he knew exactly where to start.

5.00 a.m. the next morning
The Foreign Office
Quai d'Orsay, Paris
Pierre St Martin, the Foreign Minister of France, and a future presidential hopeful, stood beside a large portrait of Napoleon placed on an easel on the left-hand side of his lavish office. Before him stood M. Gaston Savary, the tall saturnine head of the French Secret Service – the Direction Générale de la Sécurité Extérieure (DGSE), successor to the former, internationally feared SDECE, the counter-espionage service.

27

The two men had never met before, and the elegant St Martin, was, quite frankly, amazed that he had been summoned to his office at this ungodly hour of the day, apparently to converse with this . . . this spy from *La Piscine* – the kind of man patrician politicians in London refer to as 'Johnny Raincoat'.

La Piscine was the government nickname for the DGSE, so-called because of the proximity of the bleak 10-storey Secret Service building to a municipal swimming pool in Caserne des Tourelles. M. Savary operated out of 128, boulevard Mortier over in the 20th *arrondissement*, about as far west as it is possible to go and still be in the City of Light. It was not the kind of neighbourhood in which you'd expect to find an urbane Foreign Minister. The suave and expensively tailored M. St Martin had never been to *La Piscine* before.

Nonetheless, they had both been ordered to the sumptuous offices on the Quai d'Orsay by none other than the President of France himself. And the current incumbent of the Elysée Palace was due here in the next few minutes.

M. St Martin, who had spent the night at the apartment of an actress generally considered to be one of the most beautiful in France, was a great deal more irritated by the intrusion into his life than M. Savary.

Both men were around the same age, fiftyish, but the Secret Service chief was a lifelong career officer in undercover operations. For him the call in the middle of the night was routine. No matter the time, he was instantly operational, and he had for 10 years been responsible for the planning of black operations conducted on behalf of the Government of France, using both military forces or civilian agents.

A lithe, fit and slightly morose man, M. Savary had even taken part personally in various French adventures. He would, of course, admit nothing, but he was reputed to have been operational in the attack and subsequent sinking of the Greenpeace freighter the *Rainbow Warrior* in Auckland Harbour, New Zealand, in July 1985. Interference with the Pacific nuclear tests conducted by France? *NON! JAMAIS!* was M. Savary's response to that.

'Would you care to remove your raincoat?' asked the Foreign Minister. 'Since we are shortly to be in the presence of our President?'

Without a word Savary took the coat off and slung it over the back of a near-priceless Louis XV chair.

St Martin stared at the spy's raincoat over the back of chair, and winced. He pressed a button to summon the butler to bring them coffee, but his main intention was to get rid of the offending garment owned by Jean-Claude Raincoat or whatever his damned name was. M. St Martin had always held a sneaking regard for the Bourbons and their excellent taste in furniture.

'I don't suppose you have slightest idea what this is all about?' he said.

'Absolutely none,' replied the intelligence chief. 'I just received a telephone call from the Palais de l'Elysée and was told the President wished to see me in your office at 5.15 a.m. Here I am, *n'est-ce pas?*'

'My summons was exactly the same. My mobile phone rang at 1.30 a.m. God knows what this is all about.'

'Maybe Le President is about to declare war?'

'There is always that possibility.'

Savary smiled for the first time. But just then their coffee arrived, for three, as requested. And M. St Martin asked the butler to pour two cups before instructing him to hang the raincoat in the hall closet.

Almost immediately a phone bell rang on his enormous desk and a voice announced that the presidential car had arrived at the portals of the Foreign Office. Pierre St Martin poured the third cup of coffee himself.

Three minutes later he was astonished to see that the President was entirely alone: no secretary, no aides, no officials. He closed the door himself and said quietly, 'Pierre, Gaston, thank you for coming so early. Would you please ensure our discussion is conducted entirely in secret? Perhaps a guard outside the door?'

St Martin spoke briefly into the telephone, handed the President a cup of coffee and motioned for everyone to be seated, the President on a fine upright drawing-room chair, the Secret Service chief on the Louis XV piece lately occupied by his raincoat, while the Foreign Minister himself retreated behind his desk.

'Gentlemen,' said the President, 'approximately two hours ago one of the most important princes in the Saudi royal family left my residence to fly home in a French Air Force jet to Damascus, and then in his own aircraft to Riyadh. His visit with me was so private, so confidential, not even the most senior members of staff at the Saudi Embassy here in Paris were aware of his presence in the city.

'He came not only to inform me that the financial excesses of the Saudi ruling family would shortly bankrupt his country, but to propose a way to resolve the problem – to the very great advantage of himself, and, it must be said, for France.'

St Martin swiftly interjected. 'Doubtless inspired by that young Saudi prince who nearly sank the *Queen Mary* last week?'

'I think so,' replied the President. 'But the problem of 35,000 princes, all members of the same family, spending up to a million dollars a month on fast living, has been vexing the reformist element in the Saudi Government for several years. According to my visitor the time has come for that to cease.'

M. Savary spoke for the first time. 'I imagine he mentioned the Saudi King is heavily protected by a fiercely loyal Army, Air Force and Navy. So, if I follow your line of thinking correctly, an overthrow of that part of the family is more or less out of the question.'

'Indeed he did, Gaston. He mentioned it in great detail. And he pointed out that the only person in the entire Kingdom who could pay the armed services is

31

the King, who receives all the oil revenues of the country and pays all the bills for his family.'

'So the armed services would be most unlikely to turn against him,' said M. Savary.

'Most unlikely,' agreed the President. 'Unless for some reason the vast revenues from the oilfields ceased to exist . . .'

'And the King could no longer pay them, correct?' said M. Savary.

'Precisely,' replied the President.

'Sir, I have no doubt you are as aware as I am that those Saudi oilfields are guarded by a steel ring of personnel and armaments,' continued Savary. 'They're virtually impregnable, understandably, since the whole country is 100 per cent dependent upon them, from the richest to the poorest.'

'Well, we have not reached that point in the conversation yet, Gaston. But I would like to inform you, in the broadest possible terms, what the prince was proposing.'

'I, for one, am paying keen attention,' said Pierre St Martin.

'Excellent,' replied the President. 'Because the information I am about to impart might be of critical importance to our nation. His Highness Prince Nasir proposes the following. Someone hits the oilfields and knocks out the main pumping station and the three or four biggest loading terminals on both the Red Sea and the Persian Gulf.

'Two days later, with Saudi Arabia's economy effectively laid to waste, a small, highly trained fighting force attacks the Saudi military city in the south-west of the country near the Yemen border, and, while the military is in disarray, another highly specialised force goes in and takes Riyadh.

'They knock out a couple of palaces, eliminate the royal family, take the television station and the radio station and sweep the Crown Prince to power. He then appears on nationwide television and announces he has taken control, and the corrupt regime of the present King has been summarily swept away.'

'And you are proposing we somehow take part in all this?' asked St Martin, incredulous.

The President paused. 'Certainly not. I am merely suggesting we examine the feasibility of it.'

'And if the military coup was carried out, with our assistance, and the prince takes over Saudi Arabia, what could be in it for us?' asked Gaston Savary.

'Well, as his best friends and closest allies, and a sworn opponent to the ambitions of the United States, France would be awarded every single contract to rebuild the oil installations, and we would become the sole marketing agents for all Saudi Arabian oil for the next 100 years. Anyone wishes to buy, they buy it from us. Which means we effectively control world oil prices.'

'And how long would it take us to rebuild the oil installations?'

'Perhaps two years. Maybe less.'

'And what about that big Saudi Army and Air Force?'

The President shrugged. 'What about them? They would have no alternative but to switch their allegiance, to serve the new King. After all, they cannot serve a dead one, *n'est-ce pas*? And no one else could possibly pay them but the new ruler. And even then things would be rather tight for a few months, until some oil began to flow, probably in the Gulf terminals.'

'You really think this could be achieved, sir?' said Gaston. 'Militarily, I mean?'

'I have no idea. But Prince Nasir does. And he says that if it is not achieved Saudi Arabia is doomed.'

'What kind of a premise will he campaign on?' asked St Martin.

'Well, he won't really need to campaign, will he? Not if he simply seizes power. But he will immediately assure the country that the massive financial stipends for the princes will end forthwith. Which will save his treasury maybe $250 billion a year.

'He will also advocate an immediate return to pure Muslim worship of the Wahaabi persuasion. You understand: strict rules of prayer, no alcohol, the unquestioned word of the Koran and the teachings of the Prophet. There will be no more cosying up to American politicians, and basically the country will return to its Bedouin roots, to the old ways of life.

'They will heed the call of the desert, and bring up their children according to the old traditions, as indeed Prince Nasir has brought up his own. And there will certainly be no more financing of terrorism. And no further need to pay vast sums of protection money to groups who might otherwise attack Saudi Arabia. I am referring, of course, to hundreds of millions of dollars directed to al-Qaeda.

'Once Prince Nasir has severed his ties with the United States, there will be no further danger from the fundamentalist groups. And of course we may also expect far greater Saudi support for the Palestinians.'

'But surely this will cause chaos on the world oil markets?' said St Martin. 'Absolute chaos.'

'I have no doubt it will. But this won't affect us, because we will rid ourselves of our Saudi contracts long before anything happens. We will sign new two-year agreements with other Middle Eastern countries for all of our oil and gas requirements. That way we will ensure the continuation of oil into France during Saudi Arabia's period of rebuilding, and procure new and better contracts more favourable to our country.'

'But what about the world oil shortages? This would just about bankrupt Japan, and cripple even the mighty economy of the United States. Our European partners will also be hurt. Gasoline could go to $150 a barrel.' St Martin was just beginning to look particularly distraught.

'I agree,' said the President. 'But if Prince Nasir is correct, all this will happen anyway, if the Saudi population takes to the streets in protest against the royal family. As for the oil prices going through the roof

– well, can you imagine anything more appealing to the country which effectively controls world sales of Saudi oil?'

'But, sir,' said St Martin, 'the Saudi fields are the only stabiliser in the entire world's markets. Remember how they saved the day by producing millions of extra barrels in 1991, and then again after 9/11 when they pumped almost five million extra barrels to save the market? Petrol prices hardly went up by a single franc.

'Saudi Arabia *is* the world market, the saviour of the world's economy in times of crisis. It's the only nation which can produce extra oil. What are its reserves? Two to three million barrels a day, if necessary, at any one time? Can you imagine the reaction of the United States if anyone ever found out we were in any way implicated?'

'What if no one ever found out we were implicated?' replied the President. 'What if no one ever knew? What if it all appeared to be just an Arab matter – a military coup, by the people, against their corrupt rulers; a kind of insurrection which spread, most unfortunately, to the oil wells?'

'Sir, do you think it possible such a momentous action by France could ever be kept secret?'

'Again,' said the President, 'I cannot be certain. But the reason we are in this room, at this unearthly hour of the day, is because we have been asked for help by a senior representative of one of our major trading partners . . . a partner which would feel obliged, in future, to purchase all of its military hardware from

France – warships, fighter aircraft and weaponry worth billions.

'Therefore, gentlemen, I ask you to please find out what we can do, how quietly we can do it, and whether we can stay sufficiently remote so as never to warrant suspicion of – how shall I put it? – any questionable dealings.

'Meanwhile as far as I am concerned this conversation never took place. You are the only two people in France who know anything of the prince's visit, and of the proposals he made. Perhaps you would be good enough to contact me when you have gathered your thoughts.'

And, with that, the man who considered himself to be the most powerful figure in the European Union stood up, replaced his coffee cup on the tray and walked to the door.

Neither Pierre St Martin nor Gaston Savary could recover swiftly enough even to open it for him. Both the French Foreign Minister and the head of France's Secret Service were in shock. They stood open-mouthed at the departing President, momentarily stunned by the enormity of the task he had set them.

'*Sacré merde!*' muttered Pierre St Martin.

Friday morning, 9 May
Paris
Gaston Savary was alone, driving his black Citroën staff car through heavy commuter traffic into the remotest outpost of the north-west suburbs of the city. He was

going against the incoming traffic but it was still outlandishly busy, with queues of buses, vans and trucks all the way, as always, in both directions. More than three and a half million people fought their way into, and out of, Paris every working day.

He reached the outer suburb of Taverny and drove up to the guardhouse at the entrance to one of the most secretive compounds in Europe – the headquarters of France's Commandement des Opérations Spéciales (COS), the joint service establishment which controlled the worldwide special ops activities of all three French armed forces.

As head of the largely civilian French Secret Service, Gaston Savary was a regular visitor, and both duty guards wished him '*Bonjour*' before waving him through to a waiting escort who stepped into the front seat of the Citroën.

They drove towards the offices of the 1st Marine Parachute Infantry Regiment, the prime special ops unit in France, the direct equivalent of Britain's SAS and the USA's Navy SEALs and Rangers. A formidable black ops outfit, it clandestinely provided special training and even assistance to foreign countries; in addition, it also provided offensive action, if called upon to, as it had been in West Africa in 2008. It also conducted its own military intelligence gathering and in recent years had been at the sharp end of most French counter-terrorist operations. Two heavily armed helicopter squadrons stood under its command.

Gaston Savary instructed his escort, a young Army

lieutenant, to park the car. He let himself out at the main entrance, where another young officer greeted him and took him immediately to the special ops C-in-C, General Michel Jobert.

The two men were old acquaintances but nonetheless Savary handed over a letter, certified by the office of the Foreign Minister of France, instructing the general to work carefully and in the strictest confidence with the bearer, examining the project scrupulously, before arriving at one of two conclusions: possible or impossible.

And so it was that, in the most clandestine manner imaginable, France's two most senior undercover operators began their feasibility test on behalf of their government; and in a sense, on behalf of Prince Nasir Ibn Mohammed of Saudi Arabia.

In the next 15 minutes General Jobert's dark bushy eyebrows rarely resumed their normal position on the lower part of his forehead. He was truly astounded at the scale of the proposition. Gaston Savary counted at least a dozen softly exclaimed '*Mon Dieus*'.

But the proposition was real enough: the President of France wanted a professional opinion; could the Saudi oil industry be brought to its knees, by military attack, for a period of around two years? And whether in the ensuing days, with the Saudi economy in ruins, it would be possible to subdue the Saudi armed forces and then take the capital city of Riyadh? All without France appearing to have the slightest involvement.

The first three proposals – the oil, the surrender of the Army and the capture of Riyadh – were probably possible. In the measured opinion of General Jobert the collapse of the economy would leave an army somewhat disinclined to fight anyone. The problem was the fourth: could France somehow make it all possible, with a substantial military involvement, and yet still remain anonymous?

On further reflection, General Jobert thought 'absolutely not'. So did Gaston Savary. Which essentially meant that, if he took their advice, the President would have to decline the offer of the Saudi prince to make France its sole supplier of future military hardware, and the sole world agent for all Saudi oil products. And that particular '*Non*' would ultimately represent the rejection of an opportunity for the hard-pressed French Republic to earn several hundred billion dollars. That was one scenario both Jobert and Savary suspected might not sit too well with a President whose country had been known to operate almost exclusively out of a sense of unfettered self-interest in recent years.

The general, who, until that moment, had as yet not received the slightest indication as to why he was meeting Gaston, read again the second page of the letter from Pierre St Martin. It contained an outline of the requirements which Prince Nasir considered necessary to cripple the Saudi oil industry.

Priority number one was the destruction of the world's largest processing complex at Abqaiq, situated 25 miles inland from the Gulf of Bahrain.

Abqaiq was the destination of all crude oil from the Saudi south, particularly from Ghawar, the most productive oilfield on earth. Beneath the shifting desert sands, right here, 60 miles south-west of Dhahran, lay 70 billion barrels' worth of oil.

Close to Abqaiq was Pump Station No. 1 which sent some 900,000 barrels of light crude per day 700 miles up and over the Aramah Mountains, to the Red Sea oil port of Yanbu al-Bahr. If Pump Station No. 1 went down, the massive loading terminals of both Yanbu, and, 90 miles to the south, Rabigh, would be finished. So would the huge refineries in the area, including the enormous complexes at Medina and Jiddah.

The general continued to read, his expression changing frequently as he took in what was in essence the scenario outlined by Prince Nasir to the President at the Elysée Palace earlier that week.

'You want me to hit that lot?' he asked incredulously, once he had finished reading. 'That's probably 10 different targets. Three would be difficult. I suppose we could get three hit squads in there. But they'd need backup and the explosive would weigh God knows how much. We'd need 40 men in each team. But 10 targets? *Mon Dieu!* I'd say that would be impossible. We'd have a better chance bombing it.'

'That, of course, is out of the question,' said Gaston Savary. 'Remember, the President's main requirement is secrecy. If we sent in a squadron of fighter bombers, they'd know the nationality of the attackers in about 10 minutes. The Saudis have a lot of very sophisticated US-built surveillance kit.'

Both men ruminated on the apparent hopelessness of step one and a mood of tacit acceptance prevailed. The critical path of the operation required a succession of 10 swift, devastating hits on the greatest oil-producing network in the Middle East. And so far as General Jobert could see, it was militarily impossible, either by land or by air. Impossible, at least, without getting caught.

General Jobert paced the room. He was an impressive man, not tall but built like a middleweight, with thick black curly hair and a swarthy complexion, very French, equally pragmatic, with the merest suggestion that somewhere in the family tree there may have lurked a North African ancestor.

His appearance was in stark contrast to that of the lean, pale-skinned, 6 foot 2 inch Gaston Savary, whose mournful expression concealed a keen sense of irony and a somewhat sarcastic sense of humour. However, this particular morning they were thinking as one, both of them aware that outright rejection of the President's request would not be a good idea. For either of them.

The general pondered further. Land attack? *Impossible.* Air attack? *Non, absolument non.* Then he brightened a little. *How about by sea?*

Gaston Savary looked up sharply. 'You mean frogmen, brought in by submarine, swimmers who could fix sticky bombs on the offshore rigs?'

'*Exactement!*'

'Have you checked the depth of the water lately? I mean, around Abqaiq, which is not only in the middle of the desert, but also the key to the entire operation?' Gaston loved the rhetorical question.

But the general smiled; it was the smile of a man one move from checkmate. 'As a civilian, you of course do not understand everything about the military mind,' he said. 'However, you will have heard of cruise missiles. And these days there are some very effective ones, that fly out of nowhere.'

'In these days of intense surveillance, nothing comes out of nowhere,' replied the Secret Service chief. 'There's always someone watching.'

'True,' replied the general. 'But the chances of detecting a missile fired from a submerged submarine are slight. I'm talking about a missile programmed to fly over the ocean and then over the middle of the desert. I assure you no one will pick that up. The element of surprise is too great.'

Savary knew when he heard something important being said. He paused for a moment, nodding his head slightly. And then he asked, 'Do you really think we could put a submarine in the Gulf without anyone knowing? And then have it unleash a barrage of cruise missiles at the shores of Saudi Arabia without anyone finding out?'

'They'd find out when the oil terminals, pumping stations and refineries went up in smoke. But they'd never, in their wildest dreams, guess who the culprits were, and, above all, how they'd done it.'

'And what about the other coast?' asked Gaston Savary. 'The Red Sea? You can't even get in there without travelling on the surface.'

General Jobert shrugged. 'A submarine would be logged through Suez. But so would many, many other ships. But it would not be logged through the southern end. The Red Sea can be traversed underwater, and it is not unusual for a French submarine to make that journey. Also, the Red Sea is extremely deep in places.'

'And we also have the justification of a motive in our favour,' said Savary. 'We are great friends with Saudi Arabia. And why would anyone, in their right mind, want to blow up the oil system which keeps not only us but most of the civilised world in business? No one would suspect us. No one.'

'I have no doubt the President of France considered that most carefully before he asked us to conduct this feasibility test.'

'Do you think the whole operation could be carried out using cruise missiles alone?'

The general frowned. 'I cannot say, but my instinct is, no. We certainly could hit the refineries, and the pumping stations, because pinpoint accuracy is not a requirement. But the loading platforms and offshore rigs would require real accuracy, and I don't think we could count on a cruise to hit such a small target in exactly the right place. And, anyway, someone working on the rig might see a wayward cruise come in. They're supposed to be accurate to 10 metres. But that's too big a margin if you're trying to hit the upper deck of a drilling rig. Better to attack from below the surface.'

Gaston Savary could see why Michel Jobert had been made a general, and he could most certainly see how he came to spearhead the French Army's special forces.

'Well, General,' he said, 'I think we must agree it is the most interesting plan. Because, if it succeeds, the new King of Saudi Arabia will owe France *everything*. Certainly we will have enormous power over him, because he could *never* admit he was the mastermind behind the destruction of his own country's oil industry.'

'Well, no, he could not,' replied Jobert. 'And that would mean French companies would undertake the entire rebuilding programme. There would be huge contracts awarded to us, just as the Americans claimed almost all the rebuilding contracts for Iraq after the last Gulf War.'

'And there'd be a lot of very grateful French companies,' said Gaston. 'And the riches for the oil industry would be incalculable. Imagine owning the sole marketing agency for all Saudi Arabian oil. *Mon Dieu!* That would be something, eh?'

'And I would not be surprised if that led to a long and comfortable retirement for both of us' said the general. 'But, for now, let's not get too excited. I would like to call Admiral Pires over for half an hour.'

'I don't believe I know him.'

'He's COMFUSCO.'

'The Navy's special ops outfit?'

'*Exactement.* Commandement des Fusiliers Marine Commandos. Admiral Pires is the head of it. But he's an ex-submariner. And right now he is in over-all command of all naval assault commandos, plus the Commando Hubert divers unit and the Close Quarters Combat Group – that's naval counter-terrorist, both assigned to COS.'

'That's every kind of assault from the sea, correct?'

'*Absolument.* That's beach reconnaissance, assaults on ships, intelligence gathering, amphibious landings, small boat operations, raids, rescue ops, and of course Combat Search and Rescue – CSAR.'

'Of course,' said Gaston, who was, despite his experience, always amazed by the military's detailed, meticulous operational structures.

A young lieutenant put his head around the door to announce that Admiral Pires would be with them in 10 minutes.

Privately, Gaston Savary thought the entire scheme was a boundless exercise in naked ambition which would probably end up being abandoned. As a kind of super-policeman he was used to bureaucrats conducting relentless searches, desperately trying to find reasons not to do things. If ever there was an oppportunity to say no, this was surely it. Offhand he could think of about 10 reasons himself.

But, like many of his fellow spies and spy masters, Gaston was an adventurer at heart. And he knew how to work the system. No one had asked him to blow up the oilfields. He had merely been requested to find out if it was possible to do so

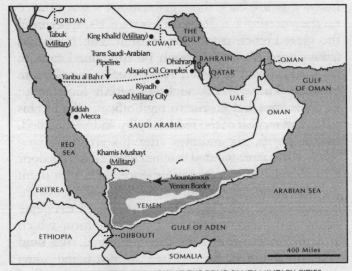

THE ARABIAN PENINSULA MARKING THE FOUR SAUDI MILITARY CITIES

47

without getting caught. And he was most certainly doing that.

Admiral Georges Pires arrived on time, with the flourish of a man who had better things to do than talk to Secret Servicemen. His splendid family summer home – going back three generations – was situated on the waterfront at St-Malo, less than 100 miles from the great French naval base at Brest. The Navy had always been his life, although he had found time to be married and divorced twice, before his fortieth birthday. There was a slightly roguish look about Georges Pires, but his rise to high office in the principal assault section of the French Navy had been exceptionally swift. Six minutes after his arrival, having received a sharply worded briefing from General Jobert, he was reduced to complete silence.

'*Mon Dieu!*' he exclaimed, once he had gathered himself. 'That is the most dangerous plan I have ever heard.'

And Savary gave him the benefit of his own wisdom. 'Admiral,' he said, 'we are not being asked to blow up half of Saudi Arabia. We are merely being asked to decide if it could be done, in secret. To the inestimable advantage of France.'

'Well, technically we could put one of our new SSNs into the Gulf, making an underwater entry through the Strait of Hormuz. It's deep enough, and it's been done before.'

'Is that one of the old Rubis Class boats?' asked Savary.

'No, no. It is one of the new Project Barracuda boats we have been building in Cherbourg for several years. You may have been briefed about them. We have just two which will become operational this year. They're bigger than the old Rubis, around 4,000 tons, nuclear hunter killers with torpedo and cruise missile capabilities. They actually carry 10 MBDA SCALP naval missiles. That's a derivative of the old Storm/Shadows. They're good, quiet ships with excellent missiles. We're conducting sea trials right now off the Brest Navy yards.'

'How would you consider the likelihood of getting in and out of the Gulf undetected?' asked the general.

'Oh, very good. And the missiles are all pre-programmed. Yes, I suppose we could launch them at a given target along the Saudi coast.'

'Would anyone see them in flight?'

'Most unlikely. The Saudis are quite sophisticated, but I'd be very surprised if they picked up low-flying missiles like these on radar. They would not be expecting such an attack.'

'Certainly not from their next King,' said Savary, helpfully. 'Any thoughts on operations on the other coast?'

'The Red Sea?' asked the admiral. 'Well, that is more difficult, because you'd come through the Suez Canal on the surface. But I don't think that would attract undue attention. And you might manage to exit the southern end off Djibouti at periscope depth; assuming you wanted to stay out of sight. That's the

Bab al Mandab, the narrow strait which leads out into the Gulf of Aden — shallow, sometimes under 100 metres deep.

'Anyway, a half-submerged submarine might look a bit suspicious to the American radar, *if* they picked us up — especially with oilfields ablaze 400 miles astern of the ship. It would probably be better just to go straight through, on the surface, in the normal way, the very picture of innocence.'

Gaston Savary really liked this suave and know-ledgeable admiral who looked extremely young to be holding such high office and rank. But he was not young in thought, and he had grasped the significance of the problem very swiftly, as indeed had General Jobert.

'I should like to speak to Admiral Romanet first,' said Pires, looking at Gaston. 'He's our Flag Officer Submarines in Brest. And I don't want to second-guess him. But I would say we could hit our missile targets on both coasts from submerged SSNs. And certainly, in my own area of operations, we could send in teams of commandoes to take out the loading platforms and offshore rigs . . . the Saudi Navy has never been up to much. They'd be no trouble whatsoever.'

The admiral paused, looking thoughtful. Then he said, 'Those platforms are big constructions, though. We'd probably need a mix of RDX — research-developed explosive — TNT and aluminium. And the frogmen would have to swim in with 25kg watertight satchels. And we'd use timers, so the swimmers and

50

perhaps an SDV, and the submarine, could get clear before the blast. But we could do it. Most certainly we could do it.'

Admiral Pires again paused. And then he added, 'But the Navy's role is only the beginning, correct? And so I will leave you, while I confer with Admiral Romanet.'

'I'd prefer it if you brought him here,' said General Jobert. 'I think at this early stage, while we are just starting to understand the situation, all discussions should remain under one roof.'

'Aha,' said Admiral Pires. 'Already we are slipping into the black ops mode; already it is occurring to you that we may be ordered actually to carry out this assault on our Arab brothers in the desert. Or at the very least, on their oil wells.'

'That's the trouble with you guys. You always say yes,' said Gaston Savary.

'That's because we are loyal servants of the Republic,' replied the general. 'We are here to do the bidding of the politicians. And we try, if asked, to achieve the impossible.'

'But half an hour ago you thought this would be impossible without getting caught.'

'I do not think that now,' replied the senior commander of COS. 'I believe we could smash the Saudi oil industry with missiles and frogmen from those two SSNs. And never be detected.'

Gaston Savary stood up. 'Gentlemen,' he said, 'I have been entrusted to conduct this study on behalf of the Foreign Minister and the President himself.

51

I would be grateful, Admiral, if you would stay for the second part of our discussions. I have enjoyed listening to your views and I think you may have more ideas to give us.'

Savary was not the first high-ranking French official to single out the forty-six-year-old Georges Pires as a top-flight military intellect, a career officer who could yet find himself in the Palais Bourbon as a member of the French Parliament.

'Honoured, sir, I assure you,' replied the admiral.

Savary continued. 'Perhaps, General, you could now outline for us anything you may know about the Saudi military defences, on land, I mean.'

'Yes, of course,' he said. 'Let me switch on this big-screen computer and I will tell you what I know; it is fairly standard but will at least show you the size of the task.'

General Jobert stood back and, with an officer's wooden baton, pointed to the map of Saudi Arabia. 'They have an overall strength of around 126,000,' he began. 'That's the four elements – Army, Navy, Air Force and the Royal Saudi Air Defence Force.

'They don't have regular garrisons. The Army is widely dispersed but its strength is concentrated at four large military cities, built at huge expense in the 1970s and 80s with the assistance of the United States Army Corps of Engineers. The first one to note is right here . . . Khamis Mushayt, in the mountains of the south-west, about 100 kilometres from the Yemeni border.

'The second is up here at Tabuk, which protects

the north-west of the country – in particular these routes which lead in from Jordan, Israel and Syria. A third site, Assad Military City, is at Al Kharj, 100 kilometres south-east of Riyadh, right in the middle of the desert. That's where the Saudi's national armaments industry is located.

'But the really big one is right here . . . facing the border area towards Kuwait and Iraq, right outside this city marked here – Hafa al Batin. This is the King Khalid Military City. You can see it's sited, deliberately, near the Trans-Arabian Pipeline – TAPLINE – which connects the big southern oil centre of Ad Damman with Jordan.

'King Khalid Military City is huge. It houses something like 65,000 people, military and civilians. It's got everything – cinemas, shopping arcades, power plants, mosques, schools, the lot. It's built in the shape of a massive concrete octagon, with several smaller octagons inside it. Right outside the main complex they have a hospital, a racecourse, maintenance and supply areas, underground command bunkers and the anti-aircraft missile sites.

'Gentlemen, you will *not* be attacking the King Khalid Military City.'

'What's the surrounding country like?' asked Admiral Pires.

'Wide-open desert, swept by radar, no cover. We'd be facing the Saudi missiles and artillery.'

'Can they shoot straight?'

'Most certainly.'

Admiral Pires smiled. 'Gentlemen,' he said, 'we

will not be attacking the King Khalid Military City.'

'Are they all like that?' asked Gaston Savary.

'Not quite so bad. But none of them is likely to be easy. Not for a small group of Special Forces. To tell the truth, Gaston, I can see no way for any small group to take, and force the surrender, of these strongholds. The Saudis have excellent communications and air cover. In the end, we would not have a chance.

'And in addition they have a well-armed National Guard which is specifically tasked with defending the oil installations. The Saudis are not stupid. They know those huge complexes are their lifeblood, and they've protected them very thoroughly.'

'What's their Air Force like?'

'Very modern. Well-equipped. US and British fighter bombers. F-15s, Tornadoes. Strong offensive capability. They also have airborne surveillance and tactical airlift capability. In brief, the Royal Saudi Air Force can move people around at will, they can see from the sky and they have a serious strike force.'

'My notes from Prince Nasir say the Air Force bases may be vulnerable?' said Savary.

'Well, maybe. But they have two substantial air wings – the F-15s and the Tornadoes. And they are divided into strike force air bases at each of the four military cities. It's a bit confusing, but they call the base at Khamis Mushayt the King Khalid Air Base. Same name as the place in the north. You understand? Down here by the Yemeni border.'

54

'That King Khalid must have been quite a leader,' said Savary. 'Half the country's named after him. But this is the air base Prince Nasir mentions. He clearly thinks it's vulnerable.'

'We need to have a very careful look,' said General Jobert. 'Very careful indeed. Because it must be obvious to each of us that the consequences of any French soldier being caught, captured or even killed would be absolutely calamitous for France. The Americans would immediately surmise we had blown up the oilfields and there'd be all hell to pay.'

'It sounds to me as if the destruction of the oilfields is several times more important than everything else put together,' put in Admiral Pires. 'Just imagine. The lifeblood of the people suddenly gone. An entire nation, the majority of whom can never even remember poverty, suddenly facing the fact they could all be back on camels. No oil; no wealth; no more prosperity. I think the nation would go into shock.'

'That's Prince Nasir's view entirely,' said Savary. 'He thinks the armed forces will not have the will to fight. For whom? For a penniless king, no longer able to pay them?'

'More like a dead, penniless king,' said Admiral Pires. 'Because if this goes ahead, the Saudis will obviously rally to the cause of the Crown Prince. Especially if he promises to end the patronage of the royal princes, and to put the country back together. Let's face it, he's the military's only hope.'

'That is all true,' said the general. 'The collapse

of the Saudi economy would be an earth-shaking event. But there still has to be an armed attack, to subdue the Army and the Air Force, then to capture the main palaces in Riyadh, and take out the King and his principal ministers. In the end, you always have to win it on the ground.'

'According to Prince Nasir,' said Savary, 'the feeling against the King is so strong, the people are so angry, that they would rally to the cause of *anyone* who could help them to get rid of the royal family. And Crown Prince Nasir is extremely popular.'

'Which leaves us with two tasks,' said Admiral Pires. 'Number one: to get into the King Khalid Air Base and either take or destroy it. Then, almost simultaneously, to capture Riyadh and remove the King of Saudi Arabia from office.'

General Jobert smiled. 'One thing, Admiral. Taking the air base needs to be so decisive it will cause the entire military city at Khamis Mushayt to cave in – and then cause the other three military cities to come to the conclusion there is nothing left to fight for.'

'With Prince Nasir on television appealing for calm, assuring everyone he has everything under control, it just might work,' said Admiral Pires. 'So long as the collapse of the oil industry has the shattering effect we think it will.'

'The point is,' suggested Savary, 'this whole thing has to look like an entirely Arab operation. It will simply appear that the Crown Prince has pulled off a palace *coup d'état*. For the good of the people. And that may be an end to it. It just so happens Prince Nasir chose France to help his country get back on its feet. America is not the only country that can take what it wants, when it wants, you know.'

'So long as no one gets caught, eh?' muttered the general.

'Precisely,' responded the admiral. 'So long as no Frenchman is ever discovered anywhere near the action.'

'And who exactly does the President have in mind for an operation like this?' asked the general.

'He hasn't even considered that yet,' said Savary. 'He simply wants to know if we think it is possible. At this stage, no more.'

'Do you have the feeling that if we say yes he will start thinking about it very, very quickly?'

'I have,' replied Savary. 'And we may as well have a few answers. So let me ask a question . . . King Khalid Air Base – who goes in, us or an Arab force?'

'Oh, that would have to be a French assault force,' said the general. 'I doubt anyone except us, the British, the Americans or the Israelis could possibly pull that off . . . but it seems so incongruous to have a French force, out there on its own, attacking that Saudi air base.'

'There would have to be some Arab involvement,' offered Admiral Pires. 'Maybe a 2/IC, or a couple of locals, men who understand command, who know the terrain and who speak the language.'

'I see that,' said Savary. 'I see it very clearly. We

could provide the force, if we approve the plan. But Prince Nasir will have to provide some leadership, or, at worse, some high-level advice.'

'I don't know that any Arab army has the kind of man we are looking for,' said the admiral. 'We need a skilled Special Forces operator, with a sound knowledge of high explosive, close-combat fighting and making detailed plans.'

'I don't think they have anyone to fit that bill,' said the general. 'And anyway, how the hell do we get in there. We can't suddenly drop 60 parachutists into Saudi Arabia. Much too risky.'

'Then they'd have to come in by sea,' said Admiral Pires. 'But it would be difficult by submarine. The SDV only holds half a dozen men. A ferry service like that would take hours. And they couldn't swim in. Too far. Too dangerous.'

'That's the kind of problem which gets solved by an Arab who knows the territory,' said Admiral Pires. 'And understands what's required. The kind of Arab who probably doesn't exist.'

'I know of one,' said Gaston.

'Oh yes?' said General Jobert.

'He's the Commander-in-Chief of HAMAS. His name is General Ravi Rashood. From what I hear, he's ex-British SAS. He could do it. The Americans think he's pulled off some terrible stuff over the last few years. He could take the air base.'

'But would he?' wondered the general. 'Why would he?'

'Because he's a fanatical Muslim fundamentalist,'

replied Savary. 'He hates the Americans, and he wants them out of the Middle East for ever. And he knows that, without Saudi support and Saudi oil, they would have to go. I think you'd find General Rashood more than willing to talk . . . but I think you'd have to pay him, and HAMAS, for the privilege of his involvement.'

'Hmmmm,' mused the general. 'Interesting.'

'And now,' continued Savary, 'for the biggest question of all: who commands the Saudi mob in Riyadh? Who recruits, organises, arms and rallies thousands of citizens who hate the King but have no idea what to do?'

'I know one thing,' said Admiral Pircs. 'You need a top-class soldier for that. And top-class soldiers become familiar to many people. In all of France, it might be impossible to find such a man, with the right qualifications and a suitably low profile. Those kinds of leaders become public figures. And one sight of this man leading an attack on the Saudi royal family would end all of our chances of anonymity.'

'All that you say makes good sense, Admiral,' said Savary. 'But there must be someone. A trained fighter, somewhere, who has seen combat but has not reached the highest rank. Someone who has perhaps retired in recent years. Someone who might consider undertaking such an operation for, say, $10 million. Enough to allow him to live the rest of his life free of all financial worries.'

All three men grew silent, pondering, perhaps, the potential destruction they could unleash if they made the recommendation to the President of France that he so clearly desired. Savary seemed to be at a loss but the two military men ran their minds back over a working lifetime in the armed forces.

Eventually, surprisingly, it was Savary who spoke up. 'There was such a man, you know, who worked for my organisation, Secret Service, the DGSE. I never met him: he was mostly based in Africa, rose to be deputy regional director of a large area, northern, sub-Saharan and western Africa. He operated out of Dakar, Senegal.'

'Did he have combat experience?' asked the general.

'And how,' replied Gaston. 'I believe he started off in the Foreign Legion. And I think he distinguished himself in Chad, you know that battle against the rebels at Oum Chalouba in 1986. He was decorated as quite a young officer for conspicuous bravery. I'm not sure what he did after that, but he definitely joined the Special Forces.'

'Do you remember his name?' asked Michel Jobert.

'Yes. He was Moroccan by birth. Gamoudi. Jacques Gamoudi. Had some kind of a nickname, which for the moment escapes me.'

General Jobert ruminated. 'Yes, Gamoudi. I think I've heard that name. He was involved with COS, after his service in the Legion. But I can't remember precisely what he did.'

He walked over to a computer desk at the far end of his office and tapped in some keywords. 'This ought to come up with something,' he said. 'It's an amazing piece of software: gives detailed biographies of all French serving officers of the past 25 years.'

They waited while the computer buzzed and whined. Then the screen brightened. 'Here he is,' said the general, quietly. 'Jacques Gamoudi, born 1964 in the village of Asni, in the High Atlas Mountains. Son of a goatherd who doubled as a mountain guide.'

'Hell, that's a big step. Moroccan farmboy to a commission in the Foreign Legion before he was twenty-two.' Admiral Pires was baffled. 'Those guys can't usually speak French.'

'Looks like he had some kind of sponsor. Man called Laforge, former major in the French Parachute Regiment. He was wounded in Algeria in 1961, medically discharged. Then he and his wife bought some kind of a hotel in the village and young Gamoudi worked there. Looks like Laforge helped him join the Legion.

'Jesus. There's a copy of his original application form, Bureau de Recrutement de la Légion Etranger, Quartier Vienot, 13400 Aubagne. That's 15 miles from Marseilles. He went down there a few weeks later in 1981, passed his physical tests and signed on for five years.'

'You're right,' said the admiral. 'That's a hell of a piece of software.'

'Any sign of his nickname?' asked Savary. 'I'd know it if I heard it.'

'Can't see it,' said Michel Jobert, scrolling down

the screen. 'Just a minute – this could be it. Does *Le Chasseur* sound familiar? There's a bunch of mercenaries he led in some very fierce fighting in North Africa. According to this, they always called him *Le Chasseur.*'

'That's him,' said Gaston thoughtfully. 'Jacques Gamoudi, *Le Chasseur.*' So saying, he drew his index finger across his throat in the age-old gesture. There could be no doubt about the reputation of Colonel Gamoudi. *Le Chasseur.* The Hunter.

CHAPTER TWO

One month later.
Early June 2009

The trouble with *Le Chasseur* was that he had essentially vanished into the crisp, thin air around the high peaks of the Pyrenees, somewhere up near the little town of Cauterets, a ski station 3,000 feet above sea level, hemmed in by 8,000-foot summits.

It was common enough knowledge that Colonel Jacques Gamoudi had taken early retirement from the Army, and headed with his family to the Pyrenees where he hoped to set himself up as a mountain guide and expedition leader, much as his father had done before him in faraway Morocco.

An inspired piece of guesswork by Gaston Savary had brought him, in company with Michel Jobert, to the town of Castelnaudary, 35 miles south-east of Toulouse, where *Le Chasseur*'s military career had begun. Quartier Lapasset, home of Foreign Legion's training regiment, was in Castelnaudary, and the young Gamoudi had spent four months there as a recruit.

Savary and the colonel had made extensive

inquiries, and not without some success. But there was no detail, only that Jacques Gamoudi, with his wife Giselle and two sons, now aged around eleven and thirteen, had headed east into the mountains, maybe four years earlier, and had not been seen since. Only one man, a veteran Legionnaire colonel, thought he had heard that the family had settled near Cauterets.

And so it was that their staff car was now winding its way through the spectacular range of mountains which divides France from Spain. They took no driver and Savary himself was at the wheel. Things had moved forward in the three months since they had first discussed the operation in Saudi Arabia.

Now the pressure was on, applied directly by the President of France. Their mission was simple: find Colonel Jacques Gamoudi. Savary was beginning to wish he had never suggested the man's name in the first place. They were not only lost: it was growing dark, they had no hotel reservation, and, generally speaking, they only had the vaguest idea where they were going.

Cauterets had seemed a reasonable plan, and they had run south-west from Toulouse for more than 100 miles into ever higher ground. And now they were driving through steep passes south of Soulom, climbing all the while, up past rugged, treeless peaks. 'This road ends at Cauterets,' said the general helpfully.

'So does the world, I shouldn't be surprised,' replied Savary, a note of irritation in his voice as he stared ahead at the darkening mountains. 'God knows how we'll ever find this character.'

'Oh, let's not be negative,' said the general. 'I doubt there are that many mountain guides in the area. And they'll all know each other.'

'You'd need to be a mountain guide to live up here,' said Savary, a Parisian to the tips of his highly polished loafers. 'Shouldn't be surprised if the whole population consisted of mountain guides.'

General Jobert chuckled. Twenty minutes later, now in the pitch dark, they ran past a sign which said, at last, CAUTERETS. And there before them was the brightly lit resort town with its cheerful hotels, bars and restaurants.

They drove on down Route 920 and swung on to the Place Maréchal Foch. Straight ahead of them were the lights of the Hôtel-Restaurant César, and simultaneously both men exclaimed, more or less in unison, *This'll do for us*.

Anxious to disembark after their long journey, they heaved their bags out of the car and found their way to reception, where they booked two rooms and reserved a table in the surprisingly crowded dining room.

Twenty minutes later, a few minutes before ten o'clock, they were dining in the best restaurant Cauterets had to offer. As they unwound after their long hours on the road, both men pondered their next move. They had made it to Cauterets — not without some difficulty — but now came the hard part: how to find Jacques Gamoudi.

Between courses, Savary tried an elementary check of the telephone book, but there was no Jacques Gamoudi. In fact, there was no Gamoudi whatsoever. If *Le Chasseur* was living up there in the mountains, it was safe to say he was probably using an assumed name.

'You know, I've never asked you, Michel, but what was Gamoudi actually doing for the Special Forces after he left the Foreign Legion?'

'Well, he had a glowing service report,' replied the general. 'And he quickly made the 1st Marine Parachute Infantry Regiment. He was recommended for a commision, which is a considerably more difficult task than a similar rank in the Foreign Legion. So he went to the French Military Academy at St-Cyr, in Brittany.

'From there he went to the Central African Republic and was promoted to major at an incredibly young age. He commanded his squadron in a highly dangerous long-term reconnaissance operation. That led to the successful evacuation of 3,000 French civilians, and a crushing defeat of the FACA – a rebel movement and a very nasty bunch.

'They decorated him again and then he was invited to join the Secret Service, which he did. In June 1999 he masterminded the rescue of the US Ambassador from the Congo. The French special ops team accompanied the diplomat to the Gabon, but Colonel Gamoudi stayed behind and directed the remaining French troops, the ones who had done the fighting.

'He earned his nickname *Le Chasseur* in the murky world of North African politics where regional conflict was rife and rebellions frequent. He was always in the thick of it, frequently commanding ex-French and Legionnaire officers fighting as mercenaries, protecting French oil interests, and private French companies with involvement in the diamond industry.

'They say he was even involved in a truly daring plot to assassinate the President of the Ivory Coast five years ago.'

The general hesitated briefly, before adding, 'Jacques Gamoudi always seemed particularly at home in a Muslim environment. And I'm telling you. One way and another, he was one hell of a soldier.'

'I imagine it can take its toll, a life like that,' said Savary. 'In that awful climate, forever watching your back, always concerned for those who rely on you . . .'

'No doubt,' said the general. 'I understand many people were most surprised when he turned his back on the Army. But he was, apparently, disenchanted. And wanted nothing more to do with it.'

'It's often that way with very brave men,' mused Savary, drinking his wine. 'That sort seem to wake up one morning and wonder why they are doing so much more than everyone else, for the same basic salary. He might be a hard man to turn around. Unless we have a lot of money.'

'We do have a lot of money. And I assure you the President and his royal cohort from the Saudi desert will not hesitate to spend it, if we can persuade them that Gamoudi is the right man to take Riyadh.'

Surreptitiously, the general laid three photographs on the table. 'Take another good look at these, Gaston. Because I think he might even deny who he is when we find him.'

'*If* we find him,' said the Secret Service chief. '*If* we find him.'

By now it was a little after 11 p.m. As they left the dining room, the general asked the head waiter if he had heard of a man named Jacques Gamoudi. Colonel Jacques Gamoudi. He was greeted with the blankest of Gallic looks. No, he had never heard of him. A discreet glance at the three photographs also failed to jog his memory. It was a pattern which would be repeated with the concierge, the receptionist and indeed the owner. None of them had ever met *Le Chasseur*.

The following morning dawned bright and warm, and under cloudless skies the two men made their way up to the cable cars which linked Cauterets to the Cirque de Lys, the point of departure for a skier's paradise, 25 miles of some of the best slopes in the region. Close season though it was, the cable car station was a regular starting-point for mountain guides, and a gathering place for walkers and climbers from all over Europe.

For two hours, Gaston Savary and General Jobert stood beneath the great peaks, mingling with the guides. Their question was the same as that of the night before: had anyone seen this man? A photograph held discreetly in the palm of the hand elicited no positive response, no furtive look, even, of deceit or secrecy. *Le Chasseur* had surely vanished, if indeed the Legionnaire in Castelnaudary had been correct in the first place. By lunchtime the two searchers were pretty certain the man had been mistaken.

There were just a few hikers gathering now, and they appeared not to have a guide who would walk with them. At least not an adult one. There was a boy of about fourteen showing them a map, but that was all.

It was perhaps their last hope. As the hikers moved off, Savary walked over to the boy who was now folding his map, still clutching his 10-euro tip.

Gaston wished him '*Bonjour*' and showed him the photographs. Without hesitation the boy exclaimed, 'Hey, that's a good picture of M. 'ooks.'

'Monsieur *who*?' said Savary.

'*Hooks*,' he emphasised. 'He's a mountain guide, lives over in a tiny little place called Héas, right up in the mountains, far above Gèdre. That's him. Definitely. The man in your picture.'

'Do you know his first name?'

'No, no. He's M. Hooks. No one calls him by his first name.'

'Has he lived there a long time?'

'Not too long. But I remember when he came. I was ten, and I was in M. Lamont's class. I used to live over at Gèdre, and my school went on a few expeditions to the mountains around the Cirque de

Troumouse. M. Hooks was always our guide. He takes all the school parties up there.'

'Where exactly did you say he lives?'

'Héas, it's called. It's not much – just a few houses with a shop and a church. You go south from Gèdre. It's on the map, on the way to the highest mountains around here. But you could go right past without noticing the village.'

Savary thanked the boy and gave him another 10-euro note. Two hours later he and General Jobert were driving along a slow, winding mountain road approaching the small town of Gèdre along the tumbling Gavarnie River.

There was only one road out of the town, heading south towards the Spanish border, back into the highest peaks. Gaston filled up the car with petrol and noted the signpost reading CIRQUE DE TROUMOUSE. Underneath it was written HEAS 6KM.

This was another mountain road even more twisting than the last. All around were great craggy escarpments, almost bare of trees, offering grandeur rather than beauty. And this little road would eventually become almost a spiral as it headed up into the astonishing 10-kilometre wall of mountains which formed the Cirque de Troumouse.

Héas was the last stop before the big climb. And such was the traffic up there to see the views that the French had shrewdly made the last stretch a toll road up to the edge of the Cirque.

Gaston Savary and General Jobert pulled into the village a little before three o'clock in the afternoon.

They inquired at the shop about M. Hooks and were politely told by a woman that he had gone into the mountains that morning with a coachload of schoolchildren and their teachers. He usually returned to Héas at around 4 p.m. Meanwhile they could certainly talk to Mme Hooks, who had just gone to meet her two sons off the school bus from Gèdre, and would be home in a few minutes . . . four houses up the street on the left. Number 8.

Savary thanked her and bought a couple of cartons of orange juice. They sat on a wall outside in the sunlight and drank them, waiting for a lady with two children to come up the hill towards them.

They did not have long to wait. A slender, pretty woman, late thirties, laughing with two young boys, appeared almost immediately. General Jobert stepped forward with a cheerful smile.

'Mme Hooks?' he asked.

'Yes,' she said, carefully. 'I am Giselle Hooks.'

'Well, I hope I haven't startled you. But my colleague M. Savary and I have come a very long way to see your husband on a most urgent matter.'

'What about?' she said. 'You are looking for a guide through these mountains?' One glance at them told her otherwise.

She appraised the two men, noting their excellent manners, their well-cut clothes and polished shoes, and indeed the big Citroën government car parked conspicuously outside the shop. Every sense told her these were men from the military, but she chose not to betray her thoughts.

'Not exactly,' said the general. 'But we have something to tell him which he will most certainly find interesting.'

Knowing better than to antagonise such people, Mme Hooks said quickly, 'Please come up to the house, and we will have some coffee . . . this is Jean-Pierre, and this is André, our sons.'

The general raised his hand in greeting. 'And this,' he said, 'is a very important Frenchman from Paris. M. Gaston Savary.'

They walked about 50 yards up a slight incline and entered through a gate into a small walled garden which surrounded a white stone house with a red-tiled roof, a classic French Pyrenean building.

The living room was also classic French country style, large with a heavy wooden dining table at one end and a seating area around an enormous brick fireplace. The kitchen was in an adjoining room, through a beamed archway, and all the furniture was of the same high quality. Beautiful rugs, possibly North African, were spread over the oak floorboards. A large framed photograph of M. Hooks and his new bride, taken in 1993, hung on the wall beside the kitchen.

General Jobert noted instantly that Hooks had married in the dress uniform of the 1st Marine Parachute Infantry Regiment. Mme Hooks took the boys into the kitchen.

She emerged with a tray bearing four mugs, three of them full, and a coffee pot. She assured them that her husband would not be long. 'That school bus he's on is supposed to be back in Gèdre by four o'clock.'

She was right. Four minutes later, the door opened and Jacques Hooks, a bearded man of medium height, and not an ounce overweight, walked in. He was wearing strong leather boots, suede shorts and a T-shirt, with a green rucksack over his shoulder. Jammed into his wide studded belt was a large sheath knife.

M. Hooks was surprised but remembered his manners. 'Oh,' he said, 'I was not expecting visitors. *Bonjour* . . . I am Jacques Hooks.'

General Jobert was the first to his feet. '*Bonjour*,' he said. 'My name is Michel Jobert, and this is my colleague Gaston Savary. We have come a very long way to see you . . .'

M. Hooks seemed momentarily to freeze. His face was expressionless. Then he said, 'I don't suppose there would be much point in hiding my true identity from you. I'm assuming you are both from some branch of the military, but I should warn you right away. I have no idea what you want with me but I am retired. I have a wife and family, as you see. And I have no intention of leaving my little mountain paradise.' Catching his wife's eye, he motioned for her to join the two boys in the kitchen.

Gaston Savary held out his hand. 'Colonel Gamoudi, I'm honoured to meet you,' he said. 'For what it's worth, I'm head of the French Secret Service. And General Jobert here is Commander-in-Chief of the 1st Marine Parachute Infantry . . . your old regiment.'

'Of course I knew exactly who General Jobert was the moment I walked in,' said Jacques Gamoudi. 'I stay in touch with a few old comrades, you know. And I most certainly would recognise my former commanding officer.' He smiled gently, poured himself some coffee and shook his head. 'But I'm happy in the mountains. It's a good place to bring up a family. It's clean, there's no crime and the people are friendly. I'd like to keep it that way. Now, tell me: what brings you to Héas?'

Gaston Savary took in the man before them, observing the heavy forearms, the bull neck, the wide swarthy face. He noted too the jagged scar below his right ear, the tight military-cut hair, the straight back of his natural stance. The hard brown eyes. Ex-Foreign Legion, ex-Special Forces, ex-mercenary in North Africa. Parachutist. Combat fighter. *What the hell did I expect him to look like? Yves Saint Laurent?*

'Before we go on,' Gamoudi said, 'I should perhaps explain I am not hiding in any way. But in my line of business you make many enemies, and so I changed my name. I thought it wiser not to return to Morocco, since I was in North Africa on behalf of the French Republic for so long. You will understand what I, am saying.'

The two men from Paris nodded. Then the general spoke.

'I will let M. Savary outline for you the background

74

to our visit. It involves a foreign country, and, indeed, the President of France . . .'

And for the next 10 minutes the Secret Service chief outlined the problems now facing Saudi Arabia: the prolific spending of the royal family, the monumental cost of that family, the deep unrest within the Kingdom, the savage cuts in personal income from the oil, the offensive ties to the United States of America, the loss of the true Islamic religion in favour of the ideals of a different, godless world to the west.

Jacques Gamoudi nodded. One of four million Muslims resident in France himself, he still tried to adhere to the dictates of the Koran, although it was difficult to attend a mosque up here in the mountains. But his parents had been devout in the teachings of the Prophet, and there was no question in the mind of Colonel Gamoudi: *There is only one God. Allah is great.*

On their twice-yearly trips to Paris, one of them at Christmas with the boys, Jacques always took his wife to the great Paris mosque, with its towering, 100-foot-high minaret, located directly opposite the Natural History Museum in the Jardin des Plantes. As the home of the Grand Imam, it was extremely important to Jacques that he attend the mosque whenever he reasonably could.

Years of military service in North Africa had kept his religious beliefs alive, and he understood implicitly what so many millions of Saudi Arabians felt about their ruling family. He could not imagine life without the Koran and its teachings, but he could imagine the desolation any Muslim might feel watching the systematic erosion of their religion, in the day-to-day life of a country like Saudi Arabia.

'There are many great problems in Saudi Arabia,' he said, 'but I am at a loss to understand why they should concern me, and why you have come all this way to see me.'

'Well, Jacques,' said Savary. 'Let me put it very simply. Three months ago the President of France had a private visit from one of the most senior princes of the Saudi royal family. As a result of that, he has asked us personally for our help in overthrowing the present regime and returning the Saudis to their Bedouin roots. That is why we made a point of seeking you out ourselves – not for a second did we consider sending someone else – to talk to you. You will understand that the fewer people who know about this the better. And now General Jobert will explain to you what has happened so far, and what we intend to do to help them.'

What followed in the next 10 minutes was possibly the most astonishing thing Colonel Gamoudi had heard in his not uneventful life. He listened wide-eyed to the plan for the Navy to knock out the entire oil industry, bringing Saudi Arabia financially to its knees.

He nodded in general understanding of the plan to hit the air base at King Khalid Military City when the Saudi armed forces' morale was at its lowest ebb. And he indicated his general acceptance of the need

76

to take Riyadh, for the people to rise up and perhaps storm the palace. And all this in the moments before the Crown Prince appeared on television to announce he had, with the backing of a small number of military commanders, taken control of the country and that the old King, one of his 100-odd uncles, was dead.

He also understood these two men were here, in his home, seeking his advice.

But when General Jobert coolly told him that he, Colonel Jacques Gamoudi, was the man chosen by the French Army to command the operation in Riyadh, he almost choked on his coffee.

'*ME!*' he shouted. '*YOU WANT ME TO CAPTURE THE CITY OF RIYADH?* You must be dreaming.'

Put as bluntly as that, Gaston Savary thought they might all be dreaming. But General Jobert was dead serious. 'You have all of the necessary qualifications, Jacques. And we believe you will be leading a revolution against which there will be no opposition . . . we expect the Army to have given up by then . . . you just need to take the palace . . .'

'But what about the guards? . . . What about the King's bodyguards . . . what about the protectors in the palace . . . ?'

'I don't recall such trifling matters ever having discouraged you before,' said Michel Jobert.

'*TRIFLING!*' snapped Jacques. 'About a hundred armed men with AK-47s firing 1,000 rounds a minute at you.'

'I was rather thinking we might hire one of those Muslim suicide bombers,' said the general. 'Have him flatten the main royal palace without much fuss.'

'General, am I supposed to be taking this seriously? I mean, who's going to arm this mob? Who's going to train them? Get them to move forward as a fighting force? What about supplies? Hardware? Ordnance?'

'I assure you, Jacques, there will be plentiful supplies, every last request granted. For this operation no expense will be spared.'

'Well, General. When I read about it in *Le Figaro* at least I'll know what's happening. But I could not possibly take part, not in any way whatsoever. I'm retired now. I don't have the stomach for it any more.'

'But you are still a young man, Jacques. What are you, forty-five? And, by the look of you, very, very fit. Climbing mountains all day, you should be.'

'General, I want to make myself very clear. I cannot, *will not*, be involved. I have my wife and family to consider. General, I would not undertake this for a million dollars.'

Michel Jobert smiled but said nothing for a few moments. Then he spoke. 'How about ten?' he said.

On a day of truly outlandish suggestions, this one beat them all.

'*HOW MUCH?*' exclaimed Jacques.

'I think you heard me,' said General Jobert. 'How about $10 million, with a further $5 million bonus when Prince Nasir assumes the throne of Saudi Arabia?'

Jacques Gamoudi was stunned into silence. He stood up and walked from one end of the room to the other. He paused, shaking his head, reflecting on the outrageous proposition. It was outrageous in its assumptions; outrageous in its arrogance; outrageous in its rewards; outrageous in every way.

The Moroccan-born colonel had been around in his time, but never had he heard anything quite to match this. He spoke slowly. 'You want me, General, somehow to smuggle myself into Saudi Arabia, then into Riyadh, then find myself a head-quarters, and start recruiting people to join a popular revolution. And, when I have enough, to attack the royal palaces?'

'Please don't be absurd, Colonel. You will not be alone. As a guest of Prince Nasir, the Deputy Minister of the Armed Forces, you will be there on a bona fide matter. You will be flown into Saudi Arabia by private jet provided by the French Air Force. You will be chauffeur-driven to a small palace on the outskirts of Riyadh. There you will meet the Saudi military commanders loyal to the Crown Prince, and there too you will meet the terrorist commanders, most of whom have connections with al-Qaeda. And there you will be briefed as to the size of your force and its assets.

'From then on, you will decide what you require. Transport. Armoured vehicles. Perhaps some artillery, which is currently being stored in the desert. Helicopters. Maybe tanks. Everything is available. But you will mastermind the entire operation.

Communications, and above all, the attack on the King's palace. Anything you ask will be provided.'

'And for all this I am to be paid $10 million, and five more when Prince Nasir takes over. And what then? Do I remain in Riyadh?'

'No. You leave, probably within a few days. A French Air Force jet will be awaiting, to fly you directly home to Pau–Pyrénées Airport.'

'And who's supposed to take out the King and his immediate family and advisers?'

'I think that is an honour we would leave to you. Because that way there will be no mistakes,' said Gaston. 'Your reputation precedes you.'

Jacques Gamoudi poured himself another cup of coffee. 'How long would I be in Riyadh?'

'Several months. You would be attended at all times by personal bodyguards, with a staff of perhaps six former Saudi Army officers, hand-picked, men who know and love the country. But men who are tired of the King and his entourage.

'You would move around locally with a driver in a Saudi government car. There are plenty of them in Riyadh. Yours would be provided by the Crown Prince. For longer journeys you would be provided with a helicopter and a pilot. Royal Saudi Air Force, courtesy of Prince Nasir. You will get to know him well.'

'And if I refuse?'

'You won't, Colonel. You are a devout Muslim. Islam needs you. It is sounding the call for battle. And you will, as you always have, answer that call.'

'But there must be others? Younger officers. Men who are just as well qualified.'

'We have chosen you, Jacques. And we have informed only two people of our choice. The President of the French Republic and the Foreign Minister of France.'

'Ah, nobody important then,' said Colonel Gamoudi ironically. 'It's nice to keep things on a low level, eh?'

'And the money?' pursued the general.

'Well, of course, the money is enough to tempt any man. But why dollars?'

'You mentioned dollars first, Jacques. You said *not for a million dollars* – and I went along with that because ultimately you would be paid in dollars, by the Saudis, through us, for the good of France.'

'Do I still have a choice? What if I do refuse?'

'I think that would be spectacularly unwise,' said the general. 'You are the man we have selected. This is the biggest operation for France since World War II. It means more to us than any action by a French Government since we joined the European Union. It will seal our prosperity for the next one hundred years.'

'Yes, I suppose it would.' And again Colonel Gamoudi seemed overwhelmed by it all. He stood up and paced the room again, eventually turning around and asking, 'But why me?'

For the first time, the general spoke with an air of impatience. 'Because you are an experienced combat fighter. You understand command, and you under-stand a sudden and ruthless assault on an objective.

81

You know how to deploy troops. You understand the critical path of any attack, you know what cannot be left undone. Not least, you are an expert with high explosive.

'Even more importantly, you are a Muslim, and you are expert at working with Muslims, at home in their own environment. With the massive military and financial backup of France and Saudi Arabia, there is an excellent chance that our mission will be accomplished.'

Jacques Gamoudi stood still. And then he said, 'How and when would I be paid?'

Sensing a weakening of Gamoudi's resolve, Gaston Savary took over. 'You will receive $5 million upon your verbal agreement to undertake the task. This will be wired into an account opened in your name at the Bank of Boston at 104, avenue Champs-Elysée. It will be an account solely controlled by you. Once the money is paid, no one can touch it except for you and your wife, unless you specify otherwise. There will be irrevocable documents to that effect.'

'And the second instalment?'

'That will be wired into the same account 48 hours before your attack commences. And you will be in a position to check its arrival. Plainly, if it does not come you will not launch the attack.' Gaston Savary paused. 'Jacques,' he said, 'I assure you, your paltry sum of $10 million dollars is the very least of the problems facing the French Government and the incoming Saudi regime at this time.'

'Would I be obliged to keep the money in France? Perhaps to avoid taxes?' asked Colonel Gamoudi.

'Colonel,' said General Jobert, 'you will have a letter, signed by the President of France, absolving you from all French government taxes for the remainder of your lifetime, and that of your wife.'

Jacques Gamoudi whistled through his front teeth. 'And my bonus?' he asked.

Savary sensed a sea change at last. 'That will be presented in the form of a no-refund, no-recall cashier's cheque to be held by your wife. But dated for one month after the operation. She will be given the cheque at the precise time we pay the second $5 million instalment.'

'And if the attack should fail?'

'Our emissaries will call at the house to retrieve the cheque.'

'And if I should be killed in action?'

'Your wife will keep the cheque and deposit it in her account in the Bank of Boston.'

'And what if the attacks from the sea should fail, and the Saudi oil industry is somehow saved?'

'If that happened the operation would be cancelled. You keep the initial $5 million and come home.'

'And the second $5 million?'

'We are paying $10 million for you to launch the attack, and take Riyadh,' said Gaston flatly. 'Clearly we don't pay if you do not attack. And the attack would be impossible if the King remained in control of the Army, which he would if the oil keeps flowing. Everything depends on the destruction of the oil industry.'

'You make it very clear, and very tempting,' said Jacques Gamoudi.

The men from Paris listened as he then proceeded to justify to himself the reasons why he might accept the job.

'We fight a weakened enemy. Maybe one with no stomach for the fight. I think your Saudi prince is correct – no army wants to fight for someone who may not pay them. It knocks the stuffing out of them. Soldiers too have wives and families, and I think the Saudi Army may feel they have no alternative but to join the new regime. That way they still get paid.

'A popular rising by the people is often the easiest of military operations. Because there are too many reasons for their opponents not to fight – one of these is usually money, the second is usually more important: all soldiers have a natural distaste for turning their guns on their own people. They don't like it. And quite often they refuse to do it.'

Taking advantage of a pause in conversation, Gaston Savary stood up and Michel Jobert gave a suggestion of a nod.

'Jacques,' said Gaston, 'I have no doubt that you will want to discuss this with your wife. We were thinking in terms of one week. I am going to give you two business cards: one is for me and my personal line, the other is for the general and his private number at COS headquarters. If you decide to go ahead, you will call one of us, and say very simply that you wish to talk. Nothing more. You will then replace the telephone and wait.

'Meanwhile, remember: the only people in the whole of France who know anything of what we have just told you are the President, the Foreign Minister, the three people in this room and two admirals of the French Navy. That's seven. I need hardly mention you will say nothing to anyone. But of course we know you never would. We know your record.'

And with that the two men from Paris stood up and shook hands warmly with the mountain guide. But before they left, Gaston had one last question. 'Jacques Gamoudi,' he said. 'Why Hooks? A curious name for a Frenchman to adopt.'

Colonel Gamoudi laughed. 'Oh,' he said, 'that was the name of the US Ambassador we successfully evacuated out of Brazzaville in the Congo back in June 1999. Fourteen US citizens altogether. Ambassador Aubrey Hooks was a good and brave man.'

Two months later
August 2009
It had been a long, painstaking, somewhat intensive road to Bab Touma Street in the old part of the city of Damascus. There had been a zillion contacts with Hezbollah, even more with the militant end of the Iranian Government. There had been countless clandestine talks with contacts inside al-Qaeda, mostly orchestrated by Prince Nasir. And finally a succession

85

of e-mail exchanges with the leaders of the most feared of all terrorist groups, HAMAS.

But Gaston Savary and General Michel Jobert had finally made it. The Syrian government staff car, carrying two local bodyguards and the two Frenchmen, slowed smoothly to a halt outside the big house near the historic gate in the city wall. This was the discreet and well-guarded home of the HAMAS commander-in-chief General Ravi Rashood and his beautiful Palestinian wife Shakira.

Prince Nasir had been insistent. *We need this man. He will bring us military discipline, and he will bring with him heavily armed, experienced Arab freedom fighters. We cannot destroy a military air base with amateurs, and this HAMAS C-in-C is the best they've ever had.*

And now Gaston Savary and General Jobert were about to meet him, on his own ground. But, nonetheless, as allies. France's roots in Syria went very deep, but the key to this forthcoming conversation rested on one simple fact – there could never be an Islamic nation stretching from the Arabian Gulf to the Atlantic end of North Africa so long as Saudi Arabia operated with one foot in the United States of America.

Every Islamic fundamentalist knew that; every Islamic fundamentalist understood there was something treacherous, un-Arab, about the way the Saudi King both ran with the fox and hunted with the hounds.

And now these two Frenchmen were here, about to enter the lair of the most infamous terrorist the world had ever known. And they were bringing with them, perhaps, a formula to change everything. Savary and Jobert would be made very welcome by General Rashood, the native Iranian who had once served as an SAS commander in the British Army.

The door was opened by a slim young Syrian wearing Arab dress. He bowed his head slightly and said quietly, 'General Rashood is awaiting you.' They were led down a long, bright, stone-floored corridor to a tall pair of dark wooden doors. The young man opened one of them and motioned for the Frenchmen to enter. Their two bodyguards provided by the government took up positions outside.

The room was not large and General Rashood was alone, as agreed. He sat at a wide antique desk, with a green leather top. To his left was a silver tea service which had been brought in as the government car arrived. To his right was a service revolver placed on the desk next to a leather-bound copy of the Koran.

Ravi Rashood arose and walked around the desk to greet his visitors. A thickset man, with short dark hair and an unmistakable spring to his step, he wore faded blue jeans and a loose white shirt. '*Salaam alaykum*,' he said, *Peace be upon you*, the traditional welcome of the desert.

The two Frenchmen greeted him in return and General Rashood poured mint tea into little glass cups in silver holders. 'Welcome to my home,' he said gracefully. 'But time is short. You should not linger here, for many reasons. In Damascus the walls and the trees have ears and eyes.'

'It's not so different in Paris,' said the French Secret Service chief. 'But Paris is bigger, and therefore more confusing.'

General Rashood smiled and spoke quietly and to the point. 'I have of course been briefed very carefully about your plan. I have studied it in all its aspects. And I believe every Arab of the Islamic faith would welcome it. The antics of the Saudi royal family really are too excessive, and, as you know, there can be no real prospect for a great Islamic state so long as Riyadh allows itself to be ruled by Washington.'

'We understand that only too well,' said General Jobert. 'And as the months go by, and the situation grows worse, the King, it seems, will tolerate anything from the younger members of his family. I expect you read of the death of one of the princes off Monaco? The King simply refuses to discuss it. According to our sources, the Crown Prince, Nasir, is the only hope that country has of growing up and taking its place at the centre of the Islamic world where it belongs.'

'I understand we are looking at the destruction of the oil industry,' Rashood replied, 'followed by a military attack on one of the Saudi military bases, then the capture of Riyadh and the overthrow of the royal family.'

'In the broadest terms, correct,' said Michel Jobert. 'The main thing is to take the oil industry off the map for maybe two years. Because as soon as that is achieved the King will automatically be weakened badly. In Riyadh the mob is almost at the gates even now. The looming bankruptcy of the nation should be sufficient for them to welcome a new regime with open arms.'

'I don't think we can attack one of those military cities,' said General Rashood. 'They are too big, too solidly built and too well defended. Have you thought about the air bases?'

'Exactly so,' replied General Jobert. 'We think the King Khalid Air Base at Khamis Mushayt is the one for us. If we can hit and destroy the aircraft on the ground, and achieve the surrender of the base, I think we could launch a separate squad at the command headquarters of the main base and demand the surrender.

'Remember, they will already know we've hit and crippled the oil industry, and they'll know we've hit and destroyed a large part of the Saudi Air Force. I think they might be ready to surrender. And if Khamis Mushayt surrenders, that would probably cause a total cave in of the Army, especially as the television station will by now be appealing for loyalty to the incoming new King.'

'Yes, I think all that follows,' said General Rashood. 'But what precisely is it you wish me to do?'

'I would like you to train and command the force which assaults the bases at Khamis Mushayt. And we would like you to be in constant communication with the commander in charge of the attack in Riyadh, and to move in to assist him in the final stages of the *coup d'état* in the capital.'

'And where do I get the force to attack Khamis Mushayt? I would need specialists.'

'French Army Special Forces,' said General Jobert. 'Well-trained, experienced fighters with expert skills in critical areas. We would also expect you to bring perhaps a dozen of your most trusted men. Your guides inside Saudi Arabia will all be al-Qaeda who will provide back-up fighters if required.'

'We'll need several months for training and co-ordination,' said General Rashood. 'Where will we train?'

'France. Inside the classified areas where we pre-pare all our Special Forces. Top secret,' replied General Jobert. 'Most of it inside the barracks of the 1st Marine Parachute Infantry.'

'And then?'

'Final training will be at a secret camp in Djibouti. From there you move into Saudi Arabia.'

'How exactly?'

'With respect, we would leave that to you. You have greater experience and knowledge of the field.'

General Rashood nodded gravely. 'And your budget? I imagine there will be no restrictions.'

'Absolutely not. What you need, you get.'

'And for myself? Do you have a figure in mind for my services?'

'In such a patriotic mission for the Islamic cause, we wondered if you might consider doing this for nothing.'

'Wrong.'

'You wouldn't? Not for the ultimate creation of an Islamic state?'

'Not even for that.'

'A shame, General. I was led to be believe you were an idealist.'

'In some ways I am. But if I manage to achieve our objectives, I imagine there will be billions of petro-dollars flying around in favour of France. Otherwise you would not be here. You are not idealists. You are in it purely for gain. And I do not work as an unpaid executive for greedy Western states, although I appreciate the philanthropic nature of your request.'

'Then do you have a figure in mind?'

'A figure on the value of my life? Yes, a lot.'

'How much?' asked Savary.

General Rashood was succinct. 'My price is $10 million. And if I am successful I expect a bonus payment.'

General Jobert nodded.

'In addition, there is HAMAS; we would need to pay perhaps 20 men in the region of $100,000 each.'

'What do you think HAMAS would require?' asked Savary.

'For the loss of their commander-in-chief? For maybe six months? I'd think another $10 million.'

'That's a great deal of money,' said General Jobert.

'Not to the Saudis,' said General Rashood. 'And don't try telling me France is paying, because I know that could not be true.'

'And your bonus?'

'If we take the southern bases, and I successfully help your commander in Riyadh, putting a new king on the throne of Saudi Arabia – another $5 million.'

'I think that too could be arranged,' said General Jobert. 'We would require you to make a brief trip to Paris in the next few weeks to meet our Riyadh commander. You will be working closely together in the coming months. Speed is of the essence.'

'If you can guarentee absolute security and secrecy, that would be my pleasure,' said General Rashood. 'But now you should leave. We will continue to communicate through the Syrian Embassy in Paris. And I will confirm the agreement of my masters in the HAMAS council.'

They shook hands on the agreement, then the two men hurried from the house and into the waiting car, which would take them directly to the airport and the waiting French Air Force jet, bound for Paris.

4 p.m., Wednesday 26 August 2009
Damascus International Airport
Daniel Mostel, aged twenty-four, was one of a few thousand Jewish residents of Damascus. His well-connected parents, who ran a highly successful car-hire company with excellent government contracts, preferred the relaxed religious attitudes of Syria's principal city and had always resisted the temptation to emigrate to Israel.

Daniel worked in air-traffic control and had ambitions of one day becoming a pilot. He spent most of his evenings studying to take the Air France examinations. At weekends he attended a pilot training school out at the other airport, Aleppo, east of the city.

Although Daniel's family had been in Syria for several generations, his maternal grandfather had lived in Israel during the Arab-Israeli wars of 1967 and 1973. His stories of Israel's courage had so moved his grandson that, as a result, Daniel Mostel was now a member of the *sayanim*, that secret, worldwide Israeli brotherhood whose members would do *anything* in the name of their country.

Daniel Mostel was a fanatic for the cause of Israel. He had often considered leaving Syria and returning to his true home but his main contact in Mossad knew he was more valuable to Israel right there in the control tower of Damascus International Airport, staying alert and watchful. Daniel had never breathed a word to his parents about his involvement with the *sayanim*.

And at this particular moment during that hot afternoon he was greatly confused by the presence of an Air France jet airliner, a European Airbus, standing away from all the other aircraft, with no passengers, and nothing, so far as he could see, in the way of a flight plan.

Shortly after four o'clock he saw the air crew plus two flight attendants board the jet, and 10 minutes later a black Syrian government car pulled up at the

93

foot of the steps leading up to the forward section. A single man stepped out of the back of the automobile and climbed nimbly up the steps, without looking round. He carried a small leather holdall and wore faded blue jeans with a white shirt and a light-brown suede jacket.

Daniel saw them close the aircraft's main door immediately, then he watched it taxi out to the end of the runway. Two stations down from his own, he heard his boss say firmly, '*Air France zero-zero-one cleared for take off.*'

Daniel had not the slightest idea who was aboard that aircraft, but he knew there was only one passenger. And it was a big plane to be carrying a single person.

He knew it was unwise to ask too many questions about what was going on. It was plainly none of his business. And to make such an inquiry might only bring suspicion upon himself. General Rashood had most certainly been correct about one thing – the walls and the trees did have ears and eyes in Damascus.

Daniel took his break at 5 p.m. local time. He left the airport for 10 minutes, driving out to a lonely part of the desert, and there, using his mobile cell phone, he called a very private number at the western end of the city, out on Palestine Avenue. He reported the departure of the Air France flight, giving the serial number painted on the fuselage, the zero-zero-one flight number, which was plainly invented, and relaying the information that a government car had delivered its only passenger. Took off to the west, 1630.

Twenty minutes later, Mossad agents were being alerted in Cairo, Tripoli, Baghdad, Tel Aviv, Rome, Nice, Paris, London and Amsterdam. Mossad disliked anything clandestine being conducted by anyone in their territory, and this venture had all the hallmarks of secrecy on an international scale. The signal to the agents was simple: find out who's on board Air France zero-zero-one out of Damascus.

And since the brotherhood of the *sayanim* was active in just about every airport and flight checkpoint in Europe, it took only half an hour to establish the flight was on its way to Paris, where it was due to land at 7.30 p.m., a two-hour time gain on a five-hour flight.

Waiting up on the viewing deck at Charles de Gaulle airport and watching through binoculars with several other plane-spotters, Simon Baum was not just a member of the *sayanim*: he was the bureau chief of Mossad's entire Paris operation located in the basement of the Israeli Embassy.

He saw the Air France flight come in to land, right on time, and he guessed correctly that it would taxi somewhere close to the area in which a French government car was awaiting, close to where a young baggage handler, also a member of the *sayanim*, was standing behind a line of in-flight catering carts, hidden from view, holding an extremely expensive digital camera, with a long-range lens.

95

The baggage handler watched the aircraft taxi into position no more than 40 yards from his position. The main cabin door opened and a flight attendant stepped outside and waited at the top of the steps. He aimed the camera straight at the door as the passenger appeared . . . *click* . . . *click* . . . *click*. The passenger turned away to speak to the flight attendant. Then back toward the terminal building. *Click* . . . he was caught once more, then twice as he came down the steps. But then the man turned away, towards the awaiting car. The car was snapped for good measure, and then two more frames through the rear passenger window as it sped away towards the private entrance to the airport. Nine shots. Within 20 minutes the camera would be back with M. Baum, and the baggage handler would have earned his payment.

The government car passed through the guarded gates swiftly and immediately a black Peugeot fell in behind and tracked its quarry all the way along the main road into the northern suburbs of Paris. From there the government car turned west and headed across the top of the city towards Taverny, where it sped down two quiet streets and swung into the guarded gates of COS.

The pursuing car did not follow into the final approach road but swerved away to the south, back to the central part of the city and the Israeli Embassy.

But Mossad now knew two things. First, the mystery man from Damascus was ensconced in the Commandement des Opérations Spéciales in Taverny.

And second COS *really* did not wish anyone to know his whereabouts.

Simon Baum knew it would be extremely difficult to track anyone in France whom the military did not wish to be tracked. If the mysterious visitor from the desert was going anywhere internally, he would travel by military jet or helicopter.

Simon Baum would rely on the *sayanim*, and in the meantime he would send the airport photographs over the internet to all his main offices and agents in France, and something might break loose. He held out no real hope that the visitor was of any special interest to him or his organisation, but Mossad had not earned its fearsome reputation by not bothering. It had become the world's most notorious intelligence network because it missed nothing, left nothing to chance and solved all problems to the best of its ability.

And so the airport photographs were circulated throughout the vast network of the Israeli Secret Service. And, curiously, the first coded e-mail came back from headquarters in Tel Aviv. It said simply: 'Visitor to Paris, General Ravi Rashood, C-in-C HAMAS, aka Major Ray Kerman of British SAS. Eliminate.'

Simon Baum stared at the name of the most wanted man in Israel, Major Ray Kerman, who had jumped ship in the battle of Palestine Road in the West Bank city of Hebron three years earlier. Kerman, who had hit Israel's Nimrod Jail and released every one of the most, dangerous political prisoners in the entire country.

Kerman, scourge of the US West Coast, the most wanted man in the entire world. And here he was, having dinner in the Paris suburb of Taverny with French military chiefs, under strict government protection. Simon Baum could not believe his eyes at the name on the screen before him. But Mossad did not make mistakes. If they said it was the HAMAS C-in-C, then that's who it was.

But ELIMINATE! *Mon Dieu!* They must be joking. At any rate. Not this trip.

Simon did not sleep that night. He remained in his office in the bowels of the Israeli Embassy, sipping cognac poured into dark Turkish coffee, what Parisians call *café complet*. He constantly checked his e-mail.

But the night was quiet and so was the new day. Simon worked restlessly, checking dozens of communications until the early afternoon when he finally dozed off in his office. He was asleep at his desk when the long-range French Marine Commando helicopter, the SA 365–7 Dauphin 2, clattered into the sky above Taverny, bearing the COS director General Michel Jobert and the HAMAS general Ravi Rashood along the first miles of their long journey to the south.

They flew to the eastern side of Paris, well clear of the heavy air traffic around Charles de Gaulle Airport, and set a course due south. It would take them east of the city of Lyons, then down the long Rhône valley all the way to the delta in the glistening salt marshes of the Camargue. From there they would swing east along the coast, across the great bay of Marseilles and into the small landing area the Foreign Legion operated at Aubagne, 15 miles east of France's second city.

It could scarcely have gone more smoothly, except for a certain Moshe Benson, an air traffic controller at the small regional airport near the village of Mions, eight miles south-west of Lyons' main St-Exupéry Airport, and thus considerably closer to the flight path of the Marine Commando helicopter.

Moshe Benson picked it up on the airport radar as it clattered 10,000 feet above the vineyards of Beaujolais. He realised instantly it was military, not transmitting, and not offering any call sign to this particular control point. This was slightly unusual, even though in France the military were apt to operate with a degree of independence.

Moshe Benson made a routine call to the control tower in Marseilles to report formally that a fast unidentified helicopter had just come charging through his air space and they might keep a watch for it. He told them he assumed it was French military.

Meanwhile Simon Baum was awakened by one of his agents to learn that a Marine Commando Dauphin 2 helicopter had taken off one hour ago from the Taverny complex and appeared to be heading south. The Mossad chief immediately called four *sayanim* at various airport – Dijon, Limoges, Lyons and Grenoble. The only one who could help was Moshe Benson.

Simon Baum knew the range of the Dauphin was less than 500 miles and that Marseilles was 425 miles south of Paris. Unless it was going sightseeing along the Riviera, that particular helicopter was bound for Marseilles, or, more likely, the military base at Aubagne.

Baum called two of his top agents in Marseilles and told them to get out to Aubagne on the double. He checked his man in the main city airport, Marseilles-Provence, and put him on full alert, though he did not expect the Dauphin to fly in there.

Thus, by the time Generals Michel Jobert and Ravi Rashood touched down in Aubagne in the gathering dusk, there was a black Peugeot discreetly parked along the main road to Marseilles, 200 yards beyond the main gates to the Foreign Legion garrison. Through powerful binoculars, Simon Baum's men had watched the Dauphin land and now they were watching for an army staff car to leave the garrison bearing at least one, and possibly two, passengers.

They had only four minutes to wait. And when General Jobert's Citroën began its 15-mile journey into the city, there was a Mossad tail right behind, with two of Simon Baum's most lethal operators in the two front seats. They were not so much agents as hitmen.

They drove directly into Marseilles and ran west down the wide, main boulevard of La Canebière towards the Old Port. With the busy harbour in front of them, they turned right and made their way to the north side, to the Quai du Port, and immediately turned away from the water, into the labyrinth of streets, home to some of the best restaurants in Marseilles.

The army staff car came to a sudden halt outside the world-famous fish restaurant L'Union, and both General Jobert and General Rashood stepped out and hurried up the front steps. They were inside, with the big mahogany doors closed behind them, before their Mossad trackers had turned the corner.

But Simon Baum's men had seen the car backing into a parking space not 20 yards from L'Union's main entrance and they guessed the passengers had already made an exit. Agent David Schwab jumped out and waited outside the restaurant while his colleague, Agent Robert Jazy, parked the car and returned on foot.

Five minutes later both men went into the panelled bar area of the big, noisy restaurant and identified General Rashood from the airport photographs they had received from Paris on the internet. Neither of them could identify General Jobert, and the third man, now speaking to the two new arrivals from Paris, was unknown to them.

Neither Mossad agent knew it but they were witnessing a minor piece of secret history: the first meeting between General Rashood and Colonel Jacques Gamoudi, the two men who would command the military assault on Saudi Arabia.

In two separate places, 25 feet apart at the long polished wooden bar, the five men sipped glasses of wine from the vineyards of the Pyrenees, until, shortly after 7.30 p.m., General Jobert and his companions walked out of the bar into the main restaurant and were led to a wide, heavy oak table in the corner of the room, covered with a bright red and white check tablecloth. Two flickering candles were jammed jauntily into the necks of empty bottles of Château Petrus, the most expensive Bordeaux in France.

The three men occupied three sides of the table: neither had his back to the arched entrance across the room. Colonel Gamoudi and General Rashood had already established a mutual respect and were locked in conversation mostly involving the armoured vehicles necessary to storm Riyadh's main royal palace from the front. General Rashood favoured a quieter entry against unsuspecting guards, who could then be taken by surprise, with an armoured vehicle jamming the main gates open.

Jacques Gamoudi was inclined to hit those main gates with a tank, and have his infantry charge from behind that heavier armoured vehicle, moving straight ahead, firing from the hip.

'My approach is less likely to cause us casualties,' said Ravi. 'Because that way we'll call all the shots, with a huge element of surprise. A tank's damned noisy and likely to alert the entire place.'

'It also has another bonus – it terrifies people,' replied Colonel Gamoudi. 'And may even cause a quick surrender of the palace guards.'

They ordered quickly and simply: Italian *antipasti*,

a steaming bowl of *bouillabaisse* for three and white wine from Jurançon.

'I think one of our main problems will be getting the guys in for the hit on the King Khalid Air Base,' said Ravi.

'*Bouillabaisse* – air base – it's all beginning to sound the same to us, heh?' laughed Jacques. 'And the sea's the key to both operations.'

Michel Jobert laughed, and the conversation turned to the sticking point – the entry into southwestern Saudi Arabia. 'It's all very well for you, Jacques Gamoudi,' said Ravi. 'Your guys are in and ready, as soon as you arrive. I have to get my squad into the country, and it's not going to be easy. I don't know if the Saudis can fight, but there's a lot of them. And we have to be extremely careful.'

'That's true, General,' replied Colonel Gamoudi. 'Because my operation depends entirely on the news from Khamis Mushayt. It's critical the Saudi Army in Riyadh understands there has been a major surrender in the south. And critical they know it before my opening attack.'

Ravi nodded in agreement, but signalled silence as the waiter arrived with their main course. The conversation took a more light-hearted tone. The principal decisions had been made, Ravi and Jacques had accepted their commission, and the plan would be executed as masterminded by Prince Nasir. If there was going to be a time to step back before the attack, this was it.

It was then that agents Schwab and Jazy appeared

in the waiting area to the main dining room; now they were wearing long black leather coats, which they had not been wearing in the bar. And they were standing in the slightly raised entrance at the top of the two wooden steps which led down into the dining area.

They were facing Jacques Gamoudi, head on, from a distance of around 100 feet. They stood to Ravi's left and to General Jobert's right. Gamoudi was staring back at them, when, to his amazement, he saw each of them swiftly draw AK-47s from inside the front flaps of their coats. He could see the unmistakable shapes of the short barrels being raised to shoulder height.

With the instincts of the lifelong combat soldier he grasped the heavy table and hurled it foward, sending wine, *bouillabaise* and God knows what else crashing to the floor. With his left hand he grabbed Ravi by the throat and with his right he grabbed the general, hurling them both down.

The opening burst from the AK-47s smashed a line of bullets clean down the middle of the hefty table top which now acted as a barrier between Ravi, Jacques and Jobert and the flying lead from the Kalashnikovs. All three of them could hear the bullets whining around the room. Behind them two waiters had gone down, blood pumping from their chests.

It was a scene of carnage. Crockery was shattered, bottles of wine smashed, women screaming, everyone rushing or crawling for cover. Another ferocious burst of fire confirmed that the hitmen were making their way across the restaurant. Jacques Gamoudi drew the only weapon he had, the big hunting knife he took with him into the mountains, and Ravi Rashood pulled his service revolver from the wide leather belt, near the small of his back.

Colonel Gamoudi snapped, 'It's you they're after, *mon ami*. I'll take one, and you shoot the other soon as you can see him. General Jobert, stay right there behind the table.'

And with that the iron-souled mountain guide crashed under the adjoining tables until he reached a solid white column in the centre of the room. The precise path of Jacques Gamoudi was made plain by the sheer volume of destruction he left behind him on the floor of the restaurant, overturned tables and chairs, magnificently cooked seafood, burning candles mostly extinguished by wine and the contents of ice buckets.

But it was impossible to shoot him as he dived beneath the tables, staying low, hammering his way forward. However, the Mossad men gave it their best shot and bullets richocheted in all directions.

Agent Jazy now hung back, at once looking for the charging Gamoudi and trying to provide cover for his partner, as David Schwab moved forward for the kill, towards the upturned table behind which his quarry was crouching.

But somehow Jacques Gamoudi got around behind Jazy, and he leapt at him with the bound of a mountain lion. He plunged his knife deep into the man's throat, ripping the windpipe and jugular. Jazy had no time to scream. He dropped his weapon and fell back dying in the mighty arms of *Le Chasseur*.

Agent Schwab turned around and swung his rifle straight at Gamoudi who was using Jazy as a human shield. He hesitated for a split second and Ravi Rashood, moving even faster than Gamoudi, dived horizontally out from behind the table and shot him clean through the back of the head, twice. A line of bullets, hopelessly ripping across the timbered ceiling, was the Mossad man's only reply.

The entire room was now bathed in blood. Fifteen diners were injured, five of them seriously, and four staff were dead, including the head waiter, who had been caught in the opening crossfire. Such was the speed of the battle, no one had yet called either an ambulance or the police. Surviving staff members were either in shock or still taking cover.

Colonel Gamoudi and General Rashood hauled Michel Jobert back to his feet and they grabbed the two fallen AK-47s as all three of them ran for the exit.

Alerted by the sounds of mayhem from within the restaurant, their driver had moved the car to the entrance of the building. As they piled into it, General Jobert snapped, 'Aubagne. And step on it. Back roads. Stay off the highway.'

And at high speed they headed out of Marseilles; they were men above suspicion, two decorated French Army officers, one of them serving at the highest possible level, and an Arab general called in to assist

France in a highly-classified operation, presidential edict.

'Trouble, sir?' asked the driver.

'Not really, Maurice. A pair of amateurs made a rather silly error of judgement,' said Michel Jobert. 'Not a word, of course. We were nowhere near Marseilles.'

'Of course, sir. I know the rules.'

CHAPTER THREE

Thursday 19 November 2009
National Security Agency
Fort Meade, Maryland

Lt. Commander Jimmy Ramshawe, personal assistant to the director of the world's most sophisticated intelligence agency, was looking for the third time that Fall at a sudden, sharply upward spike in world oil prices. He had noticed one in September, another in October and here was West Texas Intermediate trading futures today at almost $53 a barrel on Wall Street's NYMEX exchange.

It was the same story on the International Petroleum Exchange in London. Brent Crude had actually hit $55 in the City earlier that morning before New York had opened for trading. In mid-afternoon it fell back to $48.95. The pattern was not drastic, but it was steady.

Somewhere in the world, perhaps shielding behind international brokers and traders, there was a new player in the market. And, as Jimmy Ramshawe put it, *the bastard's buying a whole lot of oil. And he's doing it on a damn regular basis . . . I wonder who the hell it could be.*

Gas was now $4 a gallon at the pumps in the United States, which was pleasing no one, especially the President. In Britain it had hit the equivalent of almost $9. And so far as Jimmy could see, it was all caused by just one big player, in the futures market, on both sides of the Atlantic, buying, buying, buying, driving up the prices.

Lt. Commander Ramshawe could not fathom how the buyer had managed to keep it all so secret. The sheer volume of oil futures being purchased was of mammoth proportions: someone who thought he needed an extra 1.5 million barrels a day, or almost 40 million barrels a month.

'Multiply that bastard by forty-two,' muttered Jimmy to himself, 'and you've got some bloody mongrel out there trying to buy one and a half billion gallons of gas every month. Christ! He must have a lot of cars.'

The initial suspect, in the young lieutenant commander's opinion, had to be China. *A billion bloody cars and no oil resources. But then,* he thought, *they wouldn't do it like that. Not out there on the open market buying high-priced futures. They'd cut some kind of a deal with Siberia, or Russia, or the Central Asians around the Baku fields. It can't be them.*

And it could hardly be Russia, which now had all kinds of oil resources from the Baku fields. Great Britain? No, they still had their own North Sea fields. Japan? No. They had very cosy long-term contracts with the Saudis for both gasoline and propane. So who? Germany? France? Unlikely. Especially France which for years had been reducing its oil requirements in favour of nuclear-powered electricity plants. But he reckoned it had to be one of them because no other countries could play on that scale.

The young lieutenant commander had other things to do at that moment but he immediately put in two routine calls, one to the International Petroleum Exchange in London, the other to NYMEX in New York, leaving messages for his contacts on both numbers to call back the National Security Agency at Fort Meade.

Jimmy knew both men, having talked with them during various oil crises before. He did not want this to be official. He just wanted someone to mark his card on who might be the unexpected major buyer in the world oil market right now, the guy driving up the prices; not to earth-shaking levels, but enough to cost a lot of people a great deal of money.

Lt. Commander Ramshawe knew there were always reasons for things. When someone was in any market, buying heavily, there was always a solid reason. Just as when someone was out there selling, there was always a reason. And in Jimmy Ramshawe's global view, those reasons needed to be located and assessed. As his boss Admiral George Morris so often said, *Damned good intelligence officer, young Ramshawe*.

It did not take him long to get his answers. Roger

Smythson, a very senior oil broker in London, said he could not be certain but the buyer who was unsettling the London market was undoubtedly European. He had already run a few traces and it looked like France.

Orders, he said, were coming in from brokers based in Le Havre, France's biggest overseas trading port, which contained the largest of all the French refineries, Gonfreville l'Orcher. In Roger's view the fingerprints of TotalFinaElf were all over some huge trades made from that area.

From New York, the suspicion was the same. Frank Carstairs, who worked almost exclusively as a dealer for Exxon, said flatly, 'I don't know who it is, Jimmy, but I'd bet a lot of money it's France. The orders are all European, and there's a big broker down in the Marseilles area who's been very busy this past couple of months.'

'That's a major oil area, right,' said Jimmy. 'TotalFinaElf country, right?'

'Oh, sure,' said Frank. 'Marseilles handles around one-third of all France's crude oil refining. Terminals at Fos-sur-Mer, that's us, Exxon. Berre, that's Shell, Le Mede, TotalFina, and Lavera, BP. They got a damned great methane terminal down there and an underground LPG depot the size of Yankee Stadium.'

'That's liquid petroleum gas, right, Frank?'

'You got it, Jimmy. Mostly from Saudi Arabia, like the majority of French oil products.'

'Thanks, Frank. Don't wanna keep you. Just wondering what's going on, okay?'

As soon as he put the phone down on New York, Jimmy logged on to the internet and checked the energy status of France, the fifth largest economy in the world and also one of the largest producers of nuclear power.

He read a pocket summary of the recent history of the French oil giant Total. It had merged with the Belgian company Petrofina in 1999, then merged again, with Elf Aquitaine, to create, unimaginatively, TotalFinaElf, the fourth largest publicly listed oil company in the world – right after ExxonMobil, Royal Dutch Shell and BP.

TotalFinaElf had proven reserves of 10.8 billion barrels and production of 2.1 million barrels a day. It owned more than 50 per cent of all the refining capacity in France. It was the seventh largest refiner on earth. And, finally, it was a major shareholder in the 1,100-mile pipeline out of Baku, through Georgia to Turkey's Mediterranean port of Ceyhan.

Christ! thought Jimmy. *They're big enough, but why? France uses only 1.9 million barrels a day, and if push comes to shove their own oil company produces more than that. Beats the hell out of me, unless they're closing down their nuclear power plants and switching back to oil.*

So far as Jimmy could see, this was a highly unlikely scenario. France had reduced her oil usage in the past 30 years from 68 per cent of gross energy consumption to around 40 per cent. But she still imported 1.85 million barrels a day, mostly for road, rail and air transportation. As a nation she was totally reliant on imported oil, the vast bulk of it coming from Saudi Arabia, with some from Norway and a very small amount from other producers.

France generated 77 per cent of her electricity from nuclear power, and she was the second largest exporter of electricity in Europe . . . *they're not going to close down the bloody nuclear plants, are they?*

Same night, 7 p.m.
Chevy Chase, Maryland
The big colonial house which stood well back from the road, fronted by a vast lawn and a sweeping blacktop drive, was not an official embassy of the United States. Though no one would have guessed it.

There were two armed special agents, one just inside the wrought-iron gates, another in a black government automobile near the front door. There were surveillance cameras set into the gables of the house, laser beams, alarm bells and a highly sophisticated electronic security system.

And the visitors were legion. In any one month, the agents at various times waved through cars from foreign embassies, cars from the Pentagon, cars from the National Security Agency, cars from the CIA and cars from the White House.

When Admiral Arnold Morgan (Retd) was in residence, there were a lot of people with a heap of problems who needed the advice of the old Lion of the West Wing. And since many of those problems had a direct bearing on the health and wellbeing of the United States of America, the admiral usually agreed to give people the time of day.

113

As retirements go, the autumn of the admiral's life was full of bright colours. The former National Security Adviser to the President was still in action, unpaid, but still growling . . . *I wouldn't trust that sonofabitch one inch.* So much for the President of one of the richest states in the Middle East . . . *Who! That dumwit couldn't fight his way out of a Lego box, never mind build a decent nuclear submarine.* So much for the science and research director of the world's fourth largest Navy.

Admiral Morgan was like a desert sheik dispensing wisdom and guidance to his flock at the weekly *majlis.* Except the admiral's flock was worldwide, with no racial boundaries. There were probably 10 foreign armed services, allies of the United States, who preferred to check in with the admiral before making any major decision. The same applied, often, to the President of the United States himself, Paul Bedford.

Most of the admiral's guests came at their own request, but the visitor tonight was there as an old friend, invited for dinner by Admiral and Mrs Morgan, the beautiful Kathy who had served as his secretary in the White House with the patience of Mary Magdalene.

General David Gavron, the sixty-two-year-old Israeli Ambassador to the United States, was unmarried, though there were at least two Washington hostesses who were all but certain he would marry them. He loved dining with Arnold and Kathy and he always came alone. The three of them met quite often, occasionally at their favourite Georgetown restaurant, sometimes at the Israeli Embassy three miles north of the city and sometimes here in Chevy Chase.

It was growing cold in Washington and Admiral Morgan reckoned he was in the final couple of weeks of his outdoor barbecue season. On the grill were five enormous lamb chops – which would be eaten with a couple of bottles of Comtesse Nicolais's 2002 Corton-Bressandes, a superb Grand Cru from her renowned Domaine Chandon de Brialles, in the heart of the Côte de Beaune.

Arnold was a devotee of the comtesse's red burgundy and considered lamb chops to be utterly incomplete without it. Which meant the chops were incomplete about a dozen times a year, because, at around $100 a bottle, even Arnold considered Corton-Bressandes a touch extravagant for regular drinking.

However, he had purchased a couple of cases of the 2002 several years ago and he took great delight in serving it to special guests, like David Gavron, who had introduced him to the perfect, silky desert wines of the old Rothschild vineyards 15 miles south-east of Tel Aviv. Admiral Morgan's cellar was never without a case of that.

Tonight it was a very relaxed dinner. The wine was perfect and the chops outstanding. They finished with a piece of Chaumes cheese and drank the last of the burgundy. By 11 p.m. they had retired to the fireside in the timbered book-lined study and Kathy served coffee, a dark, strong Turkish blend which David himself had brought as a gift.

They were discussing their usual subject — terrorism — and the sheer dimension of the pain in the ass it caused all over the world, the cost and the inconvenience. Which was, after all, what terrorists intended.

Quite suddenly General Gavron asked, 'Arnold, have you heard anything more about our old friend Major Ray Kerman?'

'Plenty,' replied the admiral. 'Too damned much. Volcanoes, power stations and God knows what. But we never really got a smell of him. He's an elusive sonofabitch.'

'We nearly had him, you know,' said the general. 'Damn nearly had him.'

Arnold looked up sharply. 'What do you mean, nearly had him?'

'Nearly took him out.'

'You did? When? Where?'

'Couple of months ago. Marseilles.'

'Is that right? I never heard anything.'

'I'm not surprised. But do you remember an apparent gangland killing in a restaurant? Bullets flying. Customers injured, staff dead?'

'Can't say I do.'

'No. The French police covered it up pretty tight.'

'You've lost me, David — what about Kerman.'

'The night before the killings, we picked up Kerman arriving in Paris. On an empty Air France flight, big European airbus, no other passengers. Then we located him again at the French Foreign Legion training base at Aubagne, just east of

116

Marseilles. Remember, we want Kerman just as badly as you do.'

'And then?'

'We sent two of our best agents in.'

'Assassins?'

'Agents, with a . . . well . . . a flexible agenda.'

'And what happened?'

'They were both killed stone dead in some kind of a shoot-out. But of course no one knew who they were. The French police announced it was a gangland killing, involving drugs, tried to blame one of the dead waiters.

'We never even knew what was going on 'til we saw police pictures of two dead men being carried out of the restaurant. They were never even released, far less published, but one of our field officers saw them and immediately identified one of the bodies on the stretcher, throat cut wide open.'

'Christ!' said Arnold. 'What about the other guy?'

'Also dead. Two bullets to the back of the head, fired from a semi-automatic Browning high-power pistol . . . 9mm. The SAS has used them for years, but not many other modern forces do.'

'None of this was in the newspapers, right?'

'Certainly not. For some reason the police, or the French Government, someone, wanted this thing played right down. We of course were not anxious to have the names of our dead agents plastered all over the place. And they carried no identification with them.

'We just decided to let it ride. And the French kept

it quiet for us. The bodies apparently vanished. And no one ever heard anything more. But it was Kerman we were after. And Kerman, I believe, whose finger was on the trigger of his trusty Browning service revolver.'

'You think he cut the other agent's throat?'

'No. That must have been his buddy, whoever that was.'

'Jesus. Sounds like another SAS man,' said Arnold.

'Doesn't it? But Hereford has reported no one else missing. Whoever it was, it was a very professional response. We have never before lost agents armed to the teeth with AK–47s to a couple of amateurs having dinner, armed only with a pocket knife and an old-fashioned pistol.'

'You think Kerman's still in France?'

'I don't know. But he left from Damascus. That's where we logged on to him. But our people did not see him return. He could be anywhere.'

General Gavron could not have known about the devious way General Rashood had made his escape from France – the long car journey back to Paris; the first-class seat on board a regular, crowded Air France flight to Syria; the French Secret Service steering the HAMAS assault chief through security, complete with his Browning 9mm; the two accompanying bodyguards from the 1st Marine Parachute Infantry Regiment, all three wearing Arab dress. It all looked too normal at Damascus Airport, way too normal to attract the attention of Daniel Mostel.

'Kerman,' said Arnold. 'He's like the goddamned

Scarlet Pimpernel, going back to his native France without leaving an address!'

'Someone had it, that's for sure,' replied the Israeli general. 'But now the trail's gone cold.'

'So we're back where we started,' said Arnold. 'He might be in Syria. But it could be Jordan, or Iran, or Libya. Or even Cairo. And now France.'

'Yes. But that was a damn funny business in Marseilles, Arnie,' said the general. 'I mean, what's Kerman doing in France in the first place? And what's he doing in a Special Forces aircraft? Landing at a Foreign Legion base? And who was he dining with? And how come he has the obvious protection of the French police, not to mention the French Government?

'That restaurant was the scene of a colossal crime. And the police refused to release any information whatsoever. A lot of people were hurt, some killed, but they would not even name the dead. I mean my agents.'

Admiral Morgan smiled. General Gavron still regarded himself as the head of Mossad, even though he had retired from that position several months ago. *But I guess*, thought Arnold, *when you've fought a tank battle alongside 'Bren' Adan in the Sinai, been wounded, decorated for valour, and put your life on the line for Israel, you're apt to take even its minor problems very personally.*

He looked into the wide, tanned, open face of the Israeli. He probed those bright blue eyes for a sign of disquiet. And he found it. David Gavron was bitterly

119

unhappy that one of Israel's greatest enemies might be planning another operation.

Arnold could see almost straight through the former Israeli battle commander, as if the unacceptable thought was reflected in those piercing eyes . . . *What the hell was Kerman doing in France, smuggled in, and probably out again, all with government protection?*

The following morning Lt. Commander Ramshawe's phone rang before 0800. He recognised the voice instantly. 'Morning, sir,' he greeted the former Director of the National Security Agency.

'Jimmy,' said Admiral Morgan. 'Do you remember a couple of months ago reading anything at all about a gang shooting, something to do with drugs, in Marseilles, southern France?'

'Nossir. Doesn't ring a bell.'

'It was pretty big. Like 15 injured and maybe six dead in a real bloodbath in some restaurant near the waterfront.'

'Still doesn't ring a bell, sir. But I'll get right on it, check it out. Do you have a more precise date?'

'It was in the last week of August. Restaurant called L'Union. Police apparently wanted it kept quiet. They released no information at all. But Mossad lost two agents, both killed in the fight. One of them had his throat cut. They reckon the other one was shot by Major Ray Kerman.'

'Jeez,' said Jimmy Ramshawe. 'Here he comes again.'

'Precisely my thoughts. See what you can dig up. You and Jane want to come over for dinner later? We'd be glad to see you. And we're getting to the end of the grilling season. How about some New York sirloin steaks? Keep your strength up.'

'Sounds great, sir. We'll be there. Second dogwatch. Three bells, right?'

'Perfect. 1930. See you then, kid.'

Jimmy Ramshawe had absolutely no idea why, but whenever the Big Man came on the line a ripple of excitement swam right through him. The unerring instinct of Admiral Morgan for real trouble was infectious. And so far as the young lieutenant commander could remember, he'd never been wrong.

And another thing. What was with this Marseilles bullshit? He hadn't thought about the place from one year to another and now he'd heard it big time, twice, in 24 hours. The bloody French were up to something, he surmised. The old admiral didn't come in with requests like that unless something was afoot. He made a mental note to air his concerns about the French to Admiral Morgan.

But the trouble with France was, he couldn't really read the language. What he needed was an English-speaking newspaper which might carry the story. He logged on to the internet and whistled up the foreign pages of the London *Daily Telegraph*.

Result: one big fat zero. *Not a bloody line about a mass murder. Bloody oath, they're getting slack over there.*

Born in America of Australian parents, Jimmy still spoke with the pronounced accent of New South

Wales. His fiancée Jane Peacock was the daughter of the Australian Ambassador in Washington. Both of them loved to have a pop at the Brits for being incompetent and inept. And an unreported mass murder in the next door country would do Jimmy fine for a few hours.

Bloody pom journalists. Wouldn't know a truly significant story if it bit 'em in the ass.

He actually knew that was not true, but it amused him to say it, even under his breath. Anyway, beaten by the system, he sent for a translator and keyed his internet connection into the news pages of *Le Figaro*, last week in August. *Le Figaro* was better than the *Telegraph*. But not much.

It reported a serious shoot-out in L'Union restaurant in Marseilles, a commonplace occurrence in a city historically known for its connection to crime, drugs, smuggling and other nefarious activities.

The newspaper claimed 15 people had been admitted to hospital and some of them had been released that night. It also believed there were TWO fatalities (Jimmy's caps in his report) when it was clear there were more. Because they named the dead waiters, but not the Mossad agents.

The whole thrust of the story was an intergang battle involving drugs, professional villains, killing each other. It was of no significant interest to ordinary citizens. And the innocent bystanders caught in the crossfire? Those who survived would receive generous compensation from the restaurant's insurance company.

The headline in *Le Figaro* ran over just one column on page 7. It read: GANGLAND KILLING IN MARSEILLES — *Diners in L'Union restaurant hurt in crossfire.*

There was no follow-up on any of the next five days. 'Well, I guess that's the bloody end of that,' said Jimmy to himself.

Well, nearly. Because the young intelligence officer who enjoyed the ear of the mighty had received this story from the mightiest of all, Admiral Arnold Morgan himself. *And the great man does not go real strong on half-measures*, he thought. *He called me because he wants some bloody answers. And he wants 'em quick, like by dinnertime tonight. That's why we're going to his house, right?*

He immediately told his translator, a twenty-three-year-old civilian graduate named Jo, to get on the line to directory inquiries in France and get the number of L'Union restaurant in Marseilles. He then told her to make the call and to put it on the speakerphone in the middle of his desk.

And he listened with interest as the phone rang on the faraway south coast of France and was answered on the fourth ring.

'*Préfecture de Police, Marseilles.*'

'Tell 'em you want the restaurant, not the bloody gendarmes,' hissed Jimmy.

Jo struggled boldly but was told firmly, 'The restaurant is closed. We have no information about its reopening.'

'Tell 'em you don't understand why a closed

123

restaurant has its phone calls automatically diverted to the police station,' hissed Jimmy.

But again Jo encountered a brick wall – 'I have no information on that,' replied the Marseilles gendarme.

'Pull rank,' said Jimmy. 'Tell 'em who we are. And then tell 'em we want to know precisely how many people were killed in the mass murder at L'Union because we believe at least one of them may have been a United States citizen.'

Jo went right ahead, beginning, 'Sir, this is the Director's office at the National Security Agency of the United States of America in Washington, DC. You may call back to verify if you wish. But we want some answers, and if necessary we will go to presidential level to get them. Please bring someone of senior authority to the telephone.'

'*Un moment, s'il vous plaît.*'

'Beautiful, Jo, that's my girl,' grinned Lt. Commander Ramshawe. And in the background they both heard a voice say, '*Sécurité Américaine.*'

And then a new voice came on, speaking excellent English. 'This is Chief Inspector Rochelle. How may I assist?'

Jimmy took over. 'Thank you for coming to the phone, Chief Inspector. My name is Lt. Commander Ramshawe and I'm the Assistant to the Director of the National Security Agency in Washington, DC. I thought I was calling L'Union restaurant, but we came straight through to you. I would like to know exactly how many people died in that shooting in the restaurant two months ago? We have reason to believe one of them was an American citizen.'

'*Non, monsieur*. That is not the case. There were two members of staff, one of them the head waiter, both French, killed instantly. And then two more staff members died in hospital. They also were French, and both known to me. No member of the public, injured in the shooting, died later in the hospital. That's four people dead altogether, all French. The whole thing was drug related.'

'I see,' said Jimmy. 'And what about the men who came into the restaurant and carried out the shooting. Were they arrested?'

'Unfortunately not, sir. They all got away. Three of them. And our inquiries have led us to a drug gang in Algiers, where we are continuing the search. The perpetrators of the crime are known to us. And have been for several years. But these people are very elusive.'

'Are you absolutely certain that no one else except members of staff were killed?' asked Jimmy.

'*Absolument*,' replied the chief inspector. 'You see, only the staff were standing up. Everyone else was sitting down. The bullets hit the waiters.'

'Do you think the Algerians got their man?' said Jimmy.

'I think so. One of the waiters was under observation by us. But I am not at liberty to name him for obvious reasons. However, we think the assassins achieved their objective.'

'Very well, Chief Inspector,' said Jimmy. 'Thank

you for being so helpful. I will make my report on the basis of the information you have given me.'

He replaced the phone, saying under his breath, 'That is one lying French bastard.'

'I'm sorry, sir?' said Jo.

'Oh, nothing really. It's just that when you get told that a renowned international intelligence agency has just had two of its agents murdered on a certain day, at a certain time, in a certain place, there is an extremely high likelihood of that being true. When a French policeman then tells you it never happened, there is an extremely high probability of that being a fair dinkum whopper.'

Jo laughed. 'Well, the first man we spoke to was obviously in a defensive mode. But the Chief Inspector seemed relatively forthcoming.'

'No doubt,' replied Jimmy. 'But he was still telling a flagrant lie.'

And then he said, 'Jo, I've got a plan. You go and rustle up a couple of cups of coffee and we'll see if we can get one of Langley's finest around to that restaurant.'

Four minutes later he was outlining the story to the European desk of the CIA, who had a good man in Marseilles. In fact they had two, both in residence. Sure, they'd get right on it, especially if the Big Man was interested. They'd do some snooping, see if anyone knew anything, maybe someone who was working on the refurbishing of L'Union.

★   ★   ★

4 p.m. (local), Friday 20 November
Rue de la Loge, Marseilles

Tom Kelly, a Philadelphia-born journalist, had been twenty-nine years old and preparing to marry a Bryn Mawr history teacher when he fell in love, helplessly, with one of her French students. She was Marie Le Clerc, aged twenty-one, from Marseilles.

Tom bagged his job, bagged the history teacher and followed Marie home to France. There he married her, found himself a job as news editor on a local paper, then moved to head up the political desk of the *Le Figaro* in Paris. From there he drifted into a close relationship with two CIA agents, primarily because he was a fountain of knowledge about politics in the capital city.

At which point the CIA requested he come to Washington where he was cleared for security and stationed back in Marseilles with a very useful freelance contract from the *Washington Post*. Tom was thirty-six now and he and Marie had two children and lived close to her parents in the western suburbs of the city.

Right now he was making his way along rue de la Loge towards L'Union. He could see it about 50 yards ahead. There was a white truck outside and two ladders were jutting out through the wide open front door of the restaurant. Men at work, he thought.

When he reached the entrance, he turned left, up the steps and into the main foyer. There was a strong smell of paint, and a deafening screeching sound

127

from the main dining room where two men were sanding the oak floor. Above him were two painters, on scaffolding, working on a beam, which he did not know had recently been decorated with a stream of bullets from an AK-47.

No one took a blind bit of notice as he strolled across the room inspecting the refurbishments. He could easily have been one of them. He wore dark-blue trousers, matching wool sweater and a light-brown leather jacket.

Eventually someone noticed him and came over, inquiring if he could help. René was his name, an electrician by trade.

Tom's French was excellent and he came straight to the point: he identified himself and told René he was trying to find out how many people had been killed that August night, since his government believed one of them might have been an American citizen.

There seemed to be no one around in authority, and René was glad of the break and happy to help. 'I don't really know myself,' he shrugged, 'but Anton, up the ladder with the paintbrush, he may know. His brother was a friend of the waiter who died in hospital . . . let me call him down.'

Anton descended from the ceiling by way of the scaffolding and shook hands with Tom. 'Six people died in here that night, including the two guys who came in with the Kalashnikovs. One was shot and one had his throat cut.'

'Anton, how do you know that?'

'Because we all went to the funeral of Mario, and another guy who worked here saw the whole thing and he told us at the reception. He said the two guys who came in with the guns were both killed – he thought by the men they had come to assassinate. He said they weren't just crazies. They were professionals who had come to kill someone specific.'

'And Mario was still alive when they carried him out?' asked Tom.

'Yes. Unconscious but still alive. But the guy at the funeral said there were six bodies carried out. He remembered because only four of them went in an ambulance. He said the other two were taken away in a police van.'

1300 (local), Friday 20 November
National Security Agency, Fort Meade, Maryland
Tom Kelly's report came in from the CIA's European desk immediately after lunch. It confirmed what had been obvious to Lt. Commander Ramshawe from the start: six, not four people, had been killed in L'Union. The French police had gone in and cleared out the bodies of the two Mossad agents and were saying nothing about it to anyone.

And, if they knew, they were most certainly saying nothing about the man they had come to kill. Admiral Morgan's man had been positive those two assassins had come for Major Kerman.

And if, thought Jimmy, *it was straightforward, why had not the French authorities simply admitted there had been an attempt on the life of the ex-British SAS major, which had failed, and somehow Major Kerman had made his escape?*

Only one answer to that in Jimmy's opinion: the bloody French knew darned well Kerman was in that restaurant, and probably at their invitation, since they had taken very large steps to hush the whole thing up.

So why did France arrange a secret meeting with the most wanted terrorist in the world? That was a question to which there would be no answer. The French were not admitting he was in the country, not admitting someone had tried to kill him and very definitely not admitting he had more than likely killed one of the assassins.

This was, the lieutenant commander knew, the end of the line. The French were saying nothing. The two Mossad men were dead. And no one knew where Kerman was. Nor the identity of the men he had been having dinner with in L'Union restaurant. To pursue the matter further would be a monumental waste of time, especially since Mossad would not wish to publicise the death of its agents.

Nonetheless, Jimmy logged all of the information on to his private computer files and downloaded a copy of the CIA report to show Admiral Morgan at dinner that evening.

7.30 p.m., same night
Chevy Chase, Maryland
Jimmy Ramshawe and Jane Peacock were in luck tonight. Admiral Morgan was a friend of both their

130

fathers and he elected to push the boat out one more time with a couple more bottles of Comtesse Nicolais's Corton-Bressandes. Jimmy's eyes lit up at the sight of them warming gently by the log fire in the study.

He helped the admiral barbecue the steaks, mostly by holding an umbrella against a chill late November rain, then moving in with a wide platter Kathy had kept in the warming oven.

The four of them knew each other well. Jane, who looked like a surf goddess right off Bondi Beach, loved to go shopping with Kathy in Georgetown because the admiral's wife kept her on the straight and narrow, fashionwise; helping her choose items she knew would be acceptable to Ambassador Peacock, dispenser of the allowance, financer of the ruinous college fees she annually required.

Kathy hated having live-in help and preferred to manage her own kitchen, so after dinner she and Jane tackled the clearing up while the admiral and Jimmy retired to the study.

They sat in front of the fire and Arnold Morgan came swiftly to the point. 'Okay, Jimmy, tell me what you found about the murders in L'Union restaurant?'

'All calls to the restaurant are routed directly to the Marseilles central gendarmerie. When you call, a policeman answers the phone. And when he does you are told nothing. No one knows anything.

'But there's a Chief Inspector Rochelle who seems helpful but is clearly lying. He says there were four deaths that night. All French, all staff. Two died in the restaurant, the other two in hospital. There were not four deaths. There were six.'

'How'd you find out,' asked Arnold.

'Well, I spoke to the Marseilles cop myself. Then I had Langley put one of their guys on it in the city. And he did a damned thorough job. Got into the restaurant and interviewed one of the workmen painting the place. And the workman had met a member of staff at the funeral of a waiter.

'This was a guy who ducked behind the bar during the shooting. He told the CIA agent there were six dead men altogether. He saw four of them carried out to ambulances, and two others loaded into a police wagon.

'Anton – that's the workman I spoke to – saw the whole thing. He says two guys came in with Kalashnikovs, started shooting, and were then both killed by the guys they had come for. I brought you a copy of the CIA report.'

'Well, that fits in exactly with the story I was told originally,' said Arnold. 'And I'm afraid it's the end of the trail. The French are never going to say anything. And neither Mossad, nor even the Israeli Government, could possibly ask them.'

'No, I suppose not,' said Jimmy. '"Oh, by the way, messieurs, we just sent a couple of hitmen into a crowded restaurant in the middle of Marseilles, and after they'd shot half the staff and half the customers, they ended up dead themselves. Anyone know what happened to 'em?"'

Admiral Morgan chuckled. Young Ramshawe's keen, swift brain often gave way to a caustic Aussie humour. And it always amused him. But right now, he was pondering what he knew was a far, far bigger question.

'The thing is, Jimmy,' he said, 'we have to believe the Israelis when they say they located Kerman in France, and certainly the savage response to the Mossad hitmen bears all the marks of that particular terrorist. But the main thing for us is to find out what he was doing in France. Who was he seeing and why?

'A guy like Kerman, or General Rashood, whatever the hell he calls himself, must understand the dangers of any kind of travel. He could be spotted by anyone. He's obviously better off skulking around the goddamned kasbah or somewhere in the desert.

'But he made this journey. Apparently in an otherwise empty Air France passenger jet. A damned great Airbus all on his own. Someone at a very high level in France wanted to see him quite badly. And they are never going to admit it. Any inquiry from us would be like talking to the Eiffel Tower. We'll get nothing.

'And quite honestly, Jimmy, I think it's just a waste of time pursuing this further. Let's just file it and watch out for the slightest sign of further developments.'

'Guess we can't do much else, sir. But, Christ, wouldn't you just love to know where that bastard is right now?'

'I dearly would, Jimmy. But I guess he's not in France any more. Not after those shenanigans in Marseilles.'

At that precise moment, 11 p.m. on the night of 20 November, Admiral Morgan was entirely correct. Less than three months later he would be wrong.

2300, Tuesday 2 February
10,000 feet above the coast of southern France
General Ravi Rashood was in company with eight of his most trusted HAMAS henchmen, three of them known al-Qaeda combat troops, plus three former Saudi Army officers. They were just crossing the Mediterranean coastline in an AS532 Cougar Mk 1 French Army helicopter, a high-performance, heavily gunned aircraft which had just made the 380-mile crossing across the sea from Algeria.

The Cougar had taken off from a remote corner of the small regional airport of Tébessa, situated at the eastern end of the Atlas Mountains, where the high peaks began to smooth their way down to the plains of Tunisia.

General Rashood and his team had made a deeply covert journey that day, from a small airfield outside Damascus, in a private air charter flight, unmarked by any livery, straight along the North African coast to Tripoli. There the Cougar Mk 1 had met them and flown the 250 miles to their first refuelling point at Tébessa.

Right now they were coming into Aubagne, the Foreign Legion base where the general had found himself six months before on the day of the shoot-out at L'Union. Tonight, however, no one would disembark. The helicopter was immediately refuelled for the flight north to Paris.

Under cover of darkness they would land at around 0300 at the French military's special ops base in Taverny, north of Paris, their home for the next two weeks.

At this point, the Arab freedom fighters accompanying the general wore Western civilian clothing, mostly blue jeans, T-shirts and sweaters. But for all that it was an intensely military journey. Every man had a map and they were studying the same thing – the huge King Khalid Air Base beyond the Saudi Arabian military city of Khamis Mushayt.

The helicopter made a wide circular sweep around the west of Paris, crossed the Seine and headed in to land across the foggy fields above the Oise valley. They grabbed their bags the moment the helicopter touched down and were shown immediately to barracks not 100 yards from where the Cougar had landed.

It was now 0245 and General Michel Jobert, the commander-in-chief of the base, was there in person. He smiled as he shook hands with General Rashood, to whom, in a sense, he probably already owed his life. They had not seen each other for six months.

Both officers climbed into an Army staff car and were driven to the French commandant's residence where the HAMAS C-in-C would live during the forthcoming period of intense training. In the morning they would meet, for the first time, the 48 highly trained combat troops of the 1st Marine Parachute Infantry Regiment with whom they would fight in the battle for the airfield at Khamis Mushayt.

Ravi Rashood and Michel Jobert sat before a log fire and sipped a warming *café complet*. Each had been amazed at the way the French Government, and indeed the police, had kept the lid on the murders in the L'Union. And each of them understood only too clearly the dangers of General Rashood travelling outside the Arab world.

Ravi's journey from Damascus in August had been careful. But not careful enough. This time the journey was indeed untraceable. It was obvious they had been attacked by Mossad agents in Marseilles. Since then they had been at pains to ensure that no such ambush would occur before the operation. 'It would be nice if we could avoid running into a couple of assassins trying to blow our heads off,' said Michel Jobert. 'Especially since Jacques Gamoudi is not due here until next week.'

Ravi grinned. 'He was very efficient that night, hah?' he said. 'I think that character might have hit us but for the table Jacques threw forward.'

'Think! I can tell you he *would* have hit us,' said the general. 'I never even saw them. And, *mon Dieu!* Was Jacques ever handy with that damn great knife of his!'

'Saved us,' said Ravi. 'I'm glad he's on our side.'

General Jobert, despite being the Special Forces

mastermind behind the plan to topple the Saudi monarchy, could never accompany his men on the mission. Should he be captured or even killed, France's complicity in the operation would be made abundantly clear, and the position of the President of France – who, it was also emphasised, was to appear innocent of all knowledge of the assault – would be made untenable.

As for the French troops who would take part, well, the 1st Marine Parachute Infantry Regiment would send them in without identification. They would conduct the operation within hours of arriving on Saudi soil and then leave immediately. Unlike Ravi Rashood, who would have to do rather more to earn his millions of dollars reward.

Later that morning General Rashood and his 11-man team from the desert gathered for a briefing before they met their 48 French comrades who would join them on the mission. They had breakfast together in a mess hall and then reported to an underground ops room in which were arranged seven rows of eight chairs each. At the front of the room were two tables, behind which were two large computer screens.

One showed the south shores of the Red Sea with the old French colony of Djibouti to the west, and, to the east, the mysterious desert kingdom of the Yemen, the earliest known civilisation in southern Arabia. The other showed a much smaller-scale map of the Yemen border with Saudi Arabia, stretching along the eastern coastline of the Red Sea.

When the team was assembled, Generals Rashood

and Jobert came in, accompanied by three French Special Forces commanders, all majors in their early thirties, Etienne Marot, Paul Spanier and Henri Gilbert. Today everyone, including the new arrivals from Arabia, was in work uniform: boots, combat trousers, khaki shirts and wool sweaters with black berets.

The eight HAMAS/al-Qaeda men were seated in one row, three back, and, while each of them had a smattering of French, directly behind them were two Arabic-speaking ex-Foreign Legion troops who would act as interpreters.

The heavy wooden doors were closed behind them and two guards were on duty outside in the well-lit passage. Two more stood guard at the head of the short flight of stairs which led up to the corridor beyond the officers' mess.

General Jobert began the briefing, informing them that this was not nearly so dangerous an operation as it might have appeared. Certainly they would need to be at their absolute best in combat, but by the time they launched their assault Saudi Arabia would be in chaos and the lifeblood of the oil wells would have ceased to flow. The King would be under enormous pressure to abdicate and the entire Saudi military would be a state of mass confusion, unsure who they were working for.

Nonetheless, this was a room full of tension, as many young men prepared themselves to fight, hundreds of miles from home, in a small group, in territory they had not seen before.

'I am sure,' said General Jobert, reassuringly, 'the Saudis will be wondering who they are expected to fight for – the old regime or the incoming one. And according to our principal source, the man who will become the new King of Saudi Arabia, Crown Prince Nasir, the army in Khamis Mushayt will be happy to surrender. It will comfort you to know that the Crown Prince is constantly being apprised of our plans at all times. You can be sure that your success will meet with his approval and his gratitude.'

He told them that in the broadest possible terms they were expected to attack and destroy the Arabian fighter bombers parked at the King Khalid Air Base five miles to the east of Khamis Mushayt.

'A separate force is then expected to occupy the headquarters of the Army base and demand their surrender,' he said. 'This will almost certainly mean taking out the guard room, and possibly the senior commanding officers. General Rashood will personally lead this section of the operation.'

The general then handed over to the most senior of the ex-Saudi officers, Colonel Sa'ad Kabeer, a devout Muslim, descendant of ancient tribal chiefs from the north, and an implacable enemy of the Saudi royal family. Colonel Kabeer had commanded a tank battalion in Saudi's Eighth Armoured Brigade in Khamis Mushayt. He would lead the opening diversionary assault on the air base.

Colonel Kabeer rose to his feet and nodded a greeting to the men before him. And then he told them, encouragingly, 'The Saudi Army has always suffered from a great shortage of manpower. Thus there is always weakness. In addition, the head of the armed forces is a prince of the royal family, as are numerous C-in-Cs and batallion commanders.

'We should remember that at the time of our opening assaults, every one of them will be terrified that their enormous stipends from the King are about to end. It would not greatly surprise me if several of them flee the country before we fire our opening shots. I am in complete agreement with Prince Nasir, the Crown Prince, that the Saudi Army will cave in the moment we attack. So we should conduct our operation with maximum confidence, knowing that right is on our side, and so is the incoming ruling government.

'I should like to begin by outlining the precise location and state of readiness of our target . . .' The colonel stepped back and pointed to a spot on the second computer screen.

'This is Khamis Mushayt. It is located in the mountainous south-west of the country in the Azir region. This, by the way, was an independent kingdom until 1922, when Abdul Aziz captured it. The entire area still has very close ties to the Yemen, from where we launch our assault.

'There is huge hostility to the Saudi King down here, because they believe he has abandoned his Bedouin roots and sold out to the West. In the totally unlikely event of failure, there will be no hostility to us locally, I am certain of that.

'Khamis Mushayt, right here, is a thriving market

town with a modern bazaar. The population is around 35,000, and the town is situated 2,200 metres above sea level. Except for March and August when it rains like hell, it has a moderate climate and there is a lot of agriculture and vegetation — should we need to cover.

'The Saudi Army's Field Artillery and Infantry Schools are both located at Khamis Mushayt. It's also the headquarters of the Army's Southern Command. There are three brigades deployed here in the south to protect the region from any invasion from the Yemen. The Saudis have, rightly, never trusted them. There's the 4th Armoured Brigade at Jirzan on the west coast, the 10th Mechanised Brigade at Najran in the mountains, and the 11th at Sharujah to the east . . . right here on the edge of the Rub al-Khali, the Empty Quarter.

'Now, you should all take a note of the GPS numbers for the King Khalid Air Base in case anyone gets lost. It's precisely 18.18N 29.00' — and 042.48E 20.01'. The base controls all military air traffic in the area. There is, by the way, no commercial traffic. That all goes to Abha, 25 miles west.

'At King Khalid we're looking at two flying wings. One with McDonnell Douglas F-15s. The other with squadrons of British Tornado fighter bombers. In addition, there are elements of the 4th (Southern) Air Defence Group to provide protection from air attack on the airfield. We should probably knock that out very quickly.'

General Rashood, who would assume overall

command of the three attacks, then stood up to discuss deployment. 'As you can see,' he said, 'we have a 60-strong squadron. Six of these will command a small headquarters, central to our communications with each other, and with Colonel Jacques Gamoudi in Riyadh, if necessary. There will be no direct communications with France under any circumstances whatsoever.

'The remainder of you will be split into three troops, each of 18 men. Each group will arrive on station separately because it's far less risky that way.

'The first diversionary attack will be on the air base main entrance, and carried out by a group of al-Qaeda fighters which will rendezvous with us when we arrive. They will provide our explosives, detonators, detcord and timing devices, all acquired locally. And when they launch their own attack at the gates, they will use small-arms grenades and hand-held anti-tank rocket launchers.

'Meanwhile, Troops One and Two will cut their way through the wire and into the air base on the far side. They will proceed to eliminate all the aircraft they can see, both on the ground and in the hangars. We already have excellent local charts and maps of the airfield which will be distributed later. At the rear of the room you will see that large model, which looks like a layout for model trains. It is in fact a very good scale model of the base.

'At the conclusion of the raid, which I anticipate will face only very light opposition, both the airfield

142

troops will move up to a secure point halfway between the base and Khamis Mushayt.

'Shortly before that, Troop Three, led by myself, will attack the main military compound. We will blast our way into the barracks and secure the headquarters. We will inform anyone still standing that the King Khalid Air Base has fallen. Half the fighter planes in the Saudi Air Force will have been destroyed – with luck there will still be a fierce red glow in the sky, to reinforce that message, especially if we locate the fuel dump.

'And then we will demand surrender, before we blow the place to pieces. We'll force them to take us immediately to the commanding general and his deputy – that's two arrest parties of six each – and we'll hold them at gunpoint until the C-in-C broadcasts to the entire complex ordering a complete surrender. If they resist, we'll execute them. Which will terrify everyone else. But don't worry, they'll surrender. They're only toy soldiers.

'One thing to remember on a mission as highly classified as this: we leave no colleague on the battlefield. Anyone hit, injured or dead will be brought out and returned with the squadron to France. That's one thing we can learn from the US Navy SEALs. In their entire history, they have *never* left a man behind.'

Already those with whom General Rashood would fight were beginning to smile and talk among themselves. For the first time, they began to feel that they could pull it off. And perhaps the most important issue was the new concept of strong local support, the explosive coming from people in the town who hated the King. There was the readiness of the al-Qaeda fighters, Saudis, who would be joining them. And above all there was the feeling that they were representing the next King. This was not some mere terrorist attack on the innocent. This was proper soldiering. With proper objectives. Conducted under professional military commanders.

But for the first time, now, each man in the room began to appreciate the enormity of the task that lay before them; became aware of the huge political and global consequences of success – never mind failure – in their forthcoming mission.

'Do you know how we will get in there without anyone knowing?' asked someone.

'No,' replied Ravi sarcastically. 'I thought we'd just hang around and see if there was a bus going our way . . . you have any spare Saudi riyals? We might need them for the fares.'

The whole room collapsed into laughter as the tension eased. Despite the brutal reputation of the trained killer who stood before them, Ravi Rashhood always knew how to speak to his team.

'Just checking,' replied the trooper. 'I'm used to coming in by parachute. And I didn't think you'd think much of that.'

'Correct, soldier,' said Ravi. 'If it eases your mind, the answer to your question is, by sea.'

'Not swimming, sir? The Red Sea's full of sharks.'

'Not swimming,' replied General Rashood, smiling. 'Something more dangerous than that. But with a much better chance of survival. We won't be dealing with that part of the plan until next week.'

General Jobert formally thanked the HAMAS commander and then outlined the ground which would be covered over the next two days. 'The first session this afternoon will be devoted to commands,' he said. 'Troops One and Two, both on the airfield and during preparation, will speak only French since the majority of these specialist troops are from the 1st Marine Parachute Infantry Regiment.

'Troop Three, commanded by General Rashood, will comprise mainly Arabic-speaking personnel with some French support from this base. All of them, however, speak English, which is the native tongue of the general himself. Therefore we have decided that, throughout the mission, those under General Rashood's command will converse only in English.

'However, any communication back to your six-man headquarters must be in French, and for that reason Major Etienne Marot will serve as General Rashood's number two, with special responsibilities for communications. Do not, however, allow that to blind you to the real reason he is here. Major Marot commands the Army's Special Operation Light Aviation Detachment – that's a helicopter assault team. His business is to arrive in places when he is not expected.'

That comment provoked more laughter, and Major Marot himself, a tall, lean career officer from

145

Normandy, allowed himself a wry smile beneath his wide black moustache.

'I wish now to deal with our fall-back positions,' continued General Jobert. 'These are outlined on the maps you will shortly be given. By this I mean that should Troop Three run into a 5,000-strong Saudi Army guarding the barracks throughout the night, plainly we would not carry out our attack. But, as you are aware, we do not build operations such as this without considering every possiblity of entry, action and escape.

'Before I hand over to your divisional commanders, I would just like to confirm that we expect the complete surrender of Khamis Mushayt to lead to a general surrender of the entire Saudi military machine. But remember – the actual assault on the royal palaces in Riyadh does not even begin until your mission is complete.

'This is a just and proper war, born of the most terrible extravagances by just one family, to the utter detriment of the people. Everything depends on your work in Khamis Mushayt. That will be the military start of the chain of events which will bring a new, enlightened reign to Saudi Arabia . . . a new King, who is already a great friend to France, and indeed to all devout Muslims throughout the Middle East. You surely go with the blessings of your God.'

General Jobert once again took his seat and General Rashood introduced the next speaker, Captain Faisal Rahman, a distant relative of the royal family who

146

now commanded a battalion of al–Qaeda fighters based in Riyadh.

Like everyone else, Captain Rahman was dressed in semi-combat gear. He rose to his feet and wished everyone *as salaam alaykum*, the traditional Bedouin greeting, which was accompanied by another gesture familiar among desert Arabs, the right hand touching the forehead and the arm coming downwards in a long, graceful sweep.

'I should like to tell you of a vacation in Spain made in recent years by a King of Saudi Arabia,' he said. 'He arrived in a private Boeing 747 accompanied by an entourage of 350, and three more aircraft, one of which was kitted out as a hospital. His vast retinue swelled to over 3,000 in a few days. There were over 50 black Mercedes cars, and an intensive care unit and operating theatre built into his woodland palace near Marbella. This building is a replica of the White House in Washington, where else?

'It cost $1,500 a day in flowers! What with the King's water being flown in weekly from Mecca, his lamb, rice and dates coming in from other places in Arabia, the King's bills were knocking hard at almost $5 million a day. By the time the enormous court of Saudi Arabia left Spain they had banged a hole in $90 million.

'The Spanish have a name for any and every Saudi ruler: King Midas. And there are those among us who think this entirely unnecessary. This lunatic expenditure, reckless extravagance, founded on wealth essentially bestowed upon us by Allah himself.

'It's not as if the King earned it, or even won it. He was given it, at birth. In our view he is the custodian and guardian of the nation's wealth. It's not his to fling around any way he wants. And it certainly ought not to be at the disposal of his 35,000 relatives, who somehow believe they have the right to do anything they damn well please with it either.

'I don't know if you are aware but every last member of the Saudi royal family travels free on the national airline, Saudia. Well, there are more than 30,000 of them now, and since it is customary for princes to have a minimum of 40 sons, sometimes 50, there may be 60,000 of them before long. That's 200 of them flying free every working day of the year. And since most of them fly at least 20 times a year, that's 4,000 of them every day! Jumping in and out of aircraft free of charge. I have one question? Is that in any way reasonable?'

The al-Qaeda commander paused. Many members of his audience were shaking their heads in astonishment and disbelief. There were also nods of approval at his words. The numbers he quoted were indeed shocking. But there was a more shocking one yet to come.

'Twenty years ago,' said Captain Rahman, 'my country held cash reserves of $120 billion. Today those reserves are down to less than $20 billion . . .' He paused to let this information sink in.

'The battle we are about to fight in the hills of

south-western Saudi Arabia, and in the streets of Riyadh, is not revolution, nor even *jihad*. We are fighting to purify a country which has been poisoned.'

A young French soldier, deadly serious, called out, 'And there really is a feeling in the country that this will help us to achieve our victory?'

'Stronger than you will ever know,' replied the captain. 'In the religious schools all over the country they are turning out young men who have been taught to follow the old ways, the customs of the Bedouin, the ones which represent our roots.

'We are by nature people of the desert but our enemies in neighbouring countries are closing in around us. Almost the whole of Islam believes we have betrayed the Palestinians, failed to help them in the most terrible injustices committed against them by the Zionists.

'Other Arab leaders feel we have allowed the humiliation of Islam. And in a sense that is precisely what the government of Saudi Arabia has done. We were all born to be a God-fearing nation, following the words of the Koran, the teachings of the Prophet, helping the poorer parts of our nation, not spending $90 million on a vacation like some King Midas.'

At this point General Rashood himself looked up. 'Every Arab knows the situation in Saudi Arabia cannot continue. There is too much education for that. I believe I read somewhere that two out of every three Ph.D.s awarded in Saudi Arabia are for Islamic studies. The Saudi Arabian royal family's greatest threat is from within. The clerics are teaching truth. It's just a matter of time before the whole thing explodes.'

'Just a matter of time,' echoed Captain Rahman. 'And I believe we will hasten that time. And the good Prince Nasir will come to power and make the changes we must have . . . I know this seems a very ruthless, reckless way of attaining our ends, but it is the only way. And the new Saudi ruler will owe a debt of gratitude to France which may never be repaid.'

The captain hesitated before adding, with a smile, 'But I understand he will most certainly try.'

General Jobert stood up and spoke. 'I will now call out the members of each group. Your commanding officers have given this considerable thought. But the three troops of 18 men have very different tasks, and the command headquarters situated in the hills close to the action also has a critical role to play.

'Please now, everyone pay attention while I make a roll call . . . *Troop One, air base assault . . . commanding officer Major Paul Spanier . . .*'

0830, Sunday 7 February
Port Militaire, Brest
Two hundred and fifty miles to the west of Paris lay the sprawling headquarters of the French Navy around the estuary of Brest, where the Penfeld River ran into the bay. This was the western outpost of Brittany, home of France's main Atlantic base, where they kept the mighty 12,000-ton Triomphant Class ballistic missile submarines. Not to mention the main

150

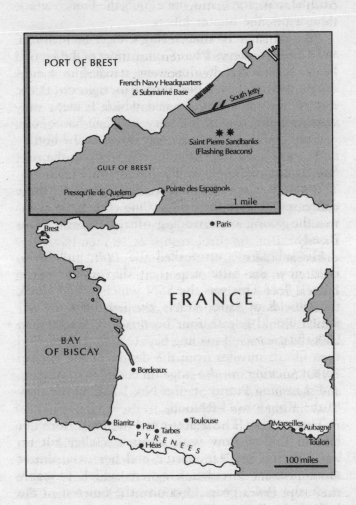

PORT OF BREST

French Navy Headquarters
& Submarine Base

South Jetty

★ ★
Saint Pierre Sandbanks
(Flashing Beacons)

GULF OF BREST

Pressqu'île de Quelern   ● Pointe des Espagnols

1 mile

Brest   ● Paris

FRANCE

BAY
OF BISCAY

● Bordeaux

Biarritz   ● Toulouse   Marseilles ● ● Aubagne
Pau ● Tarbes   ● Toulon
P Y R E N E E S
Héas

100 miles

Atlantic strike force, and, since 2005, the French attack submarines, the hunter killers.

Admiral Marc Romanet, Flag Officer Submarines, and Admiral Georges Pires, Commander of the French Navy's special ops division, were standing in a light drizzle wearing heavy Navy topcoats, right out at the end of the south jetty beyond which France's submarines swung to port for entry into their home base.

They could see her now, way down in the bottle-neck, more than two miles to the west, on the surface, making six knots up the channel in 20 fathoms. Through the glasses Admiral Romanet could see three figures standing on the bridge. One of them he knew was the young commanding officer, Captain Alain Roudy.

His submarine was called the *Perle*, hull S606, right now the most important ship in the entire French fleet. This was the SSN which would attack the oilfields of Saudi Arabia, the lethal slug of war which would release four boatloads of frogmen to blast the great Gulf loading bays to smithereens. And then fire its missiles from the depths of the Persian Gulf, knocking out the huge oil complex of Abqaiq, and slamming Pump Station No. 1 halting the flow of the Kingdom's lifeblood,

This was her. The 2,500-ton *Perle*, fresh from her refit in Toulon, now with a much smaller but no less powerful nuclear reactor, and her new, almost silent primary circulation system which probably made the *Perle*'s propulsion unit the quietest in the entire undersea world.

She'd been down in France's Mediterranean Command Base for her major refit for almost six months. And she was a lot more important today than she was last May when she had gone in. At that time it had been assumed the Saudi mission would be carried out by one of the brand-new boats scheduled to come out of Project Barracuda. But that programme had been subject to mild but critical delay, and Prince Nasir could not wait.

He had been to see the President three times. And three times the President had insisted the Navy move fast, in two oceans, and cripple the Saudi oil industry before the New Year of 2010 was more than three months old.

The three men who had been appointed to deal with that request were the two admirals who now stood at the end of the south jetty, and their guest, who was at that moment sheltering from the rain in the Navy staff car parked beneath the bright, flashing harbour warning light at the tip of the jetty: M. Gaston Savary, France's Secret Service chief.

Admiral Pires had invited Savary to visit because he knew the pressure under which the President had placed him. He considered that the least he could do was to show Savary the underwater warship upon which all of their hopes, and probably careers, depended.

Tonight there would be a small working dinner at Admiral Romanet's home, where Savary would meet the commanding officer and much would be explained. This was to be the first briefing for Captain

Roudy. And, privately, Gaston Savary thought he would probably have a heart attack. It was not, after all, an everyday mission.

'*Gaston, come out here!*' called Georges Pires. '*I'll show you our ship.*'

Gaston Savary stepped out into the rain and took the proffered binoculars. He stared out down the channel, and saw the *Perle* sweeping through the water, a light bow wave breaking over her foredeck, the three figures up on the bridge, in uniform, looking ahead.

They stood in the rain for another 15 minutes, watching the submarine drift wide out to her starboard side, staying in 100 feet of water, as she skirted the St-Pierre Bank, a rise in the ocean floor which shelved up to only 25 feet in two places.

Almost directly south of the harbour entrance she made her turn, hard to port into the channel, and headed in. Her jet-black hull seemed much bigger now and more sinister. She was in fact the most modern of the Rubis/Améthyste Class, commissioned back in 1993. But naval warships do not get old: they have everything replaced. And now, the *Perle* not only packed the normal hefty punch of her Aérospatiale Exocet missiles, which could be launched from her torpedo tubes, she also carried a new weapon . . . medium–range cruise missiles.

These could be launched from underwater, under satellite guidance, and literally hammer into a target several hundred miles away, travelling at Mach 0.9, just short of the speed of sound.

She looked a symbol of menace. And, according to the rare communications she made with her base, while crossing the Bay of Biscay for home she had performed perfectly. And, above all, quietly.

The Toulon-based engineers at the Escadrille des Sous-Marins Nucléaires d'Attaque (ESNA) had done their precision work superbly.

'That looks like a dangerous piece of equipment,' said Gaston Savary as she came sliding soundlessly past the jetty.

'That *is* a very dangerous piece of equipment,' confirmed Admiral Pires, as he turned seawards, to return the formal salute of Captain Alain Roudy, high on the bridge.

CHAPTER FOUR

There were five men, each of them sworn to secrecy, each of them in uniform, standing around the wrong end of Admiral Marc Romanet's long dining-room table. The other end contained five place settings and two bottles of white burgundy from the Meursault region.

But this was officially pre-dinner. And down there at the business end was spread a whole series of naval charts and photographs now being studied carefully by the two admirals, Romanet and Pires, plus Captain Alain Roudy and Commander Louis Dreyfus, commanding officer of the *Améthyste*, the *Perle*'s sister ship.

These were the two submarines selected by the French Navy to cripple the economy of Saudi Arabia and half the free world. Or, put another way, to free up the wealth beneath the Saudi Arabian desert for the overall benefit of the Saudi nation. Or, alternatively, to

156

return the Saudi Government to the ways of Allah and to the purity of the Prophet's words. It all depended upon your point of view.

The fifth member of the group, Gaston Savary, was standing behind the naval officers, sipping a glass of burgundy and listening extremely carefully. He would be before the French Foreign Minister, M. St Martin, in Paris the following afternoon, for a debriefing. The decision of the four men with whom he was dining tonight would decide, finally, whether this mission was Go or Abort.

The subject on the agenda was the Red Sea, 1,500 miles of water forming Saudi Arabia's western border. With the Suez Canal providing the northern entrance, the French submarines would, by necessity, make the journey on the surface.

They would travel separately, probably two weeks apart. Only the *Améthyste* would remain in this deep but almost landlocked seaway to carry out its tasks. The *Perle* would continue on and exit the Red Sea at the southern end, before proceeding up the Arabian Gulf and into the Strait of Hormuz, en route to its ops area north of Bahrain.

The question was, could Captain Roudy make the southern exit underwater out of the range of prying satellites and American radar? Or would he need to come to periscope depth, in order to move swiftly through the myriad islands which littered the ancient desert seaway, before making his run out through the narrows and into the Gulf of Aden?

With the sandy wastes of the Yemen to port, the

Perle would pass to starboard the long coastline of the Sudan, then the equally extensive shores of Eritrea, then Djibouti, before making the deep-water freedom of the Gulf of Aden. But the final 300 miles, past the Farasan Bank and islands, followed a route where the water shelved up steeply on the Yemeni side, from 3,000 feet sometimes to 20 feet, which was precisely its depth off Karmaran Island.

The exit from the Red Sea was a long trench, narrowing all the way, with the island of Jabal Zubayr stuck right in the middle. Then there was Jabal Zugar Island and Abu Ali Island, both with bright flashing warning lights which were quite useless to a submarine trying to crawl along the sandy depths of the 600-foot deep channel. The rise of Hanish al Kubra was a navigator's nightmare, almost dead centre in the channel, now only 300 feet deep and only about a mile wide.

However, there were two navigational channels here. One, with routes north and south, ran to the east of Jabal Zugar, close to the Yemen. It was shaped in the dogleg of the island's west coast. The other marked channel ran 25 miles to the south-east, and skirted the western side of Hanish al Kubra. Essentially it comprised two narrow seaways, north/south, 14 miles apart running alongside a series of rocks, sand-banks and shoals. These were the most tricky parts because of the narrow channels, which skirted a couple of damned great sandbanks, one of them only 65 feet from the surface. However this stretch, which required the greatest navigational care, was the final black spot for the submariner.

Thereafter, both south routes converged into a 45-mile-long marked seaway, which suddenly shelved up again, to less than 150 feet, but had the advantage of being dead straight all the way to the southern Strait, gently falling away again, to a depth of 600 feet.

In places it narrowed to a few hundred yards, with a very shallow shoal to port, but it ran on into the Strait of Bab al Mandab and then into the Gulf, into depths of 1,000 feet plus, right off Djibouti – and the US base, west of the Tadjoura Trough.

'Think you can handle that, Captain Roudy?' asked Admiral Romanet.

'Yes, sir. If those chart depths are accurate, we'll get through without being seen. Under seven knots in the shallow areas, but we'll be all right.'

'The charts are accurate,' confirmed Admiral Romanet. 'We sent a merchant ship through there a month ago using sounders all the way. We checked depth against chart depth from Suez to Bab al Mandab. The charts are correct.'

'Thank you, sir,' said Captain Roudy. 'Then the GPS will see us through the southern end. I'll run with the mast up.'

'Very well,' replied Marc Romanet, who was well aware of the tiny GPS system positioned at the top of the periscope of the refitted Rubis. It was not much bigger than a regular hand-held unit, and it would stick out of the water a matter of mere inches.

The *Perle*'s CO had plenty of depth for that. And that minuscule system, splashing through the warm, usually calm waters of the Red Sea, would always put Alain Roudy within 30 feet of where he wanted to be.

'Before we dine I would like to go over the plan for the *Améthyste* which will be following you through the Suez Canal almost three weeks later,' said the Admiral. 'Commander Dreyfus, you will, of course, run straight down the Gulf of Suez along the Sinai Peninsula and into the Red Sea at the Strait of Gubal.

'Have you done it before?'

'No, sir. But my executive officer has. And so has my navigation officer. We'll be fine.'

Admiral Romanet nodded and looked back to his chart. 'Your ops area is around halfway down the Red Sea, in waters mostly around 500 metres deep. We have decided this is not a perfect area for an SDV – swimmer delivery vehicle – and our Rubis submarines are anyway not ideally equipped to carry one. Instead our SF will make the transit from the submarine in two Zodiac inflatables, six men to a boat. The outboard engines run very quietly and the guys can row in the last few hundred yards for maximum silence.

'We have targets at Yanbu and Rabigh, enormous terminals, with these huge loading docks, in the picture here . . .' The admiral pointed with the tip of his gold ballpoint pen. 'They will be separate operations, 90 miles apart. The plan is to attach magnetic bombs to the supporting pylons, using timed detonators, and then have the lot crash into the sea at the same time.

'At 1900, as soon as it's dark, the Special Forces will leave the submerged submarine, which will be stopped around five miles offshore. That gives them a 15-minute run-in, making 30 knots through the water. Two boats. The submarine will wait, pick them up, then travel quietly down to the loading bays at Rabigh, arriving at around 0200.

'There is no passive sonar listening in that part of the Red Sea, nothing before Jiddah, 110 miles further on where the Saudi Navy has its western Navy HQ. That's a big dockyard, with vast family accommodations, mosques, schools and so on. But its only real muscle is three or four missile frigates, all French-built, bought directly from us. We know their capabilities well. And anyway we're not going that far south.

'The chances of the Saudis picking up a very quiet nuclear submarine, running several miles offshore, are zero. And even if they do, there's not much they can do about it. They have virtually no ASW capability. And even if they did send out a patrol boat, even a frigate, for whatever reason, we'll either hide, easily, or sink it.'

Commander Dreyfus nodded. 'Same procedures as Yanbu for the Special Forces. Send in two Zodiacs and wait?'

'Correct. Then you will move out to sea . . . you'll be around halfway between Yanbu and Jiddah . . . make your ops station somewhere here . . .' The admiral pointed again to the chart. 'Correlate your timing,' he said. 'With the bombs on the loading dock pylons. I want them all to go off at precisely the same time.

'So you will open fire simultaneously with the cruises, seven and a half minutes before H-Hour on the pylons. You will fire three pre-programmed batteries – four missiles in each. The first four straight at the Jiddah refinery, then four at the main refinery at Rabigh. And one into the refinery at Yanbu . . . right on the coast . . . here . . . directly north of your hold-area position.'

'Fire and forget, sir?'

'*Absolument!* The moment the birds have flown, steam south-west, out into the deepest water, then proceed south towards the Gulf of Aden . . . stay submerged all the way. Then move into the Indian Ocean. Proceed south in open water, still submerged, to our base at La Réunion 300 miles off the west coast of Madagascar, and remain there until further notice.'

'Sir.'

'I think, gentlemen, we should dine now. And perhaps outline our plans for the Persian Gulf with Captain Roudy as we go along? *D'accord?*'

'*Dac,*' said Georges Pires, employing the slang word. 'I agree. This kind of talk tends to dry the mouth. I think a glass of that excellent Meursault up there would alleviate the problem perfectly.'

'Spoken like a true French officer and gentleman,' said Gaston Savary.

Admiral Romanet seated himself at the head of the table with Georges Pires to his left and Gaston to his right. The two submarine commanding officers held the other two flanks. Almost immediately a white-jacketed orderly arrived and served the classic French dish *coquilles Saint-Jacques* — scallops cooked with mushrooms in white wine and lemon and served on a scallop shell with piped potato.

He filled their glasses generously, and for all four of the visitors they might as well have been dining in a top Paris restaurant. The main course, however, provided a sharp reminder that this was a French naval warship base, where real men did not usually eat *coquilles Saint-Jacques*.

Admiral Romanet's man served pork sausages admittedly from Alsace, not with the traditional Alsace sauerkraut, but rather with onions and *pommes frites*. It was the kind of dinner which could set a man up, just prior to blowing out the guts of one of the largest oil docks in the world.

The golden brown sausages were perfectly fried, and they were followed by an excellent cheese board, containing a superb Pont l'Eveque and a whole Camembert . . . *les fromages* — one of the glories of France. And only then did the waiter bring each man a glass of red wine, a 2002 Beaune Premier Cru from the Maison Champney Estate, the oldest merchant in Burgundy.

Admiral Pires considered that, one way and another, the Submarine Flag Officer at the Atlantic Fleet Headquarters in Brest was a gastronomic cut above the hard men who lived and trained at his own headquarters in Taverny.

But Admiral Romanet, a tall, swarthy ex-missile director of a nuclear boat, was still concerned with the business of the evening. He had exchanged the wine glass in his right hand for a folded chart of the Persian Gulf waters to the east of Saudi Arabia. And he now considered he knew Captain Roudy sufficiently well to address him by his first name.

'Alain,' he said. 'I think we have established that your exit from the Red Sea can be conducted submerged. And, as you know, it's a 2,000-mile run from there up to your ops area in the Persian Gulf.

'As you also know, it's possible to enter the Gulf, via the Strait of Hormuz, underwater. The Americans run submarines in there all the time. However it's not very deep, and some of the time you'll have a safety separation of only 35 metres in depth, which does not give you a lot of room, should you need to evade.

'However, I don't think anyone will notice you because they won't be looking for you. The Iranians on the north shore are so accustomed to ships of different nationalities coming through Hormuz, they are immune to visitors.

'Your real difficulties lie ahead . . . up here, north of Qatar. And that's your new ops area. You'll need to run north, straight past the Rennie Shoals . . . right here . . . marked on the chart. You'll leave them to starboard but I don't think you should venture any closer inshore. You want to stay north, right around this damned great offshore oilfield . . . what's it called? The Abu Sa'afah. There'll be some surveillance there, and it's marked as a restricted area, so you'll stay as deep as you can.

'Now, the main tanker route is right here . . . this long dogleg, about a mile to starboard. It's half a mile wide coming out and about the same running in. It's deadly shallow, between 25 and 35 metres, which you don't need. And all around it, the deep water is starting to run out. This is a dredged tanker channel and it's the only way inshore if you want to stay submerged, at least at periscope depth.

'It would be nice to put yourself right here . . . in 35 metres of water, north of that sandbank. But it's too far off the Saudi coast – it would give the Special Forces team a near 14-kilometre run-in to this long jetty – that's this black line on the chart . . . the main loading dock, one mile offshore from the huge Ra's al Ju'aymah oil complex. That's the biggest liquid petroleum terminal in the world. There's Japanese tankers as big as Versailles pulling in there night and day.

'And so, gentlemen, the *Perle* must make her run-in down the tanker route . . . that's about nine kilometres, and we'll have up-to-date data on how busy that route is at night. But the Saudi tanker docks are *always* busy, so we must assume that a run south to our holding point will entail running between the very large carrier crafts – the VLCCs.

'You'll cut into the channel here . . . 2,000 metres north of this flashing red light, marked number two.

165

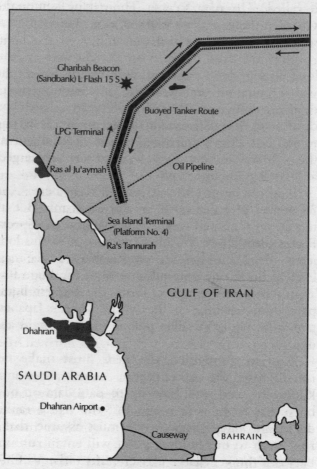

Gharibah Beacon
(Sandbank) L Flash 15 S ✳

Buoyed Tanker Route

LPG Terminal

Ras al Ju'aymah

Oil Pipeline

Sea Island Terminal
(Platform No. 4)

Ra's Tannurah

GULF OF IRAN

Dhahran

SAUDI ARABIA

Dhahran Airport ●

Causeway

BAHRAIN

THE TANKER ROUTE LEADING TO THE GREAT SAUDI ARABIAN OIL TERMINALS

Then you'll cross the tanker route, watching carefully to starboard, heading straight towards this light on the Gharibah Bank . . . see it, Alain, right here?'

'Okay, sir. Six quick flashes and then the light, correct?'

'*C'est ça*. And then you run south down the ingoing channel for about five kilometres to your first drop-off point. Exactly here . . .'

'Do we leave the main channel to reach that point, sir?' asked Captain Roudy. 'I mean when the Team One Special Forces depart the submarine?'

'I don't think so. It's too shallow beyond the marked sea lanes. The lack of depth will drive you to the surface. And we cannot have that.'

'You mean we let them out right in the main tanker channel?'

'No choice. But they have very speedy boats, and you'll wait for a break in the traffic, and then move fast. It's a two-boat mission. We're talking minutes here. Not half-hours.'

'So Team One will be right in the middle of the main tanker route when they set off?' confirmed Alain Roudy, a shade doubtfully.

'Yes, they will. But it's well buoyed. Plenty of lights and warnings. Anyway, those SF guys know what they're doing. But we will want two boats on that target; I think Georges thought four men in each?'

'I did think that, Admiral,' replied Georges Pires. 'Although we could probably achieve our mission with seven men in one boat. But that leaves no margin

167

for error. We definitely take two boats, just in case we have a problem, equipment failure or something. I'm talking rescue. We leave no one behind, no matter what happens.

'As soon as Team One is gone, the submarine turns south and runs on down the ingoing right lane. You'll have to put a mast up from time to time for a visual. But remember, in these waters, you have no enemy. You are *le prédateur*, and there's no one to stop you. The issue here is that no one must know you exist, *n'est ce pas*?'

'No sir. So we don't wait around for the Special Forces at the first holding point? The one you've marked right here? I mean for them to return?'

'No, you leave them, immediately. Proceed south for another five kilometres, to the very end of the tanker route. Then you cut through this narrow seaway between these shoals into an area which is, again, more than 30 metres deep, two miles north-east of the main tanker anchorage.

'Look . . . right here, Alain . . . at this point Team Two will be less than a mile from the enormous Sea Island terminal, perhaps the most important part of this mission. As you know, we are going to blow it up. It's a massive loading structure, stands a little over one kilometre offshore from the biggest oil exporting complex in the world, Ra's Tannurah. Sea Island is known as Platform Number Four, and it pumps over two million barrels a day into the waiting tankers.

'Now, at this second holding point, the Zodiacs

have a very short run-in to the target. No more than 800 metres. We have been studying a progression of satellite pictures to see how light it is on that terminal. My own opinion is the frogmen will have to swim the last 300 metres. Just depends on the degree of darkness.

'But they will accomplish this very swiftly. There will be six swimmers, carrying six bombs through the water. Each man fixes one bomb to one of the six principal pylons. It's a magnetic fix. Then he sets the timer and leaves, being very careful to keep the light-blue wires as well hidden and deep as possible.

'All this must be precisely coordinated with Louis Dreyfus's operation in the Red Sea. Because when they blow, they must blow absolutely together. It is essential these huge explosions cripple the oil industry all at the same time.

'So the moment the timers are fixed, the frogmen head immediately back to where the Zodiacs are waiting. It should take them only two minutes to reach the submarine, climb aboard and start back up the channel to the previous holding point, one hour north, and pick up Team One, which will be there by this time, after their much longer Zodiac journey.'

'If that liquid petroleum terminal goes up,' said Gaston thoughtfully, 'Prince Nasir will have lit a blowtorch from hell. It will probably light up the entire Middle East.'

'The Sea Island terminal would also have a fairly spectacular edge to it,' said Captain Roudy. 'Imagine a million barrels on fire out in the ocean. That would be quite a sight.'

'But I am afraid you will not see it, Alain,' said Admiral Romanet, smiling. 'When Team Two is back inboard, you will have the *Perle* steaming away, straight back up the tanker route, directly to the missile-launch point right here . . . 34 kilometres east of the terminals.

'That's going to take you five hours at tanker speed of 10 knots. You'll need to be on your way by 2300, in order to launch the cruises at 0400. The bombs on the pylons probably want a seven-hour time delay. But you'll work that out.'

'And, of course, we leave the datum immediately after firing the missiles?' asked Captain Roudy.

'Of course. You target the pipeline, the inland pumping station and the Abqaiq complex. They will explode simultaneously with the pylon bombs. At which time you will be 34 kilometres away, heading quietly east, well below the surface. The Saudi oil industry will blow to smithereens within four minutes of your departure from Holding Point Three, the firing area.'

'Sir,' said Captain Roudy, returning in his mind to the place which worried him most, 'do we get the Zodiacs back inboard when the SF guys return?'

'No time. Scuttle all of the boats. Same for Commander Dreyfus. Get the frogmen back in, and take off, back up the tanker route.'

'And then head east, through Hormuz and south

to La Réunion, submerged all the way?' asked Captain Roudy.

'You have it, Captain. Then you take a vacation, and in a few weeks bring the *Perle* home, around the Cape of Good Hope.'

'Well, sir, that sounds like a very good plan. And of course we do have that priceless element of surprise on our side. No one would ever dream a Western nation would be crazy enough to slam Saudi Arabian oil out of the market for two years.'

'Correct,' said Gaston Savary. 'It would seem like that British proverb . . . er . . . cutting your nose, to spite your face . . . but not in this case. I understand France's need for oil products has been taken care of. We have signed agreements with other countries to supply us with oil and gas, therefore we do not need Saudi oil for several months. And when it comes back on stream, it will effectively be ours to market, worldwide, at whatever price we fix.'

'What about OPEC?' asked Commander Dreyfus.

'I don't think Prince Nasir, the new King, will want to compromise his position with France, not to placate his fellow Arab producers,' replied Admiral Pires. 'This is the most extraordinary military action, It could only have been created by a potential new King. It is also devilishly clever – a plan direct from *le diable*.'

'Except that at the heart of it all lies an honourable objective,' said Admiral Romanet. 'To restore the best elements of the Saudi royal family, and to give the people a new, enlightened ruler: our friend, the Crown Prince.

'Gentlemen,' he said. 'I think we should raise a glass to the takeover by Prince Nasir, and, of course, to the . . . er . . . prosperity of France.'

1030, Tuesday 23 February
French Foreign Legion outpost
Djibouti, Gulf of Aden

Former SAS Major Ray Kerman had made his headquarters 18 miles north of Moulhoule, close to the Eritrean border, on the northern Gulf Coast of Djibouti. He had chosen the partly garrisoned Foreign Legion outpost of Fort Mousea because the training of his 54-strong assault squad would attract less attention there.

Here, in one of the hottest places on earth, even in the cool season the temperature rarely dipped below 90 degrees. They were only 11 degrees north of the equator, and in summer the heat was around 106 degrees day after relentless day. The entire country had only three square miles of arable land and it seldom rained. Ray Kerman imagined he must have been in worse places than this tiny desert republic, but, offhand, he could not recall one.

His squad had been in hard training now for many weeks. The men had willingly driven themselves across various different terrains; pounding the pathways through the Taverny woods; fighting the Legion's obstacle courses down in Aubagne; and then hammering their bodies through the heat of the rough desert tracks around Fort Mousea.

To his men he was known by his formal

name, General Ravi Rashood, Commander-in-Chief of HAMAS. Even the more senior French officers now referred to him as General, and every day he joined them in their relentless military training. Some of them had served in the Foreign Legion and understood how hard life could be. But nothing, repeat nothing, had prepared any of them for the regime of fitness required by a former SAS major.

They were getting there now. Many of the assault team members possessed power which bordered on animal strength. They could run like cheetahs, fight like tigers. Even the Iron Man from the Pyrenees, Colonel Jacques Gamoudi, who had visited for two days that week, was deeply impressed by the level of their fitness.

Out there on this burning shore they practised every form of assault-troop warfare, building temporary 'strongholds', designed only to be attacked by their own colleagues. All through the dark hours, they would watch, wait, study the stars and the cycles of the moon, slowly growing into their chosen roles as predators of the night.

They learned to cut wire, silently, within earshot of their own sentries, sharp, but unheard. They learned to move quietly across rough ground, on their elbows, armed to the teeth. They learned to attack from behind, with the combat knife. They learned priceless skills in near-silent communication one to the other. And they learned expertise in explosives. Some were just refreshing their knowledge and training. Others were rookies at the combustion game. But that would soon change.

Above all, they learned to listen in the dark; to the soft breezes of the desert, to the approach of a distant vehicle — with the wind and then against it. Because the sound was different. They could recognise the snap of a breaking twig at 40 yards; they could discern the sound of a footstep on the sand. By the end of February, General Rashood's men were supremely attuned to the rhythms of the night.

By day, they were trained physically, starting every morning at 0500 before the sun was up, jogging, sprinting, press-ups, finishing with a four-mile run into the desert and back. There was a two-hour break, before an enormous lunch, the food being flown in from France twice a week in a French Air Force jet. The curious observer might have noticed the more frequent arrival of a French aircraft but, if so, little was made of it. No heads were turned, no questions asked. And as a result of the frequent drops, no group of combat soldiers was ever better fed: the French Republic had invested heavily in these men.

An entire barrack-room block was converted into a kitchen. Cooks and orderlies were flown in from Taverny as temporary members of the existing garrison. There was meat aplenty: beef, lamb, sausage, fish, chicken and duck. If a man wanted a fillet steak every day, he could have it. But the salad, spinach, cabbage, beans, brussels sprouts and parsnips were compulsory. In addition, there was also French bread and milk and fruit from all around the Mediterranean. Plus gallons of fresh fruit juice, tea, coffee and cream.

The camp ran entirely on two large generators, driven by diesel engines. Every afternoon, after the late two-mile run, there was a briefing before dinner, where General Rashood and the commanding officers would go over the plan of attack. Again and again.

The assault on Khamis Mushayt would begin on the night of 25 March. And on this particular evening at 1700, 23 February, General Rashood was presiding, speaking in English which all the Arab warriors understood, as well as most of the French. There was a translator present for those who spoke neither. He outlined the various points of departure, informing them for the first time that they would make the 250-mile journey from Fort Mousea in 70-foot long dhows, the traditional craft of the Red Sea and the one least likely to attract attention. Each man would be disguised as a Bedouin, wearing traditional Arab robes.

General Rashood's dhows would make this journey from Djibouti and run north, crossing one of the narrowest points of the Red Sea from west to east, and then sailing up the long coast of the Yemen. General Rashood spoke clearly, precisely.

'These craft make a fairly steady seven knots,' he continued. 'In a light westerly breeze that is, straight off the desert. That is normal for these parts. The journey to the north coast of the Yemen will take us less than two days, and we will leave in relays from here, beginning at first light tomorrow morning.

'The first convoy will consist of three dhows, carrying my Troop Three and the command staff of our headquarters. That's 24 in each, eight per dhow. I do not want everyone concentrated together, in case anything unexpected happens. Each man will take his personal weapons – AK-47, service revolver and ammunition, combat knife and hand grenades. We will take food for 17 days, plus water, radios, cell phones, bedding and first aid requirements. At no time will any dhow be out of sight of the other two.

'Troops One and Two will leave two days later, each of them in two dhows. That's two leaving around 0600, and two more at 1400. All the dhows will land on an isolated stretch of coastline in northern Yemen, each troop in a separate location. Again, I am trying to avoid a concentration of personnel and equipment. I am not concerned about being attacked. I am worried only about being noticed. Your landing sites have all been selected following extensive study of reconnaissance photographs, taken especially by French Air Force surveillance aircraft.'

Everyone nodded in understanding and agreement. 'And now,' said General Ravi, 'comes the bad news. I have wracked my brains for a comfortable, unobtrusive way of getting into southern Saudi Arabia from the coast of the Yemen. But there is none. There are hardly any roads except the one along the coast, and that carries whatever traffic there is between the two countries. Which means it is busy; that rules it out for us.

'We can't go by air, because the only landing places are Saudi-controlled. We daren't risk helicopters because they're too noisy and may easily be located by military surveillance around Khamis Mushayt. So that means we'll have to walk.'

'How far is it, sir?' called one of the Saudi troopers.

'Only 110 miles as the crow flies,' General Rashood replied. 'But in reality we'll be covering over 130 miles, perhaps even as much as 150, depending on the terrain. We must walk through the mountains, and it will take us 10 to 12 days. Anything we need, we carry, and that means heavy bergen rucksacks, and there are not many armies which could do it.

'The terrain is tough, with steep gradients, and the heat unbearable. But we are not ordinary forces. We're Special Forces. And we're about to find out how we got the word Special next to our names. No one else could do it, except us.'

Again the assembly of brutally trained men nodded in agreement. 'Twelve miles a day does it, right, sir?' one of General Rashood's HAMAS freedom fighters called out.

'Correct, Said,' replied the general. 'Sometimes it will be easier, marching along the high ground. Other times it will be much more difficult. Maybe down to one mile an hour on the steep escarpments. But overall we'll aim for 14 miles a day, and some days we'll cover perhaps 20, and others only four. But we'll make it. We have to make it.'

He waited for the translators to finish. There were no questions. The general continued. 'Each troop will take a different route from the Yemeni coast through the mountains to our RV, which is four miles south of the King Khalid Air Base. Al-Qaeda guides will be out in the mountains to bring us in. There is already a carefully selected "hide", and everyone will have a minimum of 24 hours to rest up before the attack. Most of us should get a little longer than that, but there will be recces throughout each night — around the air base and along the road which leads up to Khamis Mushayt.

'By the time you reach the RV, you may have used up your food and water. Do not worry. There will be fresh provisions awaiting us courtesy of the Foreign Legion through Abha airfield, to the west of King Khalid. Al-Qaeda have transported it by camel up through the foothills to our rendezvous point.

'There will also be local maps for each man which I'll distribute in a moment. You will see there's a road leading up to the base which we ignore. We will come cross-country to the village of al-Rosnah, then cross a secondary mountain track and into wild country above another village called Elshar Mushayt.

'From there we look down through the hills, and see in the distance the military base to the left and the airfield to the right. It's a perfect spot for us. And the people of both these little places probably know we're coming and will be ready to assist.

'Once we're in those hills we're more or less safe. Just so long as we shoot straight and hard on the night of 25 March.'

The hours between 0200 and 0400 were spent breaking camp, the 24 men packing their equipment and provisions — ammunition, bedding, food and water — as efficiently as possible.

An hour before the sun rose above the Red Sea to the east they were driven down to the seaport on the north side of Moulhoule, where the three dhows awaited them. They had to walk the equipment out to the boats along the long jetties, and General Rashood himself supervised the seating of the soldiers and storing of their supplies.

Each of the 70-foot dhows was arranged for eight men to rest up during the two-day voyage. Awnings were erected on poles to protect them from the pitiless sun out on the water. The moon was already setting as they pushed out into the offshore waters of the Bab al Mandab Strait, running slowly north, sails high, in 20 fathoms and a light breeze.

The dhows sailed around 400 yards apart, and, by 0630, with the sun now just visible above the eastern horizon, they made their starboard turn, towards the brightening sky, each hidden man with a Kalashnikov inches from his hand, each man with a hand grenade in his belt.

To a passing ship the three dhows could be nothing but peaceful traders, plying the old routes, probably carrying cargoes of salt from Djibouti up to Jizan. They certainly looked nothing like an assault force

179

about to attempt the capture of Saudi Arabia and the overthrow of the King.

This was the unobtrusive start of a famous land attack: three Arab dhows, their cargoes under awnings, elderly captains at the helm, sons and family tending the huge sails as they slipped through the wavelets on a hot, serene morning. It was a timeless, almost biblical scene in the Red Sea, one that would have been seen down the centuries; not a semblance of menace, even in these dangerous times in the Middle East.

But General Rashood's instructions were clear . . . *if any intruder gets within 100 feet, civilian or naval, eliminate the crew and sink the ship. Instantly.*

Thursday 4 March
Port Said, Egypt
They logged the French nuclear hunter killer submarine the *Perle* through the northern terminal of the Suez Canal shortly before midday. Captain Roudy would make most of the 105-mile journey on the bridge. But first he dealt with the formalities in Port Said, coming ashore and speaking personally to the customs officers and inspectors from the Egyptian naval base, situated beyond the vast commercial network which controlled the canal.

Nowadays, Egyptian officials rarely boarded a naval vessel making the transit; this was largely because of objections voiced by the Russians who had always used the Canal to transfer ships from the Black Sea and Mediterranean to the Arabian Gulf.

Captain Roudy watched one of the Egyptian Navy's Shershen Class fast-attack Russian gunboats move slowly by, heading south, and shook his head at the age of the craft. 'Probably 40 years old,' he told his XO. 'I wonder if they've updated the old missile system – they used to to be aimed manually, like bows and arrows!'

Egypt had no interest in the French submarine, signed the papers, issued the permits and informed the entire world by satellite that France had just sent a hunter killer from the Med into the Red Sea. There was nothing sinister about that. They did it by international agreement, like many other guardians of sensitive waterways around the world.

They were underway by 1230, and the *Perle* set off south on the surface towards the halfway point of Ismailia at the top of Lake Timsah. By nightfall they were on their way down to the Great Bitter Lake, and at 0200 they came through Port Taufiq and ran into the Gulf of Suez. The water was still only 150 feet deep throughout the entire 160-mile seaway, but it was littered with rocky rises and a couple of wrecks, not to mention several sandbanks. In addition, the seaway was narrow and the land along the Sinai Peninsula shelved gradually into the Suez Gulf on the portside. It was no place for a submarine.

Captain Roudy kept the *Perle* on the surface until they had moved through the Strait of Gubal and into the deeper waters of the Red Sea, where the sea bed sloped sharply to a depth of 2,000 feet. And at 1709 on Friday afternoon, 5 March, Alain Roudy ordered the French submarine to dive, all hatches tight, main ballast blown.

Bow down 10 . . . make your depth 200 metres . . . speed 12.

Aye, sir . . .

Until then, the speed, direction and position of the *Perle* had been public knowledge. But shortly after 5 p.m. on that Sunday afternoon, this was no longer so. Now no one knew her speed, or direction or position in the water. And certainly not the intentions of her captain.

Those watching the satellites might have assumed she was headed south into the Gulf of Aden. But the important thing was that no one knew for certain. And no one ever would know either, since the *Perle* would not be seen or detected again; not that month anyway.

In fact, she would not be seen until the second week in April when she was scheduled to arrive in La Réunion. And, by then, the world would be a very different place. Especially if you happened to be a member of the Saudi royal family, or indeed the President of France.

Five days later, as Captain Roudy was working his way south down the Red Sea, underwater, the *Perle's* sister ship, the *Améthyste*, was ready to clear the submarine jetties in the naval harbour of Brest in western Brittany.

It was 0500, not yet light, but a small crowd had

gathered under the arc lights to see them off. Just families, the shore crew, a few engineers who had conducted her final tests, and, to the surprise of some, the head of the French submarine service, Admiral Marc Romanet.

They'd begun pulling the rods the previous evening to bring the *Améthyste*'s nuclear reactor slowly up to temperature and pressure. Commander Dreyfus had already finalised the next-of-kin-list, which detailed the names, addresses and telephone numbers of every crew member's nearest relatives, should the submarine, for any reason, not return. It was standard procedure.

Mme Janine Dreyfus, aged thirty-one, mother of Jerzy, four, and Marie-Christine, six, was at the top of the list. All three of them stood now with the other families in the pouring rain under a wide umbrella, awaiting the departure, watching her husband and their father, who was standing with the officer of the deck and the XO, high on the fin, speaking into his microphone.

At 0515 the order was issued to 'Attend Bells'. Eight minutes later, Commander Dreyfus snapped to the engineers, 'Answer Bells.' The XO ordered, '*Lines Away*', and the tugs began to pull the *Améthyste* away from the pier.

The strong, gusting south-west wind off the Atlantic swept the rain almost sideways across the hull, and Commander Dreyfus, the collar of his greatcoat up, cap pulled down, waited for the tugs to clear before calling . . . *10 knots speed.*

The great black hull swung to starboard in a light churning wash and she moved silently forward in the rain, across the harbour, towards the outer point of the south jetty, then out into the main submarine roads of the French Navy.

She swept wide of the St-Pierre Bank and then steered two-four-zero, south-west down the narrow waters of the Goulet, her lights just visible in the squally weather. Some wives of crew members stayed to see them finally disappear. Janine Dreyfus and her children were the last to leave.

Commander Dreyfus finally left the bridge as they approached the light off Pointe de St-Mathieu, at the south-western tip of the Brest headland. And then he ordered the ship deep, on a long swing to starboard beneath the turbulent waters of the outer Bay of Biscay, and then south to the endless coast-lines of Portugal and Spain and the Strait of Gibraltar.

1500, Friday 12 March
North-western Yemen

This was the hottest day yet. General Ravi Rashood and his men were still walking. They had been going for almost 10 days now, up through the mountains, ever since the landing on the deserted beaches north of the Yemeni town of Midi, four miles from the Saudi border at Oreste Point.

Only the supreme fitness of the men had kept them going. The concentrated food bars they car-ried with them had maintained their essential bodily requirements, but the last two days had seen some weight loss and the general was anxious to reach the RV.

No one had complained as they trudged up the high escarpments, heads down, hats pulled forward, day in and day out, guided only by the general's compass and GPS. But when elite troops like these ask for rest, you give it to them immediately. And General Rashood noticed these requests were now becoming more frequent.

The temperature was constantly in the low nineties, and the Army bergens the men carried on their backs were growing lighter as they consumed their supplies, but it was not enough to make the march much easier.

Their weapons were slung across their backs, and each man carried a heavy belt of ammunition across his chest. They took turns, in four-man groups, carrying two heavy machine guns, set on leather grips, for 30 minutes at a time. Their fortitude was a testimony to their training and discipline.

General Rashood knew they still had another four miles to cover before dark. Almost 30 miles behind him he knew Team Two were moving slightly quicker under the command of the teak-hard former Legionnaire Major Henri Gilbert. His own tireless number two, Major Etienne Marot, was in satellite communication with Henri every two hours.

The final group, Team One, commanded by Corsican-born Major Paul Spanier, was 12 miles in arrears of Major Gilbert, and moving faster than all of them, along a different route. That was the nature of a march like this: everyone began to get slower.

Team One could see the sun was just beginning to sink into the Red Sea, several miles to their left, when two lone camel riders appeared on the horizon. They were moving with the slow sway of the Bedouin, in the unchanging rhythm of the centuries. And they were not on the same track as General Rashood's men: they were coming from the north-east, across rough, high desert sand, littered with boulders, virtually no vegetation, leaving a dusty slipstream behind them. Sometimes the riders disappeared with the undulation of the ground, but the dust cloud never did.

Ravi checked them out through binoculars: both were armed, rifles tucked into leather holsters in front of the saddle. The general ordered everyone off the track, to the right, down behind a line of rocks . . . *weapons drawn* . . . *action stations*.

Slowly the riders advanced on their position. They made no attempt to conceal themselves. They drew right alongside the rocks and dismounted. The leader spoke softly . . . *General Rashood. I am Ahmed, your guide.*

Password? snapped the HAMAS commander.

Death Squad, replied the Arab.

And General Ravi advanced from behind his rock, right hand held out in greeting.

'*As salaam alaykum*,' responded the Bedouin. 'We have brought you water. There are only two miles left of your long journey.'

186

'I am grateful, Ahmed,' said the general. 'My men are tired and thirsty. Our supplies are low.'

'But ours are plentiful, and they are very close by now. Let your men drink . . . and then follow us in.'

'Did you see us from far away?'

'We saw the dust, and we saw movement along the track from more than two miles away. But we never heard you, not until now. You move very softly; you move like the Bedouin.'

'Some of us are Bedouin,' replied the general. 'And we are pleased to see you.'

Ahmed's companion, a young Saudi al-Qaeda fighter, had pulled two plastic three-gallon water containers from his camel and set them up on a low rock for the men to drink. That was two pints each, and there was not much left after 10 minutes.

Then they picked up their burdens again, the two Arabs remounted and they set off, as always moving north, and the ground began to fall away in front of them as they approached the hide the al-Qaeda men had built.

At first it was difficult to discern. Not until they were within 100 yards could they make out its shape, a crescent of rocks guarding the rear, and a solid rock-face 150 feet to the south, overlooking a dusty valley. Beyond that were low hills, and in the far distance there was flat land, too far away to see the aircraft hangars on the King Khalid base.

Inside the hide there were wooden shelters about eight feet high, with nothing but a back wall. The other three sides were open, with poles holding up palm-frond roofs which were covered in bracken. There was one square earth-coloured tent, again with bracken on the roof, which appeared to contain stores. Big cardboard containers could be seen through its open flaps.

Off to the left there were several small primus stoves for cooking. A fire was out of the question here: its smoke would clearly be seen in the crystal-clear blue skies from both the air base and the army base, nearly five miles away.

This rough hide, set in the foothills of the Yemen mountains, would be home to the French-Arabian assault force for the next 13 days. And it would be a time of intensive surveillance of the bases, checking every inch of the ground, studying the movements of the Air Force guards night after night, observing the movements in and out of the main gates, noting the lights which remained on all night.

When Captain Alain Roudy's missiles slammed into Abqaiq's Pump Station No. 1 in the small hours of Monday morning, 22 March, General Rashood's hitmen would be ready.

0900 (local), Monday 15 March
Central Saudi Arabia
The main road leading to the ancient ruins of Dir'aiyah, 20 miles north-east of Riyadh, was closed. At the junction with al-Roubah Road just beyond the Diplomatic Quarter a Saudi military tank stood guard. Two armed soldiers were talking

to three officers from the *matawwa*, the Saudi religious police. Almost to a man the *matawwa*, strict enforcers of the equally strict interpretation of the Koran, supported the creed of Prince Nasir. Above the group was an official looking sign which read 'ROAD TO DIR'AIYAH CLOSED OWING TO RESTORATION'.

Motorists who stopped and claimed to be going on further than the famous ruins were allowed to pass, and were given a permit to be handed in to the guards stationed two miles from the ancient site. No one would be permitted to leave their vehicles. And it was the same coming south from Unayzah.

When the highway reached Dir'aiyah there was a road block in both directions. Uniformed soldiers prevented anyone going down the track which led west from the main highway. They collected passes and politely told motorists the reopening of the ruins would be announced in the *Arab News*. Of course, most drivers did not care much when they reopened, and any tourists had been stopped miles away, on the edge of the city.

Anyone who gave any thought to this might have wondered about the iron-clad security which now surrounded the very first capital city of the al-Saud tribe. Dir'aiyah, the Kingdom's most popular archaeological site, was under martial law. Not since the Turkish conqueror Ibrahim Pasha ransacked, burned and destroyed the place almost 200 years ago had a Saudi army seemed so intent on defending it.

In effect, Dir'aiyah was no more than a ghost

town. In 1818 Ibrahim had demanded every door, wall and roof be flattened. His marauding army pounded the walls with artillery, even destroyed every palm tree in the town, before they marched back to Egypt.

The palm trees came again but the Saudis never wanted to rebuild what had once been their greatest city; instead they elected to start again with a new capital to the south, Riyadh. And for more than 180 years Dir'aiyah stayed as it had been left: the remnants of the old buildings, a mosque, the dwellings, the military watchtowers, the shapes of the streets, an entire cityscape, all open to the skies.

It was a place where life had become extinct, no more than a sand-blown Atlantis, with only the sounds of shifting feet as tourists with their cameras shuffled around one of the former glories of Arabian history.

Until the day Colonel Jacques Gamoudi showed up.

Gamoudi had arrived on a scheduled Air France flight from Paris to King Khalid International Airport on 2 December and had been in residence in Riyadh ever since. His appearance in the Saudi capital went unnoticed. He took a taxi from the airport and checked into the busy Asian Hotel off al-Bathaa Street.

It was two days before he met up with three emissaries from Prince Nasir, and that was in the Farah, a local restaurant on al-Bathaa Street, resplendent with large red and white Arab lettering above the door, enhanced by a large picture of a cheeseburger. From then on things took a turn for the better. That afternoon he moved into a beautiful house, behind high white walls and a grove of stately palm trees.

He was given a communications officer, two maids, a cook, a driver and two staff officers from the al-Qaeda organisation, both Saudis, both natives of Riyadh. One of them was the brother of Ahmed, General Rashood's guide, 700 miles away in the foothills above Khamis Mushayt.

And for two weeks they studied the maps, looking for an ideal spot to store armoured military vehicles, several of them carrying anti-tank guns, and possibly six M1A2 Abrams, the most advanced tank ever built in the USA. Saudi Arabia's armoured brigades owned more than 300 of these battlefield bludgeons, half of them parked in lines at Khamis Mushayt.

They also needed a place to stockpile light and heavy machine guns, for later distribution, and for hand-held rocket and grenade launchers. Not to mention several tons of ammunition and regular grenades. Much of this arsenal was currently in storage in the military cities under the watchful gaze of Saudi Army personnel sympathetic to the cause of Prince Nasir.

The questions were – when could the cache be moved? And where could it go?

Jacques Gamoudi called staff meetings, sometimes attended by six, even eight, specially invited al-Qaeda revolutionaries. He conferred with his small specialist team, and he spoke encrypted to General Rashood in the south. There was no communication whatsoever with France.

One night there was a sudden visit from Prince Nasir himself and Jacques expressed his concern about the principal problem: how to move the hardware out of the military stores and place it all under tight control, ready for the daytime attack on the reigning royal family and their palaces.

The Prince himself had masterminded the acquisition of the weapons and he had called on his loyalists to store and protect them. Curiously, that had not been difficult. All of it had essentially been stolen from the Royal Saudi Land Forces, which, awash with money for many, many years, were apt to be relatively casual with ordnance.

For two years there had been the most remarkable nationwide operation of pure deception going on in Saudi Arabia. One by one, battle tanks had gone missing from the big southern base at Khamis Mushayt, driven out, straight through the main gates, on massive tank transporters and driven north to Assad Military City at Al Kharj, 60 miles south-east of Riyadh, where the national armaments industry was also located.

No one bothered to inquire when the tank was loaded on the transporter by regular soldiers. The sentries never even questioned the drivers as the huge trucks roared out through the gates. And certainly the guards at Assad never even blinked when a Saudi Army transporter, driven by serving Saudi soldiers, hauling a regular M1A2 Abrams tank bearing the insignia of the Saudi Army, drove up and banged on the horn. They simply waved them through.

The tanks were parked in a neat group out on the north side of the parade ground and everyone assumed someone else had issued the order. Such things can happen when half the population hates the King and all he stands for. And even then, only if they think there is a real chance of a regime change.

No one ever said anything. Hardly anyone even noticed. And it was the same with hundreds and hundreds of weapons, boxed, crated, and moved from base to base, always placed in a spot which everyone assumed had been designated by a senior officer. In fact, those spots had been designated by no one.

Prince Nasir's secret arsenal was there for all to see. But no one really saw it. There were thousands of rounds of ammunition, packed into the storage centres at Assad. Another huge cache of weapons had been driven to the southern warehouses in King Khalid Military City itself. But there was no paperwork. It was all just there, like everything else. And no one would miss it when it went, in the two weeks leading up to 25 March.

Now it was time to move. And the prince and his advisers had each assumed, like the Saudi guards and quartermasters, that someone else had that under control too. In fact, no one had it under control, even though it was the first question

Colonel Gamoudi asked . . . *Where's our base camp?* *. . . from where do we launch our attack? . . . where's our command headquarters? . . . does it have communications? . . . if so, let's test them right away. You can't have a decent revolution if you can't talk to each other.*

From the very beginning the Saudi rebels had been bemused by the forthright military opinions and questions ground out by the ex-French Special Forces commander.

And the trouble was, he could not solve the problem. It was the Saudis who knew the territory, the Saudis who knew the available strongholds and houses. It was they who were supposed to be telling Jacques where to make his headquarters, not the other way round.

By late February things were growing tense. Hiding boxes of ammunition, and even cases of light machine guns, was one thing. Disguising a damn great Abrams combat tank in someone's front yard, on the outskirts of Riyadh, prior to charging straight down the Jiddah Road with guns blazing on the morning of 25 March . . . well, that was rather a different matter.

Colonel Gamoudi had marked up various possibilities, big houses with big gardens behind high walls. But he did not like any of them. It was always in his mind . . . *one careless word from a servant, one sighting by an unsuspecting passer-by . . . one friend of the family loyal to the crown . . . that was all it would take.*

And he told the prince of his concerns. He told

him he needed a base, where the public could not go. It had to be near a main highway, and it needed to be absolutely impenetrable by prowlers or sight-seers. That meant it needed to be a place which could be cordonned off, for an obvious reason, one which would cause no consternation among the public.

'Sir, do you have the power to select somewhere, and have the authorities deem it off-limits until further notice? Somewhere we can start moving into, somewhere we can move the ordnance . . . somewhere from which we can attack . . . ?'

Prince Nasir pondered for two hours. He paced the room and sipped coffee. He pored over the map of the city and its environs. And at 2.30 a.m. he stood up and smiled. 'Yes,' he said. 'I have it. I am, after all, head of the National Guard, and I have many serving officers loyal to me. The *matawwa* are also fiercely loyal to me. No one would think twice about it if we closed an historical site for restoration. I would not even need to tell anyone.'

Which was why, on Monday 15 March, there were eight MIA2 Abrams tanks parked bang in the middle of the ancient ruins of Dir'aiyah, and why the eighteenth-century mosque had a new roof of camouflage canvas to shelter the hundreds of tons of materiel hidden behind its great sandstone walls.

And why the ramparts of the old city were again manned by heavily armed guards – huddled behind high rocky outposts, with searchlights front and centre, all powered from the electric cable that once

195

fed only the kiosk which sold guidebooks and cold drinks to tourists.

Even Ibrahim Pasha would have thought twice about an attack in the year 2010: any intruder caught trespassing within a quarter of a mile of Dir'aiyah was essentially history.

Colonel Jacques Gamoudi had a grudging admiration for the thoroughness of Ibrahim's attack, but he was mortally grateful for the high section of the city wall he had left intact. He now had a total of 25 armoured vehicles parked inside at the base of the wall. And every hour, military vehicles arrived with more and more ordnance.

Le Chasseur, working from a specially built wooden office, logged and recorded every single delivery. The walls were pinned with maps. He knew the location of the most important palaces he must take. He knew where the radio station was. He was briefing his drivers, and, above all, his tank commanders. There would be casualties, he was certain of that, and he was amazed at the volunteers who came forward to pilot the aircraft he wanted driven directly into the principal palace.

It seemed that no matter what he asked for it was provided. The Moroccan-born colonel knew in his own mind that he was ready to take the capital of Saudi Arabia.

0100, Wednesday 17 March
25.50N 56.55E. Speed 12. Depth 50
Captain Alain Roudy's submarine was steaming into

196

the Strait of Hormuz, the great hairpin-bend gateway to the oil empires of the Middle East. The *Perle* ran 50 feet below the surface, holding course three-one-five, slightly to the Iranian side of the seaway. Right now they were not trying to evade or avoid anyone's radars or watchdogs.

They were leaving a very slight wake on the surface, but one which was discernible only to the expert eye. This did not include tanker captains, or their afterguards, and there were no patrol boats in radar sight, either from the Iranian or Omani navies.

There was a massive LPG tanker making 10 knots, way up in front, and 20 minutes earlier they had passed a 350,000-ton Liberian registered VLCC heading south about four miles off their port beam. Alain Roudy knew the seaway would probably grow busier as they headed into the mainstream north–south tanker routes inside the Gulf, but, for the moment, the *Perle* ran smoothly underwater in 30 fathoms, oblivious to wind, waves and tide.

They would begin their turn to the left 200 miles hence, to the north-east, west of Ra's Qabr al Hindi, the jutting headland of the Musandam Peninsula, the northernmost point of the Arab sultanate of Oman and a closed military zone. Captain Roudy would probably encounter Navy patrols off here, and he would accordingly slow right down, wiping that faint but, to these people, telltale wake clean off the surface.

From there the submarine would head west, steering course two-six-one, slowly, only seven knots, directly towards the Saudi oilfields. It was a 520-mile run, 170 miles a day, which would put them comfortably in their ops area in the late Sunday afternoon of 21 March. Just west of the Abu Sa'afah oilfield, that is; five miles east of the world's busiest tanker route, the one which led down to Saudi Arabia's Sea Island terminal.

On board the *Perle* were 16 men from Commander Hubert's D'Action Sous-Marine Commando (CASM), underwater action commando. The French Navy's crack combat diver capability, they were right up there with the US Navy SEALs and Britain's SBS.

Twelve of these frogmen, the swimmers who would hit the oil platforms, came direct from CASM, Section B, Maritime Counter-Terrorism, which was a bit rich under the present circumstances.

The other four, expert boat drivers and communications personnel, had been seconded to the mission from Commander Hubert's specialist Second Company. They were the four best men in the critical fields of placing the Zodiacs inch-perfect in the right place, and staying in communication with the swimmers and the mother ship.

The hitmen had been very self-contained on the journey out, quiet, thoughtful and rarely seeking conversation with the crew. But everyone understood why. These 16 men represented the front-line muscle of the mission. Should they fail, or be hit by gunfire and wounded, or even killed, the result would be an absolute catastrophe for the Republic of France.

Everyone appreciated what these swimmers were expected to accomplish and also the dangers they faced. Of course most of the crew knew the precise identity of the target.

But submariners are apt to be extremely intelligent, and there was no one aboard the *Perle* who did not understand the men from CASM were most definitely going to hit something hard. That was the critical path of the mission, the sharp end. Black ops men, in all the Special Forces in all the major navies, are allergic to failure.

Commander Jules Ventura, a thirty-two-year-old bear of a man from Provence, swarthy, taciturn, half-Algerian, would lead the divers to probably the more dangerous offshore LPG terminal at Ra's al Ju'aymah. The submariners who served Jules, and talked to him, already regarded him as a god. Which was the one thing that actually made Big Jules smile.

1630, Thursday 18 March
25.40N 35.54E. Course one-four-zero
Speed 7. Depth 400
The *Améthyste* crept slowly through the warm waters of the Red Sea, 340 miles south-south-east now from Port Said. There were almost 600 fathoms below her keel, and her new nuclear reactor was running sweetly. She made no sound in the water, and the biggest excitement so far on this journey was when they passed, briefly at PD, within five miles of the flashing light on the jagged El Akhawein Rock jutting up from the sea bed at latitude 26.19.

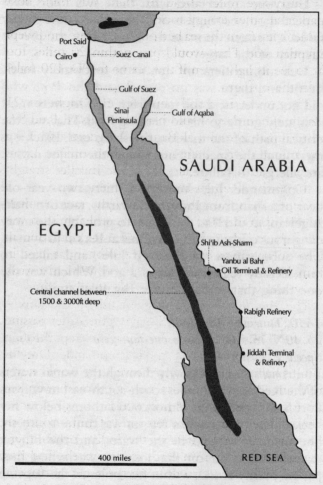

Port Said

Cairo •

------- Suez Canal

------- Gulf of Suez

Sinai
Peninsula ------- Gulf of Aqaba

SAUDI ARABIA

EGYPT

Shi'ib Ash-Sharm

Yanbu al Bahr
• Oil Terminal & Refinery

Central channel between -------
1500 & 3000ft deep

• Rabigh Refinery

• Jiddah Terminal
& Refinery

400 miles

RED SEA

THE NORTHERN END OF THE RED SEA

Thirty-five miles ahead of them was their next marker, another craggy rock, Abu El Kizan, scything suddenly up from the sea bed on the desolate sandswept Egyptian side. They would pass within 20 miles, too far to see its light, even if they came to PD, 120 miles from the ops area.

They were in good time for the night of 21 March, when they would blast the massive Red Sea oil terminal at Yanbu al-Bahr to kingdom come – a few minutes after their commanding officer, Louis Dreyfus, had fired a volley of cruise missiles straight at the Yanbu, Rabigh and Jiddah refineries.

Generally speaking, the *Améthyste* was a more cheerful ship than the *Perle*. But then her mission was infinitely less dangerous, since she was operating in deep open waters, in a lonely sea – lonely, at least, in terms of warships, against a country which had a weak Navy and was inexpert in the use of submarines.

The *Améthyste* was the biggest fish in the tank – so long as there were no US Navy submarines passing through. Thus she had no enemies as she crept through these international waters. And if Commander Dreyfus and his helmsmen held their nerve, they would never have any enemies, because no one would even see her for the next four or five weeks.

And when they did, thousands of miles south in the warm western waters of the Indian ocean, there would be no reason on earth to suspect she had had anything whatsoever to do with the night of stupendous combustion which had destroyed Saudi Arabia's oil industry. That was, surely, just an 'Arab thing'.

Commander Dreyfus and his senior officers understood that extremely well. The sense of real danger, that knife-edge existence, always present in the *Perle* as she picked her way through the Gulf of Iran, was missing from the *Améthyste*.

Which was why the *Améthyste* was a very cheerful ship. And why the dark, lean and droll commander of the frogmen, Lieutenant Garth Dupont, aged thirty-one, spent many hours playing bridge with his colleagues and the crew, though for stakes about 26,000 times lower than those wagered by the late-lamented playboy, Prince Khalid bin Mohammed al-Saud, in the classy environs of Monte Carlo.

In fact the entire sum of the cash wagered by Garth Dupont and his pals on the 3,000-mile voyage from Brest added up to 1/1,000th of the money blown in half an hour in Monte Carlo by the Prince Khalid (deceased) and HRH Princess Adele, late of south London.

CHAPTER FIVE

0030 (local), Sunday 21 March
Northern perimeter King Khalid Air Base

General Rashood, Major Marot and their two senior French explosive experts were lying flat among the dust, bracken and rocks, beyond the high wire fence which guarded the air base from attack from the rear.

They were watching for the umpteenth time the guard change in the base. It took place at this time every night, at which point a Saudi Air Force jeep drove half a dozen men right around the perimeter.

They always drove fast, always with the jeep's main beams raised; they were always noisy and their lights cast a useful illumination on the aircraft parked out on the north side of the airfield.

General Rashood and his command team had spent many weeks studying the field from satellite photographs, and, however many training flights took off and landed at King Khalid, there always seemed to be the same number of fighter bombers on this station – 40 US-built F-15s and 32 British Tornadoes.

The US aircraft were arranged in five rows of

eight, the British jets in four rows. Very occasionally wide hangar doors, 200 yards away, were opened, and it was possible to see three more fighter aircraft inside. It may have been a service rotation, or just running repairs to active aircraft. General Rashood could never quite tell whether they were the same ones or not, because he only saw them every three days, and his view was head-on to the identification numbers.

The attack was to begin four days from now on Thursday 24 March. And tonight's final recce was critical, to make certain none of the airfield routines were broken. The guard changed at the regular time, the aircrew in the brightly lit hangars and workshops stopped work at 1800, and the base was more or less asleep soon after midnight.

On Thursday night the 12 top demolition men in Major Paul Spanier's Team One, operating in pairs, were going in here. Their task was to work their way down the lines of F-15s. Simultaneously, Major Henri Gilbert's Team Two demolition experts would be in among the Tornadoes, prior to the opening frontal attack on two hangars, one of which they had never seen opened.

General Ravi had his own idea of sequence, which was for bombs to be set on the engines of the standing aircraft, with timers set for detonation at 0100 Friday. That was 72 explosions, which, given the jet fuel on board, ought to create a blast visible from space.

He was allowing a generous 15 minutes per aircraft which meant each team had one hour and 30 minutes to set the explosive on six of them. In addition, Ravi allowed four minutes more on each aircraft for the teams to remove wrenches, screwdrivers, pliers and bits of cut and spliced detcord. That was almost two hours per team to take care of the fighter bombers. Thus the frontal hit on the hangar doors would take place at 0100.

Tonight's first tasks were principally about time, checking that from the guard change at 0030 it would take exactly 14 minutes for the jeep to speed out past the only spot among the parked aircraft where intruders could be seen.

Busy demolition men tend to get preoccupied but on Thursday night each man would have a tiny beeping alarm on his watch which would sound at 0042, the signal for everyone to hit the deck, lying flat in the dark until the Saudi Air Force's final patrol was past and on its way back to the barracks.

Ten minutes earlier, the first moment that jeep had driven by the hangars, General Rashood's two detcord men would be at the great sliding doors and winding the high explosive around the locks. When the aircraft blew, the doors would blow too, and the spare men from Teams One and Two would be in there with bombs set for five minutes.

As the staff of the airfield charged out to witness the total demolition of the 72 aircraft on the field, they would see the hangar erupt in a fireball. And then the fuel dump, which was situated on the eastern edge of the airfield and would probably provide the biggest explosion of all.

Meantime, the al-Qaeda fighters who were sched-uled to open up a diversionary fight at the gates at 0050, thus preoccupying many of the guards, would now be assisted by the spare men who had blown the hangars.

Their orders were to move fast through the air-port buildings and return to the main gates with hand grenades to blast both guard rooms, thus entrap-ping the Saudi defenders front and rear. At 0055 the al-Qaeda men were to fight their way inside the base carrying two heavy machine guns and open fire on the accommodation block and communication rooms without drawing breath.

That, reasoned General Rashood, would effectively be the end of Saudi resistance: almost every aircraft on the base blown to pieces, the hangars destroyed, most of the guards dead or burned, buildings on fire. What was there left to defend? If it wasn't the end of Saudi resistance, something had gone drastically wrong.

Right now he was certain they had thought of everything. The charts of the airfield back in Taverny had been completely accurate, the scale model they had studied had been perfect. The surveillance photographs had been remarkably helpful, and the detailed plans of both the F-15s and the Tornado fighter jets, provided by Saudi sympathisers inside the base, were a priceless guide to the demolition men.

Nonetheless, General Rashood was still lying in the dirt outside the wire on the northern perimeter of the airfield. He felt that he knew the place better than his own home back in Damascus.

Through his binoculars he watched the jeep with the new guard detail drive from the guardhouse to the gates. Then it picked up the men coming off duty and drove them back to the accommodation block. Six more guards then boarded the jeep and it swung around and headed out on to the airfield. It always drove down the main runway and then picked up the narrow perimeter road and made a circuit of the whole air station.

Tonight the general was making a final decision on where to station two of his men lying flat, machine guns ready, just in case it was necessary to eliminate the six guards in the jeep. For a few days he had considered the best spot might be in the bracken, right inside the fence.

But on reflection, watching the angle of the jeep's lights, night after night, he decided there was perhaps a one in 10 chance the beams might pick up a movement in the bracken. And then they'd have uproar on their hands before the aircraft demolition team had completed their work.

The Saudis might even have time to communicate and turn on the airport floodlighting system, maybe even send for help from the military base which would have helicopter gunships down there in about 10 minutes.

The prostrate general shuddered at the thought. It could all go wrong, right here on his patch. And he could not tolerate that. No, the two HAMAS bodyguards protecting the men in among the aircraft would take up position behind the wheels of the aircraft nearest to the perimeter path.

That way there was no possibility of being seen, not in the dark, and they would be only 50 feet from the jeep as it passed. Plainly, it would be slightly hairy for the two bodyguards operating five feet below a ticking time bomb in the aircraft's engine.

But these were professionals, and they would be safe on the guard stations until 0055 when it would be time to run like hell, out under the wire with the 24 demo guys, and into a big Saudi army truck which had been hidden in the desert for three weeks and would be on station to get them out and back to the hide.

Ravi intended to put his main wire cutter on duty at the fence at all times. Everyone would go in through a small gap in the fence, three feet by four, two at a time at 2300, and then it would be put back lightly to avoid any detection by the occupants of passing jeeps.

The moment the last one had sped past, almost certainly travelling too quickly for proper observation, the wire man would complete cutting a huge gap, 10 feet wide by 12 feet, so that the getaway truck could practically back in.

Now, as he lay there deep in thought, the lights of the jeep lit up the northern perimeter road. Ravi Rashood watched the range of its beam every inch of the way, and as it roared past all his instincts were confirmed. The bodyguards would take up station on Thursday night behind the landing wheels of the F-15s.

Between now and then, the surveillance team would switch their attention to the military base, five miles away. In General Rashood's mind the airfield plan was complete. Now he had four days to refine his plan for the assault on the Khamis Mushayt army headquarters, and the subsequent, vital surrender of that sprawling Saudi military base.

1830, same day, Dir'aiyah
In the past few days, Prince Nasir had arranged for a succession of heavy-duty construction hardware to arrive at the outer walls of the ancient ruins.

There were a pair of bulldozers, two cement mixers, various trucks with commercial names printed in Arabic, three vans, a pile of scaffolding, and, since yesterday morning, a crane which looked as if it could lift the Hanging Gardens of Babylon.

There could be no doubt there was serious restoration work afoot out here on the edge of the desert. No reason whatsoever why the main road out of Riyadh should not be closed to any vehicles not passing straight through the area.

Shortly after dark, the white-robed prince himself arrived for a conference with his forward commander from the French Pyrenees.

'Ah, Jacques!' he greeted the French colonel. 'Come and talk to me out beyond the ruins . . . walk with me to the temporary home of a true Bedouin . . .'

And he placed his arm around the shoulders of Jacques Gamoudi and together they walked out between the shattered buildings of the ancient city, continuing for perhaps half a mile where a three-sided tent had been erected, in front of which was a gigantic Persian rug, spread upon the sand.

There were probably 15 close friends in attendance, mostly political and religious advisers and relatives of the prince. And Colonel Gamoudi was perfectly at home among them. Above his regular combat gear, he now wore the traditional red and white *ghutra*, secured by the *aghal*. He looked what he now was – a freedom fighter in the cause of Islamic fundamentalism.

Prince Nasir loved the desert. Those who knew him well talked often of his hatred of the gaudy palaces of the royal family. It was said that when he first entered his own new official residence, on the outskirts of Riyadh, he had taken one look at his sumptuously decorated bedroom and walked out of the door, marching along the upstairs corridor until he came to a small, almost bare, spare room. 'I'm happier in here,' the great-great-grandson of Ibn Saud had declared.

Behind the tent, Jacques could see the cooks labouring over modern barbecue grilles; he could see the line of Range Rovers parked nearby; he could smell the roasting lamb; and he could see the great bowls of dates and the tall glasses of iced camel's milk.

He sometimes had to give himself a reality check.

And this was one such moment, as he stood next to a royal family of Bedouin, robed, speaking quietly close to the timeless oasis of Dir'aiyah. It was a scene which had scarcely changed for thousands of years. Except for the Range Rovers and other, occasional, modern trappings.

And he stared at the tall bearded prince of the blood who accompanied him, and he watched the deference bestowed upon him, the gentle bowing of heads, the graceful sweep of the right arm from the forehead. The murmured *as salaam alaykum* from the robed brethren.

And four days from now he was to try and capture their country for them, with tanks, high explosive, gunfire and mayhem. '*Jésu*,' thought Jacques. '*What could I have done to deserve all this?*'

But now the prince was bidding him be seated, and he was placed next to Nasir on the vast rug set upon the hot sands. Above them the sky was clear and the temperature was rising by the day in the central desert, now five weeks on from the cold nights of mid-February. Tonight it was around 81 degrees. A pale moon was rising above the endless shifting dunes to the south-east, and the great revolutionaries of the Saudi royal family were relaxed.

Which was a sight more than Jacques Gamoudi was. He had spent the last weeks scheming and planning a simultaneous attack on several targets. His advisers had promised him that he would have an army to help him. But he had yet to see that army. He knew there were immense stores of small

211

arms and ammunition in the city, and he of course could see the heavy artillery he had around him, the armoured vehicles and tanks.

When the time for the attack came, *Le Chasseur* would make no mistakes. So long as he was obeyed, he would take Riyadh. But where the hell was his army? That's what he wanted to know. So far as he could tell he had about 24 known fighting men, all Saudi, all al-Qaeda, most of whom he saw every day. The rest was a mystery.

And since he was probably going to take to the streets four days from now, he ventured to ask Prince Nasir whether he was absolutely sure the army would show up.

The prince smiled, thoughtfully chewing some dates. 'Jacques,' he said, 'you will have an army of thousands, a great army which will sweep away everything in its path. And you will lead them, and explain to them the critical targets you have chosen. They will follow you and your chosen commanders, and you will be astounded at their bravery and determination.

'And remember, as you look around this very oasis, when Dir'aiyah fell to the army of the Ottoman Empire in 1818, that was the *only time* in recorded history that the heartland of Saudi Arabia has been conquered by a foreign invader. And it's never happened since. My people, in time, conquered this land, they took almost the entire Arabian Peninsula. We are warriors, and we understand, to a man, that you will lead us in our fight this week.'

Colonel Gamoudi thought that was all very well. And he was used to Prince Nasir's flowery language – the language of an idealist. And he looked the Crown Prince of Saudi Arabia straight in the eye, and said softly, in French, 'où qu'ils soit' – wherever they may be.

'Jacques,' said the prince, 'as you know we have been stockpiling arms in the city for many weeks. We have vast caches of weapons stored in two houses in the Makkah Road. We have them on al'Mather Street and al-Malek Saud Street. Our main ammunition dumps are in great houses on Olaya Street. I'm talking about AK–47s and hand grenades. But we have hand-held rocket and grenade launchers as well.'

'Sir,' said Colonel Gamoudi, 'you will remember I asked about the possibility of a suicide bomber aiming a plane straight at the main royal palace. I still think that's the quickest and most effective way of spreading instant chaos. And striking at the heart of the rulers. Is that likely to happen?'

'So far, we have only 230 volunteers for perhaps the greatest act of martyrdom in our history. They are men who understand they will be saving their families, their friends and their country. They are all Wahaabis, which is the true Islamic teaching of our nation. Any one of them would be proud to answer the call of the three trumpets before crossing the bridge into paradise.'

Jacques brightened considerably. 'But, sir,' he said, 'when will our great army begin to muster? Remember, I've never even seen it.'

'Jacques, I have observed you since you have been here, and I have observed the great importance you attach to communications. I have seen you demand the most expensive cell phones, radio and satellite communications in the world . . . and I know you have briefed your commanding officers in the greatest detail.

'Each of the men you speak to every day, the Saudi officers who will fight for us, the men who masterminded the acquisition of the arms, have an area of the city which they control.

'And many, many people understand something is going to happen soon. On Wednesday night after ten o'clock the people will begin to gather their arms at our safe houses all over the city.

'Jacques, when you lead our convoy of tanks and armoured vehicles down the main road and into the city, they will come from every dwelling in Riyadh. They will come in their thousands, and they will flock behind your battle tanks, and they will march with you and your high command. And they will follow you into the mouth of hell.

'Oh yes, Jacques Gamoudi. They will come. They will most definitely come . . . *Bismillah*, in the name of God.'

Colonel Gamoudi brightened some more. But he said, 'You mean, I will never see this army until it falls into line behind our artillery?'

'No one will ever see this army until it falls into line behind your artillery. We must both have faith.'

Right now Jacques understood why he was being

paid a minimum of $10 million to organise this people's revolution. It was Sunday night, and he knew that on Tuesday morning $5 million would be paid into his private account in the Bank of Boston in the Champs-Elysée. He also knew his bonus cheque of an additional $5 million was being handed to Giselle at their home in the Pyrenees.

She would instantly call and inform the Bank of Boston that her cheque had arrived. At 2 p.m. here in Saudi Arabia, given the three-hour time difference from Paris, Jacques would dial the bank's number on his cell phone and tell the operator, 'Extension 387'.

The reply would be simple . . . *Three eight six*. And he would cut the call off. *Three eight six* meant his account showed a balance of $10 million, and they had heard from Mme Hooks that she now held an irrevocable cashier's cheque for $5 million to be deposited on the day King Nasir assumed power.

Either that, or he, Jacques Gamoudi, was on the next plane out of King Khalid for Paris, $5 million richer and no further obligations. The money from the French Government, he knew, would be there.

'Your Highness,' he said, 'I have faith in you. And I have faith in the officers I have met here in Riyadh. I have been impressed by their planning, and their staff work. Each of them knows and understands our objectives. I am sure that on Friday morning they will confuse and demoralise our enemies, with their audacity and daring.'

Prince Nasir smiled. 'Then your opening attack

will follow the master plan you have worked on?' he asked. 'The military vehicles will leave here in convoy the moment we hear that Khamis Mushayt has fallen? Two combat tanks and eight vehicles will head cross-country, straight to the airport, and you head into the city where Colonel Bandar's brigade will peel off and go directly for the principal television station?'

'Correct,' replied the French colonel. 'It is essential we control the airport, and hold power over all public communications. Major Majeed will take the airport by storm, and it will surrender easily. But I have instructed 10 al-Qaeda commandoes to go straight to the control tower and capture it with gunfire, if possible with no damage to the equipment.

'Colonel Bandar will take television Channels 1 and 2 by force of arms, but hopefully without loss of life. If he drives that Abrams tank straight through the front door they'll surrender, believe me. Journalists only die by accident, not from choice.'

'And the remainder of the convoy?' asked the prince. 'Will that advance into the city for three miles as you suggested, as if in a military parade, right to the edge of the central area?'

'Yes, sir . . . while it gathers our followers. But then it will swing left, back on to al'Mather Street and return north, to join the four main battle tanks and the six armoured vehicles we leave back at the junction of the Jiddah Road.'

'Good, very good. And then?'

'I lead the convoy to the east, straight around the Diplomatic Quarter, and into the area where the main palaces are located. Major Abdul Salaam's brigade and a substantial group from the Makkah Road immediately hit the Prince Miohd bin Abdul Aziz Palace where the full morning council meeting will be taking place before the King's arrival at 1300.'

'And attempt to capture them, round them up?' asked the prince, perhaps considering the fate of his several cousins and childhood friends, who would be attending that meeting.

'Absolutely not,' replied Colonel Gamoudi. 'That's our first objective. We go in hard – rockets, grenades and gunfire. We take out every single person in the building and then knock as much of it down as we can. We cannot allow the officials inside to live, for fear of later uprisings, and we do not want the building. That palace and all of its occupants is on our critical hit list. To seize a ship of state, you first smash its rudder.'

The prince nodded. 'And then?'

'We pass two more minor palaces as we go out to the east and we take them by force of arms. I do not expect many important people to be in them. We wipe them out and anyone who may later bear arms against us. But we avoid civilian casualties wherever possible.'

'Do we destroy the buildings?'

'No. We need those big buildings to set up our new command posts. And, once we've taken them, we push right on to the King, who will be in the Al Salam royal palace. And as you know, this is a substantial building. I will press the red button on

217

my comms system and the suicide bomber will take off instantly from the airport, which by now we control.'

'Straight at the palace?'

'Straight at the upper levels of the palace. I'll take care of the lower levels, and the guards.'

'And the King and his family?'

'The King dies. And so do any princes serving him. If the great man is as smart as I think he is, he'll already have evacuated many of his family. Probably within hours of the oil bombardment on Thursday morning.'

'And the families, Jacques? The King's wives and many children . . . if any of them are still there?'

'Sir, if you had asked me to slaughter women and children, there would be a different commander sitting here with you. And I would be with my wife and children in the Pyrenees . . .'

'Even for $15 million?' asked Prince Nasir.

'Even for $15 billion,' said Colonel Gamoudi, quietly. 'I'm a soldier, not a murderer.'

Prince Nasir again nodded his head, gravely.

'And when the palace falls?'

'I recall Major Abdul Salaam, to organise a total occupation of the building. I have detailed six al-Qaeda staff officers to assist him in this. All prisoners will be marched to the smaller royal palace half a mile down the road where they will be held under guard.

'I will then open a new communication centre in the second palace, and Colonel Bandar will transport television crews there, and you, sir, will make your first broadcast to the nation, informing the populace that the King has fallen, and the city is in the hands of the armed forces of Prince Nasir Ibn Mohammed al-Saud, the great-great grandson of Ibn Saud. And you will address them with your message of hope, inspiration and future prosperity.'

'And you, Jacques, what further mayhem have you in mind for my country?' smiled the Prince.

'I will regroup my army, sir, hopefully with many more trucks and transports and make my way to the south-west, to downtown Riyadh, where we take and occupy several places, no more firing unless there is serious resistance. And if there should be, I am afraid we must be utterly merciless.'

'Which places?'

'Oh, the big shopping centres, the council building, King Fahd Medical Centre, the Post Office, the bus station and railway station. The Central Hospital, because there will certainly be casualties.'

'And the main army? The ones in the other great military cities of Saudi Arabia?'

'That will all be taken care of by General Rashood. He will compel the commander-in-chief of Khamis Mushayt to speak to his opposite number in Tabuk, informing him that Khamis Mushayt has fallen to the troops of the Crown Prince.

'He will also tell him the King has been removed, and that his great friend Prince Nasir implores him and his men to change their allegiance immediately, particularly as the Prince is the only man in the world who can pay them and take care of their families. The King is dead. Long live the King.'

Crown Prince Nasir remained slightly quizzical. 'And you are not concerned that the opening action in this great saga is all concentrated around the east side of the city, while the central area scarcely knows what's going on?'

'Not with a man like General Rashood taking care of the rest of the Saudi armed forces, sir. To take any country, you must first cut off its head. That's the King. When he falls, everything starts to cave in. You will rule Saudi Arabia by Friday afternoon.'

Prince Nasir rose, and he beckoned to *Le Chasseur*. 'Come, Jacques,' he said. 'It is almost eight o'clock. And I would like you to pray with us . . .'

'Thank you, sir,' replied the devout Muslim from Morocco. 'I would be greatly honoured.'

The great bond of Islam seemed to engulf him alone, as he stood next to the Arab prince, out there on the shifting sands around the oasis of Dir'aiyah.

1900, same day, Sunday 21 March
24. 10N 37. 35E. Speed 5. Depth 100
The *Améthyste* moved slowly through the dark waters west of the jagged island of Shi'ib ash sharm, guardian of the 10-mile long deep-water bay along the coastline north of Yanbu al-Bahr.

Shortly after 1900 in the evening, with night settling heavily over the ocean, Commander Dreyfus ordered his ship to the surface and the French nuclear hunter killer came sliding up out of the depths of the flat, calm Red Sea to take up her ops station. Water cascaded off her hull as she shouldered aside the ocean, moving forward slowly, making as little surface commotion as possible for a 2,500-tonner.

Just ahead they could see the warning light on Sharm's rocky headland, flashing every few seconds, casting a white light on the glinting waters, mostly to warn tanker captains of the dangers inherent in not making a sharp landward turn.

Shi'ib ash sharm sat five miles off the shore, directly west of the loading platforms which serviced the world's biggest oil tankers at the far end of the 700-mile trans-Saudi pipeline. That pipeline ended at the port of Yanbu, having snaked across the vast central desert and over the Aramah Mountains, all the way from Pump Station No. 1, near Abqaiq.

To reach the main loading terminal at Yanbu, tankers had to make a hard turn, at either end of Sharm, from the north or south. For the SF insert that night, Commander Dreyfus had chosen the northerly route, a three-mile-wide seaway, between the island and a large shallow area, which had to be avoided by the VLCCs and most certainly by the *Améthyste*.

The water was beautifully flat, and the rising moon to the east, from behind the mountains, was casting a pale light on the narrows. The submarine was just about invisible, its black hull casting no shadow on the surface. But inside there was a frenzy of activity.

Several hands were already hoisting and hauling the deflated 22-foot Zodiacs up through the big

221

hatch on the forecasing, manhandling them on to the deck, where the seamen had already brought out the electric air pumps.

The 175-hp Yamaha outboard engines, which would power the two craft, were coming up separately from the torpedo room where they had been stored for the voyage. Within moments, six engineers were out on the casing, three of them bolting the heavy motors into position on the stern, expertly clipping on the fuel lines, attaching the battery cables and ignition wires, while the boat was still being inflated.

The engines were clipped into the upward-tilt position. And two other seamen filled the fuel tanks with diesel and loaded a four and a half gallon spare fuel tank inboard each boat. Also being loaded were assault rifles, ammunition, six grenades, just in case, and the comms transmitter, which would guide them home after the bombs had been fixed.

There were also medical supplies, morphine and bottles of water, mainly in case someone was badly injured and needed to drink. The two 'attack boards' which contained the swimmers' watch and compass, both inbuilt, non-glare, were also placed on board.

The lead frogmen would swim in with the boards out in front of them, and they would especially need them if they had to exit the Zodiacs sooner than planned, for whatever reason . . . busy harbour, launch activity, anything the Zodiac captain considered might compromise the safety of the boats, if anything or anyone came too close.

When the first Zodiac was ready they pushed it to the downward slope of the deck and allowed the hard-decked inflatable to slide down into the water held secure by two lines attached to its bow, each one held by two brawny seamen.

Another two men attached and rolled a wood-runged rope ladder down the side, and the officer of the deck signalled for the first six of the Special Forces assault group, led by Lieutenant Garth Dupont, to come up through the foredeck hatch and proceed to the head of the rope ladder.

Garth was unrecognisable from the relaxed bridge player of the lower deck. He was dressed in his jet-black wet suit, hood up, goggles on his forehead, his face smeared with black camouflage grease. His big flippers were attached to his belt, and on his back, in a waterproof rucksack, he carried a massive 60lb 'sticky' bomb which would clamp magnetically to one of the giant steel pylons supporting the loading dock in Yanbu. Also on his belt was his sheathed, specially made Sabatine combat knife, and a roll of detcord, and wires, with a 24-hour timer.

His air system, the Draeger, also carried on his back, was a compact model, containing air for only 90 minutes, about twice as much as he would need. The system was a special non-bubble breather which would betray nothing to a curious sentry staring down into the water. In any event the Frenchmen would operate 50 feet below the surface which would render them invisible from the platform.

Privately all four of the frogmen hoped there would be tankers on the docks, casting huge shadows and shielding them from prying eyes. They would work in the dark, unseen, somewhere down below the tankers' keels, which would suit them perfectly.

The four swimmers would work in pairs, and when the bombs were stuck hard to the pylons the timer would be magnetically clamped to a third one, with wires running to the splice in the detcord. When the timer reached 0400 it would send an impulse into the detcord splice, which would ignite the explosive fuse.

This would streak at the rate of two miles a second straight into the detonaters fixed to the bombs, which would blast the pylons in half, probably blowing the deck on the platform into several pieces. Any ship on the dock would probably have its hull split asunder and sink to the floor of the harbour, all 300,000 tons of it, which, in time, might take quite a bit of removing.

Add to this the activity of the *Perle*'s cruise missiles which were to hit the faraway pumping station at Abqaiq and the great Red Sea port of Yanbu al-Bahr was in dead trouble – starved of oil, its loading terminal obliterated, perhaps half a million tons of shipping jamming its jetties.

Garth Dupont climbed backwards down the ladder, found his footing and slipped over the rubber hull of the Zodiac, which was still held with fore and aft lines by the seamen on the submarines.

Then, one by one, his five-man team joined him,

224

the three other swimmers, the boat driver, and the comms officer, with his GPS receiver, and mobile phone to communicate codes back to the submarine if necessary.

Seaman Raul Potier took the wheel and kicked the engine over; it started first time. If it hadn't, one of the engineers would probably have been keel-hauled. He untied both lines and expertly curled and then hurled them back on to the submarine's deck. He took the Zodiac quietly away from the hull, 50 feet out into the water, and waited.

The comms man pushed the buttons to dial the officer of the deck up on the casing, checking the phone was working. Then they reversed the process, ensuring they had two-way transmission. The second Zodiac was lowered into the water and the second half of Team One went through the same checks. When they had checked the phones once more, one to another, they set off for Yanbu.

The Zodiacs carried no running lights as they moved swiftly through the water at around half-speed, 15 knots. Garth Dupont sat next to the driver, his night binoculars trained on the blackness ahead, but his vision was not improved by the rising moon.

A mile in front he picked up the lights of a tanker, off his starboard bow, coming towards them, but he could see only her green running light and he guessed she was leaving by the southern route around Sharm. Way ahead of that was another tanker, going his way, slowly into port, probably lining up to receive, little did they know it, what would probably be the last oil from Saudi for a very long while.

Within 12 minutes they could see the lights on the loading docks, now only a couple of miles ahead across the bay, and it quickly became clear this was a busy Sunday night. Garth could pick out two tankers he thought were on the jetties, with three waiting to come in, a mile offshore out to his port side.

One mile from the jetties he ordered Raul to slow right down to five knots, then to slip in very slowly. The Navy had no indication of sonar surveillance in these waters, but Garth was taking no chances. By now it was clear there was a great deal of light on the docks, shining from both the enormous tankers and the jetty itself. And those lights seemed to spill out for two, maybe three, hundred yards into the main approaches to the Yanbu terminals.

Garth ordered the engines cut back to idling speed, just enough to hold a position without drifting. He took one final look ahead and ordered the other swimmers to action stations. The four men sat down and pulled on their flippers, fixed goggles and Draeger lines and slid softly over the side. The comms officer quietly passed the instruction to the second boat. No one shouts in black ops.

The eight men in the water came together as two groups, two leaders and two followers in each. Garth ordered them deep with a thumbs-up and they began to kick their way underwater, each of the followers swimming with their right hands on the left shoulder of their leader, in the pitch-black water 12 feet below the surface.

The leaders swam using flippers only, their attack boards held at arms' length out in front of them, like regular floatable kickboards; but these boards had instruments which showed the precise time and direction without the swimmer needing to pause to check either watch or compass.

The lead pair in each group had made the inshore journey in Garth Dupont's boat. This meant that no instructions needed be passed from one group to another. In any event the plan was simple. Each four-man team was to head directly towards the tankers, Garth's men to the one on the left, the others to the one on the right.

Given the complications of mooring lines, and propellers which could start at any time, the under-water leader had ordered them to take each tanker amidships, diving right down to the keel – 40 feet on a loaded tanker but likely to be only 30 feet on these half-laden hulls.

There would be 20 feet of water under the keels, and, once through and under the dock, the swimmers were to head to the far ends of the platform and place their bombs deep on the corner pylons, two men attending each objective.

And so they kicked in, rhythmically through the water, one pressure stroke on the flippers every 10 seconds . . . *KICK* . . . *one* . . . *two* . . . *three* . . . *four* . . . *KICK* . . . *one* . . . *two* . . . *three* . . . *four*. Kick and glide, conserving energy, all together. That

227

way they arrived on the starboard sides of the tankers at the same time; using their hands on the hulls, they pushed their way under, and Garth was relieved to find there was a long drop down to the harbour floor.

Nonetheless, it was nothing short of dead creepy down here in the pitch dark. Weaker men would have been spooked but these were strong men. On the dock side of the tanker, however, it was suddenly much brighter; if this was more comforting, it was plainly more dangerous.

Both groups now made for the seaward pylons on the two corners and were irritated at the number of barnacles on the steel. They had to scrape them off with combat knives before the bombs could be clamped on tightly. The time settings were all different in the countdown to H-Hour, 0400 the following morning: at 1956, on the first pylon, the timer was set for eight hours and four minutes. On the land-ward corner pylon, which took longer to reach, it was set for seven hours and 57 minutes. They then made their way under the platform to seek out the next four pylons.

And there the clamping and timing processes were repeated until all eight of the 60 pounders were in place, clocks set, the final one for seven hours and 18 minutes.

With their cumbersome loads now shed, the men headed back the way they had come, under the tankers and back out to the waiting boats. On the way in, they had kicked approximately 80 times, each kick carrying them 10 feet, or three and a half metres. On the return journey, again 12 feet under the water, they counted the kicks again.

At the count of 80 they all surfaced, now quite widely spread out. Garth reached for his bleeper to signal their position to the Zodiacs and within minutes they were safely onboard, breathing their first fresh air for well over an hour.

The Zodiacs now turned away from the Yanbu docks and made a beeline for the *Améthyste*, waiting beyond the north end of the island. The comms men were both in contact with the mother ship, and within 15 minutes they saw the rapidly flashing light signal on the submarine's foredeck.

They came alongside, grabbed the lines and began to disembark. The last men off-loaded the rifles, ammunition and equipment into canvas bags which were immediately hauled inboard. Then they took their Ka-Bar combat knives and slashed six wide gashes in each of the pressure compartments in the Zodiacs' rubber hulls. Before the hitmen had even pulled off their flippers and hoods, both Zodiacs were settled nicely in 200 fathoms on the bed of the Red Sea.

Commander Dreyfus ordered all hatches closed, main ballast opened, and took the *Améthyste* to 300 feet below the surface, running south at 12 knots, straight down to the next great Saudi loading dock in the oil port of Rabigh.

The Special Forces had dinner as soon as they returned and then settled down to two tables of bridge. Garth Dupont, flushed with what he believed to be the total success of their first mission, opened the bidding in *les picque*, spades, in the first rubber; ended up bidding six, and making one.

Amid laughter of good-natured derision, someone said he hoped Garth could count a damned sight better underwater than he could on the surface. Garth assured them he would be challenging for the Underwater Bridge Championship of France when they returned.

In fact, Garth had been asleep for only three hours when they reached the calm waters off Rabigh just after 0100 on Thursday morning. Commander Dreyfus had made fast time all along the Saudi coast, where they found the deep ocean quite deserted both on and below the surface. They picked up only two small fishing boats on their passive sonar all the way from Yanbu.

It was still only 2345 when they came to periscope depth, confirmed their GPS fix and found the quick-flashing warning light on the headland of Shi'ib al Khamsa, a small deserted island directly in front of the 15-mile-long bay which protected the port of Rabigh.

He left the island to starboard and pressed on for another four miles right into the gateway to the bay, another wide seaway, with a flashing light on the right hand side but nothing on the left, where a coastal shoal rose 350 feet from the sea bed to a level only about 100 feet below the surface.

However at that point the well-chartered bay had depths of 300 feet until quite close to the shore. And Commander Dreyfus elected to make a hard right turn, at PD, into the wide southern end of the bay. This was no cul-de-sac – not for surface ships, at least – because there was a narrow 50-foot channel at the end of Shi'ib al Bayda, one of three islands which more or less blocked the bay to the south. However, the Bay of Rabigh was a cul-de-sac for a submarine.

Commander Dreyfus thus came quietly to the surface and made a 180-degree turn in this sheltered, 'private' end of the bay. There was not a ship in sight, on radar or sonar, on or below the surface of the water. It would take him a matter of moments to go deep and vanish, heading out of the bay any time he wanted.

Rabigh was not as busy as Yanbu, principally because it had no major trans-Saudi pipeline coming in off the Aramah Mountains. Nonetheless, it could be full of tanker traffic in mid-week since it had a very large refinery. This took in crude from Yanbu and dispersed it in various forms of gasoline, petrochemicals and LPG, taking the heat off the constantly overworked terminal 90 miles to the north.

Once more Garth Dupont led his team out of the submarine and into two new Zodiacs, same procedure, all the way into the docks. But Rabigh was not as light as Yanbu, and he hoped to find an even closer holding point. However, off to the left in a holding area about two miles away, Garth could see one tanker making its way slowly inshore, but the jetties were empty.

Just one other tanker was within sight of the

frogmen, a VLCC of unknown origin, making its way out of the bay about half a mile off their port beam. The Zodiacs carried no running lights and the sky was cloudy. The warm air above the water seemed muggy, and there was no moon to cast even the faintest light on the surface.

Dead ahead the jetties looked quiet, and, about 400 yards out, Garth Dupont decided to send the hit teams overboard and down into the depths en route to the loading platforms. That way the boat drivers could hang around in the dark well clear of the distant incoming tanker which appeared to be going so slowly it might not make its mooring by the following Wednesday.

But that was the nature of VLCCs. They took about four miles to stop at their regular running speed in excess of 15 knots. At four knots, creeping into the jetties, it took them almost 45 minutes from two miles out, because they actually covered the last 200 yards barely above drifting speed.

'Be ready to leave as the tanker arrives,' Garth had stressed to his men, explaining the importance of staying deep, well under the keel of the ship, the moment it came to a halt. No heroics, he told them; no going underneath the 350,000-ton hulk while it was still moving. 'We move when that thing stops,' he said. 'Unless we can get out before it arrives.'

Thereafter they kicked their way in, just as they had done at Yanbu. They were not observed; in fact, from high above no one even had a look over the side. There were no active guards on the jetties, and the shore crews had temporarily dispersed before the new tanker arrived.

In perfect seclusion, the French divers worked underwater beneath the towering platform, and within 50 minutes they had all eight bombs expertly set, times synchronised with those beneath the loading terminal at Yanbu. And the ominous ticking of the 16 detonator clocks, deep in the water, separated by 90 miles of ocean, could not be heard by anyone.

At precisely 0400 there would be two almighty explosions on the east coast of the Red Sea; Garth wondered how long it would take the Saudi authorities to work out that there might be a connection.

By the time they reached the seaward front of the dock, the incoming tanker was moored and they had to go deep under the hull before they broke free into clear water. That was the worst part. But again there was plenty of water below the keel, and they kicked their way to freedom up the starboard side of the colossal hull.

They swam 12 feet under the surface all the way back to the Zodiacs, kicking and counting, kicking and counting. When they burst up into fresh night air, they were about 50 feet from their nearest inflatable, the sea was deserted and within 20 minutes they had reached the *Améthyste*.

Procedures were identical to those at Yanbu. They unloaded the gear, climbed on to the casing, scuttled both boats and moved to their headquarters on

233

the lower deck. Commander Dreyfus ordered the submarine deep and they moved quietly out of the bay before Rabigh.

Once in open water they steered course one-five-zero down the main deep-water seaway of the Red Sea, 400 feet below the surface. They would not see daylight again for two weeks, until they reached the French navy base on the tiny sub-tropical island of La Réunion in the Indian Ocean, 3,800 miles away.

And no one on the entire Arabian Peninsula would ever know what they had done.

Same Sunday evening, 1730, 21 March
27.01N 50.24E. Speed 7. Depth 20
Course two-five-zero
Night falls over the Arabian desert and its shores far more suddenly than in more temperate northerly regions of the globe. However, on this particular night, 25 miles off Saudi's Gulf coast, it could not come down fast enough for Captain Alain Roudy.

The forty-one-year-old commanding officer from Tours, in the Loire Valley, was for the first time in his naval career living on his nerve edges. He would never have admitted that to anyone, even to his much younger second wife, Anne Marie. Actually, *especially* not his much younger second wife.

Captain Roudy was a disciplinarian, a man cut in the mould of eighteenth-century French battle commanders. And while he understood he might have been under pressure to defeat Great Britain's Admiral

Nelson and his veterans in 1805, he reckoned he would have fought Trafalgar a sight better than the somewhat defeatist Comte de Villeneuve, who lost his ship, was taken prisoner and later committed suicide.

Alain Roudy, who still lived in his hometown of Tours was currently boxed into an extremely tough time frame. Right now it was around 5.30 p.m. and the light was still not fading over these waters, 20 miles west of the Abu Sa'afah oilfield. The *Perle* was 20 feet below the surface without a mast up, moving slowly towards the main tanker lanes which would lead him down towards the gigantic LPG terminal off Ra's al Ju'aymah.

The trouble was that he needed to be in those lanes by 1815, and every time he risked a 30-second glance through the periscope he was seeing more moving traffic than there was on the Champs-Elysée at this time on a Sunday evening.

It was supposed to be a restricted area, but he'd seen at least two patrol boats circling the oilfields, four aged freighters to the north, three big fishing dhows, a trawler and a 90-foot harbour launch, plus two helicopters heading out to the landing platform in the middle of the Abu Sa'afah field.

In only 16 fathoms of water he really should have been moving west with a continuous lookout through the periscope. But he could not risk running with a mast jutting out, which might very well betray him, or even identify him. He knew the Saudis would not have a submarine in these waters, nor probably a warship, but *les Américains . . . très furtifs.* Captain Roudy did not wish to see the Stars and Stripes represented around here in any form whatsoever, above or below the surface.

The governing factor in his operation was that he needed to be 50 miles from the datum, in the launch zone, by 0400 the next morning, Monday. And that meant all kinds of deadlines to observe . . . *must be away from the last pick-up point by 2315 latest . . . must be away from the first pick-up point by 2215 . . . must wait two and a half hours at the second point for the divers to return.*

And it all meant being in there, with those tankers, running south almost in convoy, like them, at 10 knots, not later than 1815, 45 minutes from now. Otherwise, much later that night, he would have to unleash his missiles before he reached the launch area specified by Admirals Romanet and Pires. He could not slow down, nor ask for more time, because Louis Dreyfus would be accomplishing his much easier task over in the Red Sea, and their timing had to coincide.

'*Merde*,' said Alain under his breath, glancing at his watch for the seventh time in the last 20 minutes. *If the slightest thing goes wrong, we're in real trouble.*

Fifteen more nail-biting minutes went by, then Captain Roudy called, '*PERISCOPE!*'

Aye, sir.

And once more he heard the smoothest of machinery carrying the telescopic mast upwards, to jut out of the water. He seized the handles long before they were at eye-level and took in an all-encompassing view of the surface picture. The speed and grasp that had once made him leading student at the French Navy's Ecole de Sous-Marin had not deserted him. No one then could record a surface picture in his mind faster than young Roudy. And, 20 years later, nothing had changed. Captain Alain Roudy was still the master of his profession, in all of France.

DOWN PERISCOPE!

The careful surface check took him exactly 30 seconds. And for the first time in several miles he could see nothing in any direction. It was also, he noticed, at last growing dark.

The *Perle* ran on through the dark water. There was still a half-hour's running time before he had to be in those tanker lanes. But if he was even 15 minutes late, that quarter-hour would come back to haunt him all night. Any other 10-minute delay would mean almost half an hour behind schedule. And there were still four miles in front of him, before the flashing light on the Gharibah Bank.

The waters in a five-mile radius around the submarine were palpably deserted and Alain Roudy ordered a two-knot increase in speed. That, he knew, would bring him down to the tanker throughway in good time.

Again he ordered the periscope up for as short a time as possible. And then again, even though he was still relying on passive sonar to warn him of any ship coming close aboard. Then suddenly, dead ahead, were the lights of the Gharibah Bank, fine on his starboard bow.

Come right four degrees . . . steer two-six-zero . . . make your speed six . . .

Aye, sir.

UP PERISCOPE!

Alain Roudy saw a green buoy 100 metres coming up to starboard, and he knew they were almost in the *outgoing* tanker lane. He peered through the lenses and down the route and could just make out the running lights of a massive ship heading towards them.

DOWN PERISCOPE!

Aye, sir.

The turbines thrust her forward, and the *Perle* accelerated across the outgoing mile-wide lane, travelling at about the same speed as the oncoming VLCC, a mighty 300,000-tonner riding empty, high out of the water.

No one even got a sniff of her as Captain Roudy pressed on, and then, five minutes later, took a final look at the incoming lane to the right. This was his direction and his runway. Roudy wanted a couple of miles between his submarine, for and aft, and any other ships running down to the LPG dock this eventful Sunday night.

If necessary, he would wait around to ensure he had it, but in fact the *Perle* crossed the outgoing tanker's line of approach with more than half a mile to spare, and the nearest ship to them on the dark waters of the far side was another VLCC about a mile and a half ahead.

Captain Roudy ordered a 40-degree turn to port, and the *Perle* fell in, line astern.

Steer course two-two-zero . . . make your speed 15 knots . . . stay at PD . . . mast down . . . 10 kilometres to ops area.

Two decks below, Commander Jules Ventura now summoned his men to complete their checks: attack boards, Draegers, rifles and ammunition to be loaded into the Zodiacs. Combat knives, flippers, detcord, timers, detonators, wires, cutters, screwdrivers, bombs securely packed. All six of the men going in were now barefoot in their jet-black wet suits, hoods down, goggles high on their foreheads, faces blackened with camouflage grease.

Final preparations were made for the boats. The Zodiacs would be hoisted first, then the two black Yamaha outboard engines, tuned like racing cars by the engineers, just in case. The two inflatables could probably outrun the *Queen Mary 2* over a short course – assuming, that is, that someone had by now extricated *Shades of Arabia* from her portside bow.

Three minutes later, Captain Roudy ordered the helmsman to make a hard turn . . . *90 degrees to port . . . stop engines . . . blow main ballast . . . surface . . .*

The *Perle* made her turn and came driving up to the surface, water streaming off the casing. She righted herself, moving forward, then slowly came to a complete stop, showing no lights.

On the command of the captain, Commander

Ventura led his men up the unlit companionway and out on to the casing. Strangely, this great burly, taciturn Special Forces leader was talkative now for the first time since they had left Brest.

Jules was encouraging his men, shaking hands with each crew member, thanking everyone for all they had done on the voyage, as he left the ship to face the unknown in an open rubber-hulled boat. Jules was transformed now into the mortal enemy of the King of Saudia Arabia and his Navy.

The boat driver went aboard the Zodiac first and Jules followed him, helping with the lines. When they were set to leave, the commander personally curled and threw the lines back up to the deck, then sat down and ordered the big inflatable away from the submarine's hull.

It was extraordinary how thoroughly invisible it swiftly became on the black water. But the moon had not risen yet and this was a black boat, with a black engine, carrying men in black wet suits, with black hoods and black faces. Even from 30 feet they were impossible to see.

Even the submarine, now without even flashlights on the casing, had effectively vanished from sight. Certainly, when the gigantic VLCC came rolling past over in the outward lane, no one on board the 21-storey crude oil leviathan had the slightest idea there was a 2,500-ton hunter killer within a mile of them, with men on the deck, and a black ops team about to destroy the world's premier supply of oil.

The second Zodiac came away from the *Perle*'s hull and melted into the night. The *Perle* herself came away from her holding position, and slid into the ocean, back to PD, in the down lane, about a mile in front of a new oncoming tanker and still a couple of miles astern of their original leader. All of them were on the seven-mile run to the world's largest offshore oil terminal on the man-made Sea Island.

While Team Two finalised its preparations for the insert, less than one hour away, under the command of twenty-six-year-old Lieutenant Remé Doumen, Jules Ventura and his men chugged steadily along at only five knots. They had a lot of explosive on board and a lot of time to set it. The *Perle* would not be back to collect them for almost four hours.

It was five miles down to the LPG terminal and Commander Ventura had all the time he needed to study the dock lights and find the darkest stretch of water in which to begin the mission. As he checked his attack board watch and saw it was 1915, he thought of his friend and colleague, Lieutenant Garth Dupont. Garth, he knew, was leading the identical mission on the other side of the Arabian Peninsula . . . *he's probably doing the same as me, groping about in the dark with a bomb on his back*, thought Jules.

The Zodiacs were now running over the wide shoal which guarded the eastern approaches to the offshore terminal of Ra's al Ju'aymah. At least, it guarded it from submarines, since there were only six fathoms there, and the outboards ran across it very slowly. Jules Ventura and his men finally arrived half a mile north of the loading jetties at around 8 p.m. This was a very well-lit terminal and Commander Ventura saw no reason to approach it head-on, not when he could find unbroken darkness north and south of the outer dock.

He could see now what he had been seeing on the chart for so many weeks: the long man-made bridge/causeway to the offshore jetties which ran four and a half miles out from the land and ended in a great 'V' shape at the end. He presumed the liquid gas pipes ran under the causeway and ended in the huge pumping and valve-control systems positioned on the jetty, and plainly visible to the satellite cameras.

There were two tankers in residence, one of them an 80,000-ton black-hulled gas carrier out of Houston, Texas. Jules picked out the name *Global Mustang* on her stern. But he needed light-sensitive nightglasses to do so. He checked out the bow of the tanker at the other end but he could not make out the lettering on it. Not even close. He thus concluded that the north end was darker.

'Take her in another 700 metres,' he commanded, 'dead slow, minimum revs. We'll swim the last few hundred.'

Commander Ventura was more concerned with the traffic than the light. To the north-west of Ra's al Ju'aymah there were five oil pipelines crossing the ocean floor; the Qatif oilfield; another large offshore oil rig; an anchorage area for waiting tankers, all in

242

a vast restricted area. The place was humming with small craft. Big Jules could see green and red running lights all over the place, but he had none on his Zodiacs and no one could see him.

They chugged almost silently towards the jetties, and still the great shadow of the dock hung over the water, and to the north there were no reflected bright lights beyond 100 feet. Jules called his men to action stations and five minutes later they all slipped over the side and began the swim-in, just as Garth Dupont's men had done an hour earlier, over in the Red Sea.

There was one principal difference between the two missions. In Yanbu and Rabigh, Garth's men had been ordered merely to blow the terminal out of the water, all eight bombs on the supporting pylons. Here at Ra's al Ju'aymah, there was more to it. Commander Ventura was required to blast the pumping and valve system, thus igniting the volatile liquid gas.

The terminal itself was more fragile than the docks at Yanbu simply because it was a mere seaward structure miles from the land. Out here the terminal would probably collapse with the explosions of two or three 60lb bombs. Six would make total collapse a certainty.

But Jules Ventura and twenty-three-year-old seaman Vincent Lefèvre needed to climb the structure, inside, coming up directly beneath the boots and trucks of the LPG personnel. And then they had to attach the massive timebombs right below the pumps.

'If you're going to blow the damn thing up,' Admiral Pires had instructed, 'you'd better make sure that liquid gas blows out like a flame-thrower. Our objects are twofold: to destroy and to frighten. Make sure the blowtorch at Ra's al Ju'aymah ignites.'

They had studied the layout of these jetties for weeks now and each man knew intimately the supporting pylon he sought. With all eight of the men in the water, the boat drivers and comms operators headed further out for a few hundred yards, with orders to make their way back inshore for the pick-up in one hour.

The swim-in took just two or three minutes and, as ordered, they gathered underneath the structure to hear last-minute words from Jules: 'You all know what to do . . . go in pairs to the two pylons you have been allotted and fix the six bombs. Then wait below the surface at pylon No. 4 on the chart – Vincent will be right above you, working on the two high bombs.

'Don't, for Christ's sake, let anything go off early, or you'll kill us all. We rendezvous again under pylon No. 4 and return to the Zodiacs together.'

And so they swam to their appointed stations, and, like Garth Dupont's men earlier, found they had to scrape away the barnacles in the warm water so that the magnetic bombs could be clamped on to the steel hulls.

As they expected, the tide was not yet high, and Jules and Vincent removed their flippers below the surface at No. 4. Then they unclipped the straps

244

which held the Draegers, state-of-the-art breathing apparatus weighing 30lb on a man's back but weightless in the water. Jules lashed the gear to the pylon 20 feet below the surface and they pulled on their waterlogged, black Nike trainers, kicked their way up into the fresh but dank oil-smelling air below the jetty.

The steel strut they were looking for, jutting diagonally up to the next horizontal beam, was now two feet above their heads, and both men reached up with rubber-gloved hands to grab it. From there on, it was a relatively simple 40-foot climb to the underside of the decking on the high central area of the jetty.

They reached the uppermost hoizontal, which stretched for 20 feet, four feet below the decking. Pylon No. 4 ended right here. It was about the diameter of a telegraph pole and freshly painted rust-red in colour. There were no barnacles this far above the water.

Astride the beam Jules unzipped the rubberised container which held his bomb. He gently scraped the magnetic surface with his knife and then held it to the pylon, feeling its pull as the magnets jammed it hard against the steel.

Vincent Lefèvre passed the timing device which, on this type of bomb, screwed into the casing. Both knew it could be done by hand, but they also knew that they would get a much tighter fix if they used a screwdriver. Jules turned the timer into place, and set it for seven hours and 40 minutes. He held out his hand for the screwdriver, tightened the timer and the screws which held the detcord detonator in place.

Then he and Vincent began to edge along the horizontal beam, Vincent playing out the detcord. Halfway along, they paused while Jules took a length of tape and wrapped it around the beam, holding the detcord firm and invisible from any angle.

That was when he dropped the screwdriver. It fell from his grasp and hit two metal beams on the way down with a clang before splashing into the water.

Jules had no idea if anyone was directly above them, but he instantly drew his silenced rifle from its waterproof holster on his back, and, with his finger on the trigger, stared seawards at the hull of the liquid gas tanker moored to the dock.

Then, to his horror, he heard the sound of running feet above him, a single person approaching the edge. Jules and Vincent were no more than 16 feet inward from that point when they heard a thump above them. And then an upside-down face appeared from above, and then the beam of a flashlight.

Whoever it was – military guard, gas-crew worker, tanker man – Jules had no idea, but the man was staring straight at him.

'*Who's there?*' The words seemed disembodied since the face was upside-down. But they were serious, and Jules took the only option open to him. He blew that face clean off its head with a burst of his silenced AK-47. It gave a muffled clicking sound, no more, nothing like as noisy as the falling screwdriver.

The body slumped over the edge, blood dripping 40 feet into the sea. Jules was along that beam with the dexterity of a circus tightrope walker. With an outrageous display of strength, he grabbed the throat of the man and hauled him overboard, straight down into the ocean below. Then he stood there, heart thumping, in deadly silence, wondering how many more they'd have to kill before they could get away.

To the amazement of both the commander and the Navy seaman, there was not another sound, neither from above, nor from the tanker. Whoever had seen them had been alone. There were no more footsteps above, no shouting, nothing.

Jules Ventura ordered Vincent back along the beam. Then he followed him to the junction of five steel rafters which met in one spot, right below the gas pumps. There they clamped Vincent's bomb, which needed no timer, having been especially primed to explode via the detcord charge.

Jules wound the cord around the bomb and one of the beams, finally jamming the detcord into the hole normally used for the timed detonator wires. He tightened two screws and leaned back to admire his handiwork.

One thing was for certain: when that first high bomb blew at 0400, the second one would follow, a millisecond later. He motioned to Vincent to begin the climb down, which took them eight minutes. They crossed one horizontal beam just above the water, to pylon No. 4, and then dropped back into the Gulf to collect their flippers and Draegers.

As arranged, the team gathered at the pylon, where Commander Ventura's men were anxious to know why Jules had found it necessary to shoot someone. They pointed out the body which had already drifted under the structure on the rising tide 25 feet away.

Commander Ventura's orders were brusque. They took the spare detcord and wound it around the body, a long double-thickness cord coming out from under each armpit. Two young seamen were told to drag the body under the surface, hauling it back to the Zodiacs, line-astern. Jules told them he did not give a damn about the man he had shot, but he gave a huge damn about anyone finding the body.

And so they set off, four of the divers helping to pull the corpse through the water. When they reached the Zodiacs, they took a longer line from inboard, secured it to the body and towed it back behind the rear inflatable, like a water-skier who'd fallen off his skis.

Back at the submarine, they took the same tow line and lashed the man to the Yamaha engine. He was in uniform and had plainly been in the Royal Saudi Air Force, which had responsibility for guarding and protecting the country's vulnerable oil pumping stations, processing and loading facilities and oil platforms in the Gulf.

The young Arab sank with the two little inflatable boats, straight to the bottom, in 100 feet of water, right at the end of the Saudi tanker lanes. Six hours from now many more would be joining him in death. But no one would ever know there was anything special about the loss of the young loading-dock guard.

They were all merely victims, killed in the name of the world's richest and most avaricious industry.

CHAPTER SIX

2215, same night
Off Sea Island terminal, Saudi Arabia

The last two Zodiacs were heading east now, back towards the tanker lanes. Lieutenant Remé Doumen was from the chic Atlantic seaport of La Rochelle where his father, a greatly respected local ferry-owner, was mayor.

Generally speaking, Remé had never been on the wrong side of the law in his life. But now he sat in the stern of the lead Zodiac and gazed back at the floodlit steel structure of the massive Sea Island oil terminal and tried to accept what he had just done.

He knew, in the strictest naval terms, the full dimension of his mission: he had just led a team of highly trained hitmen into the heart of the enormous construction and organised the placing of sufficient high explosive to knock down the Eiffel Tower.

Remé stared at the distant lights and at the gigantic US tanker on the jetty. They were two miles away now, but he would take to his grave the memory of that night – the pitch-black water under the ship,

Philippe's hand on his left shoulder as they kicked into the pylons . . . the knife on the steel, the tiny spotlight they used for the close electronic work, the lethal detcord, the wires, the magnetic tug of the bomb, the faint trembling of his hands as he spliced the detcord to Philippe's bomb on pylon No. 3.

Six hours and 25 minutes. They were numbers he would never forget. And now it was almost 2230. Only five and a half hours now, before the true measure of his team's work would be known, before the Sea Island terminal was blown sky high.

Would he ever tell his father what he had done? His girlfriend Annie? One day his children? Tell them of the night he became, for a couple of hours, one of the world's most prominent *terroristes*?

Of course he never would. The code of the French Special Forces, like that of all Special Forces, is never broken. And Remé knew he had to cast that word *terroriste* from his mind, for ever. He was Lieutenant Remé Doumen, loyal French naval officer, and he had just completed the most important mission entrusted to his country's Navy since . . . well . . . Trafalgar.

Remé Doumen shrugged and glanced across the water to the Zodiac, and he wondered if everyone was thinking the same, looking back at the mighty oil loading terminal, knowing it had under six hours of existence left. And that they had actually committed, with relentless precision, the oncoming outrage.

Remé had always been a very tough kid. At one

point it was thought he might represent France at rugby football. He was a medium-sized centre three-quarter, a hard, fast runner at university and coveted by the Toulouse club. But the Navy had other uses for his unusual strength, and his father, who had started life working as a deck hand on the La Rochelle ferry, was enormously impressed by the thought of having an admiral for a son. The French Navy beat the French Rugby Union comfortably.

But a *terroriste*? '*Mon Dieu!*' muttered Remé, as they came in towards the waiting *Perle*. 'I'd better avoid morning papers for the rest of my life!'

He knew he would return to normal duties. And he knew he'd get the same old feeling of burgeoning pride in his uniform, and pride in the fact that the Navy had selected him, and him alone, to lead the Special Forces in the staggering assault on the Sea Island terminal. What's more, he knew he would do it again if they asked him.

Even as he led his team up the rope ladder to the foredeck, he could sense an air of urgency in the submarine. The CO himself was out on the casing, and twice Remé heard Captain Roudy exclaim, '*Vite . . . vite . . . dépêches-toi!*'

Of course, everyone knew they were stopped in a dangerous place, in the middle of the central buoyed channel, in probably the narrowest part of the tanker route. On the bridge and on the bow, lookouts with high-powered night binoculars were sweeping the sea, for'ard and aft, for any sign of an onrushing VLCC, its helmsman 100 feet above them.

The night was cloudy and overcast, and the transfer from the boats was made in excellent time. The two Zodiacs were scuttled, but the *Perle* just beat them in the race to get below the surface, diving to periscope depth, in 15 fathoms, leaving Alain Roudy to decide whether to risk going deeper.

Right now there were 30 feet below the keel, and the CO decided to stay at PD, but to take down the mast, moving nor'nor'east up the outgoing channel at 10 knots. That way nothing would gain on him from behind, and he would gain nothing on any ship up ahead. The 10-knot speed limit, and requirement, was strictly observed along Saudi tanker routes.

It was five hours running time to H-Hour. Five hours to 0400. Five hours to the temporary end of civilisation in the free world. Certainly the end of cheap oil on the global market.

The crew of the *Perle* were not giving these considerations much thought as they pushed on up the channel. But there was a growing tension down in the missile room, where most of the operators were soon to launch all 12 of their cruises, not at some phantom practice target, as was usually the case, but this time with real warheads, packed with TNT, aimed unerringly, with precision and malice aforethought.

After eight miles Captain Roudy ordered a course change to the north-east . . . *come right* . . . *steer course zero-five-zero* . . .

And 12 miles later he elected to leave the tanker

lanes completely. With the main channel about to run due east, the CO ordered the helmsman to cross the lanes and exit to the north, making a wide sweep in deeper water for 25 miles to the missile-launch area he had been allotted, 27.06N 50.54E.

They arrived at 0340, still 50 feet below the surface of the water, unobserved by anyone since first they had gone deep in the Red Sea south of the Gulf of Suez.

Missile director . . . Captain . . . final checks, s'il vous plaît.

And for the last time, Lt. Commander Albert Paul illuminated the computer screen which showed the targets, and their numbers: Abqaiq Complex — 25.56N 49.32E; eastern pipeline — 25.56N 49.34E. The third barrage of four missiles would be aimed at 26.31N 50.01E, the Qatif Junction manifold complex, at four slightly different locations, hoping to blast the one area where the pipeline was custommade, and would take months and months to repair.

Albert Paul knew that hitting pipelines was not a great idea; nor was hitting oil wells. Both could be capped and repaired with standard equipment, which ARAMCO had in abundance. The trick was to hit the loading docks, the pumping stations and, on the Red Sea coast, the refineries themselves.

Captain Roudy's targets were supremely well selected. The Abqaiq station handled 70 per cent of the Kingdom's oil. It not only pumped from the enormous Ghawar field, over the mountains to the Red Sea coast, it also fed the entire east coast. This included

254

the loading docks at Sea Island, Ra's al Ju'aymah, and Ra's Tannurah, from which Sea Island was fed.

The pipeline out of Abqaiq was obviously critical and Prince Nasir had pinpointed it as the only pipeline to be targeted. Alain Roudy's final objective, the Qatif Junction manifold complex, directed every last gallon of oil on the east coast.

Prepare tubes one to four . . .

Aye, sir.

Ten minutes later, 0350 . . . *prepare to launch . . . tube ONE . . . TIREZ DE FUSIL . . . FIRE!!*

The first of the *Perle*'s MBDA Stormcat cruise missiles came ripping out of the torpedo tube, its aft swerving left and right as it found its bearings. It flashed upwards through the water, broke the surface with a thunderous roar and lanced into the night sky, the numbers flashing through its 'brain' as it steadied on to course two-four-zero, still climbing, a fiery tail crackling in its wake.

It hit its flying speed of Mach 0.9, 200 feet above the water, at which point the gas turbines cut in and extinguished the flames in its wake. In the warm air at sea level over the Gulf, Mach 0.9 was the equivalent of more than 600 miles per hour, which meant the missile would blast into the Abqaiq complex 10 minutes after launch.

And before it had travelled 20 miles, there were three more missiles, dead astern. The lead missile crossed the narrow peninsula of Ra's Tannurah and swerved over the Saudi coastline at 0357. It rocketed over the coastal highway and changed course, flashing through the dark skies above the desert straight at the Abqaiq complex. With 10 miles to go it made its final course change, coming in from the north-east, on a line of approach which took it marginally north of the main complex.

At precisely 0401 it smashed with stupendous force straight into the middle of Pump Station No. 1, buried itself in the main engineering system and detonated with monstrous force 360lb of TNT in a blinding flash of savagery which would have blown an aircraft carrier apart.

No one working on the station's night shift survived. All the main machinery was obliterated by the explosion. Anyone standing a couple of miles away might have been staggered by the destruction and fires which began as soon as the oil ignited. But just a short distance from the remnants of the pumps there was the fire to end all fires as Alain Roudy's second missile slammed into the central area of Abqaiq's petrochemical fractioning towers.

The huge steel cylinders, full of belting hot gas and liquids, were colossally inflammable. And they did not just burn: they incinerated into a violet, orange inferno. Even Dante would have called the fire brigade. Heavy fuel oil, gasoline, liquified petroleum gas, sulphur and God knows what else blasted into the sky. And the heat was so intense it caused a chain reaction among these refining towers, which exploded one by one in the face of the searing heat.

Everything they contained was totally combustible,

and, years later, Abqaiq would still be considered the world's largest industrial calamity, greater even than the Texas City disaster in 1947 when a tanker full of ammonium nitrate fertiliser blew up an entire south Texas town. Abqaiq now burned from end to end. Alain Roudy's four missiles had all struck home. And he was not finished yet.

The next four smashed into the eastern pipeline on its way to the Qatif Junction manifold complex. Then that too exploded in a fireball. Out to the west the flames were visible in the sky from the obliterated Sea Island terminal which seemed to blow itself to pieces at 0403 with about a square mile of oil ablaze all around it.

The most spectacular fire was off Ra's al Ju'aymah, where Jules's two high bombs had slammed the upper deck of the terminal 100 feet into the air, blown to smithereens the valve system for the petroleum gas and ignited the blowtorch from hell, as forecast six weeks earlier by Gaston Savary. It was now roaring across the water, an incinerating white gas flame two feet across at source and 150 feet long.

The jetty itself was in pieces in the water but the causeway was more or less intact and the liquified gas pipe was jutting at a ridiculous 45 degrees to the horizontal, feeding the giant flame with an unending rush of propane which no one could turn off.

Twenty minutes after the explosions had comprehensively destroyed the Saudi Arabian oil industry on the east coast, no one had yet connected the two events. No one was left alive who had been working near any of the explosion sites. The administration blocks at Abqaiq and Qatif were flattened, and anyone who was awake, even remotely close to the fires, could only stand in awe of the gargantuan flames exploding into the sky every few minutes. Situated in the middle of nowhere, Abqaiq's remoteness seemed to make the inferno it had now become blaze all the more brightly.

Indeed, the first alarm was raised in the distant city of Yanbu al-Bahr, where the loading jetties had been blown sky high by Garth Dupont's bombs. But that jetty was close to the shore and the explosion scarcely harmed any of the main parts of the town. The missiles fired by Commander Dreyfus had just hit the refinery standing a couple of miles beyond the Yanbu perimeters. And this meant the police chief and several duty officers in ARAMCO's high-security forces were more than aware that something big had just gone up.

The Yanbu police phoned Rabigh, which was in much the same condition as they were – big flames, constant explosions from the burning refineries, jetties gone. In turn they both phoned Jiddah which had, in the last few minutes, lost its own refinery, courtesy of another well-aimed cruise from Commander Dreyfus.

Everyone called the security headquarters in Riyadh where they had now heard from the town of Ra's al Ju'aymah that the LPG jetties four miles offshore had just blown up and taken a 200,000-ton tanker with them. It was not, however, until after 5 a.m. that Riyadh learned of the full catastrophe in Abqaiq.

Nearly all of the great loading jetties in the country were smashed beyond repair, the pumping system was history and the Qatif manifold would take at least a year to repair. The Saudis had always known their oil industry was vulnerable, but this was too much to comprehend.

They had plenty of security in all the complexes and yet some kind of a marauding force appeared to have breached every last line of defence. The goose which had laid the golden egg and brought unimaginable wealth to this desert kingdom, and to what was now one of the richest ruling families on earth – all 35,000 of them – had now laid another egg, which had exploded monstrously. Out in the desert, many of the oil fires would burn for weeks.

And in different seas, a thousand miles apart, two submarines of the French Navy were making their way quietly home. Indeed, on board the *Perle*, running silently towards the Strait of Hormuz, 100 feet below the surface, Jules Ventura, destroyer of the LPG terminal, had just bid an extremely modest two-no-trumps.

8 a.m., Monday 22 March
Western suburbs of Riyadh
Prince Nasir heard the news before most people, mainly because he had observers in all the selected

sites, each of them under instructions to call him immediately anything happened. This made him an extremely busy man between 0400 and 0420.

And now he sat in his study with Colonel Jacques Gamoudi, drinking coffee and watching the Arab-speaking television stations to see how the disastrous news was playing out. Most commentators had put together a conspiracy theory that the oil industry had indeed been destroyed by persons unknown.

Of course al-Qaeda was an immediate suspect, but al-Qaeda, it was known, was a shadowy organisation without a titular head, without a headquarters, without known leadership. It was a seething internal mob, angry, determined, stateless and malevolent to the rulers of the Kingdom.

And since it was funded as an organisation mostly by Saudi Arabia, or at least Saudi Arabians, it was difficult to see why on earth al-Qaeda should have wanted to cut off the hand that fed it. Certainly the activities of the assault forces of the night had in half an hour brought the Saudi economy to its knees. The question was, who were the assault forces of the night? And why had they committed this apparently motiveless act of flagrant criminal aggression?

Prince Nasir and Colonel Gamoudi watched cheerfully at the torturous writhings of the commentators, who were trying to find answers to questions that seemed unanswerable. Not to mention this: what military genius had masterminded the assaults so brilliantly that they had treated the security forces as if they did not exist?

Prince Nasir considered it an outstanding night's work. And already, on television, there were constant calls to the King to speak to his people, to give them assurances, to point the way forward, to rally the Saudi nation. But right now the King was in shock. As were his principal ministers and his generals.

And on some of the English-speaking channels political journalists were forecasting the end of the rule of the House of al-Saud. Indeed, they were forecasting the end of the Saudi economy, the total collapse of the currency, and the complete inability of the government to finance anything, now that the oil had apparently stopped flowing.

There was no word from the King, which might have been short-sighted on his part, since the nation was in the process of going bust. In fact there was no official word from anyone, until 1 p.m. when the Channel 2 newscaster handed over to a spokesman for the government, who spoke rather angrily, informing the populace that there had been an attack on the oilfields and loading docks. But he said no details were available. Channel 3, run by ARAMCO, was understandably circumspect, revealing very little.

By far the best source of information was from the English-language stations in Bahrain and Qatar, which spent the morning interviewing anyone they could contact from ARAMCO. Slowly they pieced together the shocking truth that someone had launched a spectacular assault on the Saudi oil industry, coordinating stupendous bomb attacks, all apparently to explode within 10 minutes of each other.

These stations were in constant communication with the London media and by 11 a.m. had camera crews heading by helicopter to the fires still raging on Sea Island, and to the north, the LPG terminal blowtorch. By 1 p.m. there were pictures of various Saudi oil infernos on their way around the world.

At 2 p.m. the first riots began in the capital city of Riyadh.

5 a.m. (local), same day
Washington, DC
Lt. Commander Jimmy Ramshawe was very soundly asleep in his parents' luxurious apartment in the Watergate complex, which he used as his home base. He and his fiancée Jane Peacock had been out late with friends and he had dropped her off at the Australian Embassy at 2 a.m.

He was due in his office at the National Security Agency at 7 a.m., which did not leave much time for the amount of sleep he most definitely required. In Jimmy's opinion, midday would have been a better start time.

And when the phone rang at 5.01 a.m. he nearly jumped out of his pyjamas. He jolted himself awake, instantly, like all naval officers, accustomed to the lunatic hours of the Watch, and muttered, 'Jesus, this better be bloody critical.'

The duty office at the NSA chuckled, and said,

'Morning, Lt. Commander. There's something come up I think you ought to know about right away.'

'Shoot,' said Jimmy, copying the standard greeting of his great hero, Admiral Arnold Morgan.

'Sir, it appears that someone just blew up the entire Saudi Arabian oil industry.'

'*They WHAT?*' gasped Jimmy, struggling to clear his head.

'Sir, I expect you'll want to come in right away. I suggest you turn on the television right now and take a look at CNN. They seem to be on the case pretty sharpish.'

'Okay, Lieutenant. I'm on my way. Try to contact Admiral Morris, will you? I know he's on the West Coast but he'll want to know.'

'Right, sir. And, by the way, it's the biggest god-damned fire I've ever seen.'

Jimmy hit the power button. The television was already on CNN, and on the screen he could see the blowtorch from hell, blasting into the sky above the topmasts of an enormous tanker which was sunk amid the shattered remnants of a loading jetty.

'Jesus Christ,' whispered Jimmy.

But then the picture changed to an area where the sea was on fire. Then it changed again to the huge Red Sea refineries, all of them ablaze, still exploding and showing no sign, yet, of dying down. The biggest fires of all, at the Abqaiq complex, apparently had not yet been filmed.

Jimmy Ramshawe sat up in bed in total astonishment, thoughts cascading through his mind as he tried to pay attention to what the commentator was saying. So far as he could tell bombs had gone off in almost all of the principal operational areas of the largest business on earth.

Whoever had done it had coordinated a truly sensational attack. The reporter on CNN was surmising that everything had exploded shortly after 4 a.m. Saudi time. And, so far as anyone could tell, it was an internal matter, a 'purely Arab thing'.

Jimmy Ramshawe knew, like everyone else, of the growing unrest in the Kingdom, as currency reserves plummeted and individual citizen's share of the oil wealth dwindled by the year. He'd often been told by CIA guys that the Saudis were about two jumps from having the mob at the gates.

He turned the television up full volume and tried to listen while he took a quick shower. And the only copper-bottomed truth to emerge, at least in the terms required by a high-ranking intelligence officer, was that no one had the slightest idea who was responsible, nor why they had done it, and certainly not how they had done it.

The CNN commentator was concentrating on the consequences, rather than the causes; the minor consideration of what would happen now, when someone had knocked 25 per cent of the world's oil supply off the global market.

At this stage Jimmy was not interested in the market. That, he thought, would ultimately come under the heading of 'inevitable'. What exercised him was, who had done this and why?

He dressed rapidly, grabbed his briefcase, switched off the television and headed for the underground garage. When he reached the basement he headed to the only thing on earth he loved as much as he loved Jane Peacock.

And there it was: the gleaming 13-year-old black Jaguar his parents had given him for his twenty-first birthday. It had been four years old then, with only 12,000 miles on the clock, having been previously owned by an elderly diplomat friend of his dad's. Today it still showed only 42,000 on the clock, since Jimmy only took it out of Washington two or three times a year.

He and Jane usually drove her car, a small unpretentious but brand-new Dodge Neon, which did 38 miles to the gallon as opposed to the 16 mpg he got out of the Jaguar. He mostly used it for work, gunning it along the beltway from the Watergate complex out to Fort Meade every day. He loved the stubby stick shift, the surge of power of the engine and the way it hugged the corners.

And this morning he really put it through a hard training run. On near-deserted, dry roads, and a mission of national importance. Jimmy hit 90 mph on the highway and came barrelling down the road to the main gates of the NSA like a rally driver, pulling up at the guardhouse with a squeal of well-maintained brakes.

The guard waved him through briskly, smiling cheerfully at the Aussie security officer who drove like Michael Schumacher and sat at the right hand of the NSA Director himself, the veteran Admiral George Morris.

Jimmy drove straight to the main entrance of the OPS-2B building, with its massive one-way glass walls. Behind these, up on the eighth floor, was the world headquarters of the admiral, and Jimmy took advantage of a privilege he had, but rarely used. He hopped straight out of the car and signalled one of the guards to park it.

'Thanks, soldier,' he called cheerfully.

'No trouble, Lt. Commander – gotta put those oil fires out, right?'

Jimmy grinned. It was unbelievable how news, rumour and distortion whipped around this place. Here, behind the razor wire, guarded by 700 cops and a dozen SWAT teams, the 39,000 staff knew approximately one hundred times more than anyone in America about what precisely was going on in the world. Jimmy Ramshawe had long suspected each one of the 39,000 personnel briefed at least one person every 10 minutes. The Fort Meade grapevine had an extraordinary reach.

He reached the eighth floor, hurried into his office and turned on the news. It was now 0650, ten minutes to three in the afternoon in Saudi Arabia, and the fires were still raging. The news channel had essentially dealt with the blown loading docks in the big tanker ports and was now starting to concentrate on the inferno at Abqaiq.

No one had yet turned the spotlight on the critical importance of the smashed Pump Station No. 1, but CNN had received pictures of the gigantic fire in the middle of the desert, as the gasoline, crude oil and petrochemical refining towers and storage area continued to blast themselves into the stratosphere. No one had ever seen anything like this before.

The commentator was still concentrating on the possible perpetrators, and announcing (guessing) that al-Qaeda was somewhere in the background. But you can't call up al-Qaeda and check with the press office. And there were numerous other groups of Islamic fundamentalists who might, possibly, have favoured the destruction, then rebuilding, of the world's richest oil nation.

Indeed, Prince Nasir himself had recently expressed such alarm over the situation in Riyadh that he had granted an interview to the London *Financial Times* in which he had alluded to the possibility that someone, somewhere, might actually consider the destruction of the Saudi oil industry a cheap price to pay for the removal of the profligate ruling family, and a cheap price to pay for the removal of the *status quo*.

He had made a point of saying that, whatever else, it had nothing to do with him. But his heart was bleeding for the future of his ancient land. Very definitely. And, as a loyal courtier, and a man sympathetic to the plight of his fellow citizens, it pained him to mention these unpleasant truths.

Right now, along with the rest of the world's media, CNN had not the faintest idea what was

267

going on. And as their reporters took flying leaps from one conclusion to the next, Lt. Commander Jimmy Ramshawe, who was, after all, paid to think, not show off his knowledge on television, was doing exactly that. Feverishly.

As he had driven in that morning, something sitting at the back of Jimmy's mind had been nagging him and it refused to leave off. He remembered his telephone conversations back in November with his two contacts in London and New York, following what had appeared to be an arbitrary and unexpected hike in world oil prices. Someone, he'd surmised, had been playing the futures market and appeared to be stockpiling oil, discreetly, if that were possible, but nonetheless in vast quantities.

The finger of suspicion had that day, he recalled, been pointed at France, as both Roger Smythson at IPE in London and Frank Carstairs at NYMEX in New York had confirmed. Jimmy had at the time researched France's movements on the world oil market. But when that seemed to lead him only to the inevitable conclusion that the French weren't actually doing anything illegal or untoward – and after he had been momentarily sidetracked by Arnold Morgan asking him to see what he could find out about the supposed gangland killing in Marseilles the previous August – well, he'd found himself going down a blind alley on both counts and had decided to turn back.

But things were different now. The stupendous news of the overnight eruptions in the Middle East had pushed him smartly back on track. This was something worth looking at again. Switching on his computer, he logged on to the internet and found a website to elaborate more on France's activity in the oil markets and found little of interest, save that it was still importing 1.8 million barrels of oil a day, mostly from Saudi Arabia. And by the look of the morning news that was about to come to a grinding halt, as of today.

'I wonder,' mused Jimmy, 'if everyone in the industrial world is about to have bloody kittens over this, with one exception . . .' At the back of his mind he was thinking about the country which had already made other arrangements, and no longer cared whether Saudi Arabia had oil or not. *Could the French have known what no one else knew?*

Lt. Commander Ramshawe logged that as a possibility. But then he dismissed it on practical grounds, as a bit too fanciful. *It's sure as hell too wild a theory to start ringing alarm bells. But it might be the only theory around . . . guess we'll find out.*

At 0800 he ordered coffee and English muffins. He decided not to call Admiral Morris at 0500 on the West Coast, electing instead to contact his pal Roger Smythson at the International Petroleum Exchange in London.

Roger took the call from his office inside the Exchange, and, with admirable British restraint, told Jimmy that so far as he could tell the roof had just fallen in.

'Chaos, old boy,' he said. 'Absolute bloody chaos.'

'You mean the buyers are driving the prices up?' said Jimmy.

'Are you kidding?' replied Roger. 'By the time this place opened, every single person involved in the buying and selling of oil on the international market knew the Saudis were essentially out of the game.

'I mean, Christ! Jimmy, you've seen the news! The loading docks are on fire, the terminals have been blown up and the main pump station at Abqaiq has been destroyed. Even the manifold complex at Qatif Junction is smashed beyond repair. I'm telling you, whoever did this really knew what they were about.'

'You mean an inside job, perpetrated by Saudis on the entire nation?'

'Well, that's the way it looks. And you can guess what the panic's like here. Because to people working under this roof, the words Abqaiq complex and pumping station, the Qatif Junction manifold, Sea Island, Yanbu, Rabigh and Jiddah — they're everyday currency to oil men. We know how important they are. We know if there's a problem with any one of them the world's oil supply is in trouble. But Jesus! They're all destroyed and the price of Saudi sweet crude just went to $85 a barrel, from $46 last night.'

'Has it stabilised?' asked Jimmy.

'Hang on a sec. No. It's $86.'

'What's going to happen?'

'None of us knows that until the Saudis make some kind of a statement. So far, they haven't said a thing.'

270

'What about the King?'

'Not a squeak out of him. And nothing from the Saudi Ambassador to London. No one knows what's happening, and that makes the market so much worse.'

'Well, there's not much we can tell you either,' said Jimmy. 'We were waiting for word from our embassy in Riyadh. But nothing's come through yet.'

'Hey, there is just one thing,' recalled Roger. 'You remember that time we spoke in November – about the French buying up futures?'

'Sure I do.'

'Well, I kept an eye on that. And it *was* France, definitely. And they bought nothing from Saudi Arabia, but they went in strongly on Abu Dhabi oil, and Bahrain. They bought some from Qatar, and a lot from the Baku field in Kazakhstan, which is more expensive.

'You can't help thinking, can you? Because that makes France the only player in the world market which, potentially, wouldn't be too fazed by this crisis. So far as we can tell they scooped up around 600 million barrels over the next year or so, despite their long-time contracts with ARAMCO.'

Jimmy Ramshawe hung up thoughtfully.

1500, Monday 22 March
Riyadh
The first riots after the collapse of the oil industry began in the Diplomatic Quarter of the city. A

crowd of up to 500 advanced on the US Embassy compound and began to hurl rocks at the walls.

US Marine guards retreated and then spoke to the crowd, yelling through loudhailers for them to retreat, or face a volley of gunfire. The *matawwa*, Saudi's religious police, were called but ran into a hail of rocks and missiles from the crowd. The police commanders, accustomed to cooperating with the US, requested the Marines drive back the crowd with gunfire but only over the heads of the raging populace.

It was not yet clear why the Americans were being blamed for the potential collapse of the Saudi economy, and the first volley had its effect. Most of the crowd turned and ran for their lives, but they swiftly re-formed, this time outside the British Embassy, and began shouting and chanting. *INFIDELS OUT . . . OUT! OUT! OUT!*

By now the Saudi rioters had acquired a few guns for themselves, which they began firing into the air; then someone threw a hand grenade into the embassy grounds. No one was hurt but the local guards answered with a volley of gunfire aimed at the crowd and four Arabs fell wounded in the street.

By now, the religious police had summoned the National Guard in force. Historically, the National Guard were loyal to the King, and dedicated to serving and protecting him and his family. It operated separately from the regular Saudi Land Forces, and it accompanied the monarch wherever he went. In Riyadh, the National Guard's elite force was the Royal

Guard Regiment; once autonomous, it had been incorporated into the army in 1964, but it nonetheless remained directly subordinate to the King, and maintained its own communications network and a simple brief: loyalty to the King, at all times.

It was this small but well-trained force which arrived in central Riyadh with the *matawwa* on that Monday evening. Armed with light weapons and armoured vehicles, they advanced on the crowd and drove them back.

But now the rioting populace regrouped at the major downtown junction on al-Mather Street and began marching into the main commercial district. This was a fiery dragon unsure at what it should roar.

Since the early morning the dragon had been listening only to radio and television networks talking about 'national bankruptcy', of a nation with its resources destroyed for many years to come. The terror of abject poverty – the first they had ever known – had gripped every resident of Riyadh. And then, shortly after 3 p.m., a rumour swept through the city that the banks were closing and might not open again that week.

The Saudi British Bank on the wide thoroughfare of King Faisal Street was one of the biggest buildings in the city; with its doors slammed shut, it became the target of the furious mob. The rioters now rampaged into the street outside the bank, stopping traffic, firing guns and surging towards the main entrance.

273

The Saudi police were not up to this – there were now a thousand people at least, ready to storm the bank. The police used their mobile phones to contact the guardroom at the royal palace of the King requesting extra reinforcements from the Royal Guard Regiment.

But none came, and, at 1645, four young Saudis drove a huge garbage truck straight through the main doors of the bank, setting off burglar alarms and smoke alarms and ramming the vaults closed behind a steel portcullis. The trauma to the bank's security system also activated a complete shutdown of the counter areas with steel grilles and iron-clad door-locking systems.

Inside the bank the crowd went wild, blazing away with their old-fashioned rifles, and, careless of their own safety, hurling grenades which had been acquired from those members of the armed forces loyal to Prince Nasir.

From there the crowd turned its attention on automobiles parked in the street, heaving them over on to their roofs and then setting fire to them. By 6 p.m. the entire situation was turning increasingly ugly, mainly because the mob had no real target upon which to vent their fury.

All they knew was this: someone had destroyed the only asset the Kingdom had, and the King appeared to be powerless; he had not even spoken to his people. It was almost as if the royal family had decided to batten down the hatches and wait until the crisis had blown over.

As night fell, the looting began. Armed with sledge-hammers and axes the people stormed into some of the most expensive shops in the city, battering down the doors, oblivious of the burglar alarms. They stole everything they could, then torched the shops. As darkness fell, Saudi Arabia's capital was falling apart.

It was not until 9 p.m. that the National Guard began to get a semblance of control. Many of the crowd had by now drifted away with their loot, some of it extremely valuable, grabbed from the tourist shops. The police and the small details of guardsmen began making arrests, but they were principally concerned with protecting the big downtown hotels, now bolted and barred like fortresses, with all guests on the inside.

The Al Bathaa, Safari and Asia Hotels looked like war zones with armed sentries patrolling outside.

And in the middle of all this, Colonel Jacques Gamoudi, in company with three al-Qaeda body-guards, all former officers in the Saudi Army, toured the city in a jeep, watching carefully, making notes and observing the chaos.

Every half-hour Gamoudi's cell phone rang and one of the five French Secret Service agents planted in the city to feed him information would update him on the fluctuating situation. The colonel was probably the best informed person in Riyadh among either the loyalists or the rebels.

In Gamoudi's opinion things were progressing too quickly. Prince Nasir had assured him many times that his people would take to the streets as soon as they realised their livelihoods were threatened; that, in the immediate future, the rulers of Saudi Arabia would have no money to distribute to the population.

The King himself was the principal wheel in the now threatened economy, but the other critical aspect of the financial health of the country had been the expenditure of the Saudi people themselves. The population of roughly nine million spent its annual per capita stipend of $7,000 on consumer goods. That $63 billion a year kept the commercial juggernaut moving in the overblown welfare state that was the Kingdom of Saudi Arabia. With free health-care and education and interest-free loans for buying houses – in addition to cheap electricity, telephones, water, domestic air travel, and, of course, gasoline – they had had it good. And right now, nobody knew what was going to happen.

But it went without saying that, regardless of the grim outlook for ordinary Saudis, the people most desperately affected by this unfortunate turn of events were the royal princes, thousands of them, the cousins of people like the late Prince Khalid bin Mohammed al-Saud. Having had so much, they had all the more to lose.

In his audience with the President of France at the Elysée Palace the previous summer, Prince Nasir had, in his diatribe against the profligacy and immorality of the ruling family, only touched the tip of the iceberg. It went much deeper. It was a story of almost unrelenting avarice and corruption; of princes supplementing their incomes with kickbacks from big business; of acquiring property cheaply by dint of their royal connections and the odd veiled threat; of manipulating government departments to their own ends; and, not least, of borrowing vast sums from the bank and never paying them back. To those who suffered from the activities of the ruling family it had been a protective circle which could not be broken. No one in business in Saudi Arabia dared face the wrath of the King and his advisers. The King held the purse strings and the armed forces were sworn to defend him. But now the banks were closed and their future in the country a big question mark.

That first day, there was an instant run on the currency as merchants, businessmen and other shrewd operators attempted to withdraw their funds. Currency holdings fell dramatically in just a few hours. By 3 p.m. the Saudi American Bank was forced to join the Saudi British Bank in closing its doors, not just in Riyadh but in Jiddah and Taif as well.

With the banks closing, more and more of the princes decided to cut and run. By the end of that Monday afternoon the first of the private jets were leaving King Khalid International Airport. Various members of the royal family who worked in government and in the armed services took only a short time to realise the extent of the financial crisis which was looming.

Throughout that morning, and into the early part of the afternoon, vast sums of money were being transferred by wire to French, Swiss and American banks. Entire families were preparing to leave, many of them driving towards the north-west borders which led into Jordan and Syria.

And the real trouble had not even begun.

Colonel Gamoudi continued his tour of the city, sensing with every turn of the wheels the turmoil among the population. In his opinion this situation could explode at any moment; the alarm bells ringing within the shattered portals of the big banks were sounding just as urgently in the head of Jacques Gamoudi.

He could see two main threats to the operational plans of Prince Nasir: first, the mob was about to burn down the entire city; second, the King had to be considering calling in the Army from the military cities to restore order if things did not improve rapidly. The Army was still loyal to the royal family.

That would put his own operation completely out of the question. However many rebels, anarchists and al-Qaeda fighters he had, his dozen or so tanks and brigade-strength armoured vehicles would be no match for the entire Saudi Army and Air Force.

Jacques Gamoudi could not wait until Thursday or Friday to launch his attack. This was all happening far, far sooner than anyone had anticipated.

He ordered his driver back to the Dir'aiyah base, and once there he called a staff meeting for 2200. Meanwhile, he took his cell phone out beyond the ruins and into the desert. He walked for 10 minutes, fast, along an ancient camel track. And when he was quite satisfied there was not a sound coming from anywhere, he punched in the numbers to a private line in the heart of the Commandement des Opérations Spéciales complex in Taverny, north of Paris.

He used the veiled language they had agreed upon for an emergency: '*I wish to speak to the curator, s'il vous plaît.*'

'*Speaking.*'

'*This party has started early and it's getting out of control. I think we should get moving at least a day early, maybe two days early. Can I have your agreement to proceed as I see fit?*'

'*Affirmative. I'll leave our friends in the south to you.*'

At which point the 20-second conversation ended abruptly. General Michel Jobert replaced his receiver. Thousands of miles away, Jacques Gamoudi pushed the button to end the conversation and walked slowly back to the garrison in the desert ruins.

The phone call had been critical, vital to the operation. It had been tactically sound and would govern the entire French-Saudi alliance for the next 48 hours. But it was also a calculated risk, as Jacques Gamoudi knew it to be when he made the call.

Same day, same time
Joint Services Signals Unit
Cyprus
The Joint Services Signals Unit (JSSU) was located in a very secret place. The United Kingdom's listening post in Cyprus, it was high up in the hills at

279

Ayios Nikolaos, north of the military base in the UK sovereign territory of Dhekelia, south-east Cyprus.

Here, at the crossroads of east and west, British intelligence operated a hub from which they intercepted satellite messages, phone calls and transmissions emanating from all over the Middle East. To the north lay Turkey, to the east Syria, Israel and Iraq, to the south-east Jordan and Saudi Arabia, to the south Egypt.

JSSU was manned by the cream of British electronic interceptors from all three services, the majority from the Army. They maintained a constant watch, monitoring communications around the clock, every one of the operators a highly qualified linguist, trained solely to translate intercepted messages and conversations as they are transmitted.

The satellite communications intercept ran right across the frequency, including faxes, e-mails, coded messages in 100 languages, the majority of this data being recorded on a long-running tape for later analysis. Conversations of particular interest were, however, written down by the listening operator, as they are spoken, and immediately translated.

The electronic outpost in south-eastern Cyprus was regarded as a priceless asset by British intelligence, and in turn by the National Security Agency at Fort Meade. JSSU was a part of the fabled British intelligence operation in Cheltenham, Gloucestershire, GCHQ (Government Communications Headquarters). If Cyprus was the jewel in the crown of GCHQ, in turn GCHQ was the jewel in the crown of Britain's espionage industry, which costs $1.5 billion a year to run.

It was from Cyprus that terrorists' combat communications were first breached, from tiny Nikolao where they hacked into Osama bin Laden and his henchmen in faraway Afghanistan. The US National Security Agency willingly pooled all its intelligence with Cheltenham, where the 4,000-strong workforce operated from blast-proof offices under an armour-plated roof. It was a huge new building, circular, with a round central courtyard. It was called The Doughnut.

This particular Monday had obviously been a day of pandemonium, with the Saudi oilfields destroyed and a zillion cell phone calls being made all over the Middle East. In fact, it was probably the busiest day in the Cyprus listening post since the Egyptian Second Army had rampaged across Israel's Bar Lev line in 1973.

Only now, as the evening wore on, the riots in Riyadh began to die down and businesses and banks closed, did satellite communications start to slow up. Corporal Shane Collins, a twenty-eight-year-old signals expert from one of the British Army's tank regiments, was at his screen in the Nikolao ops room checking the traffic, which was, naturally, mostly in Arabic.

He was just having his first cup of coffee of the evening when he heard a message which made him lean forward in his seat. He wrote down nothing but listened carefully, knowing it was being automatically recorded on that specific frequency.

The voice was French. Very French. *Le conservateur? La fête? En avance?* Corporal Collins pressed his 'listen again' button, and carefully wrote down the full transcript – noting the brevity, the lack of any personal greeting or even recognition.

He knew some French but not enough to be sure. He punched the brief sentences into his computer and transmitted them to the translation section on the next floor. Within five minutes it was back:

This party has started early and it's getting out of control. I think we should get moving at least a day early, maybe two days early. Can I have your agreement to proceed as I see fit?

Affirmative. I'll leave our friends in the south to you.

It was all in French. Both ends. And while Corporal Collins could not activate a trace to establish from where the phone call had emanated, he immediately called over his duty captain and reported that he had a conversation on the satellite which was plainly not just a personal call.

The captain agreed, and he lost no time in passing the text straight back to GCHQ in Cheltenham for detailed analysis. It was 2130 in Riyadh, 2030 in Cyprus and 1830 in Gloucestershire.

The Middle East Desk, deep inside The Doughnut, put an immediate trace on the satellite, searching for the starting point of the call. They established a line on the frequency, which stretched back from Cyprus, across the Lebanon coast, south of Damascus, through Jordan and straight through Saudi Arabia, bisecting Riyadh and the central desert and ending somewhere down in the Rub al-Khali, the Empty Quarter.

Somewhere along that line a Frenchman had activated his cell phone to . . . someone. GCHQ then put out a tracer to other listening posts to try and locate a different 'line' which would bisect their own, revealing the location of the French caller. No one was surprised when another listening post in north-east Africa came up with one. The lines bisected one another around 20 miles north of Riyadh.

The Cheltenham analysts asked their computerised system to make several trillion calculations in five minutes, and quickly established this was not a code, but, rather, veiled speech. 'The curator' was and would remain unknown but the experts were certain this had military overtones.

Corporal Collins had sensed it. The analysts inside The Doughnut agreed with him. No greeting, no farewell. This was a signal, not a conversation. One piece of information – the party had started early and might get out of control. One question – can we go early? One answer – yes.

But, go where? What party? Did this refer somehow to the current uproar in Riyadh? If so, who wanted to get involved? Had they tapped into al-Qaeda's command headquarters?

The British intelligence officers had been wrestling with this problem all day. Why al-Qaeda, an organisation which had received sums of up to $500 million from Saudi sources in the past 15 years? Al-Qaeda, which was comprised of Saudis, who made up the vast majority of the 9/11 hitmen back in 2001, and who, it was believed, made up almost the entire population of terrorists held at Guantanamo Bay, the US naval base in Cuba. Why on earth would al-Qaeda wish to bite the hand that fed it?

Well, if not al-Qaeda, who? The analysts at GCHQ were baffled as to motive and culprit, but they were not baffled by the innate importance of Corporal Collins's signal. And at 10 p.m. that night they relayed it on to the National Security Agency at Fort Meade. It was 5 p.m. in Washington.

The NSA ops room had been buzzing all day with a perfectly astounding lack of information about the Saudi oil crisis. No one had given serious consideration to the theory of outside involvement. It still seemed a completely internal Arab affair. Someone, for whatever reason, had apparently planted a succession of bombs from one end of the Arabian Peninsula to the other, and simultaneously blown up the entire shebang.

If there was malice, it was directed principally at the King and the ruling members of the royal family. No one, from the highest echelons of America's espionage organisations to the top brass in the Pentagon, had come up with a single feasible reason as to why a foreign power should want to perpetrate such an action.

The most available oil in the world was Saudi,

and to most countries it would be unthinkable to be without it. Saudi Arabia provided 20 per cent of the daily requirement for the USA. Without Saudi oil, France's mighty traffic network would grind to a complete halt.

And yet . . . Lieutenant Commander Jimmy Ramshawe had an uneasy feeling. Nothing about this astounding attack sat correctly with him. He had spent much of the day pulling up data on the Saudi oil defences, and there were a lot of them. Every one of those giant structures – the pump stations, the loading terminals, the refineries, the offshore jetties at Sea Island and the LPG docks off Ra's al Ju'aymah – had been heavily guarded.

According to the Middle East desks at the FBI and the CIA, you could not get anywhere near these places, certainly not by land. You simply could not reach them, not carrying the kind of explosive which would blast them to smithereens. It was downright impossible. However, it could perhaps have been done by sea, with frogmen coming in planting explosive under the docks.

The US Navy SEALs could probably have done it, or the Royal Navy. Maybe Russia, not China, but possibly France. Certainly not Saudi Arabia, a country which did not even own a submarine and certainly possessed no underwater Special Forces capability.

No. Lt. Commander Ramshawe could not figure it out. And anyway, even if the Saudi Navy had suddenly risen against the King, that did not explain how someone else had managed to hit the Abqaiq eastern pipeline amidships, then blow up the manifold at Qatif Junction, flatten Pump Station No. 1, and set fire to the biggest oil processing complex in the Middle East, the one at Abqaiq, slap bang in the middle of nowhere and operating behind a steel cordon of armed guards.

If this was indeed a purely Saudi matter, Jimmy Ramshawe considered, it had to be the biggest inside job ever pulled. And there was no motive. Not even a suggestion of one. If the action was Saudi, it was committed by a bunch of fundamentalists bent on committing financial suicide.

And the Saudis, he knew, were not regarded as stupid. He scrolled back on his computer screen and checked the strength of the Saudi National Guard, the independent force whose special brief was to guard those oil installations in the eastern province.

The Saudis were revealing no accurate numbers, but there were thousands of troops deployed by their commanders along some 12,500 miles of pipeline, which reached 50 oilfields and several refineries and terminals.

The force worked closely with ARAMCO, with its strong American connections, both financially, technologically and militarily. These people, Jimmy Ramshawe mused, could not be taken lightly.

A bunch of hitmen creeping past battalions of guards, laser beams, patrols, probably bloody attack dogs . . . then fixing bombs all over the place! Get outta here. That's just bloody ridiculous . . . especially since dozens of bombs, from one end of the bloody country to the other, went off bang within a few minutes of each other.

The Saudi National Guard was just too strong for that. The brass at ARAMCO would not have let that happen. *Jesus! These guys have bloody tanks, artillery, rockets, plus a bloody Air Force, fighter bombers, gunships and Christ knows what else! I don't buy it. And I'm not going to start buying it any time soon.*

The clincher, so far as Jimmy was concerned, was simple: the sheer number of targets hit. *You're trying to tell me, of all the guards in all of those priceless oil installations, not one of them saw anything . . . not a single warning, not a single mistake, not a single alarm. Nothing. A bunch of blokes dressed in sheets flattened and burned 25 per cent of the world's oil, and NO ONE suspected anything! Come on. This was military. Not terrorism.*

The clock ticked past 1730 and a duty officer from the international division tapped on Jimmy's door and delivered copies of the very few coded signals from GCHQ in Cheltenham, anything which might be worth his time. These were delivered twice a day, in hard copy at his request. Admiral Morris used computers, but looking at screens was not his first choice. Jimmy liked the signals 'in black and white, right where I can see 'em'.

He looked at the top sheet. He knew the satellite intercepts were arranged in descending order of importance by the NSA staff, and at first glance he could not see anything wildly exciting about this early party someone was planning to attend.

But then he looked at the notes from the British case officer which commented on the brevity of the message and the fact that it had all the hallmarks of the military. And that grabbed his attention. Then he saw the signal had been sent on a cell phone, situated 19 miles somewhere north of Riyadh and that really tweaked his interest.

After a day like today, *anything* that said 'Riyadh' was interesting. But what made his hair stand on end was the final paragraph which displayed the conversation as it was spoken. In French.

Lieutenant Commander Jimmy Ramshawe instantly put two and two together and made about 723. 'There's something going on,' he spoke to the empty room. 'There's something bloody going on. And who's this bloody curator? And who's this French bastard poncing about in the desert, sending military signals?'

Jimmy had read enough signals in his time from all over the world to recognise military when he saw it. There was the recipient of the call, the curator! *No one asks for the bloody curator. That's a pseudonym. And the question — your permission to proceed? — that's military. No one on earth talks like that except Army, Navy, Air Force. And the reply! Jesus! AFFIRMATIVE! He might as well have signed it General de Gaulle. It's all military. These clever bastards at GCHQ have hit something here. I'm right bloody sure of that. Perhaps those poms weren't so dim after all.*

The problem was, Lt. Commander Ramshawe was not sure who to talk to. Admiral Morris was still in the Navy yards in San Diego, probably out on a carrier, definitely not to be interrupted, especially by a wild, if well considered, speculation.

The lieutenant commander pondered the situation for half an hour. Then he decided there was only one person he would like to see wrestle with the problem, and he was retired. But this was right up the admiral's street. Jimmy Ramshawe picked up the telephone and dialled the private number of the old Lion of the West Wing, Admiral Arnold Morgan himself.

'Morgan – speak.'

'Hello, sir. Jimmy Ramshawe here. Have you got a couple of minutes?'

'Well, we're on our way out, so make it quick.'

Jimmy's mind jumped two notches. He would either deliver a slam-dunk sentence to seize the admiral's attention, right now. Or risk a slow-burn introduction, during which the irascible former presidential Security Adviser might get bored and tell him to leave it for another time. Jimmy knew the admiral's boredom threshold was extremely low.

Jimmy went for the slam-dunk. 'Sir, I believe it is entirely possible that the Republic of France, for reasons best known to themselves, have just blown up the oilfields of Saudi Arabia.'

He heard a snort from the admiral at the other end of the line. 'Degree of certainty, Lieutenant Commander?'

'At this stage, about 1 per cent,' replied Jimmy.

'Oh, then we should probably nuke 'em, right, Jimmy? This week or next?'

'Sir, off the record, I am trying to piece something together here. But I don't know anyone else I can talk to about this. I have some new information I really want you to think about. If you've got time. You know Admiral Morris is in San Diego, I'm sure.'

'Okay, Jimmy. I'll tell you what. Kathy and I are entertaining this evening. Why don't you join us for dessert? About ten o'clock? Le Bec Fin in Georgetown. You know the place?'

Any invitation from the admiral was good enough for Jimmy Ramshawe. 'Sir, that would be terrific. And you're gonna love this.'

'I am?'

'Well, I think so. But basically I only said that to make sure you didn't change your mind.'

When they had finished speaking, Jimmy sat down again at his desk still consumed by that signal Corporal Collins had stabbed out of cyberspace on the other side of the world. *Permission to proceed . . . affirmative.*

'I just wonder what the bloody hell's going to happen over there,' he said, again to the empty room. 'We don't know. But I'm dead certain someone does. And, anyway, who're his bloody friends in the south?'

He decided to end his 12-hour shift and make his way home for a quick bite to eat and to smarten up for the admiral. By the time he headed out again later that evening the traffic was awful and he was already ten minutes late before he came to park his

290

car. He stopped outside the restaurant and called to the doorman, 'I haven't missed Admiral Morgan, have I?'

The doorman shook his head and beckoned for Jimmy to leave the car. 'We'll take care of that, sir', he said. 'Admiral's orders.'

Jimmy entered the restaurant and was shown to Arnold's wide booth. Kathy, looking wonderful in an emerald green suit with a cream silk shirt, wore her dark-red hair long. It was apparent that their dinner guests had left. The table had been cleared and a clean white cloth spread. On it were three dessert menus, three wine glasses and a bottle of Château Coutet.

The admiral filled each glass and pushed Jimmy's across to him; he glanced appreciatively at the label and noted the Great Man had selected a 1995 Château Lafleur from the left bank of the Gironde Estuary. He sipped it appreciatively and said, 'Thank you for this, sir. Thank you very much.'

'Oh, it's a pleasure, Jimmy. Since you plan to accuse, and then guillotine, the great Republic of France I thought we might as well kiss her goodbye with a decent bottle of her own wine.'

Jimmy laughed, and said, 'Too bloody right. Those frogs might be a bit treacherous, but they know a thing or two about the grape, eh?'

Kathy smiled at Jimmy. His rough-edged Aussie slant on life sat very well on a young officer. Much as the abrasive hard-edged humour of the admiral sat so marvellously well on a man of his learning.

She thought then, as she often did, how alike they were; like a couple of college professors who thought like Al Capone, or, in young Jimmy's case, Ned Kelly. She also thought this was going to be a very interesting evening. As did her husband.

'Well, sir. I told you I had a 1 per cent certainty level. This isn't just a shot in the dark, I'm on the case. As you know we heard last November that one of the European nations had suddenly, and for no apparent reason, bought up a whole slew of oil futures on the world market. We were told it might very well be France and over the past couple of months it's emerged that it's *definitely* France.

'I found out today the French purchased more than 600 million barrels for delivery over the next year. Some from Abu Dhabi, some from Bahrain and some from Qatar, with an extra supply from Kazakhstan.

'But, NONE from their old friends, and regular oil suppliers, Saudi Arabia. And they bought enough to take care of their 1.8 million barrels a day import requirement all over again.

'I ask why. Anyone needs extra oil, you go to Saudi Arabia. They've got more than everyone else and, with a big national government contract, it's cheaper. But no, France goes everywhere else. And today, someone destroys the entire Saudi oil industry, and there's only one nation in the industrial world that doesn't give a damn. France. Because she has her supply well covered from elsewhere. In my view, France MUST have known this was coming.

292

Coincidence is too great, the circumstances too strange.'

Arnold Morgan nodded. Said nothing. Refilled the wine glasses.

'And then,' said Jimmy, 'what else do we hear? The most wanted Middle East terrorist in the world, the Commander-in-Chief of HAMAS himself, Major Ray Kerman, is picked up by Mossad at some kind of a secret meeting in Marseilles, shipped in by the French Government, via Taverny, the headquarters of their Special Forces operation.

'Then he's secretly smuggled out. Plainly with the cooperation of the French Secret Service, who proceed to tell a pack of lies the size of an adult wallaby. All about the happenings of that night, the deaths at the restaurant . . . in Marseilles . . . *France*,' he added with emphasis on the last word. 'What's the great Middle East hitman fundamentalist doing in bloody France anyway? He MUST have had their protection . . . forget that, sir. He DID have their protection.

'Which brings me to my last point. Sometime today the GCHQ listening station in Cyprus picks up this message. It's plainly military, as you will see when I show you in a minute. And it was transmitted by a bloody Frenchman from somewhere in the desert 19 miles north of Riyadh. It was also answered by a Frenchman.

'Now, how about that? And what I want to know is this? *WHO PRECISELY* was our Major Kerman meeting in Marseilles when the bullets started flying? And where is Major Kerman right now?

'And, anyway, does that not suggest to you that France is somehow mixed up in this Saudi oil bullshit – right up to the armpits?'

They all picked thoughtfully at their desserts and Arnold Morgan sipped his wine.

'Jimmy, I have not heard anything from anyone which suggests the attacks on the Saudi oilfields were conducted by anyone other than Arabs, probably al-Qaeda but most definitely by Saudis.'

'They could not have done it, sir. I've been studying the bloody semantics all day. They could not. Unless the whole country was in revolt including the Army, the National Guard, the Navy and the Air Force. Otherwise it could not have happened.'

'Why not?' asked the Admiral.

'Because it's impossible. The Saudi National Guard, which exists to protect the oilfields and the King, is a force of thousands. And they're heavily armed and well paid. They also have tanks, armoured vehicles, artillery, rockets, access to the Air Force. All of those big oil installations are strongly protected – alarms, laser beams, floodlights, patrols, probably attack dogs. The Saudis are not stupid. They know the value of their assets, and they have protected them, stringently. Trust me. I've checked it out.'

Arnold nodded. 'Keep going,' he said.

'Well, there were ferocious attacks on two massive loading platforms in the Red Sea plus three huge refineries, all of them blown to pieces. On the east coast they obliterated the Sea Island terminal, blew up the liquid gas terminal at Ra's al Ju'aymah.

'They knocked out the Qatif Junction manifold – that's the station that directs all the oil in the eastern half of the country; they smashed Pump Station No. 1, which sends every last gallon of crude right across the mountains to Yanbu, on the Red Sea, they blasted the pipeline from Abqaiq which sits in the middle of the desert, and set fire to the entire Abqaiq operation, the biggest oil complex in the world.

'It all happened within a few minutes. It was an absolute bloody precision operation. And it was not conducted by a bunch of towelheads running around the desert with bombs under their bloody togas or whatever they're called. That was military. Because not a single alarm went off, no one made a mistake, no one got caught.

'And what beats the hell out of me is, how could anyone have got anywhere near Abqaiq or Qatif, or the pumping station? They're all in the middle of dead-flat desert. There's no cover. It's swept by bloody radar and guarded by hundreds of soldiers. I do not know how it was done. But it was not done by some shifty little bastard with a bomb. This was a military operation.'

'Or a naval one,' replied the admiral.

'Sir?' said Jimmy, longing to hear the admiral utter the words which would put them, not for the first time, on precisely the same wavelength.

'If I wanted to knock out those installations,' said Arnold, 'I'd send in the SEALs from submarines to time-bomb the seaward targets. Then, on the way

295

home, I'd flatten the oilfields in the desert with cruise missiles, fired sub-surface.'

'So would I, sir. So would I. But the Saudis don't have a submarine. So it must have been someone else. And I think that someone was France.'

'If there was even a semblance of a motive, I'd say you may be right, Jim. But it beats me why anyone would want to do this. But there could be developments in the next few days.'

'Damn right, boss,' said Jimmy. 'Remember, the Frog in the Desert — he's going to the party early.'

CHAPTER SEVEN

The world oil crisis hit home very hard on Tuesday morning, 23 March. Immediately after the opening bell at the International Petroleum Exchange in London, Brent Crude, the world's pricing benchmark, hit $87 a barrel, up around $40 from the close the previous Friday afternoon. Even on the opening day of Saddam Hussein's war against Kuwait in 1990, Brent Crude had never breached the $70 barrier.

And it was not going down. If anything, it was still rising, as the big players battled to buy futures at whatever price it took. All of the major corporations which relied on transport to survive – airlines, especially airlines, railroads, long-distance truck fleets, power generators, and, of course, refiners and petrochemical corporations from all over the world.

The London market opened at 10 a.m. with the first opening bell for natural gas futures. And the last sight most of the gas brokers had seen on their television screens before coming to work had been the 150-foot blowtorch from hell, blasting from the wreckage of the LPG terminal offshore from Ra's al Ju'aymah courtesy, though of course they did not know it, of Commander Jules Ventura, French Navy.

To the brokers, that signalled the end of Saudi Arabia's ability to produce liquid petroleum gas in large quantities. And when that ten o'clock bell sounded, in the great tiered, hexagonal-shaped trading floor of the International Exchange, it simply ceased to be a trading floor. It became a bear pit.

People were caught in the crush to the lower levels as brokers fought and struggled to be heard, bidding, shouting, yelling, *UP TWO! . . . UP FOUR! . . . UP SIX! . . .* dollar amounts unheard of in the sedate and mostly unexciting world of oil futures. Those '*UP TWOS*' were normally just cents, usually trading in a slowish band between $20 and $35. Today they were not cents, they were dollars, regular greenbacks, and the yells were so loud no one heard the second opening bell, which sounded at 10.02 a.m. signalling the start of crude oil trading.

But the brokers did not need to hear it. They knew the time, and the pandemonium doubled, and an army of men in red, yellow, blue and green jackets surged forward roaring out bids for Brent Crude futures.

Exchange officials waited in vain for the chaos to die down. But it did not subside at all. It grew worse. And at 11.00, for the first time in the history of the Exchange, the bell sounded long and hard to signify trading was suspended.

Sir David Norris, Chairman of the Exchange, addressed the floor and hoped everyone would agree

298

this uproar could not be allowed to continue. He pointed out that, among other things, it was grossly unfair to those brokers and traders who might be less used to operating in the front row of a Rugby Union scrummage.

Sir David, a considerable rugby player himself at Cambridge University, where he had also won a cricket Blue, insisted that some form of order be returned to the floor. And he requested the biggest buyers and sellers attend a private conference in his office immediately.

At least this gave the market time to recover its breath. But the underlying frenzy was ever-present and the morning high of $87 never showed any sign of dropping. On London's television news bulletins that evening Sir David made a personal appearance to announce the Exchange would not open on Wednesday morning. 'Trading is temporarily suspended due to the situation in Saudi Arabia,' he said.

Many people thought the alacrity with which the New York market, NYMEX, immediately followed suit suggested that Sir David and the Prime Minister had been in direct contact with the White House in the past few hours.

With a five-hour time difference between London and New York, London opened first and set the prices, before New York joined the daily battle for America's fuel requirements. And, of course, the knock-on effect from a tumultuous day's trading, during which oil prices had tripled at source, was nothing less than shocking.

By that Tuesday evening, in the United States, gasoline was costing $8 a gallon, instead of $2.50. In London petrol prices at the pumps had tripled to a similar amount in pounds sterling. It was the same all over Europe, except for France, where prices went up less than one euro and then fell back.

Japan was in chaos. With no access to natural gas, every household in the land depended on propane gas for its cooking needs – as Prince Nasir had observed to the French President nearly a year earlier. Propane meant LPG – the stuff still thundering out into the ocean, off the oil town of Ra's al Ju'aymah whence Japan acquired a huge percentage of its daily cooking fuel.

Restaurant prices in Japan doubled, on the basis that soon no one would be cooking anything, except over a fire. There was a stupendous run on electric cookers, which would probably turn out to be a waste of time since Japan's energy grid was entirely reliant on oil and gas from the Middle East.

Right now there were 24 Japanese tankers between four and 1,000 miles from the Saudi oil ports in the Gulf. All of them were either on the verge of returning home or trying to make the journey to other terminals, in the Black Sea, or in other Gulf States. There was no oil available in the Red Sea where the two main loading jetties were in ruins.

Internationally, air fares doubled overnight, led by British Airways and American Airlines which immediately cancelled all cheap transatlantic flights. And no one could really blame them, since no one knew the price jet fuel would fetch on the market at the end of the week.

The London Stock market shuddered and the FTSE dropped 1,000 points in two hours. By the end of the day's trading, the Dow-Jones average had crashed 842 points, wiping billions of dollars off corporate values. Airline stocks caved in worldwide, no one much wanting shares in aviation companies which could not afford their own fuel.

Industries all over the world, reliant on heavy road transportation, like food, agriculture and automotives, warned of drastic price increases unless the market stablised. Shares in General Motors, Ford and Chrysler crashed around 20 per cent.

The population slowly awakened to the fact that the United States still imported one gallon in five of its gasoline from Saudi Arabia. And that particular gallon was about to vanish.

The Democratic Administration had its back to the wall. And, in a special night session of Congress, Republican Senators and Representatives railed against the lunatic left-wing protection of the virgin wilds of Alaska, where oil-drilling had been so restricted by the shrill lobbies of environmentalists.

The dire warnings of the Republicans during the first decade of the twenty-first century had just come true in a blazing inferno on the other side of the world. America was too reliant on Arab oil, and especially on Saudi oil. A reduction of 5 per cent of its daily consumption would have represented an economic crisis for Uncle Sam. Twenty per cent was earth-shattering.

On that Tuesday night at 9 p.m. the President of the United States, Paul Bedford, a right-of-centre Democrat and former naval officer, broadcast to the nation from the Oval Office in the White House. He assured the country that the United States was not entirely dependent on Saudi oil, and that US consumption had in fact been falling in recent years.

He said that in the great scheme of things, this was a mere glitch, although it most certainly highlighted the world's vulnerability to terrorism. He admitted that once again the mighty economy of America had been shaken by actions on the other side of the world.

But it was not life threatening. He appealed for calm at the pumps, restraint in driving, and sympathy for 'our very great friends, the Saudi royal family'. He said he was confident the al-Sauds would turn once more to America in the great task of rebuilding its industry which would mean profits and jobs in the US.

And he reiterated the observation of the British Prime Minister, speaking on global television a few hours earlier: 'Saudi Arabia has not lost its oil,' said President Bedford. 'It's still there, beneath the desert floor. The Saudis have suffered a temporary setback in the drilling and refining of that oil.

'With our help,' he added, 'that will be corrected in the very near future. I spoke to the King a half-hour ago. As you will all appreciate, His Majesty has probably slept little. But he was calm and measured in his assessment of the damage.

'He does not know who could wish such harm to the peace-loving peoples of the Arabian Peninsula, and, quite frankly, neither do I. But the road back to prosperity is already being constructed. American engineers will be in Riyadh with the King and his advisers before the end of this week.

'For the moment, we have lost 20 per cent of our daily requirements of gasoline. And the Energy Secretary is working on a programme of allocations which will see us through the coming months. A little restraint, common sense and consideration. That's all we need, in order to come through this.

'Right now we are opening up new markets, finding more suppliers in South America. And I am already in touch with the Russian President with regard to special contracts in the Baku fields in Kazakhstan.

'I have ordered representatives of all the big oil corporations to report to Washington in the next 24 hours, and I intend to ensure there is no price-gouging in this country. You may expect prices at the pumps to fall back. And in the wider picture of the economy, there will be corporate priorities, particularly for the major truck fleets and airlines.

'My fellow Americans, it is doubtful if the Saudis will need to provide 20 per cent of our oil, ever again. This has been a wake-up call to the USA, and I intend to place before Congress an immediate Bill to step up drilling in northern Alaska.

'I have made it my personal crusade to rid this country once and for all of dependence on Middle Eastern oil. And on that note, I wish you goodnight, and may God bless America.'

Considered by many to be as good a speech as any they had heard from a Democrat in crisis, there was only one problem: no one took the slightest notice.

All through the night there were huge lines at the pumps right across the country, the oil companies were effectively charging anything they liked and prices were spiralling upwards as if in some fourth-rate banana republic.

Under a dark March sky, the Four Horsemen of the Apocalypse rode again. As Grantland Rice once observed . . . *In dramatic lore, their names were Famine, Pestilence, Destruction and Death. But these were only aliases* . . . in the US of A, 2010, their real names were Gasoline, Diesel, Propane and Jet Fuel.

And, despite the President's appeal for calm, there was an even greater force preparing to fan those flames of fear all over the world. Even as the President wished everyone good night, newsrooms all over the country were preparing for a Bonanza of Frightening News, that priceless commodity which increases newspaper circulation and sends television ratings sky-high.

The papers were preparing to run thousands of extra copies and print advertising rates were about to hit an all-time high. And television advertising on the networks would instantly go to levels normally associated only with a Super Bowl Sunday or a Presidential Election.

Right now, the media was in fat city. And the more frightened people became as they faced a loss of mobility, the better the world's news editors and advertising execs liked it. This was the week to justify big salaries and colossal expense accounts.

Hang on to your hats, boys!

US ECONOMY CRIPPLED BY SAUDI OIL
FIRES
PRESIDENT POISED TO BAN PRIVATE
DRIVING
SAUDI OIL BOMBS BLAST US ECONOMY
OILFIELDS ABLAZE – FED WARNS
RAMPANT INFLATION
RECORD GAS PRICES IN US – AS SAUDI
OIL BURNS

Things had been calmer in Pompeii in AD 79.

2100, Tuesday 23 March
Andrews Air Base
The US Marine jet bearing the considerable figure of Admiral George Morris from San Diego touched down a little heavily. It taxied to the parking area, where a helicopter awaited him, rotors already spinning, in readiness for the short journey to Fort Meade.

The Director of the National Security Agency

had different priorities from those of both the Administration and the politicians. Admiral Morris was not concerned with inflation, prices or the economy. He wanted to know just three things – 1) Who had blown up the Saudi oilfields? 2) Why? 3) Might they do something else? Also, he hoped to God young Ramshawe was on the case.

Admiral Morris was in his office within 23 minutes of landing at Andrews Air Base. And Lt. Commander Ramshawe was on his way along the corridor with a file containing a high volume of speculation but very few undisputable facts. He went over more or less the same ground he had covered with Arnold Morgan, at the end of which the admiral said, 'Jimmy, that's all very well observed. And I'm sure you are on to something, but I don't know what. Because there appears to be no motive.'

Admiral Morris sat still for a few minutes, ruminating, as he always did when a very grave problem stared him in the face.

At length he said, 'I do agree this was a military operation. But I can only imagine it was the Saudi military . . . no one else could possibly want to smash up the oil industry. To what end? It doesn't make sense.'

'I tell you what, sir. It made sense to someone.'

'Guess so. You had a chat with the Big Man yet?'

'Yes, sir. Met up with him last night.'

'And what does he say?'

'He thinks the wholesale devastation in Saudi Arabia

could have been achieved only with submarines, SEALs, high explosives, and in the end missiles to hit the land targets.'

'That is the only way,' said the former commander of a US Carrier Battle Group. 'Unless you bombed them, which plainly no one did. And you could not pull off something like that with amateurs planting bombs in the night.'

'Well, sir,' said Jimmy, 'since we both believe Admiral Morgan is right about 98 per cent of the time, maybe we should check out the submarine theory.'

'We most certainly should,' replied Admiral Morris. 'Get on to Admiral Dickson in the Pentagon, send him my best and ask him to check the boards for all world submarines for the past month. And perhaps he could do it real fast. I don't want Arnold on the line wondering if we've checked before we have.'

The lieutenant commander was glad to have his boss back. 'Right away, sir. He'll have SUBLANT send 'em over on the link, I expect. I'll come along to your office soon as we get 'em.'

It took only half an hour, and the lieutenant commander downloaded the sheets right away and headed back along the corridor to the director's office.

There was no need to knock. Admiral Morris held no secrets from his assistant. He was on the phone when Jimmy came in and sat down in front of the huge desk, once occupied by Admiral Morgan himself.

'Okay, sir,' he said when George Morris had finished his conversation, 'I'll run through the no-hopers first. Ignoring the China seas, the Russians had a couple of Kilos in sea trials north of Murmansk, and a nuclear boat exiting the Giuk Gap heading south down the Atlantic. That was on 2 March and the satellites caught it entering the Baltic, then the Navy yards in St Petersburg, where it still is.

'The Brits have a Trident in the North Atlantic, south of Greenland, and two SSNs in the Barents Sea close to the ice cap. Nothing in the Channel, or to the south. The other European nations with submarines – that's Italy, Spain, Germany and Sweden – do not have one at sea between them. As you know the US has two LA Class SSNs with CVBGs in the Gulf, the northern Arabian Sea and south of Diego Garcia.

'The French have a Triomphant Class SSBN out of Brest, the *Vigilant*, in the Atlantic, north of the Azores, but here's the key information – this month they sent two Rubis/Améthyste Class SSNs through the Med to Port Said, and on through Suez into the Red Sea.'

'Same day, Jimmy?'

'Nossir. The *Perle* went through Port Said just before midday on 4 March, and the *Améthyste* went through last Thursday afternoon around 1400 . . .'

'Did they come back . . . into the Med, I mean?'

'Nossir. In fact, no one's seen them since.'

'You mean they went deep in the Red Sea?'

'Apparently so, sir. We had a satellite pass over the

Canal and the Gulf of Suez at around 1900 and by then they'd gone, both ships, on 4 and 18 March.'

'How about the southern end, through the Strait, into the Gulf of Aden . . . what's it called? . . . the Bab al Mandab, right?'

'Yessir. And that's a spot we watch very carefully. Every ship entering and exiting the Red Sea is monitored by us, using satellites, surface ships and shore radar. Neither the *Perle* nor the *Améthyste* has left the Red Sea.'

'At least, not on the surface?'

'Correct, sir. And neither of them has gone back through the Canal to Port Said.'

'They could, however, have made the transit dived.'

'You sure about that, sir?'

'As a matter of fact I am. There's a wide seaway out of the Red Sea, and it's mostly two or three hundred feet deep. I think most submarine COs do come to the surface . . . there's a few islands down there and you need to be careful to stay in the defined north–south lanes, and it can be quite busy. It's easier to make the transit on the surface; the water's usually pretty flat.

'But I know US commanders who have made that transit dived, and they've done it more than once . . . the entrance to the Gulf of Aden is an interesting crossroads. Once you're through, and subsurface, no one knows where the hell you're going – north, south or east. It's a great spot to get lost in.'

'Well, the *Perle* and the *Améthyste* are certainly lost, sir. There's been no sight nor sound of either of 'em. And there have been no other submarines in all the world anywhere near the Red Sea or the Gulf in the past month. Unless a couple of US commanders went berserk and decided to slam the Arabs with a few cruise missiles.'

'Unlikely, Jimmy, wouldn't you say?'

'Impossible, sir. If the oil stuff was hit by sub-surface missiles they came from either the *Perle* or the *Améthyste*, on the basis there were no other submarines for thousands of miles.'

'The snag, Jim, is, of course, we don't know where either the *Perle* or the *Améthyste* is, within thousands of miles.'

'Five gets you 20 if one of 'em's not still in the Gulf of Iran,' said Jimmy. 'And five gets you 50 if the other one's not still in the Red Sea.'

'No thanks,' said the admiral.

'What now?' said his assistant.

'Get on to Admiral Dickson again. Ask if SUB-LANT can find out whether any French submarine in the past five years has exited the Red Sea underwater.'

'Right away, sir. That'd be interesting.'

'Not proof, of course. But a little food for thought, eh?'

Lt. Commander Ramshawe headed back to his staggeringly untidy office and put in another call to the Pentagon, to Admiral Dickson, Chief of Naval Operations.

'I can't promise absolute 100 per cent accuracy on that one, Lt. Commander,' said the CNO. 'We watch that area carefully and we watch all submarines in and out of the Red Sea. We'll have computerised records of all French SSNs and any Triomphant Class. I'll have SUBLANT give you a pretty good picture of French practices going into the Gulf of Aden.'

'Thank you, sir. I'll wait to hear from you.'

''Bout an hour,' said the CNO. 'By the way – is this for the Big Man?'

'No, sir. It's for Admiral Morris.'

'Same thing,' said Alan Dickson. 'Give him my best.'

The giant shadow of Arnold Morgan which had hung over the United States Defense Department for so many years had not receded. And every senior naval officer in the country knew of his continued obsession with submarines and their activities.

The smallest inquiry from the National Security Agency involving submarines – anyone's submarines – usually prompted the question, 'This for the Big Man?' Even though Arnold had been retired for several months. Even though he had not sat in the big chair at Fort Meade for several years. He had never quite gone. And a lot of very senior people, including the President, wished to hell he'd come back.

One hour later SUBLANT put Jimmy Ramshawe's information on the net to Fort Meade. The French sent submarines through Suez and into the Red Sea about four times every six months. Four in 10 returned the way they had arrived, back through the Canal

311

and on to either the Toulouse Navy yards in the Mediterranean, or Atlantic Fleet Headquarters in Brest.

The other six always headed out into the Gulf of Aden and usually went south to the French base at La Réunion. Occasionally a French underwater ship headed up into the Gulf of Iran, but not often.

The United States Navy had no record of any French submarine exiting Bab al Mandab subsurface. According to the analysts at SUBLANT, no one particularly liked making that voyage below the surface. And, in five years, US Navy surveillance had always picked up any French submarine heading south out of the Red Sea on the surface of the water, although they had three times recorded Rubis Class ships at periscope depth on satellite pictures.

Jimmy Ramshawe hurried back to the director's office, turning over in his mind the now unassailable truth that France had put two guided missile submarines through Suez with ample time to creep quietly into position and lambast the Saudi oil industry.

That did not of course mean they had done so. *But that bloody Frog in the Desert was looking a lot more menacing right now.* At least that was the opinion of Lt. Commander Jimmy Ramshawe.

Four minutes later, Admiral Morris instructed Jimmy to keep the Big Man informed, but, above all, to find out what he thought.

*   *   *

Midday, Tuesday 23 March
Khamis Mushayt Bazaar

Mishari al Ardh, aged twenty-four, was a market trader with his father. Their stall was always busy, selling fresh dates and a mountain of local fruit and vegetables. The old town, which stood more than 6,000 feet above sea level, enjoyed afternoon rain in March and August, which put local producers way, way in front of their brethren in the hot sandy deserts to the north.

Today was especially hard work. It seemed the news from the oilfields was so bad that people had developed a siege mentality and were ordering more of everything, much more than their families required; the way it was all over the world when the normal rhythms of daily life seemed threatened. The Khamis Mushayt marketplace was seething with activity, much like gas stations in the USA.

Mishari was trying to bring order to five wooden cases of dates when a friend of his, Ahmed, a local boy, same age, came rushing through the narrow street and beckoned him to cross over and speak with him.

Both young men were freedom fighters for al-Qaeda. Mishari crossed the street and accepted the folded piece of paper and the terse instruction . . . *Get this to General Rashood on the heights, now.*

Mishari walked to his father and spoke briefly. Then he walked through an alleyway to a parking lot where the aged family flatbed truck was kept. He jumped aboard and gunned it out on to the main road, deeper into the hills, up towards the village of Osha Mushayt, which was situated a mile from the al-Qaeda hide where General Rashood and his men were preparing for the attack on the air base on Thursday night.

He left the road after three miles and headed straight down the old desert trail to Osha. When he arrived he kept going, straight through the town and out into rough desert. Five minutes later he pulled up to the guard post and was immediately waved through. He came up here most days with fresh supplies and, usually, the morning newspaper.

Mishari parked to the north of the camp and walked through to speak to the tall Bedouin who commanded it. He explained the message had been dictated through the al-Qaeda network in Riyadh, by phone to Ahmed, who had written it down and requested it be shown to General Rashood as soon as possible.

The commander thanked Mishari gracefully and went directly to the general, who unfolded the notepaper and read . . . *Situation on streets here volatile, King might want his soldiers. Can't risk that. Essential you go tonight. We have clearance from the curator. I'll go first thing in the morning. Godspeed, Ravi. Le Chasseur.*

General Rashood walked to one of the barbecues where the cooks were preparing the midday meal. He slipped the note through the iron grille and watched it curl up and then burst into flames, directly below a roasting leg of lamb.

Then he turned to the commander and said softly, 'All right, my friend. Our work is done here. Call a staff meeting right now. We attack tonight. And may Allah go with us.'

1400, same day
Riyadh
Colonel Jacques Gamoudi sat in the shaded tent which housed the crown prince out on the desert floor. They both knew the message to the general was now delivered. They could only wait to hear that Khamis Mushayt Military City and Air Base had fallen, and then they would move, hard and fast.

They had possibly 13 hours to wait, and Prince Nasir would have to retire to one of the city palaces in order to be on the spot when the news came through. It would not be necessary to wait until General Rashood made contact. The military networks would be much quicker.

But when the news did arrive, they had to launch their attack on the royal palace. And at the precise moment, Prince Nasir had to make his broadcast announcing the death of the King and the shining future which now awaited the country. They would rebuild their oil fortunes.

In accordance with our ancient laws, as Crown Prince, I have assumed leadership of our country. I have taken my vows with the elders of the Council. And I have sworn before God to uphold our laws, both secular and religious. I am both your humble servant, and proud leader, King Nasir of Saudi Arabia.

315

With those words the lives of 35,000 Saudi princes would never be the same. And never again would there be such unashamed opulence associated with the ruler of the desert kingdom. In his own way, Prince Nasir intended to avenge the disgraceful behaviour of the recent kings of his nation.

Meanwhile in the busy streets to the south of Dir'aiyah, the city of Riyadh was once more in the throes of self-destruction, vast mobs of citizens again rioting, hurling stones and bottles, overturning cars.

At 3 p.m. (local) the King ordered the Army to a state of high alert. Like everyone else, he feared some sort of invasion might be imminent. And still no one had the remotest idea who was responsible for the destruction of the oil industry.

In the military cities of Tabuk in the north-west, King Khalid in the north-east and Khamis Mushayt in the south-west, troops deployed immediately into pre-planned defensive positions. However, there were so many deficiencies in manpower and equipment that only around 65–70 per cent of the total force managed to muster.

The King ordered naval forces at sea to form a defensive line around the coast, and his Air Minister ordered surveillance flights into the air. There were not enough ships to defend anything much bigger than Long Island on a calm day, and the surveillance flights reported nothing unusual.

Even the helicopter patrols which the National Guard had ordered to overfly the city reported nothing except civilian unrest, despite one of them making a detour almost as far to the north as the ruins of Dir'aiyah. The pilot presumably considered the remains of the ancient city largely a waste of time.

There was no sign of the Saudi Air Force. Its fleets of fighters and fighter bombers remained grounded, for one critical reason. For many years the Air Force had been commanded by royal princes, many of whom had been sent to train in England. Now that these scions of the al–Saud family were quietly on their way out of the country – most notably from the Riyadh base, where they were piling into Boeing 737s, 747s, British Aerospace executive jets and other chartered aircraft – vital instructions were simply not being issued to the pilots.

The Air Force also had another Achilles heel. The ground staff had no wish to become involved in a war in which they might conceivably be bombed during the course of some kind of internal power struggle. Flight technicians, air-traffic controllers and personnel concerned with fuelling and arming the aircraft were melting away into the vast emptiness surrounding the major Saudi bases.

Behind the blasted ramparts of Dir'aiyah, under heavy camouflage, Colonel Gamoudi was bringing his force to a high state of readiness. He had great faith in General Rashood in the south, and as darkness fell his petroleum tanker teams worked on the tasks of refuelling the tanks and armoured vehicles, loading the trucks with weapons and ammunition. He had always planned to leave this part of the operation to

317

the last minute. Even if anyone had observed the convoy of petrol tankers moving through the dusk, into the ruins, it would be far, far too late to do anything about it.

Prince Nasir himself, now in combat uniform – desert boots, fatigues, camouflage jacket, with a red and white checked *ghutra* – remained at the heart of the preparations, staying close to Jacques Gamoudi, watching an outstanding professional soldier make ready to capture a city.

1900, Tuesday 23 March
Yemeni mountains, above Khamis Mushayt
Ravi Rashood and his men broke camp as dusk fell over the desert. His 60-strong troop, including his own HAMAS personnel, began the march behind the al-Qaeda militia. Each man's face was blacked up. They all carried high explosive and their own personal weapons, plus the two big machine guns between teams of four men.

They had considered making the journey to their three separate destinations using trucks, because it was so much quicker. But General Rashood had decided against this. The level of high alert in both the military base and the Air Force base was, he decided, too big a risk. 'The only thing worse than failure is discovery,' he told them. And all the senior officers agreed.

And so they faced the five-mile walk, down to the loop road which crossed the river and ran past both bases before rejoining the road it had originally left. They travelled in single file, marching cross-country, staying off the old Bedouin tracks, with two al-Qaeda outriders mounted on camels, a mile in front of the leaders, keeping an eye open for intruders.

At 2100 precisely there would be a truck breakdown to their right, two miles south of the air base, blocking the only approach from the west. They would cross the road into the rough ground surrounding the airfield, knowing there could be no danger on their right flank.

Ravi's men had watched this road every night since their arrival and nothing had ever come down from the left, from the military base itself. The general supposed there to be an internal road between the Army and the Air Force, and he placed just two sentries, with a machine gun on the left flank beside the road. If any traffic approached, both the vehicle and its passengers would be eliminated instantly.

They reached the road on time and bade farewell to the six-man command team, the men with the communications equipment which was essentially their only lifeline if things went badly wrong. The six would take up position on high ground overlooking the air base about a half-mile to the north, with the capability of communicating with the general, the al-Qaeda commander and all three of the demolition force's team leaders. They could also call up reinforcements in the town of Khamis Mushayt if there was a rescue requirement. General Rashood considered this most unlikely.

The combat teams crossed the road in pitch dark

in groups of four, making a run across the blacktop on the command of the leaders. It was 2125 when General Rashood finally crossed the road, the last man to leave the safe side of the track.

This was the point where the attacking forces broke up. Major Paul Spanier and Major Henri Gilbert separated their 12-strong groups and moved east, for the long walk around the air base to the high bracken at the edge of the wire on the north fence. The 10 men who would go in separately and head for the aircraft hangars, then help to fight for the main entrance, would move along behind them. The two wire cutters marched in the lead with the two French majors.

General Rashood led his troop to the west to take up position four and a half miles away close to the main gates of the military base. The al-Qaeda fighters, who would launch the diversionary attack at the gates to the air base, were under orders to begin at 0055, five minutes before every aircraft on the base was blown to pieces.

Meanwhile, it was al-Qaeda's task to ensure the troop carrier trucks were in position, well hidden in the desert, with drivers ready to come in and evacuate the aircraft demolition teams on the north side. The team which blew the hangars, and then assisted the al-Qaeda fighters at the gates, would ultimately leave through the hills on the north side of the road with the local forces.

Only General Rashood and his 12-strong attack squadron would remain on the ground after the air base had been wiped out. And they would be stationed before the gates of the military city.

The night was cloudy but the ground had dried out after a prolonged afternoon rain shower. It was extraordinarily quiet and General Rashood had scheduled a 10-minute break after the five-mile walk-in from the mountains, not because of the distance but because they had all carried heavy loads of explosive and arms over very uneven ground.

And at the end of this time, the general shook hands with Major Spanier and Major Gilbert and wished them luck. He said goodbye to the al-Qaeda freedom fighters and also to many of the combat troops with whom he had become well acquainted. It was unlikely he would meet any of them again.

Upon completion of the operation, the majority of his troops were being flown in three helicopters from the northern slopes of the mountains back into the Yemen. The general had authorised this because the Saudis' surveillance capability in this part of the country would be non-operational.

As no one had known of their arrival, no one would know of their departure. All the French troops would return home by air, taking off from the Yemeni capital, San'a, situated deep in the interior. Air France flew once a week to this biblical city, said to have been built by Shem, the son of Noah. This week there would be two flights.

General Rashood himself would fly in a Saudi Air Force helicopter direct from the Khamis Mushayt base to Riyadh where he would join General Gamoudi and Prince Nasir and assist with the final capitulation of the city.

Meanwhile, there was a great deal of work to do in the south-west. Major Spanier and his team traversed the perimeter of the air base and were in position by 2235. They made contact with the al-Qaeda commander who had the getaway trucks in position. He was accompanied by four armed bodyguards, two of whom would drive the trucks, and they checked radio frequencies with the senior French officer in case of an emergency.

By 2250, the wire-cutter detail had clipped out an entry point in the fence. There were no lights out here on the remotest side of the airfield, which General Ravi had considered to be absurd. But this was a very quiet place, and no one had ever even dreamed of attacking it before. Not even the Yemenis in their most aggressive mood against the Saudis.

And so, in the pitch dark, Major Gilbert and his 11 men began to move through the wire, racing inwards, away from the perimeter road, and then swerving right into the dark part of the field where the 32 British-built Tornadoes were parked in four lines of eight.

The men split into six teams of two and began their work. Four teams started at the far ends of the four lines. The other two teams concentrated on the eight remaining aircraft, the ones nearest the perimeter, the ones closest to the approaching headlights of the guard vehicles.

The teams on the Tornadoes had a far better view

of the perimeter road. It was Major Spanier's group, working in among the F-15s, who were unsighted by the 32 Tornadoes, and could not see clearly along the road which led back to the hangars.

This was why General Rashood had two machine gunners right now prostrate behind the wheels of the two F-15s closest to the perimeter. From ground level they could provide cover for both groups. But the moment Major Henri Gilbert's men had completed their work on the first six aircraft, two of the saboteurs would swap their detcord, explosive and screwdrivers for machine guns.

They would take up new positions, behind the aircraft wheels at the furthest point down the perimeter road. No chances. High-explosive men, working on targets, tend to grow preoccupied with their tasks. They need guards.

And one by one they attacked the Saudis' fighter bombers. They unscrewed the panels which protected the engines on the starboard side, clipped out a gap in the wires which ran across the side of the block and clamped on the first of the magnetic bombs which would blow up the engine. The bomb was powerful enough to split the engine in two, and also to blow out the cockpit and control panels. Under no circumstances would this fighter bomber ever fly again.

The French Special Forces were never certain how much fuel was aboard each aircraft, but they were sure that some of them were fully fuelled. Observing from the bracken, in the afternoons, with General Rashood,

323

they had noticed that some of the Tornadoes had moved straight to the takeoff point without refuelling. Thus there was every likelihood that the ensuing fires following the initial blasts would be extremely hot and would very likely leave only burned-out hulks in their crackling red wake.

The teams worked carefully, using hammers and sharp-pointed steel punches to bang a hole through each panel, through which to thread the detcord. When the bomb was fixed and armed, they refixed the panels and ran out the detcord to a point midway between four aircraft.

And there one of their senior high-explosive technicians spliced the four lines into one 'pigtail' and screwed it tightly into a timing clock. They checked their own watches, and, after the first aircraft were dealt with at 2315, they set the main timed fuse for one hour and 45 minutes. Each set of four aircraft thereafter would have their detonation times adjusted for the 0100 blast.

And despite the certainty of their operation, the definite fact that those bombs would blow up at 0100, they still made sure no bits of detcord, no screwdrivers or any traces of the operation were left lying around.

Even if they had to abort the mission, run for cover or even find themselves on the wrong end of a firefight, it remained essential that no one ever knew the French Special Forces had worked on the airfield at Khamis Mushayt.

Two patrols came and went, neither of them even

pausing as they sped past the parked Tornadoes and F-15s. Each time the jeeps set off from the hangars, the lookout men spotted them and everyone hit the ground. Each time the jeeps never even slowed down as they came past the ops area of the French majors.

At 0042 the tiny alarms went off on each man's watch, signalling the scheduled ETD of the last patrol. For the third time, everyone hit the ground, knowing that, 14 minutes from now, the jeep, packed with its six armed guards, would drive by, less then 50 feet from the demolition teams.

They also knew that, as that jeep drove away from the big doors to the two massive aircraft hangars, almost half a mile from where they were working, their own team would be into the gigantic doors, winding the detcord, setting the timers and concealing themselves in a place where they could see the blast, before charging inside to do their worst.

As the minutes ticked by, the tension rose; not because any of them were afraid of a straight fight, which they knew they would win anyway, but because of the danger of discovery. The one careless move which would alert the Saudi patrol that something was afoot, the one minute giveaway which might give the Saudis the split second they needed to report back to the military base that they might be under attack.

On came the jeep, and the men pressed their blacked-up faces into the ground down behind the aircraft wheels. Only the sentries kept their heads up, ready to machine-gun that jeep to oblivion should there be the slightest suspicion of discovery.

But it came and went as it always did. Fast and unseeing. And at the hangar doors, the French explosive team were wrapping the detcord around the locks, with one lookout on each of the field-side corners of the buildings, just in case of a foot patrol.

There was, however, no danger of that. Tonight, this Air Force base was as inefficient as it had ever been. The defection of some of their senior officers had caused a drastic effect on morale. The pilots were without proper leadership, and, while the oilfields burned, and the capital city collapsed into self-inflicted chaos, there was nothing for them to defend, never mind attack.

Air Forces need targets, and dozens of aircrew and, indeed, guard patrols, had gone missing, heading for the Yemeni mountains. The pilots, a more senior breed, had not deserted their posts, resigned their commissions or even left the area. But they were mostly asleep or sitting around talking. They were not hired to guard and service fighter aircraft. They were hired to fly them, and there was at present nothing to fly them at.

And anyway, for how long would they have their highly paid jobs, with the King reportedly on the verge of bankruptcy? In Saudi Arabia, as in all Western democracies, the media was expert at frightening the life out of the population if it could.

The Frenchmen set the timers on the hangar doors for 0100, and then headed towards the north fence to hide out while the work of their colleagues was completed. At 0100, they would take out every aircraft in the hangars, and then move towards the main gate on the southern perimeter.

At 0055 the al-Qaeda freedom fighters launched their attack on that gate. Two hand grenades were hurled into the outer sentry station, blowing up and killing all four guards. Four young al-Qaeda soldiers flew across the road and hauled back the wrought-iron gates which had not been locked while the guards were on duty.

Immediately four rocket-propelled grenades were blasted in from the other side of the road, three of them straight through the windows of the inner guardhouse, killing all six of the night-duty patrol. One of them already had the handset in his hand, in the throes of reporting the first explosion, died with the handset still in his hand, which made the opening attack a close-run thing. But the young Saudi never even had the chance to dial.

Lights instantly began to go on in the guards' accommodation block 200 yards away, out of range for the rocket grenades, out of range at least for any form of accuracy. And that was why General Rashood had insisted that, the moment those gates were open, six young al-Qaeda fighters should race through, four of them with hand-held grenades, the other two with sub-machine guns.

Simultaneously two British-built general purpose machine guns were being hauled into position on the flat ground opposite the remains of the inner

guardhouse. Occasionally criticised for its weight –
24lb, unloaded, on its tripod – this weapon delivered
devastatingly accurate firepower out to a quarter of
a mile. The SAS never went anywhere without this
tough, reliable weapon.

And now the young Saudis were running straight
into the barrels of three guards who had burst from
the accommodation block door to find out what was
going on. The first boy hurled his grenade straight at
them, but they saw him in the light from the fires
at the gate and cut him down with small-arms fire.
The three other boys swerved left and hurled their
grenades through the windows of the accommodation block, which disintegrated in a huge explosion.

The big al-Qaeda machine guns opened up inside
the gates and peppered the front of the building,
killing all three of the Air Force guards who had ini-
tially stepped outside. The last two of the six al-Qaeda
runners reached the burning building and sprayed
the far windows with gunfire, thus discouraging any
further interference.

It was one minute before 0100 and the al-Qaeda
men were running back to their fallen comrade,
confident they had stopped any communication from
the guards but heartbroken at the almost certain
death of their friend, and for one of them, a brother.

They reached him safely under covering fire from
the GPMGs precisely when the opening explosions
from the airfield detonated with savage force. The
first four Tornadoes exploded like bombs, and, since
light travels a lot faster than sound, the silhouettes

of the sobbing young Arabs could instantly be seen as they tried to drag their comrade to safety, tried to stop the blood, tried to save him from dying.

The deafening explosion which followed made a sound like another bomb. And then all the aircraft on the field blew to pieces, all within a period of perhaps 25 seconds. The skies above the airfield lit up, with wide luminous flashes reaching out along the skyline. And each one was punctuated with a mighty *BOOOOOM* as the F-15s detonated, some of them loaded with jet fuel.

Flames reached 100 feet into the air and the glow in the sky was visible for miles. At the conclusion of the eighteenth massive blast, with the last set of four fighter jets exploding, there was, for a few moments, a calm interrupted only by the crackling of the flames. And then the biggest blast of all shook the base to its very foundations.

The hangar door blew outwards and six of the French Special Forces raced forward, firing M-60 grenade launchers aimed at each of the three aircraft inside, two of them fuelled at the completion of their service. Six rocket grenades struck almost simultaneously and detonated in the midst of several hundred gallons of jet fuel.

The blast was sensational. It blew the hangar to shreds, obliterated the curved roof, which collapsed, and allowed the flames to roar skywards. The next hangar contained two E-3A AWACS, radar surveillance aircraft. And when the rocket grenades went in there, it was the final devastation for the base.

With flames raging into the sky, and almost 80 aircraft destroyed, there was hardly anything left to defend. And the final elements of the 4th (Southern) Air Defence Group, whose duty it was to protect the base from air attack, quite simply fled. Their commanding officers were long gone.

In the end, the *coup de grâce* was delivered by Major Paul Spanier himself. He stayed behind as his men charged back through the huge hole now cut in the perimeter fence, and, accompanied by two troopers, jogged for 400 yards and blew up the fuel farm with four rocket grenades. One would have probably done it, fuel farms being liable to blow themselves up once something was ignited. No Special Force squadron had ever been able to resist exploding a fuel farm, and this one proved no exception to the rule. Khamis Mushayt went up like a dream.

It exploded in a gigantic blast, lighting up the desert for several miles. Back in the barracks area of the air base running figures could be seen heading back to the main gate. This was the 12-strong force which had destroyed the hangars and were now detailed to nail down the final surrender.

The trouble was that there were no longer any Saudi Air Force guard personnel left alive, and certainly none on duty. So the Frenchmen and their al-Qaeda comrades joined forces and commandeered a couple of jeeps and headed directly to the airport's control tower which seemed to be undefended.

They ripped an anti-tank rocket through the

downstairs door, and the al-Qaeda commander grabbed a loudhailer from the jeep and demanded, in Arabic, a peaceful surrender, which he quickly achieved. The four duty officers, working high in the tower, came out with their hands up, and were swiftly handcuffed and marched ahead of the jeep to the main office block.

This building stood next door to the flight officers' accommodation. The al-Qaeda troops hurled a couple of grenades through the downstairs window of the offices; immediately the door opened and six men with their hands high walked out into the night, unarmed and unable to offer resistance.

As agreed, the al-Qaeda commander demanded to see the commanding officer of the air station, who was no longer in residence. The one remaining senior officer was forced, at gunpoint, to return to the building and communicate to the Khamis Mushayt Military City that the air base had surrendered unconditionally to an armed force of unknown nationality. The air base, he confirmed, was history. There was not an aircraft on the field which could fly.

At this precise time, there were hundreds of military personnel gazing to the east where the entire sky seemed to be on fire. There was an intense red glow reaching into the heavens, with flames raging along the horizon.

In the main communications centre a phone call confirmed what they already knew – the air base had been attacked and obliterated by an unknown force. And even as they stood, petrified by the wrath which was plainly still to come, General Ravi Rashood and his trusty fighters stormed the main gates of the military city.

They rammed the gates with an elderly truck, on the theory that it could quickly be replaced by a new army vehicle. General Rashood personally leapt from the front passenger seat and hurled two grenades straight through the windows of the guardhouse.

The two sentries on duty were cut down by small-arms fire from the back of the truck, which was now parked dead in the middle of the entrance, a favoured tactic of the HAMAS C-in-C because it stopped anyone else coming in and it stopped anyone either leaving or closing the gates.

And out swarmed Ravi Rashood's chosen men, firing from the hip, racing towards the barracks whose occupants were in the upstairs rooms staring at the inferno at the air base. General Rashood's men shot off the locks and kicked open the door. They fired several rounds into the guardhouse on the lower floor, killing four men, and proceeded up the stairs, firing as they went.

All that was unnecessary. Those in the barracks were in no mood to fight and they stood on the upper landing, with their hands folded on their heads as ordered by General Rashood's senior officers. The HAMAS chief left four men to guard their captives then turned their attention to the command headquarters.

And there they met no further resistance. The officers and soldiers on duty surrendered as soon as the doors were kicked open, and the duty officer with his skeleton staff in the ops room did the same. General Rashood demanded to know where the commanding general could be located and was told he had left.

'Who commands this place?' said General Rashood. 'There must be someone, for Christ's sake.'

It turned out to be a veteran colonel, a career officer from the old school who had served in the first Gulf War. Ravi had him brought in, with his four senior staff members, by a hastily convened arrest party of al-Qaeda troops. The general always endeavoured to keep France and the French troops as far from contact with Arab officers as possible.

This particular Arab colonel did not need much persuading. General Rashood talked to him for perhaps two minutes, outlining what his men had achieved thus far, and the general was wise enough to accept that resistance was hopeless. He agreed to order his three subordinate brigades to withdraw back to their barracks, a mile away, and to wait there until further orders were issued.

There was only one unit which did not surrender and that was the 4th Armoured Brigade at Jirzan, which the Colonel commanded. He knew that some harebrained scheme had been dreamed up at headquarters in Riyadh whereby a tank brigade would be placed in a high state of readiness in order to proceed to Riyadh in the event of a coup against the King.

This was the nearest heavy armour to Riyadh and

one or two of the more cautious members of the King's defence committee had decided to instruct the Jirzan commanders to prepare to advance on the capital by road. This would entail loading the tanks on to transporters and driving them up the coast road and then over the mountains through al Taif. It was a distance of 700 miles and would probably take a week.

It was a hopeless, last resort, completely impractical, too slow and militarily absurd. General Rashood smiled and asked who was in command at the Jirzan HQ.

The colonel named a prince, the deputy commander, and Ravi instructed him to get His Highness on the phone and tell him not to waste his time. In fact it was the phone call which turned out to be a waste of time, since the young prince had already fled to Jiddah, where he had collected his family and flown to safety in Switzerland.

General Rashood cursed. And then he issued his final command. 'Colonel, you will call the Ministry of Defence in Riyadh and instruct them that the air base here has been destroyed, and that the Khamis Mushayt Military City has fallen to the same attacking force. You will tell them that further resistance is pointless.'

The colonel was happy to comply. He was so shocked at the events of the night, so amazed at the final conclusion of his command, that he forgot even to ask the HAMAS general his name. He was so utterly relieved not to be dead, so thankful his family was safe here in the officers quarters, he had not the slightest intention of asking anyone else to die.

The colonel's plan was simple: to remain here, in position with his men until they were issued instructions from the new rulers of Saudi Arabia. General Rashood told him to keep watching the television and to expect a force of 200 al-Qaeda fighters to arrive in trucks throughout the course of the night.

'Just to keep order, you understand?' he said. 'We would not want a sudden military rising here, and for that reason I will be destroying all communications both in and out of the base. Transports will be confiscated by the al-Qaeda network, and of course there are no aircraft left.'

And, with that, General Rashood handed over command to the al-Qaeda senior officer, who shook his hand and wished that Allah should go with him on the second leg of his journey, this time to Riyadh.

By this time, the least crowded of the getaway trucks had driven around the perimeter and was parked at the gates to the military city. General Rashood, in company with his initial team of eight HAMAS henchmen, now said goodbye to six of them. The three known al-Qaeda fighters would assume command-level posts right here at Khamis Mushayt, his two Syrian bodyguards would return to Damascus and the three former Saudi Army officers who had defected to al-Qaeda three years earlier would accompany him to Riyadh.

Thus the two HAMAS men climbed aboard the truck for the drive back into the mountains, to the hide, where helicopters from the Yemen were just arriving for the evacuation. All troops would be ferried to the airfield at San'a in Yemen's old Russian Army troop-carrying helicopters, a remnant of the days when the Soviet Union had been the biggest player on the southern tip of the Peninsula, when two Yemeni Presidents had been exiled in Moscow. The helicopters were big, old but airworthy. Just. And they would fly very low, and not very fast, over the mountains, just in case.

The only other inherent risk in this evacuation was the all-seeing eye of the US satellites. But the urgency of removing the evidence of French Special Forces overrode this, and Ravi Rashood decided the risk of American detection was worth taking. In any event no one could possibly have detected the nature of the helo's cargo.

In contrast, the helicopter which would fly Ravi Rashood and his three bodyguards to Riyadh was brand new and had been flown into the military city the previous day by a two-man Saudi Army crew loyal to Prince Nasir. When it landed in the capital, it would be in the grounds of the palace of the Crown Prince.

0100 (local), Wednesday 24 March
National Security Agency, Fort Meade, Maryland
The satellite pictures coming in on the link from surveillance were at once definite, but almost impossible to believe. The United States now had vivid

pictures of all the oil installations ablaze in Saudi Arabia, but these new images were incredible.

They showed with immense clarity that the mighty Khamis Mushayt Air Base, home to almost 80 fighter bombers, had effectively been taken off the map. The base, five miles east of the military city, was on fire, the lines of aircraft blazing, the hangars collapsed with burning aircraft plainly still inside.

Lt. Commander Ramshawe, who had been in his office for 17 hours, stared at the images and for the second time checked his map. No doubt about it, that was Khamis Mushayt all right, and it had been hit by an immensely powerful enemy.

Jimmy Ramshawe could compare it only to the Israeli drubbing of the Egyptian airfields in the 1967 war. It was simply not believable, right here in the year 2010, that some country, somewhere, could go to war with Saudi Arabia, unbeknownst to the rest of the world. It could not happen. But he, Jimmy, was right now staring at the evidence.

'No,' he said loudly. 'No one could have done this, except the Saudis themselves. And that's just bloody silly.'

He called the duty officer at the CIA and spoke briefly to the Middle East Desk, and they were as bemused as he was. They were receiving reports from field agents in the Saudi capital that there was further unrest in the streets, but nothing to suggest a bombing raid in the south, comparable to Dresden in World War II.

Then he called Admiral Morris, awakening him with the words, 'Sir, I think someone just declared war on Saudi Arabia. They started off by flattening one of the biggest air bases in the country, took out 80 fighter bombers at Khamis Mushayt.'

'They did?' answered Admiral Morris, fighting sleep. 'And now I guess you're going to tell me French Combat Command sent in a squadron of Mirage 2000s and let 'em have it.'

'Er . . . nossir,' replied Jimmy. 'I thought their new 234 Rafale fighter jets were much more likely.'

The admiral allowed himself a smile, despite the gravity of the situation. 'Any intelligence anywhere on this – CIA got any clues?'

'None, sir. No one has. It just happened, apparently. Right out of the blue. But of course we need to link the destruction of the oilfields on Monday to the demolition of the air base on Tuesday.'

'Whoever did it . . . well, it's the same guys, right?'

'Plainly, sir. But this is a helluva thing, sir. The CIA told me the Pentagon is recalling all the senior brass as we speak. President's in the Oval Office by 0200.'

'Gimme a half-hour, Jimmy. I'll be right there.'

The lieutenant commander replaced the telephone and looked again at the pictures. And he wondered what was happening at the air base. According to the CIA latest on the net, there was some evidence of a firefight inside the main entrance, but nothing to indicate a bombing raid on the air base.

He sat back and thought, as quietly and as

338

rationally as he could. *If no one bombed anything, and the Saudi Army was still in place, this had to be an inside job.*

But we've just about established no one could possibly have blitzed the oilfields, except from a submarine. And the Saudis don't have one. Tonight's stuff was too precise for missiles: those lines of burning aircraft were sabotaged. Otherwise there'd be visible craters. And it only takes one man to blow up a fuel farm.

No counter-attack activity from the Khamis Mushayt Air Base . . . so far as I can see, this is an internal Saudi thing. But they're sure as hell working with someone else. And I think that someone is France.

There was one gigantic flaw in his reasoning: he knew only too well the military and political chiefs would demand a motive. And so far as he could tell there was no motive.

But that doesn't bloody mean there isn't one, he thought. *It doesn't bloody mean that at all. It just means there's no* obvious *motive. Obvious to us, that is. And that's entirely different.*

He picked up the phone and asked someone to bring coffee for two to the director's office, not that there was any danger of anyone falling asleep. *This was a huge situation in the Middle East. And Christ knows where it would end.*

Admiral Morris arrived and asked immediately to see any communication from the US Ambassador in Riyadh. But there was a full report about the unrest in the city, the mystery of the exploding oil-fields and reports of a military disaster in the south.

The ambassador, without US satellite pictures right now, knew less than they did.

Admiral Morris used a magnifying glass to scrutinise the photographs taken from 20,000 miles above the earth. 'Clinical, eh?' he grunted. 'All the parked aircraft, both main hangars, and what looks like the fuel farm. No bullshit; they only hit what mattered. And there's no sign of general mayhem on the field or the runways. This wasn't a battery of cruise missiles. Otherwise there'd be stuff all over the place.'

'Exactly my thoughts,' replied Jimmy. 'This attack was made on the ground. And no one, apparently, saw anyone coming. Which sounds impossible. Those Saudi air bases are well protected, and this one stands right next door to one of the biggest Army bases in the country. We're talking thousands and thousands of armed men.'

'Jimmy. We're not really getting anywhere . . . in this place you always have to use the Sherlock Holmes approach . . .'

'When you have eliminated the impossible, only the truth remains,' he replied.

'Precisely. So why don't we spend five minutes eliminating the impossible?'

'Righto, sir . . . number one, it was impossible for any attacking force to blow up the oil installations in the middle of the desert. Number two, it was impossible for anyone to blow out the tanker loading docks from the land. Number three, it was impossible for anyone to obliterate the coastal refineries except with missiles.'

'All correct,' replied Admiral Morris. 'How about number four? It was impossible to bomb the Khamis Mushayt Air Base without being picked up on radar. And number five, it was definitely impossible for any invader to reach that airfield with God knows how much explosive and blow every aircraft to pieces without a great deal of cooperation from forces inside the Saudi military. They must have had maps, diagrams and time for recce.'

'Correct, sir. And how about number six? Whoever launched those missiles must have done so from deep water, otherwise they would have been detected. It's impossible for the Saudi Navy to have achieved that.'

'So where does that leave us?' asked the admiral, plainly not wishing to hear an answer. 'It leaves us,' he continued, 'with one unassailable truth. Somewhere, inside the Saudi military, there is a network of mutiny against the armed forces. It leaves us with a possible leader of that network, who might wish to seize power in Saudi Arabia.

'And it leaves us with an outside country willing to help that leader seize that power. And that's gotta be a country big enough to own a Navy with a heavy submarine strike force.'

'Especially since two of 'em just went missing,' said Jimmy Ramshawe.

CHAPTER EIGHT

5 a.m. (local), Wednesday 24 March
The White House, Washington, DC

President Paul Bedford had been in his office for most of the night, reading reports, talking to Admiral Morris, talking to his defence staff and wrestling with the burgeoning economic uproar the events in Saudia Arabia were causing the rest of the world.

The trouble was, no one, not even the Saudis, knew what was going on. Certainly not the United States Ambassador in Riyadh.

But at five minutes past five, his personal assistant informed him that the King of Saudi Arabia was on the line. World leaders have no time frames. It was part of the job.

President Bedford took the call instantly, greeting the King warmly even though they had never met.

'Mr President,' said the beleaguered King, an edge of humility in his voice, 'I find myself speaking to you under the most trying of circumstances . . .'

'So I understand,' said President Bedford. 'And there seems to be a great deal of confusion about who is responsible for these attacks on your country.'

'It would seem so,' replied the King. 'But who-ever is behind this, we are suffering some very serious blows both economically and militarily. It is likely we will have no oil to export for a minimum of one year and possibly for two.'

'I understand the gravity of the situation,' replied the President, 'And it is difficult to know what to do, in the absence of a clearly defined enemy. Do you have any ideas who this might be?'

'Not exactly, although it would not be a great shock to find the leaders of some fundamentalist Islamic group at the back of it. However, I felt it wise to inform you that all of my senior advisers believe the main group must be receiving outside help from some other country.

'It simply would not be possible for all this damage to have been caused by an internal Arab group. Equally, it would have been impossible for an out-side assailant to inflict such damage without internal assistance from the Saudi military.'

'I see,' said President Bedford. 'That makes matters even more difficult. A devil on the outside, and another on the inside.'

'Precisely so,' said the King. 'I therefore conclude my throne is very severely threatened, and I am no longer certain who I can trust.'

'And that's why you have come to us?'

'The Bedouin way has always been to stay with tried and trusted friends,' said the King. 'Your country represents the best friends I have had since coming to the throne. That is why it pains me to say what

343

I am now going to say.' A steeliness had crept into the King's voice. 'I must have your assurance – the word of the man speaking for the most powerful nation in the world – that your country is not responsible in any way for what has befallen my kingdom.' There was silence at both ends of the telephone; then, 'If you can give me that assurance, I appeal to you to help me in my time of need, as I have so often helped you.'

Paul Bedford had been in the White House long enough to know that, once he had given his word, those who received it knew that his word was his bond. Without protestations of innocence – indeed, without that false air of grievance that can unwittingly be expressed by those who know they are not speaking the truth – the President gave the King the assurance he so desperately needed, the assertion of the United States' complete innocence in the whole affair.

As for the second part of the King's appeal, Paul Bedford knew that he referred to the several times the Saudis had pushed more oil on to the market when supplies had seemed threatened by the innumerable problems in the Middle East; to the many times they had stabilised the markets when oil prices seemed to be rising too drastically. Saudi cooperation with the USA had worked well for more than three decades, way beyond Paul Bedford's Administration.

But he hesitated before answering. As a former naval officer, the right-wing Democrat from Virginia understood the importance of clear-cut military objectives. It flashed through his mind immediately that he could not commit US troops to fight some kind of a phantom enemy.

And then he spoke to the King gently, and with genuine concern. 'I understand your point of view,' he said. 'And if you wished an enemy to be driven from your borders you could most certainly count on the United States to be your first ally. Indeed, we have a Carrier Battle Group in the Gulf at present, and we would not hesitate to send it to your aid.

'But it seems to me neither of us has anything to shoot at.'

The King laughed, despite himself. 'What you say is true,' he said. 'I cannot see my enemy. But I know he is there. And I am very fearful of the next few days, for I feel he will strike at my country again.'

'And even if your enemy is Saudi, you have no idea of the capability of his foreign friends?'

'Indeed we do not,' replied the King.'But we believe they were sufficiently powerful to have destroyed our oil industry. Not one of my advisers believes that much damage was done by a group of internal terrorists.'

'No,' said the President.'My people at the National Security Agency are of the same mind. And my chiefs at the Pentagon, who are more cautious in their assessments of military action, are coming around to a similar view.'

'I have never before been in such a predicament,' said the King. 'I am threatened, my country is threatened, and yet I do not know by whom. I badly want to call upon the help of my very powerful friends in the United States but I am at a loss to know what they can do.'

'Sir,' said the President. 'I have in Washington a wise and experienced expert on foreign affairs. He was the National Security Adviser to the last Republican President, and I will summon him to my office this morning and ask his advice and opinions. When we have discussed the matter in proper detail, I will return your call and give you the benefit of his knowledge.'

'You must be referring to the admiral, Mr President. Admiral Arnold Morgan? A very fearsome man.'

'Correct. Admiral Morgan has that reputation.' replied President Bedford. 'Please await my call this afternoon.'

Neither man knew that they would never speak to each other again.

0630, same day
Chevy Chase, Maryland
As a new day of uncertainty dawned, in his garden in Chevy Chase Admiral Arnold Morgan was bucking the trend. Showing no outward signs of anxiety, he was up early, indulging one of his passions – picking daffodils from the exuberant plantings which carpeted his extensive garden at this time of year.

As he entered the kitchen with his spoils, the phone rang. He set them down, telling his wife Kathy, 'Splash these out right away.' Most people would say, 'Perhaps these should be put in water.' Arnold Morgan did not 'put flowers in water'. He splashed 'em out. God knows why, Kathy thought.

He headed to the phone and groaned when it turned out to be 'the goddamned factory' . . . *just a moment, sir, the President would like to speak to you* . . .

Arnold, who had been speaking to Lt. Commander Jimmy Ramshawe in the small hours, had been pretty confident this call was coming. And essentially he had been keeping his head down.

"Morning, Arnie,' said President Bedford. 'How's retirement?'

'Pretty good, Mr President. All things considered. I've been up early.'

'I imagine you have. We all have. It's been a long night.'

'What can I do to help?' asked the admiral, amused at the assumption the President was making. 'I think I have a vague idea.'

'You're right, Arnie. Can you get over to the White House? I just had the King of Saudi Arabia on the line. And, Jesus, I'm telling you, that's one worried guy.'

'I'm not sure I can help, sir,' replied Admiral Morgan. 'But since your outfit provides me with a car and driver, the least I can do is come in and have a chat. See you in one hour.'

'Thank you, Admiral,' said Paul Bedford.

'No trouble, Mr President,' said the admiral.

★　　★　　★

Earlier (local time), same day
Dir'aiyah, outside Riyadh

It was almost dawn when Colonel Gamoudi's mobile phone sounded among the ruins of Saudi's former capital. The call came directly from Prince Nasir himself.

'Jacques?'

'Sir.'

'Everything's go. Both bases at Khamis Mushayt fell in the early hours of this morning. The airfield and all the aircraft were destroyed. The military city surrendered at around 3 a.m.'

'How about the other garrisons? Tabuk? King Khalid? Assad? Any word?'

'They have not yet surrendered. All three refused when the commanding general at Khamis contacted them and suggested this might be a good time to capitulate.'

'Okay – and do the Air Force have fighter jets in the air? Any sign of gunships?'

'No. I'm told Air Force morale is very low. Many princes have fled.'

'Any sign of significant troop movements from any of the other bases?'

'I am told absolutely not. They seem to have stuck their heads in the sand.'

'Well, sir, you're an expert on sand, so we'll take that as definite.'

The prince laughed. 'You are most amusing, Colonel, even at a time like this. But now I must ask you? When do we attack?'

'Right now, sir. This is it. I'll call you later.'

The conversation had already been too long for guaranteed privacy. Jacques Gamoudi hit the disconnect button and strode out into the open space beyond the walls of the mosque. He called all five of his senior commanders together and told them to fire up the heavy armoured division. 'We pull out in 20 minutes,' he said.

Even as Jacques spoke, Prince Nasir was on the line to the loyalists in the city, where thousands of armed Saudi citizens were preparing to march on the principal royal palace, behind the tanks.

And for the first time since 1818, the great crumbling walls of Dir'aiyah trembled to the sounds of preparation for battle, as Jacques Gamoudi's M1A2 Abrams tanks thundered into life and began moving out towards the road, passing the dozens of armoured trucks loaded to the gunwales with ordnance.

The roar was deafening as they started their engines and rumbled forward, in readiness to form the convoy which would take down the modern-day rulers of Saudi Arabia.

With only minutes to go before start time, Colonel Gamoudi moved back inside the ruins of the mosque and pressed the buttons on the dial of his cell phone. This was his final check with a small detachment of French Secret Service operators who had gone into Riyadh three weeks earlier to gather the final information Jacques needed for his assault. The colonel trusted his Saudi intelligence, but not quite as much as he trusted French intelligence.

Michel Phillippes, leader of the detachment, had little to add, except that the King had ordered the National Guard to deploy from their barracks on the edge of the city, with tanks and armoured personnel carriers.

According to Michel, the guardsmen had been tasked with protecting at all costs the al'Mather, Umm al Hamman and Nasriya residential areas. These were the districts which contained the walled mansions and gleaming white palaces of high government officials and many royal princes.

But Michel reported this had been a very half-hearted operation. A few units had deployed somewhat nervously, and immediately retreated behind the walled gardens. But other units had not deployed at all, many of their soldiers having disappeared quietly back to their homes.

He said the early morning city news had announced the major banks would again be closed for the day. But so far as he could tell, the predictable rioting and looting had not materialised. In fact all his team felt that Riyadh was unusually quiet for this time in the early morning, with the sun already high above the desert.

'Seems to us like the calm before a storm,' said Michel. '*Un peu sinistre . . .*' he added. A bit spooky.

There was, however, nothing even remotely spooky going on at Dir'aiyah. This was an army moving in for the kill. Weapons were checked, shells stored on board the tanks, the Abrams crews climbing aboard. Engines roared, small arms were primed

350

and loaded, ammunition belts slung over combat fatigues.

Every armoured vehicle was prepared to open fire at a moment's notice. The gloves were off here in Dir'aiyah, and, at 0920, Jacques Gamoudi's army rumbled out on to the highway and swung right for the capital, moving slowly, tank after tank thundering down the dusty tracks from the ruins, truck after truck, laden with trained Saudi fighters, hauling its warriors out on to the road.

And in the lead tank, his head and shoulders jutting out from the forward hatch, sub-machine gun in his huge hands, stood the grim-faced, bearded figure of the assault commander.

Jacques Gamoudi, husband of Giselle, father of Jean-Pierre and André, was going back to war. And in his wide studded leather belt he still carried his combat knife, just in case today's fight went to close quarters.

He had ordered a rigid convoy line of battle, three tanks moving slowly along the highway, line astern, followed by a formation of six armoured vehicles moving two abreast – then three more tanks – then six more armoured trucks – then three more tanks, followed by a dozen armoured trucks.

The packed troop carriers came next, with a rearguard of one last M1A2 Abrams tank. This would not be an easy convoy to attack. If anyone did feel so inclined, it was damned nearly impregnable from the front, rear and either flank. It was bristling with heavy weapons, and all of them were loaded.

Before they had travelled three miles, Colonel

Gamoudi's cell phone sounded. It was Michel Phillippes again, reporting an early morning stampede to King Khalid International Airport. It was the same at far-away Jiddah Airport from where many flights also flew direct to other countries. Expatriates and their families, executives and managers within the oil industry, even manual workers, and women, servants, teachers, secretaries and nurses, were desperately trying to leave the country.

Scores of personnel from the eastern province were streaming along the road which led to the causeway to the island of Bahrain. The much smaller airport in Dhahran was packed with people trying to buy tickets on flights out of the country.

Even the US armed forces were effectively making a break for it. Personnel from training bases across the country were attempting to reach Al Kharj, the only runway on which the US military could organise contingency plans to evacuate its troops.

Michel Phillippes had men at Al Kharj airfield where they encountered dozens of British expatriates who had been working on defence contracts. They met others who simply worked in Saudi Arabia for British Aerospace, and they were all trying to get out.

From all intelligence so far gathered, Jacques Gamoudi could not imagine any stiff military resistance that morning, except from the guards at the main royal palace. The convoy rolled on towards the northern perimeters of Riyadh.

All along the way, the armed freedom fighters waved at any local people they saw, presenting the face of friendship to everyone they passed, following Colonel Gamoudi's creed always to make a friend if you could when you were about to invade their country.

In fact the people generally assumed that this was the official Army of Saudi Arabia they were seeing. Everyone was in uniform, the vehicles wore the livery of the Saudi Army. What else could it be? If there was to be more trouble following the destruction of the oilfields, this was surely the defence force of the King, moving into position.

The first group to peel off was that of Major Majeed, whose two tanks and four armoured vehicles swung left cross-country for King Khalid International Airport, an objective they had been ordered to take by storm.

Colonel Gamoudi's convoy pressed on to the head of the Makkah Road, where a vast, somewhat unexpected throng awaited them, shouting and cheering, waving in the air the brand new rifles Prince Nasir's commanders had been stockpiling so carefully for so many weeks.

In mighty formation they marched on down King Khaled Road to the junction of al' Mather Street, where Colonel Bandar's group peeled away and headed directly to the building housing the main television stations.

Colonel Gamoudi pushed on towards the Interior Ministry with the crowd massing behind his tanks, the Saudi commanders bellowing through loudhailers for everyone to hold their fire until orders were given.

They approached the great wide entrance to the

Ministry with its massive oak doors, hand-carved in the Iranian city of Isfahan. The doorman, nervous, like most people, took one look at the incoming convoy and retreated, banging the great doors behind him.

Colonel Gamoudi immediately opened fire, slamming two shells straight into the doors, left and right, like a short broadside in an eighteenth-century naval battle.

The doors disintegrated and Jacques Gamoudi unleashed his dogs of war. Twenty-six al-Qaeda commandoes, trained in camps in the Afghan mountains, charged forward, the lead six hurling hand grenades straight through the lower windows.

The simultaneous blasts in the downstairs offices were nothing short of staggering. Office workers were blown apart, sent crashing into walls, furniture was splintered, at which point the commandoes raced into the building, machine guns at hip height, yelling . . . *'Get DOWN . . . everyone get DOWN!!'*

Two government ministers rushed from the mezzanine committee rooms, foolishly leaned over the wrought-iron handrail, and, looking below, demanded to know what was going on. They were brought down with a burst of gunfire and both men toppled over the balustrade on to the carnage below.

Six more commandoes piled in through the entranceway and headed up the stairs. Everyone was familiar with the layout of the building since they had acquired the engineers' plans, as provided 20 years earlier by the bin Laden Construction Company, which had built the palace.

And now, in a sense, they were in there fighting for the Ministry, in the name of their elusive spiritual leader whose command they now followed: to destroy the wanton, Western-influenced ruler of their home country.

The commandoes reached the second floor and waited close to the east wall beneath a huge stone archway. Three seconds later there was a thunderous blast from above as *Le Chasseur* opened fire on the third floor and two more tank shells ripped high into the building. Plaster and masonry cascaded down the stairwell.

And now the commandoes were set to take the Ministry. There were 50 of them inside now, and they moved from room to room, kicking open the doors, firing into the voids, ordering anyone still living inside to surrender.

They combed every room, swept the corridors, herded dozens of terrified workers into the downstairs foyer. Thirty-two minutes after Colonel Gamoudi's opening salvo, the Saudi Arabian Ministry of the Interior, complete with its entire staff, was the first casualty of Prince Nasir's takeover.

Colonel Gamoudi ordered the building secured. He left behind five trained commandoes plus a group of 20 armed men selected from the great throng which had followed him to the Ministry. He ordered phone lines cut and turned his tanks around in the wide courtyard. Then he headed back north toward the Diplomatic Quarter and royal palaces which lay beyond.

At this precise time, Colonel Bandar's men reached the main entrance to the television stations, Channels 1 and 2, housed in the same building. The doors were glass but Colonel Bandar, a former regular officer in the Saudi Army, elected not to take his tank straight through them.

Instead he drove up to within 10 feet and hurled a hand grenade through the open window of the downstairs mail room, which, blasted asunder, scattered mountains of paper to the desert winds. He ordered the commandoes inside the building, and they came through the doors behind four grenades which destroyed the foyer, sending an eight-foot-high portrait of the King deep into the plaster of the ceiling where it hung for a few seconds before crashing into the rubble below.

Fifteen members of staff came out with their hands high and were ordered into the street, where a guard detail lined them up against the wall and ordered them not to move. Thirty more commandoes dismounted from the troop carriers and stormed into the building. The first floor was deemed secure, and now they headed to the transmission room two floors above.

They flooded up the staircase, ignoring the elevators, and two permanent guards offered brief resistance. They were gunned down mercilessly. The leading detail of six men rammed a steel chair into the newsroom door and thundered into the long room with its sound studios at the back and newscasting sets occupying almost the entire foreground.

At first no shots were fired as two of the raiders swept the walls, ripping plugs and cables out of their sockets, tearing apart any electrical connections from the leads and wires that snaked all over the floor.

At a table in the far corner, as in the newsroom in a newspaper office, editors and reporters were preparing for the next broadcast. With the stations now quiet, Colonel Bandar's men opened fire above the heads of the terrified staff.

At this point Colonel Bandar himself, a direct descendant of the elders of the Murragh tribe in the south, strode through the door and over to the newsdesk, ordering the staff to stand up, remove their headsets and pay attention. Then he barked a question in Arabic: 'Who's the chief station editor?'

Two of the nine men pointed to different executives and Colonel Bandar shot them both down with a burst from his sub-machine gun. He asked again, and this time one man stepped forward and said, quietly, 'I am the news editor of the station.'

'WRONG!' yelled the colonel. 'You *used* to be the news editor of the station. Right now I am the news editor. You will now go with my men and have your entire staff parade in the front hall. The slightest sign of disobedience and you and any member of your staff will be executed instantly.

'The rest of you, keep your hands high, and walk slowly downstairs, no elevators.'

Colonel Bandar appointed a four-man detail to accompany the former news editor through the building, routing out the television station executives and journalists and ordering them to the front hall where they were searched and allowed to stand easy, under guard.

Twenty minutes later the colonel came downstairs and demanded that 10 transmission technicians report back to the newsroom. Ten petrified electricians stepped forward and made their way back up the stairs flanked by the colonel's guards, under orders to reconnect the broadcast units which the marauding force had been so careful to leave intact.

The rebel leader then made an announcement that the Kingdom would very soon be under the rule of the Crown Prince, who would be broadcasting within a matter of hours. He asked which of the staff would be willing to carry on as before, but under a new fundamentalist regime, and which of them would prefer to announce their loyalty to the outgoing King and face immediate execution. Not necessarily on this day, but certainly by the end of the week.

With little alternative, the staff of both Channels 1 and 2 immediately pledged undying loyalty to the incoming ruler and were permitted to return to their offices, under guard. Colonel Bandar told them to prepare an outside broadcast unit to attend the prince's palace within four hours, to make the historic first film of a nationwide address by their new ruler.

The main television stations had been captured with relatively little damage done under the circumstances. They would be up and running, albeit under different management, within two hours. And now a ring of 200 armed men was placed around the building, to await the arrival of a specially appointed public relations executive from the ARAMCO organisation.

By now Major Majeed's group was driving forward, straight at the gates of King Khalid International Airport, his convoy led by two tanks, line abreast, followed by four armoured vehicles and 100 highly trained commandoes, the leaders al-Qaeda combat troops, handpicked by Jacques Gamoudi, the rest ex-Saudi military.

To the amazement of the security staff the tanks swung into the precincts of the busy airport and headed straight for the control tower, crushing the tall, white fence as if it were matchwood. They drove on, straight at the tower, and stunned passengers boarding packed passenger jets suddenly saw an anti-tank crew launch four rockets directly at the wraparound windows high above the runways.

Only one hit. Two of the other three crashed into the building's lower floor and the fourth smashed into the huge radar installation above the ops room, which was already a scene of devastation.

All the windows had blown, mercifully outwards, but the blast had played havoc with the sensitive equipment. Computer screens caved in, alarms went off everywhere, all transmissions to incoming aircraft ceased abruptly and 14 staff were badly injured by shrapnel. Two others died instantly.

The commandoes stormed the tower, screaming

for the surrender of all personnel in air traffic control, but there were no key operatives left to surrender. The anti-tank rocket had caused complete devastation, and Jacques Gamoudi was not going to be best pleased. He had warned them to use rockets only if they met stiff resistance.

But now the control tower was wrecked and Major Majeed's men were swarming into the airport ordering passengers out of the terminal at gunpoint, instructing them to return to their homes, to the city, by whatever means they could. Airport buses were commandeered, taxis stuffed with passengers and ordered to get going.

A squad of six heavily armed al-Qaeda warriors charged through the downstairs baggage area, informing personnel to concentrate on outgoing flights. They informed staff that their priority was to get people out of the airport and swiftly on to departing flights.

The soldiers in the tower ordered electricians from the first floor ops room to switch off the runway lights. Fuelled aircraft ready for takeoff could leave; incoming passenger aircraft would not be permitted to land, in the unlikely event of there being any.

Major Majeed ordered the restaurants to stay open and he told the airport PA system to keep ferrying passengers out to Riyadh; on no account was any aircraft to land without special permission from the major himself.

Abdul Majeed wanted to ensure that private corporate jets, coming to pick up senior technical staff

360

from ARAMCO and British Aerospace, were given maximum cooperation. Prince Nasir would need such people in the very near future. One hour after his arrival, the major called Jacques Gamoudi and informed him that the airport had been successfully taken.

Back on King Khalid Road, Colonel Gamoudi's convoy was still heading north back towards the junction with the Makkah Road; there must have been 10,000 people in their wake. He ordered a halt to the convoy at that junction and instructed the now returned Colonel Bandar to take command of another tank, one armoured vehicle, plus four troop carriers and head for Jubal Prison on the outskirts of the city, where many al-Qaeda sympathisers were being held, most without trial.

His orders were terse: 'Blast your way in, and take it by force of arms. They're only prison guards, and they'll surrender. Then release everyone . . . and stay in touch.' Colonel Bandar was pleased at the prospect of driving a tank straight through a big doorway, something he had refrained from doing at the television station.

And now, with the airport, the Ministry and the broadcasting services under control, Colonel Gamoudi turned his attack towards the main objective, the palace of the forty-six-year-old King of Saudi Arabia.

But first he wanted to deal with the Prince Miohd bin Abdul Aziz Palace where Prince Nasir had told him a full morning council would be convened. Whether or not any of the royal princes in this family gathering were still there, Colonel Gamoudi did not know. But he knew this was the guiding council of the monarch. If there was ever going to be a future uprising it was likely to emanate from men in that palace that morning.

In the lead tank, now sitting up on the hatch with his machine gun held across his chest, Jacques looked every inch the conqueror, a powerful, bearded man, jaw set, riding at the head of a formation of tanks, armoured vehicles, troop carriers and thousands of born-again desert warriors. There were no signs of exuberance; they marched in silence as they moved towards the royal palace to remove the King of Saudi Arabia from his throne.

Their route deliberately took them through the Diplomatic Quarter, since Colonel Gamoudi wished to make it quite clear that all foreign governments understood the thoroughness of the takeover. Now and then small groups of embassy staff could be seen on the pavements outside their buildings, many of them no doubt mentally compiling diplomatic reports on the battle for Riyadh.

There was a small crowd outside the British Embassy and a larger crowd outside the American Embassy. Jacques Gamoudi did not want any of these people to be injured if his convoy met sudden resistance, and so he shouted at them as they passed, '*GET BACK INSIDE . . . DO NOT COME ON TO THE STREETS . . . YOU WILL BE INFORMED OF GOVERNMENT CHANGES LATER . . .*'

Unsurprisingly, none of the onlookers had the

slightest idea who he was. He spoke Arabic, with an accent, and all the armoured vehicles bore the insignia of the Saudi Arabian armed forces. But this was a sizeable convoy and it was plainly headed somewhere. And, despite the general savvy of the personnel in the embassy, who could see for themselves that something monumental was most certainly afoot, it was still extremely baffling.

As Jacques Gamoudi's tanks rolled by, it was particularly baffling for one senior US envoy, Charlie Brooks, who had served in many US embassies in North and sub-Saharan Africa throughout a long and distinguished career in the diplomatic service. It was rumoured that Charlie Brooks might be the next US Ambassador to Iran, at the new Tehran Embassy.

Charlie stared hard at the man on the tank who was yelling so vociferously at him to get back inside. Charlie was not accustomed to being yelled at. And as he looked again at the man, there was a flicker of recognition. Jacques was wearing a *ghutra* and it was quite hard to get a clear view of his face. And yet . . . Charlie felt there was something familiar about him.

His mind went back over his many postings, trying to think of anyone he might have met who looked similar. But he could not focus on an individual. At least not until the convoy was out of sight around the next corner.

And then Charlie's mind slipped back some ten years or so, to a blistering hot day in June 1999 in the Congo, the former French colony, when the US Embassy in Brazzaville had been under direct threat from revolutionary forces. He remembered the siege conditions behind the embassy walls, and he remembered the rescue. That was what he really remembered.

The helicopter clattering into the grounds of the embassy, manned by French Special Forces, their leader running into the embassy ordering everyone to grab what they could, documents and possessions, and to get on board either the helicopter or the French Army truck at the gates.

He remembered that leader, an amazingly tough looking bearded character, brandishing a machine gun, barking orders, completely in control. He remembered him on the embassy driveway, ordering the helicopter into the air. And he remembered him herding the remaining staff down to the truck, manhandling boxes stuffed with documents, and then running, jumping aboard the moving truck at the last minute.

They had made it the few miles to Kinshasa Airport, and the same French military officer was in charge, leading everyone out to the apron at the edge of the runway where the MC-130 aircraft was waiting.

If he thought hard he could recall the US Ambassador Aubrey Hooks and his staff piling up the steps into the aircraft, carrying what suitcases they could. He could hear in his mind the shouts and commands of the bearded man with the machine gun, as he urged them on to the flight.

And he recalled the team from Special Ops Command Europe, mostly Survey and Assessment personnel, also joining them, until the aircraft could take no more.

There was room for everyone except the French troops who had made the evacuation possible. And they remained in Brazzaville. Charlie Brooks remembered sitting with Ambassador Hooks as the MC-130 hurtled down the runway and banked out across the Congo River. The last sight he had had of the Congo was of the little group of French Special Forces standing outside the airport buildings, watching the flight as it left them. He did not think he would ever forget their bearded leader.

But now he was not *quite* so sure. He could almost swear the guy up on the lead tank was the same French combat soldier. He could even remember his name . . . well, nearly. He seemed to recall the French troops called their boss Major Chasser.

He just wished he could have heard him speak in his normal voice, then he would have been sure. Those instructions a few moments ago, '*GET BACK INSIDE!*', addressed to the Americans in English, did not do it. But he was still damn near certain, even after all those years, that that was Major Chasser up there on the tank.

And as a career diplomat, working closely with the CIA, he did have one overriding question . . . what the hell was he doing up there on the tank anyway, reading the riot act to locals in the goddamned middle of the capital city of Saudi Arabia? It sure beat the hell out of Charlie Brooks.

Unless France was somehow implicated in the attack on the country. But the tanks were Saudi. And no foreign nationals served in the Saudi Arabian armed forces. It didn't make sense. Even after several minutes of sustained thought, it still didn't make sense to Charlie. Maybe he was mistaken, after all. The guy did look like an Arab. But then . . . so had Major Chasser.

The big lead M1A2 Abrams rumbled on through the Diplomatic Quarter; the marching army bringing up the rear looked even larger now than it had been 15 minutes earlier. Their next stop was the Prince Miohd Palace, and from 200 yards out, with its high white walls gleaming in the sunlight, Colonel Gamoudi and the two tanks flanking him opened fire.

The shells went screaming into the walls, punching huge holes. Bricks and concrete flew everywhere. Four other shells smashed straight into the second floor of the palace. The guard post high on the outer walls crashed inwards, but this was an important place and a detachment of 12 guards rushed out to defend their royal masters.

Again Jacques Gamoudi's tanks opened fire, not this time with their big artillery, but with raking machine-gun rounds, sweeping a deadly curtain across the road and the palace gates, as lethal as the German gunners on the Somme.

The 12 guards fell in the road, and Jacques Gamoudi's tanks rolled forward, straight at the gates,

Colonel Gamoudi himself standing up for'ard, his fist raised high, shouting, '*FOLLOW ME!*'

The Abrams rammed the iron gates, which buckled and were then ripped from their stout hinges, collapsing inwards, sparks flying as they ground into the concrete paving of the driveway. The colonel leaned back and hurled two grenades straight through the windows to the left of the doorway, and the commander of the tank to his right hurled two more, all four of which detonated with diabolical force, instantly killing the staff in the guardroom and the secretariat to the right of the foyer.

The doors were flung open, and another detachment of six guards rushed out, perhaps to surrender, perhaps not. They were heavily armed but their weapons were not raised, and Jacques cut them down where they stood, round after round spitting from his sub-machine gun. No questions asked.

And now his commandoes were in, pouring out of the two troop carriers behind the lead tanks. The first four men up the steps to the building were crack ex-Saudi Special Forces, battle commanders in their own right, veterans of anti-al-Qaeda black ops in the opening years of the twenty-first century.

They opened fire on the empty foyer, for good measure spraying machine-gun rounds every which way. And right behind them came six al-Qaeda fighters, heading immediately for the stairs.

This was where the first serious problem was encountered. The guards upstairs on duty in front of the main conference room had been given possibly two minutes to man their defences; they had two heavy machine guns at the top of the stairs and with the al-Qaeda troops fighting to get a foothold on that second floor, they opened fire and blew them away, killing all six of them on the stairs.

By now Jacques Gamoudi was in the door and he saw, to his consternation, that the machine gun was now aimed at him alone. He hurled himself to the floor, sideways, away from the stairs, and somehow clawed his way through the rubble to the cover of the big reception desk, a hail of bullets riddling the wall behind him.

His other troops were under the stairs in a relatively safe position. And with no visible targets, the machine gun at the top of the stairs was temporarily silenced. Jacques Gamoudi edged his way out almost directly below the upper balcony.

Right now he thanked God he had learned in the Pyrenees to become something of a master at the great French pastime of boules, with its heavy biased metal balls and demand for devilish backspin in the long forward arching throw to the jack.

Jacques had spent many happy hours in the late afternoon with the village men back home in Héas, playing in what they jokingly called the Héas Boulodrome, a shady piece of rough, flat, sandy ground near the modest town square. It had often occurred to him that a boule was approximately the weight of a hand grenade. A bit heavier, perhaps, but not much.

He ripped the pin out of his first grenade and

tossed the bomb over the balustrade where the bodies of his men lay halfway up the stairs; it fell just below them. There was silence now in the foyer, but immediately the machine guns above opened up straight at the stairs again, where the hand grenade was rattling around.

Jacques had only a split second; he took one stride forward and hurled his second grenade, giving it a wicked topspin twist, upwards towards the balustrade. Because of its weight it did not have much spin, not like a cricket ball or a baseball. But it did have just enough, and it curled over the upper balustrade, detonating four seconds later, right after the one on the stairs.

How Jacques Gamoudi got back underneath that high balcony he never knew; only that he took off on his left foot, twisted and landed face down on the floor, eight feet behind his throwing mark. The explosion blew the upper balustrade clean off its foundation and it crashed down into the lower hall. If he had been standing there it would have killed him stone dead. He felt the ground shake as it hit the floor.

Upstairs was a scene of carnage. The palace guards were killed to a man, their two machine guns blown into tangled wreckage. Colonel Gamoudi regained his feet and roared orders to the men waiting outside the door. Three of them came bursting out of the devastated guardroom and followed him up the stairs, the other one calling for a medical detail to recover the bodies of their fallen comrades, over whom Jacques and his men were now clambering.

At the top of the stairs they paused before the big double doors which the colonel booted open and then stood back so that three grenades could to be hurled inside. There were 15 Saudi ministers, 14 of them royal princes, around the table and only two of them survived the blast, having had the good sense to seek protection under the table before the grenades came in.

They now stood up on the far side of the table and made a gesture of surrender, but Colonel Gamoudi shot them dead in their tracks with two savage bursts from his machine gun.

By now his men were fighting their way up the stairs. There was no opposition, but it did look as if the entire second-floor balcony was about to collapse. With 30 men now on the upper floor Colonel Gamoudi gave his final order to his forward commander in the Prince Miohd Palace . . . *secure the building . . . arrest anyone left in it . . . any opposition, shoot to kill . . . I'll leave a force of 100 men outside.*

The decisive action at the Prince Miohd Palace had confirmed one absence at the morning council meeting that had been correctly predicted in the forward planning – that of the King himself. He was clearly immured in his royal palace, no doubt fearful for his life after the staggering events of the past two or three hours, about which he must by now have heard.

Colonel Gamoudi called together the senior staff

officers still serving in the front line of the battle with him. And he checked the road maps, pointing out the two minor palaces sited along the route to the Al Salam royal palace, where he expected to find the King.

Again his instructions to his commanders were terse. He reiterated the need to cause as little bloodshed as possible and to inflict the minimum amount of damage on the palaces themselves.

'Tell the staff to remain in place – any royal princes, take prisoner . . . but I doubt there will be any. You'll want a force of maybe 40 people for each palace. No more. The new King will make his first broadcast to the people from one of them.'

And with that Colonel Jacques Gamoudi headed back to his tank for the one-mile journey to the residence of the King. They had not travelled more than 100 yards before the next serious problem appeared in the sky overhead – a lone Saudi military helicopter, not on their own aircraft list but which appeared to be taking an unusually close look at the moving revolutionary army.

Jacques Gamoudi raised his binoculars and checked the clattering chopper which was now flying low, about 300 feet above his tank. The numbers on its fuselage did not correspond to any of three choppers run by Prince Nasir. So far as Jacques could tell, it might be arriving to evacuate the King and he could not tolerate that. But before he could call up two or three stinger missiles and attempt to shoot it down, it flew off, straight towards the palace.

And then, before Jacques could finish cursing, two more Saudi Army helicopters came battering their way over the horizon, flying low above the buildings. Again Jacques Gamoudi raised his glasses and this time he could see clearly the insignia of the King's Royal Regiment painted on the rear of both helicopters.

He assessed, correctly, that this was an operation to evacuate the King. The two helicopters, giant troop-carrying Chinooks, followed the first much smaller one directly along the road to the palace, and Jacques saw them hovering, preparing to land inside the walls which surrounded the royal residence.

This was now an emergency. Speed was of the essence. He ducked back inside the tank, seized the communications system and shoved down the red button. Twenty-one miles away at the King Khalid International Airport, an ageing Boeing 737, takeoff priority number one, began to roll down the main runway with two young al-Qaeda men at the controls, making their last ever journey, the one before the three trumpets sounded, summoning them across the bridge, into paradise and the arms of Allah.

The Boeing banked hard left, racing east across the northern approaches to the city. Laden with fuel, it came in low over the desert making 300 knots. Colonel Gamoudi halted his convoy 1,000 yards short of the palace, awaiting the arrival of the suicide bombers tasked with the responsibility of slamming their aircraft into the building.

It was a four-minute flight from the airport and

everyone saw the silver passenger aircraft flying what appeared to be straight towards them. It came in low, drawing a bead on the great curved dome of the central part of the building, and everyone held their breath as it screamed above them losing height, its engines howling.

Inside the cockpit, the pilot sensed he was too high. He throttled back and forced the nose down, increasing the revs on those mighty Pratt and Whitney engines. Too late. They were still too high. With 400 yards to go the pilot hauled back on the throttle, cut the engines altogether and the Boeing lurched into an all-engine stall.

The nose came up as the aircraft dropped 50 feet like a stone. And then it made a perfectly hideous belly-flop landing, bang on top of the dome, and burst into flames. The dome collapsed, killing anyone still remaining on the upper floor. The Boeing lurched left, and then tipped right, landing on its wing, which spun it around hard.

It hit the ground with a mighty crash, levelled a grove of palm trees and flattened five parked Mercedes-Benz staff cars. The eight-man guard detail at the rear of the palace was killed instantly, but the objective of the entire exercise, the King and his most trusted advisers, was unharmed, as they hurried out of the building towards the waiting helicopters.

There were 18 of them, but no women or children, the King's family having escaped four hours after the military bases at Khamis Mushayt had fallen. But there was still a substantial group, and space on the helicopters was tight. There were packing cases of priceless jewels and artefacts to be loaded before the passengers could board.

Colonel Gamoudi was quite certain of the Chinooks' mission, and he urged his task force forward, heading for the palace gates. He could see the black smoke rising from the grounds in the rear of the palace, but even from half a mile away he knew the Boeing had not accomplished its allotted task.

And now his prize might be slipping away. The very last thing a new King needed was a very much alive old one. Even the British had drummed Edward VIII and his American girlfriend straight out of the country once they had decided King George VI would become the rightful monarch back in 1936.

It would be the most awful blow to King Nasir if the deposed ruler was somehow to continue living high off the hog in Switzerland, spending some of his multi-billion fortune, while he, Nasir, struggled to put Saudi Arabia back on its feet. One way or another Jacques Gamoudi had to nail the departing monarch. And he had about 10 minutes, maximum, in which to do it.

And now he could see the third helicopter circling, hovering and then dropping down to land behind the high walls, in the vast front garden before the palace. '*Merde*,' he muttered, frantically signalling to all drivers to make all speed to the gates of the King's residence.

Engines howled, but the palace was still three minutes away. And it was still one minute away when the air was split by two more enormous explosions. Flames and black smoke rose into the air, but no one could see what had happened behind the walls.

They reached the gates and smashed their way through amid scattered gunfire from the remaining palace guards who had taken refuge inside the downstairs floor of the palace. Colonel Gamoudi's men returned fire with heavy machine guns and quickly silenced the defenders who appeared to have no further desire to stick their heads above the parapet.

The scene in that front yard was one Jacques Gamoudi would remember for the rest of his life. The two Chinooks had been blasted beyond recognition, there were six dead robed Arabs lying on the ground, and, off to the right, leaning somewhat casually against a palm tree, was the unmistakable figure of the former British SAS Major Ray Kerman, in company with one of his HAMAS bodyguards. They were both holding smoking anti-tank rocket launchers.

'Afternoon, Jacques,' said General Rashood. 'I thought I better get rid of those two Chinooks for you. You don't mind, do you?'

Jacques Gamoudi was almost speechless. '*Jésus-Christ!*' he exclaimed. 'Did you just get here in that third helicopter?'

'How the hell do you think I got here,' said the general, looking surprised. 'On the bus?'

Gamoudi shook his head and laughed. But then the enormity of his problems came cascading back upon him, and he suddenly shouted, in a loud, involuntary voice, '*Jésus-Christ*, Ravi . . . *WHERE'S THE KING . . .! WHERE THE HELL'S THE KING?*'

'He's in there,' replied the general, nodding towards the palace.

'*How do you know?*' asked Jacques, his voice again rising.

'Mainly because I just saw him go in there,' said Ravi. 'With a group of five bodyguards. The King was carrying an AK-47.'

'But what if he escapes? Out the back way or something?'

'He can't. I just sent three of my commandoes to seal off the rear entrance. Anyway, I'd guess it was too bloody hot to get through the gardens. There is, I expect you noticed, a 200-seater Boeing 737 with about 400 tons of fuel on fire under the date palms.'

'So we'll have to rout him out, right?'

'Yup. Do you guys want me to give you a hand?'

'*Mon Dieu!* Was Général de Gaulle French?' he replied. 'You need a machine gun?'

'What d'you think I need, a bow and arrow?'

Jacques ignored the sardonic humour of the victor of the battle for Khamis Mushayt and headed back to his waiting chiefs of staff. Someone fetched a machine gun and ammunition for General Rashood, and an al-Qaeda soldier turned up with a diagram of the royal palace.

Jacques Gamoudi had seen the plan of the palace

before but had never thought he would need it. He had counted on the suicide bomber to inflict fatal damage on the huge royal residence. He had assumed a final intervention by the forces of Prince Nasir would be strictly routine.

But things were now very different. The palace had been seriously damaged high up on the dome, and there was obviously going to be masonry all over the top floor. But the first two floors, which contained 27 bedrooms, probably remained unscathed, and it was likely the King's personal bodyguard, numbering at least 20 armed members of the Royal Regiment, would put up a desperate fight to protect their forty-six-year-old ruler.

They might even have pre-planned hiding places, like the priest-holes in certain houses in England where Catholic clergymen hid from the malevolence of Henry VIII in the sixteenth century.

Colonel Gamoudi did not think much of the prospect of chasing the King up some chimney, or into some dungeon. And neither, for that matter, did General Rashood. They studied the floor plans of the sprawling palace. It was a maze of corridors, great yawning state rooms, dining rooms of unimaginable luxury. And below were kitchens and storage rooms. There was a long arched walkway to one side of an interior courtyard, and Jacques Gamoudi shook his head in frustration.

And what was the King doing right now? Was he speaking urgently on the telephone, perhaps informing the world of his plight? Maybe he was telling his friend the President of the United States that his palace and his regime were under attack by a bunch of lunatics, and the United Nations must somehow save him?

Worse yet was the possibility that the King's extremely shrewd army commanders were planning to hole up inside the vast building and make their escape under cover of darkness. Colonel Gamoudi and General Rashood had inflicted heavy damage and they had a popular uprising behind them, but the King was still staggeringly rich, owning and controlling tremendous military resources.

And those resources might well be capable of getting him out, and that would be the worst possible news for Prince Nasir. Both Jacques and Ravi could well imagine the King sitting in some palatial residence on Lake Geneva, not so far from his multi-billion dollar fortune, giving weekly exclusives to the world's media.

There would be headlines pointing out the tyranny, the wickedness and the savage low-life intentions of the armed thugs who had driven the rightful King of the Saudis from his peaceful and prosperous kingdom. The fall of the best friend the West ever had. The media would love it, true or not, and it could very easily cause the United Nations to condemn Prince Nasir and all that he stood for.

'Ravi, we have to get him,' said Jacques Gamoudi, grimly.

'No need to tell me,' replied the general, 'and we have to get him fast.'

'Do we charge the front door with a tank and go in with all guns blazing?'

'Sounds better than ringing the doorbell,' said Ravi. 'Let's get a half-dozen guys with anti-tank rocket launchers aimed at the front of the palace. They can open fire on the second and third floor windows as soon as we've stormed the entrance.'

'Right,' said Gamoudi. 'We don't want to drive these guys upwards into that mess below the dome. There may be good cover up there, and we don't want to fight on a bomb site.'

'Correct,' said Ravi. 'We'd better beef up that detail in the rear of the building if it's cool enough. But we don't want a lot of guys in the open. For all we know the troops inside are mounting machine-gun nests in the windows.'

'We're going to have to fight for this on the inside,' said Jacques.

''Fraid so,' said the general. 'And we'd better be very quick. I'm not much looking forward to it either.'

They selected 16 Special Forces soldiers to come in behind the tank. In the rear of them were 20 al-Qaeda and HAMAS fighters, all carrying sub-machine guns and grenades. Jacques Gamoudi would lead the troops inside, the instant they breached the entrance. He would concentrate on the downstairs areas, room by room.

General Rashood would lead his commandoes up the main stairs to the second floor. As ever, the principal danger was to the assault force, the troops who had to make it happen. The King's guard could fight a solid rearguard action, protecting their man, no hurry, until darkness came. And then they had a huge advantage, on terrain they knew backwards. There was also, of course, the disconcerting fact that no one knew what extra resources the King could call upon, including overwhelming world opinion.

Jacques and Ravi had to nail him. And they had to nail him right now. And the HAMAS general, for good measure, quoted the only rules which matter during any military coup – *Let's do it fast, Jacques, and let's do it right*.

Colonel Gamoudi clambered aboard the M1A2 Abrams. The opening assault brigades moved into formation and the engines of the tank screamed as it rolled towards the palace doors, the French veterans moving behind it.

The colonel ducked low as the iron horse slammed into the doors, smashing them inwards. And as they did so, two savage bursts of heavy machine-gun fire ricocheted off the steel casing of the tank. The tank was not damaged but the guns had them pinned down, half in and half out of the entranceway, facing into the main hall.

And now it was Jacques Gamoudi who dared not put his head above the parapet; he ordered the tank to reverse and the gun to be raised. At which point he blasted the upper balcony with four successive shells which crashed into the walls behind the gallery; in turn these caved in and caused a total collapse of the third floor in that part of the building.

There was dust and concrete everywhere, and the guns were, for the moment, silenced. The room on the second floor behind the shattered wall had disappeared. Anyone who had been in there had to be dead. But there was no sound, and Colonel Gamoudi assumed the danger up there had receded.

He signalled for General Rashood to lead his men into the devastated reception hall and to take the rest of the second floor. And he watched the HAMAS C-in-C bounding up the stairs, his troops following tightly grouped on the wide marble staircase. There was still no sound from that second-floor gallery where the King's initial machine-gun nest had been located.

Jacques split his men into two groups, one left and one right. He took the left-hand corridor and, room by room, booted open the doors and hurled a hand grenade into each. There was one aspect of this type of warfare which made the task slightly easier: no one cared who was in the rooms, or whether they lived or died, and no one cared what damage was inflicted on the palace. There was no need for restraint.

And for six rooms everything went to plan. At the seventh, Jacques Gamoudi kicked open the door, and from inside it someone threw a hand grenade. It hit the wall and clattered to the floor. Jacques wheeled around and, with his arms outspread, crashed everyone to the floor, or at least everyone he could grab, which was six of the eight.

And when the grenade detonated he lost two of his best men instantly. The rest of them climbed to their feet coated in dust, some of them cut and bruised. And as they did so, a second grenade flew out of the seventh door and rolled on the floor.

Again Jacques Gamoudi saw it and again he spread his arms, this time hurling the whole scrum in through the door opposite, slamming the heavy door, just as the grenade blasted the corridor to pieces.

Suddenly this was serious. They seized a huge piece of furniture, a chest of drawers, and rammed it against the door, just to buy them a few minutes. They were short of guns, four of them having been left in the rubble outside. They had no more grenades left and there were six of them, all but trapped, until someone could open one of the high windows, built eight feet above ground level.

They had no idea how many of the enemy were in this remote interior passageway. They knew the palace was surrounded, and they knew General Rashood was gutting the upper floor in search of the King's guard. But they themselves were trapped, with only two guns and not much ammunition.

They did not dare shout for assistance, because that would only alert the enemy as to where they were. Whichever way they looked at it, the hunter was now the hunted. And *Le Chasseur* took a very dim view of that.

The one useful aspect of this reception room was a wide serving area at the rear of the room. It was a massive marble and granite slab, behind which they could take cover, especially under heavy fire. The trouble was that it would be almost impossible to fire back against a determined enemy, since that would require them to stand up against a white marble background.

Their only chance was to shelter there until the guards moved in, then hope to take them in close-combat fighting. Everyone carried a combat knife, and they all knew how to use them.

And now they could hear the huge doors being shoved open, the massive chest of drawers being edged inwards. Gamoudi ordered his men to the floor, behind the marble serving counter.

And thus they awaited their fate, which was not long coming. When the door was open less than two feet, six men, five of them uniformed and all of them armed, slipped into the room and opened fire at the space above the granite slab.

No one moved until the commander signalled them to fan out and advance down the 80-foot-long room. In English he called out, '*Come out all of you with your hands held high . . . COME OUT! IN THE NAME OF THE KING!*'

No one moved, and then the commander spoke again: 'Should you decide not to come out, my men will throw three grenades behind that counter. We will retreat out of the door, and you will die. ALL OF YOU! NOW COME OUT WITH YOUR HANDS HIGH . . .'

And then, much more quietly, he added, 'The King wishes to see those who would be his enemies. I will count to 10 before the grenades are tossed in among you.'

There was absolute silence in the room. Privately Jacques Gamoudi thought they might catch a couple of them and hurl them back. But even he doubted they would catch all three.

'ONE . . . TWO . . . THREE . . . FOUR . . .'

And suddenly there was a slight movement at the doorway, and with one leap entered the terrifying figure of General Ravi Rashood, a black mask protecting his nose and mouth from the choking dust and cordite in the corridor, his machine gun spitting fire in a long sweep right across the line of palace guards. Ravi aimed high, as he always did, at their backs. No one had time to turn and see their executioner.

It was like a firing squad. Nothing less. And one by one the guards slumped to the floor, bullets riddling their heads and necks, blood seeping on to the white marble.

The air was clean in here, and the general pulled the mask down from his face. He walked to the line of men he had shot down in cold blood. He ignored five of them. He walked straight to the man who wore no uniform, but who, like the others, lay face down on the floor, the back of his head blown away.

He kicked the man over and stared at him, directly into the unseeing eyes of a face that was all too familiar. Prostrate at General Rashood's feet lay the body of the King of Saudi Arabia. He might have lived like a pasha, but he had died like a true Bedouin, his machine gun primed, facing his enemies. Except for the one who had shot him in the back.

'*Jésu*,' said Jacques Gamoudi, as he walked across the room. 'Am I glad to see you.'

'Yes, I expect so,' replied Ravi, in that clipped British accent of his, honed in the portals of distant Harrow School. 'But I owe you one. And I'd never say you weren't damned useful in a French bistro. Myself, I tend to excel in royal palaces.'

And with that he flung his arms around his fellow commander. Between them, they had, after all, just conquered the largest country on the Arabian Peninsula.

4 p.m., same day
Prince Nasir stood before the cameras and made his inaugural broadcast to the people of Saudia Arabia from one of the smaller palaces a mile from the former royal residence. He described the death of the King which had occurred during the People's Revolution which had been so long in coming.

And he stressed that the late King and his enormous family had done nothing but plunder and spend the vast wealth beneath the sands – wealth that belonged to everyone, not just to members of one family.

He railed against the closeness of the King and his immediate family to the United States, and how it was so much more natural for Saudi Arabia to forge alliances with closer and more traditional allies, like France.

385

He pointed out the long history of cooperation between the two countries, and told the nation he was already speaking to the French President in order to formulate a plan to rebuild the oil industry, which he deeply regretted had been the first casualty of the popular uprising. It was indeed a consequence of years of reckless living and massive incompetence by the royal family.

Where was the King when our great industries had come under attack? The Crown Prince spread his arms apart in a gesture of mock confusion.

But throughout the broadcast, Nasir gave a message of hope and optimism. And he swore to help Saudi Arabia regain its former position of wealth and influence, with a fair share of that wealth for every Saudi family. Not just one family.

He at last came to the words that everyone wanted to hear: *In accordance with our ancient laws, as Crown Prince I have assumed leadership of our country. I have taken my vows with the elders of the Council. And I have sworn before God to uphold our laws . . . I am both your humble servant, and proud leader, King Nasir of Saudi Arabia.*

CHAPTER NINE

Same day, 7.45 a.m. (local)
The White House, Washington, DC

Sitting at the wheel of their new Hummer, Kathy Morgan swung the civilian version of the US Army's fabled Humvee straight into the West Wing entrance to the White House. Next to her sat her husband, Admiral Morgan, whom the guards saluted. Whenever the great man visited Pennsylvania Avenue it was like General Eisenhower returning to the beaches of Normandy. No one caused quite the same ripple of admiration.

He said goodbye to Kathy, who was having breakfast with her mother at the Ritz-Carlton, and strode towards the main West Wing entrance. The Marine guard saluted him and held open the door, inside which the Secret Service detail, on direct orders from the President, dispensed with the requirement for a visitor's pass and escorted the admiral straight to the Oval Office.

Admiral Morgan, as he had done for so many years, walked briskly past the President's secretary, tapped on the door and walked straight in.

The President came round from the side of his desk and shook the Admiral's hand. 'Morning, Arnie,' he said, smiling. 'Right on time, as ever.'

'End of the morning watch, eh?' replied the admiral, mindful of the fact that the former Lieutenant Paul Bedford was immensely proud of having once served as navigation officer in a US Navy guided missile frigate.

The President laughed, but his smile did not last for long. He buzzed his secretary.

Then he said, 'Sit down, Arnie. I've sent for some coffee . . . you want anything to eat?'

'No thanks, sir. Coffee's fine. Guess we're talking about this Saudi Arabian bullshit, right?'

'We sure are. Just this morning the goddamned phone's never stopped ringing. Things are moving real fast. You heard any of the latest news?'

'Not as much as you have, I suspect,' replied Arnie. 'Last thing I picked up on the news was extreme fighting at the Saudi military city of Khamis Mushayt, and that the people of Riyadh appeared to be marching on the royal palace.'

'Both correct,' said the President. 'But I hear now that the Khamis Mushayt base has fallen − and so has the big Air Force station right next to it.'

'Anyone say to whom it fell?' asked the admiral.

'Ask not to whom the base fell,' intoned the President, 'because we don't know. And neither do they. But the sucker fell all right . . . our air attaché in Riyadh reckons they lost half the Saudi Air Force.'

'We got one shred of evidence of an outside foe?' asked Arnie.

'Nothing,' said Paul Bedford. 'If this is some kind of a war, it's one of the most secretive ever conducted. No one has the remotest idea who's doing the attacking.'

'Guess someone does,' mused the admiral.

'And whoever that might be,' replied the President, 'they sure as hell know what they're doing . . . I've been looking at the stats on Khamis Mushayt . . . it's a huge and remote place. And no one even knows what happened. But they all say one thing . . . it's a 100 per cent Arab matter . . . conducted from inside the country.'

Arnie nodded. 'It just may be a little more complicated than that,' he said. 'Any news from Riyadh? I heard on the news the Saudi Army might have turned on the King.'

'Well, there's some rumour the aiport's fallen to an armed assault force,' said the President.

'Do we know where the King is right now?'

'No one seems to know. But I have spoken to him. And he was not under attack at the time.'

'Is he in the royal palace?'

'I don't know that. I guess he doesn't want anyone to know where he is.'

''Specially the guys who just blew up his oilfields and his Air Force, eh?' replied Arnold.

'Right,' agreed the President. "Specially them.'

'Any sign of the King's army mounting a defence? He's got a hell of an armed force, and a lot of very sophisticated equipment.'

'This whole thing seems like a series of devastating attacks – fast, professional and very ruthless. Very military.' The President looked perplexed.

It was a few minutes after 8 a.m. At that moment his secretary pushed open the door and walked over to the television set which she tuned immediately to CNN World News. 'Sir, General Scannell just called to say it looks like the King of Saudi Arabia is dead. And he says the new King is about to broadcast.'

'Thank you, Sally,' said the President, turning with the admiral towards the screen, where the anchor man was formally announcing the death of the Saudi ruler.

The new King is fifty-six-year-old Nasir Ibn Mohammed al-Saud, a devout Sunni Muslim and a cousin of the slain King. He has been Crown Prince, heir to the throne, for almost 20 years and, like most of the Saudi royal family, he is a direct descendant of the Founder of the Kingdom, the legendary desert warrior, Abdul Aziz, known as Ibn Saud.

'And now we'll go live to Riyadh, where King Nasir is making his first address to the nation, and hopefully we'll have some real information on how all this took place.'

The screen flickered and suddenly the picture appeared of a bearded Arab, his robes white, with a red and white checked *ghutra* on his head, speaking to the people of Saudi Arabia.

The President and Arnold Morgan watched together as King Nasir spoke of his regret at the death of his cousin, but nonetheless confirmed that what had taken place had been a 'people's revolution', launched by thousands of citizens who could no longer acquiesce to the profligate spending of their ruler.

He sent his message of hope for the future, but both men frowned when the new King stated that France was his nation of choice to help rebuild the Saudi oil industry on both the east and west coasts of the Kingdom.

It was well known that Prince Nasir was a reformer, a Muslim fundamentalist guided by the teachings of the Koran who most certainly would not tolerate the spectacular levels of spending achieved by the royal princes.

It was also well known that he was a man of prayer and abstinence, that he despised the godless and material ways of the West. What perhaps came as more of a surprise was his statement that he wanted the United States out of the Middle East, and with it an end to terrorism.

But first he wanted a legal, internationally recognised Palestinian state. It was clear that now, for the first time, the Palestinians had an ally in the most powerful nation on the Arabian Peninsula. And at the head of that nation there now stood a man who cared nothing for the US or for Israel.

This was bad news for the man sitting behind

the desk in the Oval Office. And it was bad news for the United States, where gasoline was currently commanding nearly $10 a gallon at the pumps. And the President made his feelings plain to Admiral Morgan.

'Seems to me there's only two parties doing well out of this,' replied Arnie. 'France, and that goddamned Nasir up there with his goddamned self-satisfied smile.'

'And his goddamned fleet of limousines, private jets and servants,' added the President.

'Yeah, and yet he says he has no interest in all of that,' said Arnie.

'Of course. But absolute power gets awfully addictive. And you cannot fault the lifestyle. He'll get to like it.'

'Well, I really hope you're right, Mr President. Because if you're not, and he really is the man we think he is, we're in real trouble.'

'You mean no more Saudi oil?'

'Well, that too. But also because Saudi Arabia has always been the missing piece in the jigsaw puzzle of the Middle East. Apart from the very small nations, we have always had the Yemen, Iraq, Jordan, Syria, Kuwait, the Arab Emirates, Iran, Egypt, Libya and most of North Africa. And, basically, you know more or less where you are with all of them. They form one huge block of Islamic nations.

'But in the middle of them stands Saudi Arabia, which in modern times has always been neither one thing nor the other. No longer a fundamentalist

Muslim nation, always a serious friend of the West, a group of devout Muslim princes, who own a fleet of the most expensive yachts in the world. Young men who profess devotion to the word of the Koran, but live like Riviera playboys at the King's expense.

'Saudi Arabia, our friend and ally, has always been the one huge thorn in the side of the Muslim republics. The one nation always out of step, the royal family which plays both hands against the middle. In short, the Saudis are a pariah to those who wish for a great Islamic empire stretching from the Red Sea to Morocco.

'And some very influential Muslims have long hated the sight of them – guys like old bin Laden, even Saddam, the HAMAS leadership, Hezbollah, all the supporters of the *jihad*. They hate Saudi Arabia for its endless wealth, its willingness to work with the West, and, above all, its refusal to back any Arab action against Israel.

'Mr President,' said Arnold Morgan. 'That all ended about 10 minutes ago. This Nasir character just laid the last piece of that Muslim jigsaw.'

Paul Bedford stood up and walked the length of the Oval Office. 'But what about the oil crisis, Arnie? What the hell's going to happen about that?'

'Mr President, you are going to get the blame for that.'

'*ME?*' exclaimed the Chief Executive. 'How are they going to pin this one on me?'

'Think about it, sir. The American people are

going to put up with a $10 a gallon gas crisis – for a little while. And then you're going to start hearing . . . *well, what the hell's the President doing about it? Why doesn't he negotiate with King Nasir? Why can't he be like other Presidents, stay friends with Saudi Arabia?*'

'I guess other Presidents have coped with that.'

'Not quite,' said Arnold. 'Because this one is going to smash the world economy. It won't smash us, but it'll go damn close. Inflation will run amok, corporations will go bust and the stock market will cave in. There'll be a run on the dollar and our trading partners all over the world will be unable to pay us. This is a global financial crisis.

'And you, Mr President, face the prospect of being swept away in the torrent . . . a reviled figure in history . . . the President who let it happen . . . unless you do something about it. And damn fast.'

'Okay, let's talk this through. Right here we're dealing with a guy dressed in a sheet who wants to live in a tent in the desert. And he plainly wants nothing to do with us. And the oil belongs to him. What's the best way forward from here?' The President was just beginning to get rattled.

Admiral Morgan climbed to his feet and stared across the room at the loneliest man in the world, who was standing, hesitantly, beneath a portrait of George Washington.

And Arnold Morgan clenched his fist, spitting out the words, '*LEADERSHIP*, sir. You have to raise your sights. Never mind that damned Arab and his oil. You gotta stand up and say, *I'M NOT HAVING IT. NOT AT ANY PRICE. NO ONE HAS THE RIGHT TO SMASH THE WORLD'S ECONOMY. AND HE'LL EITHER NEGO- TIATE WITH ME, OR I'LL KICK HIS ASS . . .'*

The President started to speak, but Arnold was not quite finished. He returned to his chair before resuming more quietly. 'And then, if we have to, we'll take his oil away, and send the bastard back into the wilderness. Because any other course of action is ultimately unacceptable, to the world that is. Not just us.'

'Arnie, if you're saying what I think you are saying, don't go any further. I am *not* going to war with Saudi Arabia.'

'Sir, we don't go to war with Saudi Arabia or with the Middle East. We merely show them an iron fist. It might be to some desert chieftain who thinks he can murder hundreds of thousands of people. It might be to a guy who has too many military ambi- tions and too many weapons. Or it might just be to someone we happen to think is unstable and dan- gerous to his neighbours. Either way, because of the effect of oil on the world's economy, we just cannot let things go unchecked.

'And when some crazy prick under a palm tree thinks he can blithely wreck the economy of dozens of countries, just because he happens to have been born on some sandhill on top of a geological phenomenon . . . well . . .'

The President took advantage of Admiral Morgan's

brief pause. 'That's when the oil becomes a *world* asset,' he concluded, 'rather than a national asset. And that's when we deem his stewardship of that oil has been abused, and that's when we move to stabilise the world once more.'

'I couldn't have put it better myself, Mr President.'

The President smiled to himself. God, but Arnold Morgan was a stubborn, opinionated old bastard. Then he thought of the strenuous days ahead of him, of the whole country, and his look darkened.

Arnold Morgan seemed to read his mind. 'Mr President,' he said, 'you know this better than I do. It's a question of getting your thoughts straight; you must be guided by two outstanding points of principle – *if this Nasir character thinks he can screw up the world just because he feels like it, and if he thinks he can mess with the President of the United States, he'd better think again.'*

The President nodded. 'I sometimes think you forget I am the leader of a political party which stands to the left, that believes in freedom, help and education for all the downtrodden peoples of this earth, including some of our own. It is not in our nature to go around crushing those who might seem to stand in our way . . .'

Arnold Morgan looked up and glared. Most of the world probably knew about his feelings for the left. 'Mr President. With respect, the left has never been correct about anything. Not about the economy, not about the military, not about business and certainly not about geo-politics. The left has screwed up and that's why the Soviet Union and just about half of Europe almost went bankrupt. The creeds of the left are not something I'd have on my mind right now if I were you.'

President Bedford sighed and shook his head. Then he listened as the admiral gave his forthright, considered opinion about the way forward in the gathering crisis, reiterating his belief that, whatever happened, the President was the man upon whom all the blame for the oil crisis would fall. Unless he acted quickly and positively.

'Arnie, this is all supposition. We still have not discussed how bad it will all be.' He allowed the admiral to continue. With a fifth of the world's oil suddenly missing, he heard him say, that meant going elsewhere for oil, to Central and South America, perhaps even to Kazakhstan.

The President interrupted Admiral Morgan in full flow, reminding him a little impatiently that, had he cared to listen a few nights earlier, he would have heard him assure the American people that overtures had already been made to the Russian President about contracts in the Baku oilfields and that new markets were even now being explored in both Central and South America.

The admiral brushed that aside. 'Okay, but there's more to it. This Saudi Arabia business is going to rumble on. It's going to take certain countries to the brink – Japan, India and Germany among them. And when the Saudis eventually get their oil back on line, there are going to be plenty of people clamouring once more for oil. They'll want it cheap and they'll want plenty of it. And right now I see the US standing at the back of the line.'

'If Nasir wants to sell it without us, he'll go ahead and do it?'

That was Admiral Morgan's line of thinking exactly. And if that was the case, the President had to take an aggressive stance, to meet Nasir head on. He had to assume that, since he appeared to be the one person to benefit most, the newly crowned King was at the heart of recent events in Saudi Arabia. The finger pointed unwaveringly at his person. Furthermore, it was becoming more and more apparent that he had operated with outside help.

'That's exactly what the late King said when I spoke to him a few hours before he died. He said that his senior advisers believed that whoever was responsible had to be getting outside help from some other country. He had no idea who it might be, but he talked of a devil on the outside and another on the inside. He seemed almost resigned to his fate. So,' he said reflectively, 'how would you advise me to proceed in this aggressive stance you want me to take?'

'Sir, you must locate the country which made possible the overthrow of the Saudi royal family, the one which precipitated this crisis. That way we have a target, a political whipping boy, someone we can rail at, even attack. This will demonstrate that the United States has a President who will not put up with subversive bullshit, which does so much harm to so many millions of people.

'We are often accused of being the world's policeman. And a lot of people do not like that. But when someone commits an international crime everyone waits for the policeman to arrive. And they wait for him to handle it.

'So you accept your responsibility, face up to the problem and deal with it. That way, all criticism of you will evaporate. You'll deflect it on to the people who committed the crime. And because you're smart, they'll take the rap for everything. We'll just look like the good guys, the people who went in search of truth, and afterwards, perhaps, revenge.'

President Bedford allowed the admiral's words to sink in. They made good sense. Then he fired his own, killer question back at Arnold Morgan. 'Do you have an idea who might be King Nasir's partner in crime?'

'Not for certain. But if I had to put my last dollar on anyone, it would be France.'

'FRANCE!' The word seemed to explode from the lips of the President.

Admiral Morgan spoke of his suspicions and those of the National Security Agency; of the missing submarines; and of the likelihood that the Saudi oil installations had been slammed by cruise missiles delivered from below the surface of the ocean. And he talked of the apparently inspired decision by the French to divest themselves of reliance on Saudi oil several months earlier.

He reminded the President of the sheer impossibility of a successful attack on well-defended mainland oilfields in the desert kingdom. And he concluded, 'Only from the sea, Mr President, only from the sea.'

Although he had left the Navy some twenty years ago, the President had maintained more than a working knowledge of his own country's Navy and he had, of course, been kept informed about those of other nations by his advisers. He knew that the Saudi Navy did not possess submarines; and, moreover, that the shallow coastal waters of the Arabian Peninsula, especially those on the Gulf side, were not suited to submarine activity. He listened as the admiral assured him that the NSA was certain that, whoever had fired the missiles at the oilfields, they had fired them from underwater. And they had not been fired from a Saudi ship.

But he remained unconvinced by the theory that the French were involved. 'Okay, they changed their oil-buying policy just in time. But that hardly makes them guilty of crimes against mankind.'

'No, of course it doesn't. And I admit we have no proof it was French submarines that fired the missiles.

'But there were two French Rubis Class ships in the area, and both have disappeared. Either of them, or even both, could have done it. And there was no other submarine within thousands of miles with the same capability. Except our own. And I happen to know we're innocent.'

For the umpteenth time since he'd come in to the White House, President Bedford wished that he had Arnold Morgan with him as his personal adviser. His perspicacity, wisdom and sureness of touch – even if he did sometimes seem to trample all before him – made him invaluable. But the President was wise enough to know that he would never be able to tempt the admiral out of retirement. For one, his wife would never put up with it.

'Do you have any further opinion on French involvement in this latest catastrophe?'

'Yes, sir. Yes, I do. The NSA is working on a very curious satellite signal they picked up emanating from an area north of Riyadh, night before the battle for Khamis Mushayt. Some kind of coded message the Brits picked up at that hotshot little listening station they maintain in Cyprus.'

'Why is that significant?'

'Because the transmission was in French. Coded French.'

'I hadn't heard about that.'

'I don't suppose you would have until they'd cracked it. The intelligence community, as you know, does not make a habit of boring the President to death with half-assed information. But I know they're on the case.'

'Your young Australian, Lt. Commander Ramshawe?'

'He's the one, sir. Shouldn't be surprised if someday he made the youngest NSA Director ever.'

'What does he think – about the overall situation regarding France?'

'He is absolutely certain the French helped the rebel Saudis. And there's another part to this conundrum. Last August, two hitmen from Mossad tried to take out the commander-in-chief of HAMAS. They failed and were both killed.'

'Is that significant to us?'

'Yes, sir. It is. Because they made their attempt in Marseilles.'

'So? Where's the connection?'

'Sir, Lt. Commander Ramshawe is curious to know what the C-in-C of HAMAS was doing in a French city, plainly under the protection of the French Government, six months before a bunch of revolutionaries took control of Saudi Arabia.'

'Right. So he sees a connection with the oil situation, France getting out of Saudi product? And the submarine possibility? And the French coded signal from Riyadh a few hours before the battle? Was the HAMAS chief involved in the command of the assault team? All that?'

'Exactly, sir. That's his line of thinking,' said Admiral Morgan. 'And remember this point, above all else: when something absolutely shocking happens on a global scale, the solution is never down to one thing. It's always down to *every* thing.

'Lt. Commander Ramshawe believes he is building a very powerful case against France. And if he can nail 'em, that's your way out of this whole goddamned mess. Because then you'll attack the French verbally, pointing out their unfailing selfishness, their total disregard for anyone else.

'And you tell the world how they helped bring down the Saudi King entirely for their own profit, never mind half the world falling into a black-out, never mind hospitals and schools closing down because of power shortages. Never mind stock market crashes, highways coming to a halt, the world's airlines grounded through lack of fuel.

'The French – the haughty, imperious French – just go along in their own sweet way, steering their own course along the road to prosperity. The Gallic pricks! And then you step up to the plate and demand, with all the righteous indignation on behalf of the United States that you can muster, that France be hauled before the United Nations to explain their conduct.

'That is your only way forward. Trust me. You cannot sit here and hope to Christ this stuff goes away. Because it's not going to.

'And if the French have really done this, sir, effectively taken Saudi oil off the world market, for their own ends, they deserve every last kick in the ass we can give 'em.'

'Yes,' said the President. 'That they do.'

Same time, same day
Wednesday 24 March
National Security Agency, Fort Meade, Maryland
Lt. Commander Jimmy Ramshawe would have been pacing his office, except the floor was such a complete mess with piles of paper that he'd probably have fallen over and broken his neck.

As it was, he sat staring at transcripts of messages and wondering why he was drawing a complete blank on every lead he had on the shattering events in Saudi Arabia.

The two French submarines were still missing. And not for the first time Jimmy counted the hours since the missiles must have been fired – 0100 local on Monday morning . . . *that's 65 hours, and all that time, the two missing Rubis Class Subs the Perle and the Améthyste were moving away from the datum, probably at a dead silent seven knots.*

Jimmy took his dividers and assessed where on the chart the submarine in the Gulf had fired his missiles, calculating they had also landed and retrieved a team of frogmen . . . *somewhere up here, north-east of the Abu Sa'afah oilfield . . . must have been somewhere up here, because they couldn't make a getaway straight through the bloody oilfield . . . they must have gone north.*

He hit the buttons on his calculator, multiplying 65 hours by seven knots . . . *455 nautical miles . . . that puts him somewhere here, through the Strait of Hormuz, and about 120 miles south-east running down the Gulf of Oman. One more day, and he's free and clear, steaming down the Arabian Sea in deep water – straight to the French naval base at La Réunion, unless I'm very much mistaken.*

Jimmy adjusted his dividers to appreciate distances in the Red Sea . . . *the second submarine fired at the same time, somewhere off Jiddah . . . and they also ran away making seven knots . . . 455 nautical miles . . . that puts them in the narrowing part of the Red Sea, off this long coastline of Eritrea and Ethiopia . . . one more day and they're through the Strait of Bab al Mandab, home free, running out of the Gulf of Aden . . . straight to La Réunion.*

Jimmy considered this was essentially a blind alley. The French would admit nothing, probably would not even reply to an inquiry from the United States. And yet he could not stay away from the possible routes of the *Perle* and the *Améthyste*.

'I just wish to hell one of the other leads would come up,' he muttered. 'Maybe a little more on the Frog in the Desert. Maybe a fix on where his message went. If we could just find out who dined with Kerman that night in Marseilles. Anything would help – and what about the new Saudi King suggesting the French were getting the cream of the rebuilding programmes in the oilfields?'

Jimmy felt he was on the right track. He was certain this was all to do with France. But, like many another detective before him, he was just waiting for a break, just a tiny chink of light in some obscure corner, which might one day illuminate the whole picture.

'Doesn't seem much to ask,' he declared to the empty room. 'Just one small break for Jim, one giant leap for the industrial world.'

At 1100 local time, right there in the National Security Agency, he got it.

The CIA were just beginning to push through the system the first-hand reports from their own people in Riyadh. That included several field officers working for ARAMCO, several informants who worked for the agency out of local businesses, banks and construction corporations, and, of course, the serious professional operators inside the US Embassy.

Most of them were Americans, and all of them were passing back their accounts of the events in the capital city as it fell to the 'forces of the people'. And there was little in dispute, since almost everyone described the military convoy led by the big M1A2 Abrams tanks, trundling through the city, taking first the Ministry, then the television stations, and finally the airport and the royal palaces.

There was of course the hair-raising account of the suicide bomber crashing into the King's palace, and there were hazy accounts of the sporadic fire fights inside the walls of the palace and the burning of the two Chinooks which many people had seen fly over the Diplomatic Quarter.

But it was the first-hand report from the veteran US diplomat Charlie Brooks which instantly caught the eye of Lt. Commander Ramshawe. Because this was a man who had served the US in many parts of the world, and understood the stakes. And what Charlie wrote, from his vantage point along the direct route of the convoy, was nothing short of riveting. At least it was to Jimmy Ramshawe.

'All of the armoured vehicles carried the insignia of the Royal Saudi Land Forces, and it was assumed we were watching a military exercise, except of course the presence of the Abrams tanks was unusual. However, I was struck by

the presence of the commander who was standing up in the turret of the leading tank. He was a heavy-set bearded guy, wearing combat gear, and a red and white Arab ghutra on his head. Like all of the other soldiers he was carrying a sub-machine gun and an ammunition belt across his chest.

'I was certain I recognised him, and of course I had to consider the fact I might have encountered him at any number of Saudi diplomatic receptions. It is perfectly normal for us to meet serving Saudi military officers. And this man was most definitely Arab in appearance.

'However, it took me a few minutes to place him. And I am now certain where I first met him. He was the leader of the French Special Forces team that rescued the staff of the US Embassy in the Congo back in June 1999. I refer to the embassy of US Ambassador Aubrey Hooks in Brazzaville where I served for several months.

'The forward commander on that leading tank was the same man. He had carried my bags into the French Army truck outside the Congo embassy. I stood with him while he loaded the boxes full of documents, and I shook his hand when we boarded the aircraft for Kinshasa. He was definitely French. His men called him, I think, Major Chasser . . .'

Jimmy Ramshawe almost choked on his stone-cold coffee.

He read the communication over and over, trying to get a handle on the stick of dynamite Charlie Brooks had sent by encrypted e-mail direct to the CIA sometime during the past couple of hours. And essentially his question was the same as Charlie's . . . *what the hell was this French Special Forces officer doing, leading an armoured convoy to attack the palace of the King of Saudi Arabia in the middle of the capital city of Riyadh?*

He realised there could be a simple explanation. There were many Middle Eastern defence ministries which had over the years employed retired Special Forces combat soldiers to help train their own armies. It was not unusual to find SAS men helping the Israelis. Indeed, Major Ray Kerman had served in just such a role.

And certainly the Saudis had employed many military, Air Force and even naval special advisers, from Great Britain, the US and, less often, France. The officer in the leading tank might well have been hired by the Saudis, after he retired from the French Special Forces.

But, according to Charlie Brooks, this guy was not serving in the capacity of a 'special adviser'. This guy, a foreign national, was commanding the entire Saudi assault force, the one which had taken down the King.

Lt. Commander Ramshawe understood something of the Arabs; he had read often of the fierce pride of the Bedouin and he loved the writing of the great Arabist Wilfred Thesiger. He knew one thing for sure – even if this was a rebel Arab army, somehow split from the main Saudi military machine, it was impossible for it to be led by a 'bloody Frenchman'.

Thoughts flooded through Jimmy's mind. *Was this the Frog in the Desert? Was this assault force in the Saudi capital half-French? Who the hell else was in those tanks? Was this a partnership between the new King Nasir and France? Or was Major Chasser just a bloke who'd emigrated to Saudi Arabia and somehow taken over the Saudi Army?*

'Bloody oath!' Ramshawe muttered. 'Charlie Brooks has sure as hell lit up my little investigation . . . I don't know where to start. . . except I have to run this Chasser character to ground in a real hurry.'

He picked up the report and headed along the corridor to see Admiral Morris, hoping to hell he was free to talk, and hoping to hell he had some hot coffee. Jimmy Ramshawe shuddered with anticipation at both prospects.

The admiral was available, but his coffee was colder than Jimmy's. George Morris read the report from Charlie Brooks and looked up sharply. 'Two priorities, Lt. Commander – one, we gotta find out about this Chasser guy. Two, have a quick word with the Big Man before you start.'

'Three,' added Jimmy, 'will I get us some hot coffee?'

'Four, thank Christ you asked,' replied the admiral.

That was typical of the repartee between the two men – the lugubrious, wise, rigidly disciplined ex-Carrier Battle Group Commander and the free-wheeling US-born Aussie, who operated on instinct and intellect, brilliance rather than structure.

'I'll call the Big Man while we're waiting,' added Jimmy.

He walked briskly back to his office, ordered coffee

for the director's office and dialled Admiral Morgan's number in Chevy Chase. No reply. On the off-chance he hit the secure line to the White House and inquired whether Admiral Morgan was there.

'Who would the admiral be visiting?' asked the operator.

'Couldn't tell you for sure,' replied the lieutenant commander, 'but I'd start with the President.'

A few moments later, the President's secretary came on the line and said politely, 'Lt. Commander, Admiral Morgan is in with the President right now. Would you like me to tell him you are on the line?'

'Please,' said Jimmy.

And within 10 seconds the rasping tones of Admiral Morgan came down the White House line to the National Security Agency, as they had done so many hundreds of times before.

'Hey, Jimmy. This urgent?'

'Yessir. One of our guys in the Riyadh embassy just filed a report identifying a former French Special Forces officer in command of the leading tank which attacked the Saudi King's palace this morning.'

'Jesus Christ! Is that right? Tell you what, stay where you are. I'll come out to Fort Meade, and we'll go over this whole French bullshit right away.'

Arnold replaced the telephone. Then he looked up at President Bedford and said, 'I'd better go, sir. We may have the breakthrough that will nail France to the wall. Can you get me a car?'

*　　　*　　　*

Half an hour later the admiral was back in his old domain at Fort Meade, sitting in George Morris's chair – where else? – reading the report from Charlie Brooks and complaining about the quality, and especially the temperature, of the National Security Agency's coffee.

Nothing much had changed since Arnold Morgan had first sat in that same chair a dozen years ago. He remained the glowering intelligence genius he always was – impatient, mercurial, bombastic, rude, and, according to his wife Kathy, adorable. Just so long as you always remembered his bite was one hell of a lot worse than his bark.

'I'll send for a fresh pot,' said Jimmy Ramshawe, picking up the phone.

'Hot, Jimmy. For Christ's sake tell 'em to make it hot. Lukewarm coffee makes lukewarm people, right?'

Jimmy was not absolutely sure he had got that. But he still snapped, 'Aye, sir.' That was the response Admiral Morgan expected, and in Jimmy's opinion it was a small price to pay for the presence of his hero.

'Jesus, we're damn lucky this Charlie Brooks was on the case,' said Arnold. 'And, of course, we have just one main objective – aside from the goddamned coffee. We must find out the precise identity of Major Chasser . . . get Charlie Brooks on the line.'

'Rightaway, sir,' answered Jimmy, lifting up the telephone and asking the operator to connect him to Mr Charles Brooks in the American Embassy in Riyadh, Saudia Arabia.

That took only three minutes. In every US embassy around the world, everyone jumped to it when the National Security Agency came on the line.

'*Brooks here. I've been expecting you guys for the last hour . . .*'

'Morning, Charlie,' said Jimmy. 'This is Lt. Commander Jimmy Ramshawe, assistant to the Director. I believe we've spoken a couple of times before?'

'Yes, we have, Jimmy. Guess you called about my report.'

'I did. Very interesting. 'Specially that bit about the commander on the leading tank.'

'That was him, I'm absolutely sure of that. Sorry I don't know his correct name, but they kept referring to Major Chasser. I spoke to him several times in Brazzaville, and he was definitely French, but he looked like an Arab.'

'You're spelling that C-H-A-S-S-E-R?'

'Well, I am. But I'm only guessing. That's what they called him. Chasser, like Nasser.'

'Charlie, we may want to pursue this further. If we do, can you give us some guidance, from back in Brazzaville, where we might dig up some detail?'

'Well, I'd have to look that up. You see I only saw him during that one day, the day we all got out. But I may still have some stuff on my computer; you know, a few names of contacts who might know more.'

'Okay, Charlie. We'd all be grateful. Maybe if I call in a couple of hours?'

'Don't bother, Jimmy. I'll e-mail you.'

'That would be great. Just one more thing . . . did you have the impression this Chasser was definitely in charge of the assault convoy?'

'Oh, there was no doubt about that at all. His tank, the big Abrams, was out in front. He was calling the shots, both to passing civilians and to the rest of the force to the rear of his armoured vehicles. I walked further up the street behind the convoy and I saw Chasser's vehicle slam straight into the gates of the royal palace. And he wasn't asking anyone's permission. Trust me.'

'Okay, Charlie. You've been a real help. We may talk later.'

'So long, Jimmy.'

The lieutenant commander replaced the telephone and looked over to the big desk where Arnold Morgan and George Morris were talking.

'He's very definite,' said Jimmy. 'The guy was called Chasser, like Nasser, spelled C-H-A-S-S-E-R.'

'And right there we got a real problem,' said Admiral Morgan, a little grandly. 'The French do not have the sound E-R . . . like we say Chasser or Nasser. E-R on the end of a word in French, any word, is pronounced AY. If this guy's name was Chasser, the French would say, CHA-SSAY.'

'Well, Charlie said he heard CHASSER, like Nasser. And he repeated it. He was certain how it sounded.'

'But he's uncertain of what he spelled,' said Arnold. 'It's elementary. The sound does not exist in French.'

Now, Jimmy thought, for a bloke whose French accent sounded like Homer Simpson trying to imitate Maurice Chevalier, the admiral was being pretty dogmatic. So he pressed on.

'Okay, sir. What's the nearest sound the French *do* have for E-R, and how do they spell it?'

'Well, they have E-U-R. As in *educateur*, teacher. Sounds much the same. But that's how they spell it.'

'How about Chasseur . . . is that possible . . . what does it mean?'

'How the hell should I know?' replied Arnold. 'We got a French dictionary around here?'

'Probably not,' replied Admiral Morris. 'But I can get one sent down in about one minute.'

At that moment the fresh coffee arrived, with, miraculously, a blue tube of Arnold's preferred 'buckshot', the little white sweetners which tasted like the sugar both his doctor and his wife had banned. Word had already hit the kitchens that the Big Man was in residence. It was just like old times.

Admiral Morris poured, Arnold stirred. And a slightly breathless young secretary from the Western European Language Department came through the door with the required dictionary.

'Let me have that, kiddo,' said Arnold, sipping gratefully. And he skimmed through the first section, French–English, for the elusive word Chasser.

And on page 74 he found it – *chasser*, the French verb to hunt, or to drive away. Pronounced, obviously, chass-ay. Right below it was the word *chasseur*, the French noun, hunter or fighter. The dictionary added *Chasseurs Alpins*, meaning mountain infantry. The feminine was *chasseuse*. But Arnold Morgan had it. *Le chasseur.* The hunter. That was plainly their man.

'And a goddamned good nickname that is,' he said, 'for a tough sonofabitch French mercenary. Question is, who the hell is *Le Chasseur*. Better call Charlie back, Jimmy. Ask him if he thinks it's possible that *Chasseur* was his nickname, rather than his real name?'

'Aye, sir.' Jimmy picked up the phone and within three minutes was once again in conversation with their man in Riyadh.

'That you, Charlie? Jimmy again. We just wondered whether you thought Chasser could be a nickname, rather than a real name?'

'Sure it could. I heard it more than once, but it could have been just the name he was usually called. Like Eisenhower was "Ike", Ronnie Reagan was "Dutch", Bush was "Dubya". Sure, it might easily be a nickname.'

Jimmy confirmed the conversation. And Arnold stood up to leave – 'Keep at it, guys,' he said. 'Watch for the submarines, and keep checking the Brits for more on that message from the Frog in the Desert. Sounds to me like *Le Chasseur* might *be* the Frog in the Desert. Stay in touch.'

And with that he was gone, and neither Admiral Morris nor Lt. Commander Ramshawe had the slightest doubt what they needed to accomplish next.

'Jimmy,' said Admiral Morris, 'we have to establish this Chasseur guy is a French citizen, and/or a French

415

resident, with a French home, and possibly a French wife. If we can't establish those things, we have nothing. Not even enough to point the finger at France.'

'You mean the ole *J'accuse*?' said Jimmy, in his Aussie accent, employing one of only three French phrases he knew – along with *Je ne sais quoi* and *Arrivederci, Roma*, the last of which he readily accepted might well be Italian.

Admiral Morris shook his head. 'Exactly,' he said. 'We must have sufficient evidence before we point the finger. And if this *Chasseur* in the front tank is really French, coupled with all the other stuff, we've probably got 'em.'

'What do we do? Get the CIA on the case?'

'Right now,' said George. 'And they start in Brazzaville, where Chasser held high command in French Special Forces 10 years ago. There must be people who remember him. There's still a major French embassy in that city. I'd say the guys could identify him with a proper name in less than a couple of days.'

'I'll call Langley right away,' replied Jimmy.

Same day, 0600 (local)
Wednesday 24 March
Brazzaville, The Congo

Ray Sharpe had been stationed in the former capital of French Equatorial Africa for two years. Here in this sweltering city on the north bank of the Congo River he had held the fort for the USA in one of the least desirable foreign postings Langley had to offer.

But Brazzaville was an intensely busy port, the hub of the area between the Central African Republic and Cameroon to the north, the former Zaïre to the east, now the Democratic Republic of Congo, and Gabon to the west. The mile-wide Congo was the longest navigable river in Africa, providing a freeway for enormous quantities of wood, rubber and agricultural goods. And an enormous amount of skullduggery. Ray Sharpe was well tuned in to the buzz of the African underworld. Sometimes he thought there was more underworld than overworld.

But today he was not stressed. For a start it was lashing down with rain, warm rain here at the back end of the season, but nonetheless sheeting, soaking squalls which rendered several highways impassable. Drainage right here was not exactly top of the line. But, for Africa, it was almost adequate.

He was sitting on the wide, shady veranda of the French colonial house he rented, and, just for a change, he was not pouring with sweat thanks to the cooling rain clouds, and he was taking a man-sized suck at his first cold beer of the evening.

Ray was a native of New England, south Boston, a devoted fan of the Red Sox and the Patriots. A burly black-haired Irish-American of forty-three, he had volunteered for Brazzaville mainly to escape a particularly messy divorce. All right, he probably drank too much, and his work took him away from his wife for much of the year, but he could not for the life of him understand why Melissa had to run off with some goddamned hairdresser named Marc – with a 'c', he always added, contemptuously.

And he was always baffled by the fact that Melissa had mercilessly skinned him alive financially. Christ! They'd been at Boston College together, where she'd been a cheerleader and he'd been a star tight-end. Their families came from the same county in Ireland, Limerick. And she'd tried to nail him to the wall.

All of which conspired to turn Ray into a classic expatriate colonial resident. Stuck out here at the ass end of West Africa, still drinking too much, missing home, but too short of serious cash, too disillusioned, and rapidly becoming too idle to return. He had learned to speak French, and he had friends in Brazzaville, but most of them were much like himself with big expense accounts and nowhere much to spend the money, except in restaurants and bars.

Still, great fortunes were made in places like Brazzaville – importing, exporting, buying dirt cheap, selling back to the USA or Europe. He'd seen it, he'd had opportunities, and there'd be more. But somehow he had never got around to making a commercial move himself. Not yet, anyway. But he'd get to it one of these days. Definitely.

Ray was just reaching into the cooler for a fresh beer when the phone rang. Who the hell was that? The beautiful chocolate-coloured French waitress, Matilda, from La Brasserie in the Stanley Hotel up the street? Or maybe even Melissa, now without her faggot boyfriend, calling for more money.

'Jeez,' he muttered, walking inside to pick up the telephone. 'Sharpe,' he said, inwardly groaning at the all too familiar . . . *Good evening, Mr Sharpe, Langley here, West African Desk . . . just a minute for the Chief.*

Five minutes later he was back in his big swinging couch, staring at his notes. *French Special Forces Commander June 1999. Evacuated the US Embassy. Envoy Brooks and Ambassador Aubrey Hooks. Believed nicknamed the Chasseur. Please trace, get real name, background and current residence if possible. Urgent FYEO. Soonest please.*

For your eyes only. Ray's eyes were a tad bloodshot, and it was still raining like hell. But he drained his beer, grabbed his light mackintosh and gunned his Ford Mustang out through the tree-lined boulevards of the biggest city in this old French colony, towards the modern-day French Embassy on rue Alfassa. He knew the resident secretariat extremely well, like every diplomat, spy and journalist.

His route took him straight through the central area of Brazzaville, which was still dominated by the Elf Oil Tower, jutting above the skyline, a symbol of French industrial power. He never gave it much of a thought, of course, and he would probably never know how significant that building was to his evening mission.

As luck would have it, most of the French Embassy staff had gone home for the evening, leaving only the

419

famously ill-tempered M. Claude Chopin on duty. Aged about ninety-four, and claiming direct blood-lines with the great composer – who was, anyway, Polish – M. Chopin was a stern French patriot, and the Republic's tricolour hung above his desk, next to a large portrait of General Charles de Gaulle. Old Claude had worked at the embassy for about 35 years and spent most of them sipping wine and griping and moaning.

He looked up, saw his visitor was the American Ray Sharpe and issued what he thought was a smile but turned out to be a suppressed sneer. '*Bonsoir, Sharpe,*' he said. '*Qu'est-ce que vous voulez?*' Which was only a marginally polite way of asking what the hell the CIA man wanted.

'C'mon, Claude, what's eating you, old buddy? I'm here on a simple mission, the smallest piece of information, that's all I want. You'll probably know it off the top of your head.'

'*Possiblement,*' replied Claude, lapsing into his usual mix of French and broken English. 'But whether I tell it to you is *quelque chose différent.*'

'Claude, I have come over to see you because it is a rainy evening, and I was just relaxing, having a beer, when I was interrupted by a phone call of such insignificance it made my hair curl . . .'

'It's already *bouclé,*' growled Claude, who was very bald and thought Sharpe's mop of curly hair made him look like a pop star.

Ray grinned. 'Seriously, old pal, you can end my problems very easily . . . you remember when the

420

gallant French Special Forces liberated the besieged Americans in the embassy right here in Brazzaville in 1999?'

'Who could forget?' shrugged Claude, his mind roaming back to those terrifying days in the 1990s when armed gangs drove around the city with their victims' severed heads stuck on their car aerials. 'Of course I remember.'

'Well, I'm trying to remember the proper name of the Special Forces leader . . . they called him *Le Chasseur* . . . the hunter . . . did you know him?'

'Of course I knew him. He was stationed here for several months. He stayed up the street at the Stanley for a few weeks — all those French officers stayed up there.'

'And, *Le Chasseur* . . . you remember his real name?'

'Why do you want to know?'

'Well, I've just been told there is to be a new Presidential Award for foreign nationals who have helped the United States beyond the call of duty.' Ray Sharpe was a think-on-your feet liar of outstanding talent. Like most spies.

'We would like to bring them to Washington, with their wives and families, and decorate them for their bravery. President Bedford insists on conducting the ceremonies personally.'

'Very commendable,' said Claude. 'And they picked *Le Chasseur* after all these years?'

'It sometimes takes a new President to recognise a debt of honour,' replied Sharpe.

'Well, I can't help you much,' said Claude. 'I heard he'd retired from the military. But his name was Jacques Gamoudi. Major Jacques Gamoudi. Everyone called him *Le Chasseur*, the hunter. He was a tremendous soldier, and a true hero, as I expect your American diplomats would confirm. Someone did tell me he'd made colonel.'

'Thanks, Claude. That's all we need. Washington will take it from there.'

Five minutes later Ray Sharpe was back on the line to the West African Desk in Langley. Three minutes after that the phone rang in Lt. Commander Ramshawe's office and a voice told him, 'Jimmy, your man is Colonel Jacques Gamoudi, but he's retired from the military. And you're right about his nickname. He's *Le Chasseur*, the hunter.'

Langley also told Jimmy that their man in Brazzaville was still on the case and would call as soon as possible with anything more he could find. And this was not long in coming. Matilda's boss, behind the long wooden bar in the brasserie at the Stanley Hotel, had been there for years and knew Jacques Gamoudi.

The barman could not be precise, but he remembered the major, as he then was, had been a light-skinned French North African, originally from Morocco.

'Was he married?' asked Ray Sharpe.

'Yes. Yes, he was,' replied the barman. 'But she never came here. I saw a photograph of her once, though. I never knew her name . . . but either her parents or

422

his . . . they lived somewhere up in the Pyrenees. I remember that.'

'How come?'

'Well, he always talked of the mountains. He said he liked the solitude. I think his father was some kind of a guide. But, anyway, he often told me when he retired he wanted to find employment as a mountain guide and he always mentioned the cool air near his wife's parents home.

'I think the terrible heat and humidity here in Africa can really get to you after a few years. Anyway, Jacques dreamed of the mountains, somewhere cold, I know that.'

Ray Sharpe got straight back on the phone to Langley, and finally returned to his beer cooler and swinging seat on the veranda at his Brazzaville home. It was still raining like hell, and he was comprehensively soaked. So he just sat steaming, and sipping, thinking about the Red Sox back home in spring training.

Lt. Commander Ramshawe studied his notes. He walked along to see Admiral Morris, and wondered, 'Have we got enough to find him?'

'No trouble, Jimmy. I'll have a quick word with our military attaché in the Paris embassy and then we'll hand it back to the CIA guys in France to finish the job.'

And in the next two hours CIA agents in France made probably 50 phone calls, and one of them came up trumps. Their top man in the French city of Toulouse, Andy Campese, was especially friendly with his opposite number in the French Secret Service.

And DGSE agent Yves Zilber, knowing absolutely nothing of the highly classified nature of the work of the *Le Chasseur*, was cheerfully forthcoming to an old friend.

'Jacques Gamoudi? Oh, sure. He and I worked together for a couple of years. I haven't spoken to him recently, but he retired from the military and went to live somewhere up in the Pyrenees, near his wife's family.

'As I recall, he became a mountain guide up on the Cirque de Troumouse – that's a massive range up near the Spanish border, in the snow. You can only get up there about four months of the year, but I think Jacques's one of the top mountaineers in the area. He lives somewhere near a little place called Gèdre.'

Just before the CIA man rang off, however, the French Secret Serviceman remembered one further piece of helpful information.

'André,' he said, 'Jacques changed his name, you know. A lot of guys retired from the service do. I might even do the same myself one day. Anyhow, he suddenly decided to call himself and his family, Hooks. I once asked him why he picked such a curious name. And he said he once had a friend of that name, out in Africa.'

Andy Campese rang off gratefully. Twenty minutes later, Agent Zilber had second thoughts about what he had said. What was a CIA man doing inquiring about a retired French Secret Service officer? It was probably nothing, but he wanted to clear himself.

Agent Zilber always reported directly to Paris, and he put in a phone call to number 128, boulevard Mortier, over in Caserne des Tourelles, in the outpost of the 20th *arrondissement*, way to the west of the city centre of Paris.

He spoke briefly to the duty officer, and, somewhat to his surprise, was asked to wait. Then a new voice came on the line and said: '*Bonsoir*, Agent Zilber. This is Gaston Savary; tell me what you have to report.'

Agent Zilber was momentarily surprised at being put through to the head of the entire French Secret Service. This was very much a case of, *WOW! Gaston Savary! Mon Dieu! The head of the DGSE – what have I said? Or, even worse, done?*

'Well, sir. A short while ago I received a phone call from an acquaintance of mine, André Campese, works for US intelligence. And he wanted to know a few details about an old colleague of ours, just a retired officer. No one important.

'And I just gave him a clue how to locate the man. It wasn't much. You know how we often swap information with the American agents. André Campese has always been very helpful to us.'

'Of course,' replied Gaston Savary, smoothly. 'What was the name of the officer in whom he was interested?'

'Colonel Jacques Gamoudi, sir.'

Gaston Savary froze. His whole system shuddered, his heart missed about six beats, his pulse packed up altogether and his brain turned to stone. At least that's what it felt like to Gaston. But he was trained to accept shock. And after a three-second pause, he spoke again.

'And for which branch of American intelligence does Mr Campese work?' he asked.

'He's CIA, sir.'

Gaston Savary, a sallow-complexioned man at the best of times, instantly turned a whiter shade of pale. He was so stunned that he gently put the phone down without making one further inquiry. Before him stood a vision of France being outlawed from the international community.

And it was his own department, the glorious Direction Générale de la Sécurité Extérieure (DGSE), successor to the sinister SPECE, which had sprung the leak.

Gaston Savary held his face in his hands and tried to breathe normally. He took an iron grip on himself and his emotions. But, in truth, he could have wept.

9 a.m. (local), the following day
Thursday 25 March
The Pyrenees
They'd been driving all night, fighting their way by car up the mountains from Toulouse, the temperature dropping and the weather deteriorating

all the way, as they climbed into the rugged high country. The 220-mile trek had taken almost seven hours, two of those hours spent on the final 40 miles running southwards and upwards along the winding, treeless road from the town of Tarbes to Gèdre.

As more than one person before them had discovered, it was not easy to find out exactly where Jacques Gamoudi lived in the mountains. But they persevered, and so it was that early in the morning Andy Campese and his colleague, a twenty-eight-year-old French-born American, Guy Roland, hit the village of Héas, entered the village store and bakery at 7.30 bought takeaway coffee, a fresh warm *baguette* and a few slices of ham.

Almost as an afterthought, Andy reached the door and called back, 'M. Hooks . . . straight on?'

'Four houses up the street on the left. Number 8.'

Andy Campese considered he had done a very cool night's work. And it certainly was cool, about 34 degrees F. They walked up to the house, which had lights on, but decided to go back to the car first, have breakfast and keep a firm watch on Number 8 until 8.30.

At the appointed hour they opened the gate and walked up the pathway to the white stone house. They'd been quick and thorough, ever since Yves Zilber had put them on the right track.

But they had been nothing like as quick as the men who worked for Gaston Savary, the men who had arrived by helicopter and evacuated Giselle

Gamoudi and her sons André and Jean-Pierre, three hours earlier.

And when the doorbell was answered, Andy Campese and Guy Roland faced a Frenchman who was most definitely not Colonel Gamoudi. He was about thirty and he wore a black leather jacket over a dark blue polo-neck sweater. His hair was cut short, military-style, and he looked like a combat soldier from the 1st Marine Parachute Infantry Regiment, which indeed he had been until six months ago.

'No,' he said in English, almost as if he knew their native language, 'M. Hooks is away on business.'

'And Mme Hooks?'

'She and the boys are visiting her mother.'

'Can you tell us where?'

'Somewhere near Pau, I think. But I have no way of contacting her.'

'And you? May we know who you are?'

'Just a friend.'

'Any idea when they might return?'

'Sorry.'

'Do you work with him up here in the mountains?'

'Not really. He's just a friend.'

'Just one thing more . . . does M. Hooks own this house?'

'I believe so. But I could not be certain.'

'Okay, sorry to have disturbed you.'

'Goodbye.'

Andy Campese was a very experienced CIA operator, and he knew for absolute certain when he had just encountered one of his own kind. The French Secret Service were parked in Jacques Gamoudi's house, there was no doubt about that. And no doubt in Andy's mind that, wherever the colonel was, it was very, very secret indeed.

He made one more stop at the village shop and inquired whether Mme Hooks had been in residence the previous day. He was told, 'She was here yesterday afternoon . . . I saw her meet the boys off the school bus. But I noticed they did not catch the bus this morning.'

'And Jacques?' he asked.

'Oh, we have not seen him for several months. He's supposed to be on some kind of mountain expedition . . . but who knows? Maybe he doesn't come back.'

Andy called Langley on his cell phone, and, at 3.45 a.m. in Washington, he dictated a short report, detailing the fact that he was 100 per cent certain Colonel Gamoudi's residence was now under the strict control of France's DGSE. He said he believed the family had been moved out in the middle of the night, probably in response to his own call to Yves Zilber.

'And they must have moved damned fast,' he said. 'We drove straight up here, from Toulouse, and they were long gone. Jacques Gamoudi himself has not been seen in the village for months. For the record he lives at Number 8, rue St Martin, Héas, near Gèdre, Pyrenees. Postcode 65113.

'The phone is listed in the book under Hooks – 05-62-92-50-66. I didn't try it because it's probably tapped, and there didn't seem to be much point. I don't even know if it's connected. Mme Hooks and the boys were definitely here yesterday afternoon.'

While Andy and Guy Roland set off briskly down the mountains back to Toulouse, the French agent at Number 8 was moving equally quickly. He hit the buttons from the house to the DGSE HQ on the outskirts of Paris and reported direct to Gaston Savary.

'Sir,' he said. 'They were here . . . 8.30 this morning. Two CIA agents inquiring about Colonel Gamoudi and his family. They were polite, not particularly persistent. If I had to guess, I'd say they were just trying to establish his residence here. They demanded no details, except who I was.'

'Which of course you did not tell them?'

'Of course not, sir.'

Gaston Savary stood up and walked around his office. There was, he knew, only one solution to a burgeoning problem. He tossed it around in his mind for half an hour and the facts never varied . . . and neither did the answer.

If the Americans know that Colonel Gamoudi was the assault commander in Riyadh, they probably also have a few other pointers to our involvement . . . that HAMAS thug from Damascus is not a problem . . . he's probably gone home already, with his troops, and will never be found – not in Syria.

The submarines are beyond detection, and, anyway, the French Navy does not answer to the Pentagon. I expect the US Government is aware of our activities in the oil market, but that's mere coincidence.

It's Gamoudi who's our problem. He's French. They have his address. And he's plainly been identified, somehow, as the leader of the Saudi revolutionary forces. If they catch him, he may very well be forced to admit everything.

Gaston Savary glanced at his watch. It was just before 9 a.m. He picked up the telephone, direct line to the Foreign Office on the Quai d'Orsay. He spoke very briefly to M. Pierre St Martin, saying, briskly, that he was coming to see him on a matter of grave urgency.

Savary was so locked in his own thoughts that he ordered a driver to take him there. This was most unusual. The Secret Service chief always drove himself, but this time he sat in the back seat turning over in his mind the very few options he had.

When he finally walked into M. St Martin's office, his mind was made up. He accepted a cup of coffee, served by the butler, and waited for the man to leave.

He then faced the French Foreign Minister and said icily, 'Pierre, I am afraid we must eliminate Jacques Gamoudi.'

CHAPTER TEN

0500, Thursday, 25 March
National Security Agency, Fort Meade, Maryland

Lt. Commander Ramshawe was on the encrypted line to Charlie Brooks in Riyadh. It was the final check required before Admiral Morris reported to the President that the NSA was 100 per cent certain the Saudi Arabian uprising had been led by a former French Special Forces officer from the Pyrenees, thus implicating France, right up to its *pantalons*.

And once more the wily US envoy had brought home the bacon. He had spent the night in the basement of the Riyadh embassy combing the yards of film shot by the security cameras mounted on the high walls of the embassy. The ones at the gate were too narrow in focus and did not cover the entire width of the road, but the wide-angled rotating camera, set just below the roof, covered the whole scene, and Charlie had in his hand a blown-up print of the convoy coming towards him, then moving away. And clearly pictured was the bearded figure of Colonel Jacques Gamoudi, machine gun ready,

432

standing up in the for'ard hatch, the lead officer in the lead tank.

The embassy camera had even recorded the colonel, in an unmistakable gesture of urgency, beckoning to the vehicles in the rear. Above him could be seen a lone helicopter, the one which circled before the Chinooks, the one bearing General Rashood. Unhappily for the US, the camera could not see in there.

Charlie Brooks told Jimmy the photographs were on their way via the National Surveillance Office, and there was no question in his mind: the assault commander was the same man who had liberated the US Embassy in Brazzaville. *Le Chasseur.*

'Hey, Charlie,' said Jimmy. 'I was just going to call you anyway. We got a name for your guy . . . does Major Jacques Gamoudi mean anything to you?'

'Gamoudi,' said Charlie. 'Give me a minute . . .' And his mind went back to those final hours in Brazzaville, the final days when the city was almost destroyed. And the scene of chaos and terror was still real to him, and he could still hear in his head the gunshots, and, if he thought hard, he could still smell the burning rubber of the upturned cars in the street. He had seen the severed heads on the aerials, watched the fury of the mob from behind the embassy walls.

And he tried to recall the first time he ever saw *Le Chasseur*, the morning the French Special Forces had come bursting through the embassy gates. There was gunfire outside, but the lunatic bloodlust of

433

the revolutionaries was no match for the steady trained fire of the French troops who drove them off.

But then he remembered – one of the French combat soldiers, the one driving the evacuation truck, had been hit as he climbed down from the cab . . . Charlie could see in his mind the man lurching in through the gates, blood pouring from a wound in his leg.

Somehow, after eleven years, he had cast that image from his subconscious. But now he remembered the French trooper going down, falling and then getting up again. He'd been standing two yards from him. And most of all he remembered the one single bellowing cry the man gave . . . 'JACQUES!'

'You got him,' said Charlie. '*Le Chasseur*'s christian name was Jacques. You can take that to the bank. And the pictures will show you, he was the assault commander in the force that stormed the Saudi royal palace.'

'And now his Pyrenean home is under the special protection of the French Secret Service,' muttered Jimmy. And then he thanked Charlie Brooks for all he had done. Lt. Commander Ramshawe had quite enough data to send Admiral Morris directly to the President. After, of course, a quick check with the Big Man.

He walked back along the corridor to the office of the director, where he knew Admiral Morris had been for most of the night. He tapped lightly and walked in, holding his dossier of information.

'Jimmy,' said George Morris. 'Have we nailed it down?'

'Definitely, sir. Just spoke to Charlie Brooks in Riyadh, and he confirms he heard Colonel Gamoudi called Jacques, very loudly by one of his troops injured in the fighting. Better yet, he's been through the film in the embassy surveillance cameras on the outside walls.

'A few of the frames show the convoy and clear photographs of Gamoudi leading the operation. He's the forward commander in the lead tank. And it's him all right.

'Back in the Pyrenees, the CIA guys ran him to ground – found his house. But the French Secret Service were already in there. No sign of Jacques, of course, but there wouldn't be, would there? He's in Riyadh helping King Nasir. The CIA agent reckoned it was a race between him and the French Secret Service, to get to Mme Gamoudi.

'The French won, and by the time our guys reached Jacques Gamoudi's village at 7.30 this morning, his family had been evacuated in the night. Now, I ask you, would the French have gone to all this trouble if Gamoudi had been an innocent mountain guide? Of course they bloody wouldn't.'

'And this was definitely Gamoudi's house?'

'Dead right it was, sir. The CIA guys checked in the village, and the French agent in the house said it was probably owned by Gamoudi, but he did not know for sure. He was probably telling the truth.'

'That'll do for us,' said Admiral George Morris. 'Now all we gotta do is find Colonel Gamoudi, and somehow get him right back here to the USA. That way we'll hang the French Government out to dry.'

'You want me to run this past the Big Man?'

'Yes, I think that would be a good idea. Meanwhile, I'm going in to talk to the President.'

Jimmy drove his black Jaguar up to the doors of the house in Chevy Chase at 0900. Two Secret Service agents escorted him through the front door to see Admiral Morgan, who was sitting by the fire in his study, growling at the *Washington Post* and the *New York Times* in that order.

The *Post* was banging on about *A FAILURE OF US DIPLOMACY IN SAUDI ARABIA* . . . and the *Times* was carping about *US FAILURE TO UNDERSTAND THE ISLAMIC MIND* . . . both of which, according to Arnold, showed the usual sad, naive, total lack of comprehension he associated with both publications.

'Liberal assholes,' he confirmed. 'Fucking dimwits could learn more from two hours with young Ramshawe than they'll ever know.'

Then he looked up and saw his visitor. 'Hi, Jimmy,' he said. 'Just thinking about you. What's hot?'

'Plenty. We just ran the ole Chasser to ground.'

'Chass-*EUR*, Jimmy. Chass-*EUR*,' replied Arnold, still sounding precisely like Homer Simpson doing his Maurice Chevalier. But he grinned, refrained from hurling the newspapers into the fire, which he felt like doing, and set them down on a small coffee table next to him.

He yelled 'COFFEE!!' at the top of his lungs, in a bold attempt to attract the attention of the sainted Kathy in the kitchen, chuckling at his own appallingness. Then he settled back and said, 'Right, Lieutenant Commander, lay it on me.'

'Well, sir. The CIA got after him in Brazzaville . . .'

'BRAZZAVILLE . . . that's some goddamned dungheap in the middle of the Congo River; how the hell did he get down there? I thought he was in Riyadh.'

'He is, sir,' said Jimmy.

'And will you, for Christ's sake, stop calling me SIR? I'm retired. I've been a friend of your father's for years. Call me Arnie, like everyone else.'

'Yessir,' said Jimmy, as they both knew he would, each of them being absolute suckers for the easy punch line.

'Right, Arnie. The CIA went to work on him in Brazzaville because that's where we know he served for several months a decade ago. Remember we only had *Le Chasseur*, nothing else.'

Arnold nodded. 'No name, right?'

'No name. But we put the local man on it and he came up with one almost immediately – Colonel Jacques Gamoudi, a Moroccan, always known as *Le Chasseur*.'

'Nice accent,' said Arnie.

'Thank you,' replied Jimmy. 'Then the CIA gave the entire French staff the task of actually tracing

437

him. And they located his family home, wife, children, the lot, in a tiny village up in the Pyrenees where he works as a mountain guide. And, guess what . . . ?'

'The French Secret Service were in that house when they got there.'

'How d'you know that . . .'

'Put yourself in their place . . . they've handpicked this superb Special Forces officer to mastermind their friend Nasir's takeover of the country. He's been out there training his troops for several months. He's probably served in the French Secret Service himself. Everyone knows him.

'Then, suddenly, up pops a US agent, from the CIA, in the middle of France, wanting to know who, and where, he is. Plainly the French will deny all knowledge of him and his whereabouts. But they know Madame Chasseur is up in the Pyrenees with her children. And they know the CIA is hot on the trail of this Frenchman who is smashing up the world's economy. What would you do, young Ramshawe?'

'I'd get up the bloody mountains real quick and get Jacques Gamoudi's family out of there.'

'Precisely, Jimmy. And then what would you do?'

'Well, I'd . . .'

'In my judgement, you would have little choice. You'd have to assassinate Jacques Gamoudi, and probably his wife as well. Because those two alone could tell the whole world what you had done.'

'But I imagine Gamoudi was very highly paid

to do no such bloody thing – by the French Government?'

'Yes, I suppose so, Jimmy. And I expect the government's secrets would be safe with him.

'But what if we got ahold of him? What if we threatened him with crimes against humanity or something? What if we got him to tell us what happened?'

'Well, in that case the Frogs might want him dead.'

'Exactly. And if they somehow assassinated him, they'd have to assassinate his wife too. Because wives who know their husbands have been murdered are likely to have a lot to say.'

'Christ, Arnie. You're saying the French might right now be in pursuit of Gamoudi themselves?'

'I should think, very definitely. If we want him, you'd better tell George to look sharp about it.'

Just then the radiant Kathy came in with coffee. She greeted Jimmy warmly and asked Arnold if he'd like her to buy him a bullhorn, just in case she was ever out of range.

The admiral stood up and put his arm around her, saying to Jimmy, 'I can't imagine how she puts up with me, can you?'

The lieutenant commander decided this was a question best left unanswered, but quipped anyway, 'I'm afraid that's the lifelong problem the lower deck has when they're dealing with an admiral . . .'

'You'll find a lifelong problem dealing with an admiral's wife if you're not careful,' laughed Kathy as she swept off the quarterdeck and back to the kitchen. 'By the way, are you staying for lunch?'

''Fraid not, ma'am. I've got to get back and it'll take me an hour in the traffic.'

The admiral sat back in his big chair by the fire. For a few moments he said nothing, apparently lost in thought. But then he did speak. 'You know, Jimmy, this is a terrible thing France has done. I guess this Nasir character has told them they'll have the inside track on Saudi oil once it's up and running, maybe even an exclusive agency. And they've always bought a lot of military hardware from the French.

'But you think about it. Can you imagine the United States doing something like that? Or Great Britain? Or Australia?

'For purely personal gain, to let the rest of the world go to hell for two years? Wiping the world's most plentiful and best-priced oil right off the map? Bankrupting little nations? Damn near closing down Japan? Hurting just about everyone? And not caring? Jesus Christ. That takes a damn special nation.'

'Sir, are you certain in your own mind – I mean as certain as I am – that France is at the bottom of all this?'

'I am certain that a group of rebel Saudis could not possibly have done this themselves. I am certain they had outside help, and I am certain that outside help came from France.'

'Is that sufficiently certain to start taking action?'

'Jimmy, I'm not the President. I'm not even an official government adviser. But if I *were* the President, I could not just sit back and see the industrial world go to hell, while France sat back eating *escargots* and getting richer and richer off the Saudi oil industry . . . No. I could not do that.'

Meanwhile, over at the White House, Admiral Morris was walking the President through the entire French scenario, explaining in detail how *Le Chasseur* had been run to ground.

When he had finished, the President wore a worried expression. It looked as if everything Arnold Morgan had warned him about had come to pass. He was about to carry the can for the collapse of the economies of the free world and of the Third World.

Through no fault of his own, President Paul Bedford stood on the verge of making a special kind of history.

'What's your take on this, George . . . I mean, what would you do in my position? Since you and your assistant seem to be the only people in the country who understand what's actually happening?'

'Sir, I'm not a trained politician. And I'm not that good at thinking like one. My task is to find out what the hell's happening, and then to try and interpret what might happen next. But you've got to take it step by step. If I were sitting in that chair of yours, I'd most certainly touch base with Admiral Morgan again.

'He's the best I've ever met at this type of thing. Especially if there's a chance we may have to kick someone in the ass.'

The President nodded. And five minutes later, just after Lt. Commander Ramshawe had left, the phone rang in the big house in Chevy Chase.

One hour later, Admiral Morgan was back in the Oval Office, briefing the President on the latest developments, among them the catastrophic collapse on the Nikkei, the Japanese Stock Exchange. In the four days since Saudi oil and gas had stopped flowing, Japan's energy analysts had been able to forecast their forthcoming power-grid shortfalls and diminishing reserves of natural gas.

It looked like a six-week problem. Which meant that around 10 May the lights would go out in one of the biggest economies in the world. Japan's reliance on Saudi oil had long bothered these analysts, and now they could see a gigantic coop of chickens coming home to roost.

And it would not be much different in the seething industrial hub of Taiwan. Nor in India and Pakistan, whose western and southern coastal areas respectively stood directly opposite the main source of all their energy, the Strait of Hormuz, the entrance to the Gulf.

China seemed to have some supplies flowing continuously from Kazakhstan, but the People's Republic was an enormous importer of Saudi oil, and right now Beijing was bracing itself for severe shortages of automobile fuel and electric power.

Indonesia had some oil of its own, but it was still reliant on Saudi production. Canada was much the same. But Europe was in trouble. The Old World had hardly any energy resources, except for some high producing coal mines in the east, and a small amount of oil left in the North Sea. Which put Great Britain in a real spot. As bad as America's.

Russia was smiling, and so were some of her former satellites along the coast of the Black Sea. And South America could probably manage without the Saudis. But the interlinked global economies of the big players threatened everyone.

As the *Wall Street Journal* observed that morning: '*The ramifications of the crisis in the Saudi oilfields are very nearly boundless. The world's leading stock markets have already shuddered, as millions of dollars have been wiped off share prices in Europe, the Far East and the United States.*

'*And the stark fact remains, this planet cannot function properly without a normal supply of oil. And for the next 12 months, there is not going to be a normal supply of oil. On a global scale, that means the only thing it can mean – bankruptcies, both large and small, market collapses, black- outs, and the failure of banks and power companies all over the globe.*'

The *Journal* did its best with some illustrations of potential disasters – '*The big bank carrying a huge debt from an airline which cannot refuel its aircraft? The major automobile manufacturers who can no longer sell product to a market that's run dry? The food industry, struggling for energy to freeze and refrigerate its product? The national supermarket chains whose cold-storage facilities keep shut- ting down? The gas stations, the trucking corporations, oil tankers themselves?*

'What happens when the industrial world starts to shut down? No one knows the answer to that. The human race is unfailingly resilient and always resourceful. But, short of war, the human race has never faced anything quite like this. And some of the most powerful industrialists in the world are surely preparing for an extremely difficult time.'

Both the President and Admiral Morgan had read the article. And despite their political views, which were often diametrically opposed, they realised that now was the time for action. Action towards France, a country that America had once considered a friend and had helped out in times of need.

The President understood that millions of Americans had never forgiven France for her dogmatic stand against the United States during the run-up to the crushing of the murderous dictator Saddam Hussein in Iraq in 2003. And nor had they forgotten the demands France had made to be given a share of the rebuilding contracts.

Seven years later, there were still restaurants in the United States which refused to serve French wine, even wine importers and wholesalers which refused to touch French products.

And here again was 'the world's most self-centred nation', this time perhaps overreaching itself in terms of pure national interest; perhaps casting itself in the role of international pariah . . . assuming someone, somewhere, felt they could prove French compliance in the takeover of Saudi Arabia.

Arnold Morgan was sure he could prove a 100 per cent French involvement. And he said to the

President, 'Sir, I am going to lay this right on the line for you. France was the nation which agreed to help Prince Nasir. Those oil installations were hit by French missiles, fired from French submarines.

'Those oil-loading platforms were blown with time bombs fixed by French underwater commandoes. Those military bases at Khamis Mushayt were attacked behind a brigade of French Special Forces, and that street rabble was marshalled into a fighting force by a former French Army officer who led the assault on Riyadh on behalf of the new King.

'During the course of the next 12 months you are going to see France move into the jockey seat in the marketing of all Saudi oil. It is entirely a matter for you whether we get left behind in the coming stampede to join the line for Saudi oil and gas.'

'And you are still absolutely convinced that the French are culpable; that we have enough evidence to accuse them?'

'Damn right we do.'

'What about the submarines, the *Améthyste* and the *Perle*? Where the hell are they?'

'One of them is heading into the Arabian Sea, the other into the Indian Ocean.'

'And what if they don't turn up at La Réunion, as you and the NSA expect?'

'Doesn't matter a damn whether they turn up or not. There were only two hunter killer submarines in all the world which could have fired those missiles. They were French, they were in the area and now they're missing, having behaved in a most unusual way.'

'Who should speak to the French?'

'You should. Or the Secretary of State. Not that it will do any good. The French will deny everything.'

'So how can we hang 'em out to dry?'

'We have to capture *Le Chasseur* and make him talk.'

'Is that likely to be difficult?'

'Extremely. Especially if the French manage to assassinate him first.'

'You think they might?'

'I would.'

President Bedford stood up and walked to the other side of the room. And once more he stood beneath the portrait of George Washington.

'Arnold,' he said. 'I am asking you to come back here as my special adviser for a few months. You can name your price.'

'Sir, I'm not good at advice. I give orders and they have to be carried out. I will not offer my views for a bunch of half-assed Democrats to sit around wondering whether to do something else.'

'How about I make you Supreme Commander of this operation, with powers to order the military into action?'

'Do you and your advisers have a veto on my decisions?'

'I would need to have that.'

'Then it's time for me to go home. If you put yourself in my hands, you also put yourself in the hands of your most senior commanders in the Pentagon. And I will not order anyone to do anything without their agreement. I work *with* the Pentagon, not against it.'

President Bedford ruminated. 'Are you suggesting I give you supreme authority to take this nation to war?'

'Of course not, sir. I am suggesting you give me supreme authority to kick a little ass with no questions asked. That way you'll save your Presidency and we'll get back to where we want to be, dealing with the Saudis.'

'Arnold, I am putting myself into a precarious position where you essentially tell me what is going to happen. Is that more or less correct?'

'Yes, it is. Because I'm not having anything to do with this, unless you give me the authority to act, and act fast. If you don't trust me, don't do it. But if you do trust me, I should decide pretty damn quickly if I were you. Because this bullshit with the oil could get right out of hand.'

'I'll put you in an adjoining office.'

'Right next to the Oval Office? Perfect. And I speak only to you. I attend no cabinet meetings, nor any other meetings. I brief you, and you take your cue from that.'

'Arnold, I would not think of doing this with any other person except yourself.'

'Neither would I, sir.'

'Salary?'

'Forget it. Just all the back-up I need.'

'Well, I guess that's a deal then. I appoint you Supreme Commander of Operation . . . what? . . . Desert Fuel?'

'How about Towelhead . . . ?'

'Jesus, Arnold,' the President interrupted. 'Let's keep personal feelings out of this. I think something less inflammatory . . .'

'Okay, let's make it Operation Tanker.'

'Operation Tanker it is; when do you start?'

''Bout 10 minutes ago. Make sure my new quarters have a sizeable anteroom for Kathy, and she'll need an assistant secretary.'

'No problem. You speaking to France today?'

'Probably not. I'm concentrating our inquiries on the land battles, and I probably won't stick a firecracker up the ass of the French until we get a sight of those submarines. Then I can act as if we know rather more than we do.'

'Uh-huh,' said President Bedford. 'And then what?'

'Oh, I don't think we'll get anywhere. The French will just do a lot of shrugging and say they have no idea what happened in Saudi Arabia. It is none of their business, *n'est-ce pas*?'

'Then what?'

'We find them guilty in the courtroom of Uncle Sam. And then, as they say in the Pentagon, we'll try to appreciate the situation.'

'Do we say anything to the media?'

'Christ no, sir. Nothing. NO announcements. NO press conferences.'

'And what about when someone notices you are

448

ensconced in the White House right next to the President?'

'You let it be known that Admiral Morgan and the President are assessing a possible problem to the United States. They are working together as two former naval officers. Admiral Morgan is an acting, unpaid adviser on a purely temporary basis.'

'Right before you have the SEALs blow up the Eiffel Tower or something?'

'More or less,' replied Arnold. 'But to set your mind at rest, we're not blowing up anything on land. But, equally, we are not anxious that France should carry on as normal, running tankers in and out of their ports with oil from Abu Dhabi . . . while the rest of us starve.'

'This is going to be interesting,' said President Bedford.

'For the final time, sir. Your only chance is to get aggressive, show your outrage, be absolutely fearless in your contempt for what France has done. Get the focus of blame right away from yourself. Shock and surprise the world as necessary.

'But look like the aggrieved party, and make a lot of noise. Above all, turn France into the enemy of the free world. That way you cannot possibly lose.'

'I'm listening, Arnie. And I know you're right. I guess it's inevitable that the United States should become embroiled in the whole affair even though they've done nothing to precipitate it.'

'Other presidents in other times have felt precisely the same,' replied Arnold. 'We gotta bite the bullet, and turn this thing around. And we have to somehow turn it to America's advantage. And that's going to cost France plenty.'

One week later
11 a.m., Thursday 1 April
The Diplomatic Quarter, Riyadh
Colonel Jacques Gamoudi amd General Ravi Rashood had been keeping their heads well down while the dust of war settled. The city of Riyadh had been quiet since the new King had taken over, and the entire Saudi armed services had agreed to serve King Nasir.

He had already announced, to a thunder of national applause, an end to the massive annual stipends to the thousands of royal princes. He further announced those royal princes who were left in the country – not many – faced a wide confiscation of their property, except for primary residences.

He advised those who could leave to do so, and immediately froze any assets of more than half a million dollars kept by any prince in any Saudi bank. He ruthlessly passed these laws retrospectively, leaving many casinos, hotels and boat marinas all over the Riviera staring at large debts incurred by the former golden boys of the Kingdom.

The King's view was simple. The princes had had their day. And if any of them had debts which they expected the King of Saudi Arabia to pay, well . . . those days were over too. They'd have to get jobs and start paying off their debts. Either that, or go and live somewhere else and keep a low profile.

He further announced that the only members of the royal family who would in future be paid anything were those who buckled down and found a way to serve a useful purpose in the Kingdom. He declared it illegal for any member of the vast former royal family to transfer money from Saudi Arabia to another country.

As for the armed services, he appealed to the Land Forces, the Royal Saudi Air Force and the Navy to remain loyal to the crown. He announced that the salaries of all serving members of those services would be paid as a matter of priority from Saudi Arabia's currency reserves. He had allocated the sum of $3 billion for this purpose in the first year.

Thus in two strokes King Nasir had rid himself of a $200 billion a year 'obligation to the princes', and gained himself a fabulously loyal national fighting force at a net 'profit' of $197 billion.

As the Saudi soldiers, sailors and airmen owed him a huge debt of honour and allegiance, so King Nasir felt towards Colonel Gamoudi and General Rashood. They were both ensconced in the big white house he had personally made available to the colonel, and their every wish was his profound pleasure to grant.

They had servants, limousines, helicopters on call, a facility at every restaurant in the city to dine at the King's expense, endless invitations to attend the palace, and if they wished to dine with the King in the desert.

King Nasir was especially fond of his comrade-in-arms Colonel Gamoudi, and he was growing to like equally well his forward commander in the battle for Khamis Mushayt. If the two leaders of the revolution so desired they were welcome to remain and make their homes in Riyadh as permanent guests of the King for the rest of their days.

If it was possible, or desirable, to recreate them in this new dawn for Saudi Arabia, the two men were the nearest thing to the most privileged of princes of the Kingdom.

The King had also moved forward on his promises to France. He had allocated $10 billion to the rebuilding of Pump Station No. 1, the Abqaiq complex, the Qatif Junction manifold, the Sea Island loading platforms, the LPG terminal off Ra's al Ju'aymah and the Red Sea refineries.

At present, there was of course a vast amount of incoming dollars still owed to Saudi Arabia, and while the King intended to increase the personal state allowances to all citizens to $14,000 a year, he did not feel able to commit billions to the rebuilding of the oil loading platforms at Yanbu al-Bahr, Rabigh and Jiddah. He would begin that work as soon as oil began to flow again.

But, true to his word, he immediately awarded all the major contracts to French construction companies, with a gigantic sum of money for advice, consultation and planning services to the giant French TotalFinaElf oil conglomerate.

It would be many weeks before the full scale of Saudi Arabia's apparent debt to France was uncovered. Meanwhile, millions and millions of dollars' worth of hardware, oil pipeline, pumping systems, excavation equipment, trucks and bulldozers were making their way systematically through the Mediterranean, from French ports to the Suez Canal.

It was boom time in the heartland of industrial France. Just as the French President had predicted, almost a year earlier, when Prince Nasir had first come calling.

Meanwhile the sun shone brightly on the Diplomatic Quarter in Riyadh. General Rashood and Colonel Gamoudi had elected to dine at one of the best Italian restaurants in the city, Da Pino, in the Al Khozama Centre, next to the Al Khozama Hotel on Olaya Street.

Once a great favourite of Saudi Arabia's ruling class, who had formerly all belonged to one family, Da Pino was now hitting very hard times, and it was easier to book a table than it had ever been. Of course, if General Rashood and Colonel Gamoudi had wished, the King would have bought it for them. However, that evening a simple dinner would suffice.

Their chauffeur drove them into the city from the Diplomatic Quarter and it was then that General Rashood caught his first glimpse of a black Citroën driving behind them before they were out of King Khalid Road. He could just see it through the passenger side mirror, and, while he was not particularly curious, he did notice the vehicle was driving up close and at one point refused to allow a white van to drift in between them.

There was a loud sounding of horns and Ravi turned to see the van driver waving his fist. They turned left at the Makkah Road, and, routinely, Ravi checked to see if the Citroën was still behind them.

It was, but as these were two of the busiest streets in Riyadh there was nothing unusual in that. However when they made their turn into Al Amir Soltan Street, Ravi was watching and he saw that the Citroën was still sticking to them closely. They sped under the big overhead junction with King Fahd Road and took the third left into the wide boulevard of Olaya Street.

They pulled up on the right-hand side, where there was ample parking space; the chauffeur would wait there until they had finished dinner. Both men climbed out on the right side, and Ravi watched the Citroën drive past and make a slow right on to Al Amir Mohammed Road. He did not give the car a second thought.

That evening they found themselves at the next table to Colonel Bandar, liberator of the Riyadh television stations, who was dining with his family. He and Jacques Gamoudi silently toasted each other with fruit juice, and introductions were made.

They all left, more or less together, just after 10 p.m., and Ravi and Jacques walked quickly through the precincts of the Al Khozama Hotel and out into the fresh night air. The chauffeur waved to them from across the street, and they stood chatting on the pavement waiting for the stream of traffic to pass.

Finally it was clear and they stepped out into the right-hand near lane, in which the traffic approached from the left. Still talking, they had set off across the boulevard when Ravi heard the squeal of tyres on blacktop, from the left, no more than 100 yards away. He stopped instinctively, but Jacques Gamoudi kept going.

Ravi turned to see an approaching vehicle which must have made zero to 60 in four seconds. Through his mind flashed the thought *black Citroën*. And he could see it bearing down on them, the driver clearly with his foot flat on the boards.

He jumped two steps forward, and, with an outrageous display of strength, he twisted, wrapped his left forearm around the throat of *Le Chasseur* and hurled him backwards. Jacques Gamoudi's head hit the ground first, then his shoulder blades.

For a split second the ex-French Foreign Legionnaire thought he was a dead man. Another half-second and he would have been. The front wheels of the Citroën brushed the soles of his feet, 18 inches off the ground, as it roared past.

Ravi leapt back on to his feet and he heard the brakes of the Citroën shriek as it skidded to a halt. For a moment he thought the driver was slamming the gears into reverse and that the car was coming back for them. They were sitting targets, all but in the middle of the road, with Jacques Gamoudi still prostrate, trying to clear his head from the almighty bang he had taken when he hit the road.

But no. The Citroën was stopped dead, but the

rear door on the right side was opening and Ravi could see the tip of a rifle, then he saw their assailant's face, a dark hard-eyed unshaven thug. Ravi Rashood, the master unarmed combat soldier from the SAS, did not hesitate.

He raced towards the car, and, with a thunderous right-footed kick which would not have disgraced a French Rugby Union fullback, he almost took the man's head off, snapped his neck and broke his jaw in seven places. The rifle, a primed AK-47, clattered to the ground and Ravi had time to grab it before the driver of the vehicle was out of the left front door and around the car holding an identical weapon.

Ravi had no time to aim or fire. But he did have time to ram the butt into the man's face. It was a vicious, high-stabbing blow delivered like a harpoonist within reach of his whale.

The blow smashed into the centre of the assassin's forehead, but he was still standing, still holding the AK-47. Now it was too late, however. Ravi was on him. He sidestepped the rifle and came over the top, planting the fingers of his left hand deep into the man's long curly hair. Simultaneously, he rammed the butt of his right palm with inhuman force into the base of the hooked Gallic nose which had briefly helped its owner look so menacing.

Ravi's blow had travelled more than a foot. And it packed unbelievable power as it exploded into the man's nostrils. It killed him stone dead, driving the nose bone into the brain, the classic combat blow of the British-trained Special Forces soldier.

456

Jacques Gamoudi sat up groggily, just in time to see his colleague kill the second of their attackers. It was the street fight to end all street fights. One kick, one hit, one uppercut. One dead, one dying. All in the middle of passing traffic.

'Not too bad,' said Colonel Gamoudi, shaking his head and grinning at the same time, 'for a guy who prefers fighting in royal palaces.'

Ravi, who was already gesticulating to the chauffeur to come and get them out of there, just said, 'Christ, Jacques. That was no accident. Someone out there is trying to kill us. And I have a feeling they want you more than they want me. You probably noticed the French car, French registration, and that second little bastard smelled like a fucking vat of garlic.'

'Try not to impugn my nationality with your English public school prejudices,' replied Jacques. 'Yes, we use a little *ail* for the flavour, but that does not make us *malodorant*.'

'Silence, Gamoudi,' said Ravi, as he hauled the French officer to his feet, 'otherwise I'll make you salute me every time I save your life. That's the second time in a week.'

'*Mon Dieu!*' replied Gamoudi, in mock exasperation. 'Where would I be without you?'

'At a guess, I'd say dead behind that serving counter in the royal palace,' chuckled General Rashood. 'Now, try to shut up, and get in the back of that car, will you – and don't get blood all over the head rest or the King will be very unhappy . . . Ahmed, give me some of those paper towels; the colonel has whacked his head.'

'I don't think his head hurts so bad as those guys' heads,' shrugged the chauffeur, passing the tissues and nodding at the two stricken assassins, one of whom was still breathing just inside the rear door. The other was lying dead below the Citroën boot.

'Probably not,' agreed General Rashood.

Ahmed took off, speeding back to the big white house on the edge of the Diplomatic Quarter. And there the two men sat on the wide rear veranda, sipping fruit juice and reflecting that perhaps Riyadh was no longer the place for either of them. Tomorrow morning they would both suggest to King Nasir that their task had been accomplished, that it was time for them to go home.

The trouble was, that little incident on Olaya Street had sown a seed of doubt in Jacques Gamoudi's mind. For a man who had spent most of his military career on the edge of violence he was nonetheless shaken by the realisation that he had just been the intended victim of a deliberate hit and run; and, when that had failed, the target of assassins armed with AK-47s. He had no idea who might be at the head of it; a man who lived as he did also lived with the threat of extinction at any moment.

His mind went back to his meeting with the two men from Paris in the Pyrenees. No reason to suspect them of foul play. But had he missed something then? Had he not expressed his loyalty to his country? Had he asked for too much in return? The money had not appeared to be a problem. No, it was absurd. What was he thinking? What about the King? Had he decided that the presence of one of the men who had put him on the throne was no longer in his best interests, was too much of a potential embarrassment? Again, it did not add up. Who then?

Whatever the case, both Rashood and Gamoudi knew that they both had to leave Riyadh. But the question was, where was Gamoudi to take refuge? He could not stay in the Middle East: too uncertain. And, despite reason telling him that the French Government could not have been implicated in the incident that evening, the instinct that he had always trusted told him that he could not go back to France: too dangerous. The French Secret Service knew where to find him; they had already pulled out the five men they had assigned to him, and they knew his haunts. They would hunt him down. It was not a situation *Le Chasseur* liked and it was not a role to which he was accustomed.

1800, the following day,
Friday 2 April
National Security Agency, Fort Meade, Maryland
'Right on time,' said Jimmy Ramshawe as he stared at the new pictures arriving online from the National Surveillance Office. The shots showed the navy base at France's old Indian Ocean colony of La Réunion. And there, tucked neatly into the submarine pens,

was the newly arrived Rubis Class hull number S605, the *Améthyste*. Out of sight for three weeks, since it had dived just south of the Gulf of Suez, but rarely out of mind. At least, not Jimmy Ramshawe's.

He had calculated the submarine had come through the Bab al Mandab sometime in the mid-afternoon of Thursday the previous week. And he'd marked his chart at a spot right off the Horn of Africa, the jutting headland of Somalia, where he'd assessed the *Améthyste* would be the previous Friday at midnight.

It was 390 miles across the Gulf of Aden – at 12 knots a 32-hour journey, he told himself. Which left them a straight 2,400-mile run down the deep and lonely Indian Ocean, probably making around 15 knots for six and a half days. On his chart Jimmy had written . . . *looking for the Améthyste in La Réunion sometime in the late evening of Friday 2 April.*

'Actually, the bastard's a few hours early,' he muttered. 'Must have been speeding . . . cheeky bugger.'

And now, he wondered, *how about her mate*? Unseen since she had been logged through Port Said on 4 March, the *Perle* had a longer journey home, through the Gulf. Jimmy's assessment had put hull number S606 well through the Strait of Hormuz the previous Wednesday. So they should have reached the Horn of Africa by Sunday 28 March.

'They got six and a half days in front of them, so I'm looking at an ETA at La Réunion sometime tomorrow evening or early Sunday morning,' he pondered. 'Jesus, if that French bastard shows up on time, for me it's game, set and match. Where the hell else have they been? And why did they both go deep in the Red Sea and stay there? None of the other French submarines making that journey *ever* do that . . . *Arnie, baby, we got 'em,*' he added.

He stared once more at the incontrovertible evidence of the all-seeing eye of the US satellite. There she was in the dockyard at La Réunion, the *Améthyste*, moored alongside her jetty, under the command of Commander Louis Dreyfus, according to the records at Port Said.

It seemed incredible, just to try and understand what she had done . . . obliterated the entire Saudi oil facilities in the Red Sea. But Lt. Commander Ramshawe knew what she had done, and, in his candid opinion, the US Navy would be justified in going right out there and sinking her, no bullshit.

But those decisions would be made by the Big Man now, and Jimmy greatly looked forward to hearing his reaction after the weekend, when it would become clear that the two prime suspects in this still baffling case were sitting in the French dockyard a couple of thousand miles south of the datum.

'They'll be there,' he told himself. 'I bloody know they'll both be there.'

He downloaded the prints and hurried along the corridor to see Admiral Morris, still staring at the satellite shots which, in his opinion, offered irrefutable evidence of French guilt in this worldwide financial horror story.

Admiral Morris studied the prints and nodded sagely. 'It's all starting to fit together, eh, Jim . . . when's the *Perle* due in?'

'Tomorrow evening, or early Sunday morning.'

'Okay, let's not make a report to Admiral Morgan until she arrives. Seems to me a double on Sunday lunchtime is a whole lot better than a single right now at dinnertime on Friday night.'

'We're going to get it, too,' added Jimmy. 'It's all starting to make sense.'

Midday, Saturday 3 April
King Nasir's palace
Riyadh

The King listened gravely to the account of the attempt on Colonel Gamoudi's life on Olaya Street that Thursday night. General Rashood and Jacques had planned to say nothing about the matter, and to make their way carefully out of the country in a few days. But the police had caused the most ridiculous fuss, and some passer-by had taken the number of their car, and Ahmed must have told about 7,000 people what had happened, because the King called Colonel Gamoudi on the Saturday morning and asked that they meet to discuss what had happened.

It quickly became apparent he had no interest in the rights and wrongs of the killings. Two of his most trusted friends had been attacked in the streets of Riyadh, and he was extremely glad things had worked out as they had.

What the King wanted to know was who had attempted to kill his friend. But when he heard the story, as recounted by Ravi, he was inclined to agree with the general's own supposition: that the culprits might have been acting on behalf of the French Government. And he did not approve of that. Not one bit.

Like them, he knew it would be pointless for him to ask the French President. No one would admit to an assassination attempt. But the reality of the incident remained. If the French had decided to take out *Le Chasseur*, they were now up against an extremely powerful enemy.

For King Nasir retained that estimable Bedouin creed of loyalty, honed over thousands of year in the desert. Arabs did not easily or willingly abandon their friends.

And so it was with General Rashood and Colonel Gamoudi. They had put their lives on the line for King Nasir and now they had become his friends. And to him this made them unique in all the world. And he would hear no word against them, and he would protect them for ever, with his life if necessary.

If the French were responsible for this outrage, they would have been wise to find that out about the new King of Saudi Arabia.

And there, in his palace, the King pledged his support for the two men who had spearheaded his revolution. He told Jacques Gamoudi he must plan an escape, and begin, somewhere, a new life.

He, King Nasir, would give him every possible assistance, including a private jet to fly out, to take him wherever he wished.

Colonel Gamoudi was deeply touched. He took the King's hand and thanked him profoundly.

And King Nasir looked him straight in the eye, in the manner of the desert tribes, and said, 'Always remember, Jacques, I am a Bedouin.'

1945, Sunday 4 April
National Security Agency, Fort Meade, Maryland
Captain Alain Roudy had made good time to La Réunion, and Lt. Commander Ramshawe was now looking at photographs of two Rubis Class hunter killers moored alongside the submarine jetties in that tiny island.

'*There* you are, you little bastard,' breathed Jimmy, staring at the close-up shot of the newly arrived *Perle.* 'Right where I bloody knew you'd be.'

He called Admiral Morris, who in turn called Admiral Morgan, and the Supreme Commander of Operation Tanker convened a planning meeting in the White House first thing Monday morning.

It was now plain to everyone that France was behind the overthrow of the Saudi royal family. And Jimmy knew this was probably it. Arnold Morgan was about to take action against the French. But this was a rare occasion when young Ramshawe could not work out which way the admiral would jump.

'One thing's for certain,' he decided. 'He's not

going to sit back and allow the French to get rich, not while half the world's struggling to keep the lights switched on.'

And it was with a heightened sense of anticipation that he arrived at the White House at 0900 on Monday morning. He and Admiral Morris arrived separately, and reported to Arnold's new quarters, where the Chief of Naval Operations, Admiral Alan Dickson, was already in conference, staring at a huge computerised map of France on a wall screen.

Arnold Morgan greeted the men from the NSA both warmly and grimly. 'I've briefed Admiral Dickson,' he said. 'And I think he agrees with me, that, for the President's sake, we have to take some action. In the modern world it is simply impossible for anyone to act with total disregard for the plight of other nations. Especially on something of this scale.

'Now, we are not going to get either an admission or an apology from the French Government. I plan to speak to the French President, but I expect him to deny all knowledge of anything.

'Thus, so far as I can see, we have several missions. One, to ensure they can't just sit back and laugh at everyone else's problems. Two, to expose and then humiliate them in front of the United Nations. Three, to teach them a damned hard lesson.'

Alan Dickson looked as if he was not sure about that. And Arnold instantly caught the doubtful look on his face.

'Alan,' he said, 'we have a very good man in the

Oval Office. He loves the Navy, he trusts us and he never allows anyone to tamper with our budgets. Through no fault of his own he is caught up in a global uproar which could finish him, if he doesn't move, and move swiftly . . .

'I think we owe him our loyalty, our brains, and the muscle of the United States Navy. Because that's the only way he'll survive. He must be seen to be furious, he must be seen to identify the culprit, and, above all, he must be seen to punish the perpetrator of this evil . . .'

Admiral Morris at once mentioned the financial problems afflicting all the big Western stock markets, and, of course, the Japanese Nikkei. An important statement was to be issued by the International Monetary Fund which was holding an emergency meeting in Switzerland later that day.

And all over the United States there were families with strong positions in the blue-chip components which made up the Dow-Jones average, and they were taking savage losses, losses unlikely to be recovered for two years, until the Saudi oil came back on stream.

'As of this moment, I am going to regard Saudi oil as a global asset,' said Admiral Morgan. 'I am going to treat the French as if they have committed a crime against humanity. And, quite frankly, I don't actually give a rat's ass what any other country thinks. I am not having the wellbeing of the United States of America jeopardised by any other nation. *AND THAT'S FINAL.*'

It sure as hell was final in that particular White House office. All three of Admiral Morgan's visitors nodded in agreement. Even Admiral Dickson, whose patriotism had just been given a sharp wake-up call.

They waited for Arnold Morgan's next jackhammer blow. And each of them stood prepared for some kind of an onslaught. But when the Supreme Commander of Operation Tanker spoke, he spoke quietly, and thoughtfully.

'I am proposing to deploy a US Navy blockade outside every French port which imports foreign oil. That includes Le Havre, at the mouth of the Seine. It contains the largest oil refinery in France at Gonfreville l'Orcher.

'Marseilles, in the south, handles 30 per cent of France's crude oil refining. There's a big terminal at Fos-sur-Mer, a Shell refinery at Berre, TotalFinaElf are in a place called La Mede, BP operate in Lavera, and Exxon uses Fos. Marseilles imports a vast amount of methane, and close to the port there's a massive underground storage facility for liquid petroleum gas; a lot of it used to be from Ra's al Ju'aymah. But the French have, of course, now made other arrangements.

'We also have to look closely at the six oil terminals in Bordeaux along the Gironde Estuary at Pauillac and Ambes – that's a major plant for liquid chemicals.

'The final spot is Brest, which as we all know is a long harbour containing the main French Navy base. But there's also a considerable oil terminal in there, which takes both crude and LPG.

'Gentlemen, I intend to place United States warships at the entrances to all four of these seaways. I realise this will only work in the short term, because France will arrange overland supplies through Luxembourg and Germany. The Belgians will also help them out since they are considerable partners in the TotalFinaElf conglomerate.

'Nonetheless, the short term will be very miserable for them. Starve those ports of oil, and the place will swiftly run dry. In the long term they'll overcome it. But right now I care only for the short term.'

'Arnie,' said Admiral Dickson, 'I realise this is purely academic. But France has a very dangerous Navy, with many ships in both Brest and Marseilles. Have you considered the possibility they may come out and attack our ships?'

'No, I haven't,' rasped the admiral. 'They wouldn't dare.'

'What if they did?'

'Sink 'em, of course. Remember, we are acting as the world's policeman, and the world is going to give its approval for us to do anything we damn well please. By the time the President has made a statement outlining the disgraceful role played by France in the current crisis, there won't be a nation on earth which disapproves of our actions.'

'I agree; attacks on policemen are generally frowned upon by law-abiding citizens. But I wonder whether we might not overplay our hand if we actually opened fire on a French warship?' Admiral

468

Dickson was slipping into an extremely practical mode.

'I would not be concerned about that. Because we would immediately issue a detailed statement about the goddamned mayhem France perpetrated on the Saudi oil installations. Our drift would be, they asked for all they get.'

Lt. Commander Ramshawe spoke next. 'Sir,' he said, 'do you have any plans to act immediately, rather than wait for the slow-burn of the blockade?'

'Funny you should mention that,' replied the admiral. 'Because as a matter of fact I do. But first I would like to brief you on the situation on the Riviera. For years France has been rolling in Saudi cash all along that coastline.

'Dozens of those young princes have kept huge motor yachts at places like Cannes, Nice and Monte Carlo. It's been nothing short of a gravy train for the French. And in turn they, of course, are swift to point out that only the French seaports can provide the level of civilised living the royal princes require.

'I thought perhaps we might humiliate France in front of the whole world, by blowing up the entire contents of those harbours.'

'Christ,' said Jimmy, 'There'd be hell to pay in reparations and God knows what else.'

'Not if no one had the slightest idea who'd done what to whom,' replied Arnold.

'Are you talking US Navy SEALs?' asked Admiral Morris.

'Yes, George. I am. And those blasts on the big pleasure yachts might be the only shots fired in this little war, but they'll cause more embarrassment to France than any other course of action we could possibly take. I also plan to check out the Gulf of St-Malo in the north. But it's only interesting if there are a lot of big foreign boats in there.

'Either way, there will be huge claims for compensation from the yacht owners. And France will have to pay, a long time before the claims reach Lloyd's of London, if indeed there is any coverage to protect people from an act of war.'

'By that time, the President will naturally have made his broadcast and blamed France for the events in Saudi Arabia?' asked Admiral Morris.

'Correct,' replied Arnold. 'And the hatred against the French will be so great among so many countries, no one will know which nation committed the atrocities in the French harbours.'

'I guess some of them will suspect the USA.'

'So they might,' said Admiral Morgan. 'But no one will know, and we'll admit nothing. And I'll tell you something else . . . most people will think it serves 'em right.'

Admiral Morris had been swept away by Arnold's arguments. He was just as angry as the Admiral for France's blatant disregard for human life, but what Arnie was suggesting was untenable. 'Listen Arnold,' he said, 'I think I know what you're doing. You're trying to provoke us into action by suggesting the most outrageous thing we could do to France. I'm not saying that I don't agree with you – an eye for an eye . . .'

There were murmurs of accord around the table.

'But we need to show ourselves as the better party here. If it ever came out that we bombed one of their harbours,' Arnold tried to interrupt Admiral Morris, who held up his hand to stop him doing so, 'I know you think that it's unlikely to come out as us, but it's *possible*, and we will look just as bad as France. We can't afford to do that.'

Arnold conceded this point. It didn't stop him from being as angry as he ever had been, but he knew he must focus his anger and put that energy into the task at hand. 'In that case,' he said to the table, 'I want to assess the possibilities of finding our friend Major Gamoudi.'

'Could I just ask what we're going to do if and when we find him?' asked George Morris.

'Sure,' said Arnold. 'We're going to kidnap him.'

'*Kidnap him?*'

'Well, he sure as hell won't want to show up of his own accord and tell us all he knows, will he?'

'Probably not. But we can't just snatch him, can we?'

'Why the hell not? Right there we're probably looking at the man who murdered our esteemed friend the King of Saudi Arabia. He'd be one of the most wanted men in the world. But we don't care what he's done. We want him to stand right up there in front of the United Nations Assembly and admit that France paid him to overthrow the King.'

'You think he'll do that?'

'I don't think he has much choice. Plainly he's a man who could be charged with anything, and we know he stormed the royal palace in Riyadh. Charlie Brooks sent us a photograph of him in the lead tank.'

'What I'm hoping is, the French make an attempt on his life, as I'm certain they will. And then we can rush in and pick him up.

'That way he'll be damn glad to shop his treacherous employers, and save his own skin by rowing in with us.'

'Well,' said Admiral Morris, 'he won't be able to return to France, will he?'

'Not likely,' replied Arnold. 'Which means we also have to get his wife and family out of the goddamned Pyrenees where she's holed up, because, if we don't, she'll be as good as a hostage. And Jacques, being the kind of man he is, may prefer to die, to save her and the kids from the malevolence of his own government.'

'How the hell are we ever going to know if France has attempted to assassinate him?' muttered Jimmy Ramshawe. 'We don't even know where he is at the moment. He was in Riyadh a week ago, but a week's a long time in the assassination game.'

At that moment, Kathy's assistant secretary tapped and looked around the door. 'Sir, there's an urgent call for Lt. Commander Ramshawe from one of our envoys in Saudi Arabi . . . would he like to take it in the outside office?'

The lieutenant commander climbed to his feet, nodding in agreement and stepped out of Admiral Morgan's new White House headquarters. He sat down at a spare desk in the outer room, and said, 'Ramshawe speaking.'

'Jimmy, it's Charlie Brooks. I'm on the encrypted line, but I'm calling because I think something very interesting happened here last Thursday night.

'There was an incident on Olaya Street, one of the main thoroughfares in Riyadh. Two men were killed in a street fight. At least, they were both dead when the police arrived, one of 'em half in the car, a big Citroën, Paris-registered. The other guy was lying behind it. They both carried Kalashnikovs and witnesses say they were killed by the man who appeared to be their intended victim.'

Jimmy listened intently at the other end of the line.

'Well, we have a few contacts at the Saudi police. For a couple of days they carried out regular investigations, just as if it was a normal killing. And, according to our man, the investigation was stopped on the direct orders of the King Apparently, the car which drove the killer away was a royal car, registered to the royal family.

'And the police say that there were two men in the car. One of them was Colonel Jacques Gamoudi. Eyewitnesses say that the Citroën tried to run both men down in the middle of the street. It missed them and that's when the fun started. Both men were killed in unarmed combat, not a shot fired.

473

Not a pretty sight apparently; one of them choked to death with a broken neck, the other had his nose rammed into his brain.'

'Jesus,' said Jimmy Ramshawe.

'And here's something else interesting. One of the eyewitnesses was a known ex-Saudi officer, a Colonel Bandar, fanatically loyal to the new King. He identified Gamoudi; said he'd served under him during the action in Riyadh. The other guy was the commander of the King's assault team in the south, the guy who took Khamis Mushayt. But he didn't know his name.'

Jimmy Ramshawe said, 'This is a very important call, Charlie. One more thing: do you have copies of any witness statements to the Saudi police?'

'Sure, I could fax them. But there's no room for doubt. That was Gamoudi all right. Don't know who his associate was, though. And the police have suddenly become real sensitive. Just an hour ago they would tell me nothing. They acted kinda scared. I guess Nasir's men are flexing a little muscle.'

'You may be right, Charlie. Stay in touch, will you? This is very important.'

Jimmy Ramshawe returned to the admiral's office and told his three superiors what he had just learned from Riyadh. It didn't take them long to come to a very useful conclusion indeed: that, far from it being some random street fight, the incident in Riyadh that night had been an assassination attempt on the life of Jacques Gamoudi.

Furthermore, the way the two would-be assassins had died shed a bright light on the identification of the other man present in the royal car as it had sped from the scene. Describing graphically the way they had met their deaths, Lt. Commander Ramshawe turned to Arnold Morgan. 'That got a familiar ring to it, sir?'

'You mean our old friend Major Ray Kerman, who specialises in such methods?'

'Our old friend Ray Kerman, sir, who flew into Paris last August, and was hunted down by Mossad to a restaurant in Marseilles which is now under the protection of the local gendarmes.'

'That's the guy, Jimmy. You think we just found out who he was with dining that night?'

'Absolutely, sir. One dollar gets you one hundred Ray Kerman and Jacques Gamoudi shared a bowl of *buoybase* that night.

'It's the specialty dish of Marseilles, sir,' he added confidently.

'Which is all the more reason why you should avoid making it sound like a submarine anchorage,' replied Arnold. '*BOUILLABAISSE, BOY! BOUILLABAISSE!*'

He still sounded like Homer Simpson doing his Maurice Chevalier, but both Arnold Morgan and Jimmy Ramshawe knew that right now the noose was tightening around the throat of the French Government.

CHAPTER ELEVEN

0900, Monday 5 April
The White House

Admiral Alan Dickson, the 56-year-old former Commander-in-Chief of the US Navy's Atlantic Fleet, was not wildly looking forward to the next 10 minutes.

As the current Chief of Naval Operations, he was about to inform Arnold Morgan he considered it too dangerous a mission to try and blockade the five major French seaports at Le Havre, Cherbourg, Brest, Bordeaux and Marseilles.

First of all, it would take half the US Atlantic Fleet of submarines to be in any way effective. Secondly, the French Navy might elect to come out and fight a sea battle. Thirdly, it would cost more money than World War II.

Admiral Dickson felt like the movie mogul who made the catastrophic loss-making film *Raise the Titanic!* – and afterwards commented *I could have lowered the Atlantic for less!*

Nonetheless, Admiral Morgan was not going to love this.

There was a chill early spring wind outside, cutting through the nation's capital, and Admiral Dickson, a heavy-set former destroyer CO in the Gulf War, still had his hands in the pockets of his greatcoat. One of them clutched the little notebook he carried everywhere, with its minute details of US Navy fleet deployments, written in his tiny, near-calligraphic hand.

The frown creasing his forehead seemed stark on skin the colour of varnished leather. But Alan Dickson was an old seadog, a man of strict, disciplined method from the New England city of Hartford. And he knew that Arnold Morgan, in this instance, was whistling Dixie. Okay. Right now Admiral Morgan had the power to do anything he damn pleased . . . but not in this man's Navy.

Alan Dickson could see war on the horizon. And while he most certainly wanted to ram an American hardboot straight up the ass of the pompous, arrogant French, he did not savour the prospect of the US Navy being hit back by probably the most efficient Navy in Europe.

Admiral Dickson knew all about the fighting capacity of the French, their hotshot modern guided-missile frigates and destroyers, their powerful fleet of submarines, and their two fast and well-equipped carriers. And he had no intention of tangling with them.

He also knew he was one of the few people in this world to whom Admiral Morgan would listen. He further knew the admiral was not a dogmatic man, but if you wished him to change course a few degrees, you'd better be heavily armed with facts, facts and more facts. Alan Dickson was certain he had 'em.

'Please go through now,' said Kathy Morgan's secretary. 'I assume you would like coffee with the Admiral?'

'Thank you,' replied Admiral Dickson as he began the short walk towards Arnold Morgan's gundeck.

'Morning, Alan,' said the occupant, without looking up from a chart of the approaches to the port of Le Havre, on the northern shore of the Seine Estuary.

'Worries the hell out of me, Alan,' he said. 'No goddamned deep water for 20 miles outside the main shipping channel – least, not deep enough to hide a submarine . . . it's gonna be hard. But we'll find a way.'

'Sorry, Arnold. I didn't quite catch that. Which port are you looking at?'

'Oh, yeah, Le Havre . . . right here on the coast of Normandy . . . in a sense, this is the big one for us . . . this is where Gonfreville l'Orcher is located, the biggest oil refinery in France.

'See it . . . right here, Alan . . . on this peninsula between these two canals . . . sonofabitch must be two miles wide . . . look at this . . . gasoline all along the north shore, this huge petrochemical complex on the south side. Starve that of crude for a few weeks . . . you got one dry-hole country.'

Arnold Morgan had never quite lost his south Texas roots.

Admiral Dickson shifted his weight from his right foot to his left. And he was grateful when Kathy Morgan herself drifted through the door carrying the coffee tray, one silver pot, two mugs, sugar, cream and a blue tube of buckshot.

'Hello, Alan,' she said. 'Nice to see you again. Black? As usual?'

'Thanks, Kathy.'

She poured two mugs of incineratingly hot coffee, the way Arnold liked it, fired two bullets into Arnold's mug; that was the one on the left, which sported an inscription in black letters which read, *SILENCE! Genius at work*, and retreated to the outer office.

'Sir,' said Admiral Dickson, seizing the bull by the horns, or at least the genius by the tail, 'it is my considered opinion that a blockade on the big French ports, would be too difficult, too dangerous and too expensive.'

Right now Arnold was somewhere along the buoyed channel, 10 miles west of Le Havre, trying to maintain periscope depth. 'Uh-huh,' he responded, half-listening, half-blowing all kingstons.

Then the shock of the CNO's words seemed to hit home. And for a moment he was speechless. He looked up. 'Did you just say what I thought you just said,' he grated.

'Yessir.'

'Well, what the hell are you talking about? I thought we all agreed our plan of action, for the President to come out and accuse France of treachery, and then to blockade her, while we're still safe in the protection of solid world opinion. Isn't that right?'

'Yessir. But I thought about it some more. A lot more. And in my view it's a very shaky plan.'

'Alan, you and I have known each other for many years. Don't tell me you're losing your nerve?'

'Nossir. I'm not at all. But when you finish looking at these charts, as I've been doing for most of the night, you're going to see problems turning up every which way.

'You've already located one of them. The vast expanse of shallow water which surrounds the port of Le Havre. I presume you would like to maintain an element of secrecy, rather than charging into the attack on the surface like a modern-day Hornblower?'

'Alan, I want you to stand there and methodically, logically, destroy my plan. That way, if I agree with you, we can get going and start again. I don't want to hear it in a disjointed way. You said, I think, *too difficult, too dangerous and too expensive*. Lay it on me in that order. And for Christ's sake stop calling me sir.'

Admiral Dickson could take an order as sharply as he could issue one. 'Arnie,' he said, 'each of the seaports involves a wide sprawling target. It's impossible, as you well know, to blockade with just one ship, even if it is a submarine. I admit you could do it, *IF* you went right ahead and sank something immediately, thus frightening the bejaysus out of everyone. But I think we should avoid that kind of first-strike violence in French waters.

'So we'd probably want two submarines at each place, Le Havre, Cherbourg, Bordeaux, Brest and Marseilles. That's 10 Los Angeles Class SSNs from the Atlantic Fleet, most of them stationed well offshore because of the depth.

'We would need back-up on the surface, mainly so that the French could see we meant business. That would probably mean five frigates and five destroyers from our bases on the East Coast. Plus two or three fleet oilers if we want them to work for several weeks.

'And even then the operation would only work off Cherbourg and Le Havre. There's a substantial French Navy presence in the port of Brest, and there's always French warships off the coast of Marseilles. Bordeaux is probably worse, because the biggest French Navy firing ranges are positioned all along that stretch of Atlantic coast and there are French warships all over the place almost all of the time.

'We'd certainly need, at the very minimum, say, six surface ships off those three places, if we want an intimidating presence.

'Arnie, in case you hadn't noticed . . . that's more than 30 US warships . . .'

'It's 35. And I had, asshole.'

Alan Dickson laughed. But he pressed on. 'My next point is the danger element,' he said, lightly. 'And, again, in case you hadn't noticed, the French have a very formidable, very modern, well-trained Navy.'

'I had, supreme asshole.'

'Well, Arnie,' continued the CNO, 'consulting my little black book here, I would like you to consider the following facts . . . the French Navy runs two carriers . . . one for fixed-wing aircraft . . . one for helicopters.'

'Right now they're both in Brest,' replied Admiral Morgan. 'The *Charles de Gaulle* with 20 Super Etendards boarded, and the *Jeanne d'Arc* with a lot of helicopters.'

'Excellent,' said Admiral Dickson. 'Which brings me to the submarine force. The French run 12 of them, all very efficiently. There are six Rubis Class attack submarines currently operational, plus two strategic missile ships, and four Triomphant Class SSBNs.

'They also have 13 operational destroyers, all of them armed with heavy arsenals of guided missiles. The latest Exocets. They run 20 guided missile frigates, stuffed with Exocets, some of them carrying the new extended range missile, the MM40 Block 3, which is probably the world's foremost anti-ship missile.'

'Is that the one with the new air-breathing turbojets, instead of the old rocket motors?' asked Arnold.

'That's right,' said Admiral Dickson. 'Damn thing flies 100 nautical miles.'

'And at high speed, I read,' replied Arnold. 'Just subsonic, but fast. Can we take it out?'

'Maybe. But it's capable of complex flight profiles. And good enough for land attack.'

'Damn thing. I guess we don't want to fool with it, unless we have to.'

'No, Arnie. We don't want to do that. And in my view it's not necessary.'

Admiral Morgan nodded, unsmiling. 'Are we ready to talk expense . . . ?'

'No. Not quite. I just wanted to throw in a couple of points about the French military philosophy. As you know, they have always retained total independence. They build their own ships, missiles and fighter aircraft. They always have. For them it's always France. Nothing else. And they're pretty damned good at it.

'It is my opinion that if we sink a French warship right off their own coast, they would fight back, probably with that damned missile. And it would not be the greatest shock in the world if they hit and destroyed a couple of our own frigates . . . And what do you want to do then? Bomb the Arc de Triomphe?'

'No.' said Arnold. 'No. I really don't.'

'Well, then I guess we have to think again. Because to my mind it's just too reckless for us to blockade France and start sinking ships. They're just a little too strong for that.'

'And ain't that a goddamned lesson for the left-wing assholes in our own precious Congress,' growled Arnold. 'In serious international discussion, even we, 100 times stronger than almost all the other nations put together, do not much want to mix it with the French.

483

'And why? Because we know they have the capacity to hit back a little too hard. And what's more they are proud enough to do it. And we do not want to get involved with such an operation. That's the precise philosophy that's kept this nation safe from foreign invasion for so long. No one wants to tangle with our military. We're just too tough.'

'I agree with you,' said Admiral Dickson. 'Which still leaves us with the problem of how to deal with the French. And it's not easy. Because once President Bedford has made his speech, and hopefully lined up the rest of the world on our side, someone needs to do something.'

'You got any suggestions?' asked Arnold. 'I know you would not have come in here on a purely destructive mission.'

'Arnie, I think we gotta hit the French oil industry at source.'

'You do?'

'Sure I do. As we know, they have replaced most of their Saudi crude oil and LPG contracts with other Gulf States. And that's their Achilles heel. That stretch of coastline is where the really big reserves are found – Abu Dhabi has an oil economy like Saudi Arabia, Kuwait has the second largest crude reserves on earth and Qatar's north gas field is the biggest LPG source in the world.

'And that's where the French have gone. And that means French-owned VLCCs moving very swiftly through the Strait of Hormuz. In my opinion, Arnie, we should take out one French VLCC right there

484

in the southern part of the Strait. Smack it hard with a torpedo. No one will know what the hell's happened.'

'Then what?' asked Arnold.

'We park a submarine at the south end of the Red Sea and wait for one of those big gas carriers to come steaming in from Qatar, en route back to Marseilles, and we whack that one as well. Then the French will know they're in trouble. But they will not be certain who their enemy is.'

'And then?' asked Arnold.

'Well, I'd guess the French will get very haughty about the entire thing. But will say nothing. Not with the whole world ranged against them. But the next French VLCC to come trundling out through the Strait of Hormuz will be escorted by one of those brand new Horizon Class destroyers which, as we speak, is with a French flotilla exercising out in the northern Arabian Sea . . .'

'Interesting,' said Arnie. 'Outstanding research. I like it already. Then what?'

'We slam the escort with a torpedo. You know, a new heat-seeking ADCAP. It'll go straight for the props. Probably blow off the stern. Put her on the bottom.'

'Beautiful,' replied Arnie. 'Then what?'

'In deference to world opinion on ocean pollution, we sink the tanker with a battery of Harpoon missiles. That way we'll set her on fire and the oil will burn instead of making a huge slick all over the goddamned Strait.'

'Yeah. I like it,' said Arnie. 'The assassin with a heart, right?'

'Yes. That's us. And that'll do it. The French will have been hit by an unseen enemy. The world will laugh. And there'll be a dozen suspects as to who committed the crime. But the French will not try again to bring oil out of the Gulf, because they will know what's likely to happen.

'And they will not want to lose another of their magnificent Horizons. So they'll just have to forget imported oil from the Gulf for a bit. Much like the rest of us.

'And, meantime, Arnie, we have to get ahold of Colonel Gamoudi and his family, and get 'em out of harm's way. Then we can hang the French out to dry in front of the United Nations.'

Admiral Morgan stood up. 'You win, old buddy,' he said. 'You're correct on all fronts. My damn plan was exactly what you say: too difficult, too dangerous and too expensive.'

'Don't beat up on yourself, Arnie,' grinned Alan Dickson. 'Every plan has to start somewhere. And you made everyone think . . . get world opinion straight, then slam the Frogs. It's just that much better to do it fast, do it hard and do it in secret. That way we answer to no one.'

Admiral Morgan grinned what he described on others as a 'shit-eating grin' and said silkily, 'We have no idea who hit the French tankers, or their destroyer, but there sure are a lot of suspects . . . heh, heh, heh.'

'If it's okay with you,' said the CNO, 'I'd like to get back to the Pentagon. We got two CVBGs in the area, one off Kuwait, another in the northern Arabian Sea. I'll have the two SSNs come down the Gulf and take up station way down the Strait of Hormuz. The second group can make its way south to Diego Garcia, and the SSNs can peel off into the Gulf of Aden.'

'You okay leaving the carrier without SSN escort?'

'Just for a few days. We'll send two more back in there from DG. That group's on station for another three months.'

'Okay. Sounds pretty damn good to me, Alan. So you may as well get outta here, and on the way out tell Kathy to have Lt. Commander Ramshawe come over right away.'

The CNO nodded and turned towards the door. As he opened it, Admiral Morgan looked up and said suddenly, 'Hey, Alan.'

Admiral Dickson turned around. And Arnold Morgan just said, 'Thanks for that. I'm grateful.'

And all the way along the corridor to the West Wing entrance, the admiral pondered the man in the new office. *In some ways he's the easiest man in the world to get along with . . . never misjudges real logic . . . never minds backing down . . . I suppose he's just not threatened. Doesn't mind being wrong. He's too damn big to care.*

Twenty minutes later, Arnold Morgan roared through the solid wood door . . . '*MRS MORGAN – WHERE THE HELL'S RAMSHAWE . . . ?*'

Kathy Morgan entered the office. 'I should think he's just leaving the beltway,' she said. 'But since I am not currently employed as a State Trooper, I have no way of knowing the precise location of his Jaguar.

'But he is on his way. I spoke to him within two minutes of your last instruction.'

'Too slow,' said Arnold. 'Empires have collapsed on delays like that.'

'So have marriages,' she replied, stalking out of the room, leaving her husband guffawing into his chart of the Strait of Hormuz.

Ten minutes later, a slightly dishevelled Lt. Commander Ramshawe hurried into the office.

'Morning, sir,' he said, dumping a pile of papers on to the large table at the end of the room.

'Where the hell have you been?' replied Arnold.

'Mostly making around 80 mph around the beltway,' said the lieutenant commander.

'Not fast enough.'

'The speed limit is 60, sir,' said Jimmy.

'Not for us, kiddo. We have no limits, neither speed, finance, bravery or daring.'

'What if a traffic cop stopped me?'

'Firing squad,' said Arnold. 'Soon as we locate his next of kin.'

'Yessir.'

'Right. Now come over here and gimme the items in order of importance we want the President to stress tonight, the stuff that makes France look bad . . .'

'Okay, sir. Mind if I start in sequential order first? Then you can decide importance.'

'Eighty miles an hour is a high speed to attend a debate . . . facts, James, facts. Lay 'em right on me.'

'Right, sir. Twenty-seventh of August. Mossad tries to take out Major Kerman in Marseilles. Question: what's the world's most wanted Arab terrorist doing in France under government protection?

'Mid-November. We notice France apparently getting out of her Saudi oil contracts, driving up the price of oil futures. As if they knew what was going to happen.

'March. The submarines coming through Suez and disappearing. The only submarines which could have hit the Saudi oil installations.

'Twenty-second of March. The Brits pick up the signal from northern Riyadh in French, transmitted requesting permission 'to go to the party early'.

'Late March. We receive photographs of the ex-French Special Forces commander Colonel Gamoudi leading the attack on the royal palace in Riyadh, in which the King is murdered. We trace Gamoudi to his home in the Pyrenees. He's a French national, living permanently in France, with a French wife and French children.

'Same time. The French attempt to assassinate him in Riyadh, when he's with the same Major Kerman, who we now believe led the attack on the Saudi military base in Khamis Mushayt.

'Last week, the new King awards all rebuilding contracts to France.

'Same time, the submarines arrive back in the French base at La Réunion. All mileages, times and distances tally with the fact they opened fire on the Saudi coastline. No other suspects.'

Arnold Morgan looked up from his notes. 'Perfect, Jimmy. I actually think it's better for the President to go in sequential order. Makes it easier to follow, and adds a certain amount of tension to the unfolding mystery.'

'I'm with you on that,' said Jimmy.

'Okay. Now you sit there and I'll write the speech in longhand. I'll want you there at all times as I come upon difficult bits, right?'

'Okay, sir. I'll get the documents in order so I'm ready to front up, on demand. No bullshit, right?'

'No bullshit,' Arnold responded. 'But go out and tell Kathy to inform the President he will broadcast live at 7 p.m. this evening.'

'Right away, sir. How about the speech-writers, sir? Do we need anything from them?'

'Frustrated poets,' said Arnold, gruffly. 'Tell 'em to send in a typist in two hours.'

7 p.m., Monday 5 April
Briefing Room
The White House
They were prowling now, the pack of newshounds Marlin Fitzwater always referred to as the Lions. The White House Press Corps was gathered at a time which was irritating for the missed-the-edition afternoon newspaper crowd, but frenzy-making for the

network television teams, and pressured for the daily newspapermen with deadlines to meet, questions to ask and stories to write.

The Briefing Room was seething. It was three minutes after seven o'clock, and the 60-odd Lions believed it was long past their feeding time. You could hear their growling out in the West Wing corridors.

To a man and woman, the newspaper Lions believed in their own importance as purveyors of the news which their organisations sold for a few cents a shot. The television reporters settled for the unquestioning general belief in Televisionland that they were indeed the gods of the airwaves.

And right now they all wanted to know why the hell the President was late. Didn't he understand their time was precious? When he kept them waiting, he kept the whole goddamned nation waiting, right?

They guessed the subject would be something to do with Saudi Arabia, since the newspapers had been filled with the repercussions of the military coup in Riyadh for several days. And this afternoon there had been yet another precipitous fall in the Dow and the Nasdaq, and news from the international stock markets was, if anything, worse. Gasoline continued at an all-time high at the pumps, especially in the Midwest.

Suddenly, however, the door behind the dais opened and the President himself walked through, accompanied only by the scowling figure of Admiral Morgan, who glared across the room, as if spoiling for a fight, daring someone to step out of line.

He rarely, if ever, deigned to speak to any member of the media, but his reputation was enormous and he was quick to bite off the head of any offending journalist. And he did not give a damn what they wrote or said about him. President Bedford had insisted Arnold accompany him into the Briefing Room from where he would broadcast tonight, live.

He had been briefed by Arnold, and Arnold alone. His instructions were clear. *You will say only what's on these sheets of paper . . . you will answer nothing from the floor . . . there will be no questions afterwards.*

As Admiral Morgan had himself put it, 'I just want to avoid someone yelling out, "*DO YOU THINK THE PRESIDENT OF FRANCE IS A FAT-ASSED COMMUNIST?*" and you reply jokingly, "I don't entirely disagree with that sentiment." And the headline screams, *PRESIDENT CALLS FRENCH LEADER A FAT-ASSED COMMUNIST.*'

At this point the President conferred briefly with the admiral, and then he stepped up to the dais and the cameras whirred. He faced a phalanx of microphones and a sea of eager but cynical faces, belonging to men and women who were ready to pounce, however limited their knowledge of the subject.

Lions are like that. If they're hungry enough, they'll go for any kill, even if the odds are stacked against them. Members of their breed call it courage, with high moral intent. Arnold Morgan had a more graphic, profane description, meaning . . . well . . . not terribly smart.

'*Good evening,*' said the President. '*I expect many of*

you will have guessed I am speaking tonight on a matter of national emergency. I refer of course to the recent events in Saudi Arabia, which have been responsible for such far-reaching economic issues for most of the free world.

'Now, the Saudi royal family has for many years operated a system of government which was not our idea of democracy. But that burning desert land is situated far away from our own, and has deep tribal traditions and cultures that we cannot hope to understand.

'They are a Kingdom, and a Muslim one at that, and they are not so many generations away from their ancient Bedouin roots. Their ways are not our ways, but they deserve our respect, and I can only say that in various times of international strife the Saudis have been the first to come to our aid.

'Nonetheless, we were aware that all was not well domestically for them, and it was not really a great surprise to students of the region when an armed uprising broke out, the royal family as we knew it was swept from power and a new King installed.

'For them the issue was a fairer system of government, with a fairer share of the wealth beneath the desert going to the people, rather than just to one family. The revolution which many of us expected has finally happened. In the long term, I for one believe it might very well be for the best.

'But tonight I am here to discuss the short term, and the crisis each and every one of us faces at the gas pumps. The severe inflation which is already happening here, in terms of air fares and all forms of travel. And the spiralling costs in electricity.

493

'I assure you this government is doing everything possible to get that under control. And in the coming weeks we will have it under control, as I promised you last week. However, tonight my talk to you has another purpose.

'I wish to inform not just citizens of the United States, but people all over the world, that the Saudi rebellion could not possibly have happened without the compliance of a heavily armed, militarily savvy Western country. And right here, right now, I point the finger at the Republic of France, which has acted in a way many of you may find unforgivable.

'The Saudi Arabian uprising was masterminded by France, executed by France and led by France. The new King was backed by France. The old King was murdered by France. And all to seize an advantage in the international oil markets when Saudi oil comes back on stream.

'I look at France, and I say again, I ACCUSE! Or, if they understand it better, J'ACCUSE!

'My fellow Americans. France did this. And you will no doubt have heard the new King Nasir of Saudi Arabia, in his opening speech, announce that France would receive all of the billion-dollar rebuilding contracts for the Saudi oil installations.'

President Bedford paused and sipped from a glass of water.

'In order that everyone should understand thoroughly how we arrived at our conclusions, I will take you through the sequence of events which led irresistibly to the culprit.

'And the first thing I would like to mention is the level of the Saudi defences around their oilfields and refining complexes. It's heavy. Military. Highly trained.

494

Essentially the Saudis have one principal asset, and that's oil. And they are far from stupid, and they know how to protect that asset.

'The only weapon which could hit those installations is a cruise missile, and it would need to be fired from a submerged submarine, not from the surface, nor from an aircraft. They would have spotted those. But they would not have spotted a submerged launch. And that's what happened. And the Saudis do not own one.

'There were only two submarines anywhere near the Saudi shores at the crucial time. And they were both French. We have their hull numbers, we logged 'em both through the Suez Canal. And we saw them go deep in the Red Sea. But we never saw them again — not until they turned up in the French base right on time having fired their missiles at the Saudi oilfields. WE KNOW WHAT THEY DID.

'And we watched the French buying oil futures last November, we watched them getting out of their Saudi contracts. WE KNOW WHAT THEY DID.

'And we took photographs of the French Special Forces commander who led the attack on the royal palace in Riyadh. We've been to his home in France. We know his name. WE KNOW WHAT HE DID.

'We know the French Government harboured and then hired the most dangerous military commander in the Arab terrorist world. We know the date and the French city where they hired him, to lead the land attack on the big Saudi military bases at Khamis Mushayt. We know his name. WE KNOW WHAT HE DID.

'We heard the last military signal from the Riyadh

commander to his French base — our good friends in the British Army intercepted it and passed it to us within a half-hour. We know what it said. And we know who said it. WE KNOW WHAT HE DID.'

The President paused to let his words, drafted and honed by Arnold Morgan, ring around the room, and, indeed, around the world.

'Many of you listening will consider that this is not the first time the French have stepped out of line with the rest of mankind. And many of you will wonder, too, if there are no lengths to which they will not go in order to remain solidly anti-American. But this time they have gone too far. They have brought the Western world to its knees, financially. But only temporarily. We'll get up.

'Meanwhile, my advisers are considering our position with regard to the French action. Right now we are about ready to declare Saudi oil a global asset. It may be that we, and our principal allies, consider the Saudis no longer competent to act as custodians of that asset. But we expect no cooperation from the French in any form.

'My fellow Americans, I am certain of our ground. I am certain of the very great wrong which has been per-petrated upon the nations of the earth. And I make no apologies for any sentence I have uttered tonight.

'I will take no questions. But I say again to the President and the Government of the Republic of France. WE KNOW WHAT YOU HAVE DONE. AND I ACCUSE . . . I ACCUSE . . . I ACCUSE.'

And with that, the Virginian Democrat Paul Bedford, the 45th President of the United States of America, turned on his heel and walked from the dais, leaving Admiral Morgan to take questions from the floor.

However, the room was in such total uproar that nothing could even be heard, never mind asked or answered. The wire service reporters had stampeded to the back of the room, and within seconds were yelling down their cell phones. The time was 7.20 p.m., a critical time in many newspaper offices. The network television reporters were dying to fire in a question which would portray them on air as focused, wise and far-sighted political observers.

Trouble was, they all went for immortality at the same time and the result was absurd. Nothing short of bedlam. Admiral Morgan shook his head and growled into one of the microphones, 'Either you guys get your goddamned act together and stop behaving like children, or I am leaving.'

That statement was not broadcast on any network. When, finally, the din subsided, someone called out, 'Sir, does the French President know what President Bedford just said?'

Admiral Morgan said, 'For all I know the French President is in the sack, since it's after midnight in Paris. But if he's sitting up in bed watching CNN or something, I guess he heard. We announced President Bedford's prime-time address several hours ago.'

'Sir, do you expect to hear from the French President either tonight or tomorrow?'

'No. Not directly. But I expect the Prime Minister of France to make a statement on behalf of his government, denying any and all involvement in the recent events in Saudi Arabia. I expect him to denounce the United States as perpetrators of a gigantic lie against the French Republic, and to call upon the United Nations to reprimand our UN Ambassador in the strongest possible terms.'

'What do we do then?'

'Shut up, Tommy, willya? Haven't you got enough of a great story without standing there saying, *And then what?* over and over? Jesus, do you guys actually get paid to go through this bullshit?'

That part was not broadcast either, on any network. But it brought a certain hilarity to the proceedings and no one was particularly surprised when the admiral shook his head and said, 'I'm outta this zoo. Go write your stuff.'

Admiral Morgan left the West Wing immediately. Kathy was waiting at the wheel of his beloved Hummer and they made the journey back to Chevy Chase together.

The fire in the study had been prepared, and all Arnold needed to do was light it and turn on the television. Mrs Newgate, their new housekeeper, employed as soon as the Morgans had returned to the White House, announced that dinner would be ready at 8.45 and would the admiral like her to open a bottle of wine?

Arnold replied that the way he felt a case would probably be more appropriate, but he would settle for a bottle of Château l'Hôpital 2000, a modestly priced red Bordeaux.

'And you'd better decant it,' said Arnold. 'Might as well drink it in style . . . Alan Dickson and I just decided not to blow the place up.'

Mrs Newgate's somewhat bewildered reply was lost in the thunder of Arnold's next words. '*JESUS H CHRIST! THAT WAS FAST.*'

At which point, Mrs Newgate, who hardly knew the admiral personally, had not moved, and for a split second she thought he was being sarcastic. But then she saw that his attention was riveted to the television screen where a man in a dark suit and a maroon striped tie was speaking rapidly in French, while a CNN journalist translated into English.

'*. . . and France cannot understand the accusations of the American President . . . our government is completely unaware of any of the actions he attributes to us . . . we know of no French commanders in Saudi Arabia, our submarines make the Suez Canal transit every month . . . there is no mystery . . . we conduct exercises in the Arabian Sea and the Indian Ocean, as they do . . . our base is at La Réunion, theirs is at Diego Garcia . . . there's no difference.*

'*And what is this signal from Riyadh they speak of? What signal? Was it in French? Who says so? And where are these photographs they claim to have? We have never been shown . . . it is absolutely preposterous that the President of the United States should level against us accusations of this nature.*

'*And I assure every citizen of this nation we shall take this matter before the United Nations in New York, and we will demand satisfaction. We will demand an apology. These charges are unfounded, and we deny them most vigorously. I am sure the Americans, with their innate jealousy of France and its civilised standards, would like them to be true. But I am afraid not, Mr President. They are lies. And I end my address as President Bedford ended his. With a repetition, n'est-ce pas? NON! NON! And NON! again.'*

'You go for it, pal,' muttered Arnold Morgan. 'You lying frog-eating bastard.'

At this point, Kathy came into the study bearing a weak, tall Scotch and soda for her husband, the way he liked it. No ice. She glanced at the television and heard the commentator saying: 'And so, the United States stands accused tonight of slandering the Republic of France and will probably have to face the censure of the Security Council of the United Nations.

'A UN spokesmen said a few minutes ago that President Bedford had made many allegations which would be difficult to prove. He added that the Secretary General was most surprised that, as a permanent member of the Security Council, the United States would choose to abuse another permanent member in this way.'

At this point, the anchor man began to turn the newscast over to CNN's United Nations correspondent, who was standing outside in the rain at UN headquarters in New York.

'Thank you, Joe.'

'You're very welcome, Fred. Perhaps you'd outline the procedures we may expect against the United States . . .'

'Be happy to, Joe . . . and I should start by saying these are very grave accusations, and I understand France has already filed a request for an emergency meeting of the Security Council which, under the Charter, must now meet inside the next 24 hours.

'The Security Council is the most powerful body within the United Nations and contains five permanent members, China, France, Russia, the United Kingdom and the United States of America. There are also 10 non-permanent members and for a censure motion to go through I am advised that a straight majority of nine votes would be required. We may assume that the USA and Great Britain will vote No to the French motion, and we may have one or two other supporters.

'However, informed opinion here at UN headquarters suggests the US will lose the vote and very probably be hauled up before the General Assembly, and be very publicly censured for making unsubstantiated allegations against a founding member state.'

'How about we substantiate them, asshole?' muttered Arnold Morgan.

Kathy made her bi-annual objection to his language, saying, 'I do wish you would not use that disgusting word so often . . .'

'Which word is that? France?' asked the admiral.

'No.'

'Well, which word?'

'I will not repeat it.'

'Well, how am I to repent and promise to be

501

better, if I am kept in the dark about the true nature of my crime?'

'You are, of course, impossible . . .' began Kathy.

'Hold it, darling . . . just for a moment . . . please . . . I want to hear what this asshole is trying to say . . .'

Kathy left the room with the words of an apparent asshole ringing in her ears . . . *Make no mistake . . . this is very serious trouble for this Administration.*

The following morning
The Pentagon
They were gathered in the fourth-floor office of Admiral Alan Dickson – Arnold Morgan, Admiral Frank Doran (C–in–C Atlantic Fleet), who had flown up from the Norfolk Naval Yards, and the Chairman of the Joint Chiefs, General Tim Scannell, who had accepted an invitation to sit in on the meeting, even though this was, at present, strictly a Navy issue.

In the opinion of Admiral Morgan the fewer people who knew about this the better. And, as Supreme Commander of Operation Tanker, he took the seat at the head of the table.

'Now, I guess we've all seen the newspapers and listened to the television broadcasts, and understand that the USA is about to come under worldwide attack inside the United Nations. I should tell you that I planned that, because what we are about to do has a good chance of being judged so shocking, no one would dream we were the culprits, since we're in so much trouble already.'

502

There was a murmuring from around the table.

Admiral Morgan continued. 'Gentlemen, we're not in any trouble. France, whatever that Prime Minister says, *did* take down the Saudi King, and it *did* plunge the world economy into crisis. And we are going to do something about it.'

He outlined the plan Admiral Dickson had masterminded. The quick hit on the first tanker carrying French crude oil to come out of the Gulf. Then another hit on the first French tanker to enter the Red Sea through the Bab al Mandab.

'That should slow them down some,' said Arnold. 'But the French are persistent. Admiral Dickson and I think the next French tanker will enter the Strait of Hormuz under escort. And that's when we cause total uproar. We hit the escort first, with a torpedo. Then we hit Tanker Number Three. And that will wrap it right up for France. They will not try to exit the Gulf with fuel oil again until we're good and ready to allow it.'

'Arnie, is this a public operation . . . like we hit and we don't care who knows it?' General Scannell looked concerned.

'Not at this stage,' replied Arnold. 'We'll launch from submarines, way under the surface, and we will not admit what we've done to anyone. We'll just let 'em all have a guessing game.'

'Torpedoes?' asked the CJC.

'Yes. Fired from several miles out. But not in the case of the last tanker. We'll hit that with three or four Harpoons, set the oil on fire, save a lot of pollution.'

'Do you intend to let anyone know it was the US of A which sank the ships?'

'No.'

'I realise this is a kind of naive question to ask in a room full of sailors,' said General Scannell. 'But how do we know if a tanker is full of French oil or not? I thought they were all registered in Liberia or Panama or somewhere. They must all look the same.'

'In a sense, they do, Tim,' replied Admiral Dickson. 'But we've been checking on both the VLCCs and the ULCCs which service France . . .'

'I take it a ULCC is much the same thing as a VLCC, but bigger?'

'Exactly: a VLCC is a very large crude carrier; a ULCC is an ultra large crude carrier, maybe up to 400,000 tons.'

'We gonna hit one of those?'

'Maybe,' said Admiral Dickson. 'But to answer your question about identifying the correct target, we've been researching the TotalFinaElf conglomerate and the methods it uses to move large quantities of oil.

'And much of it is done by a highly reputable corporation based in Luxembourg. It's called TRANSEURO, and they've run a fleet of maybe 14 or 15 tankers for years, under long-term charter to Total, mostly in the 250,000- to 300,000-ton range.

'In the trade they call it French Flag Tonnage. But these tankers ply their trade back and forth from the Gulf to Marseilles, Brest and the other

French oil ports. They can carry either crude oil or liquid natural gas. And we can identify them with no trouble, even if they choose to fly a flag of convenience.'

'We got submarines somewhere close?' asked General Scannell.

'Very close,' said Admiral Dickson. 'In fact, we have two of the best submarines in the fleet out there right now. They're in the Arabian Sea with the *Ronald Reagan* CVBG . . . the two newest Virginia Class SSNs, the *Hawaii* and the *North Carolina* . . . really great boats, 7,800 tons, submerged-launch Tomahawk cruise missiles and 38 Mark 8 ADCAP torpedoes.

'If we need four more, which I think we do, the *Cheyenne* and the *Santa Fe* . . . coupla LA Class attack submarines with the *Constellation* Group are on station in the Gulf, off Kuwait. And we got the *Toledo* and the *Charlotte* ready to clear Diego Garcia any time we need 'em. Just so *Connie* ain't hanging around with no underwater backup.'

'You don't see surface ships being needed?' asked General Scannell.

'Well, we don't want to announce our presence, and I don't see a need for us to do so. This is a very simple sub-surface operation. But we got a couple of Arleigh Burke guided missile destroyers within 200 miles.'

Arnold Morgan knew he referred to the *Decatur* and the *Higgins*, 9,000-tonners, both built in Maine, two of the most lethal warships afloat. Both armed with short-range deadly accurate McDonnell Douglas Harpoons with their ship-killing 227kg warheads, plus 56 Tomahawk ship-launch cruises. A thin smile crossed the face of the Chief of Operation Tanker.

'I may be slightly out of touch here,' said Admiral Doran, 'but can someone tell me what precisely we hope to gain from this? What good will it do us to sink French tankers?'

'Well, in part it's a point of principle,' said Arnold Morgan. 'The current financial crisis is going to get worse. There'll be shocking repercussions for people all over the world. And the basis for our actions is to hang France from the highest tree in front of the international community. That way we'll save President Bedford. If we do nothing, he'll end up getting the blame, because that's the way the world works.

'The US economy goes down the gurgler, the press, and indeed the people, will round on the President of the day and ask why he did nothing while Wall Street burned. But they can hardly do that if we got us a real live culprit out there swinging in the wind.'

Admiral Dickson interjected. 'And the humiliation of France may well pave the way for the USA to move back into Saudi Arabia, and take charge of the global distribution of the oil. We'll still pay the Saudis, same as they've always been paid, but we may just have to get into control, and make darned sure this does not happen again.'

Like all service chiefs, the admiral saw a major

506

role for the US Navy right here, and he was not about to let the opportunity slip by. 'As I see it,' he said, 'we gotta make France seem like too big an embarrassment for the Saudis, or anyone else in the oil game, to deal with.'

'Correct,' said Admiral Morgan. Essentially, we're working to a master plan, and you'll find the pieces all fall into place very quickly. There is, however, one missing piece, and we must find it.'

'What is it?' asked General Scannell.

'We have to find the French colonel who led the attack in Riyadh. His name's Jacques Gamoudi, and we need to get to his wife and children, take them to a safe house and then grab him and get them all out of the country, preferably to America. And we gotta do it before the French do. We think they're going to assassinate him; they've already tried to once.'

'The first two options are easy, the sinkings and the blastings,' said Admiral Dickson, 'but how do you think we'll get along in the kidnapping business?'

'Right now we have the CIA and the FBI working in Riyadh,' replied Arnold. 'So far as they know, Colonel Gamoudi has not yet left the city, although he might have. However, the situation, we think, is for the moment static. The French are trying to assassinate him, but he is under heavy protection from the King and is probably holed up in one of the palaces.'

'What about his family?' asked Admiral Doran.

'That may turn out to be key,' said Arnold. 'My

own view is we should snatch them, SEALs and helicopters if necessary, and get them the hell out of France. That way we got some chips. Then we somehow let Gamoudi know we got everyone safe in the USA, and all he has to do is locate us, somehow, somewhere, and he's safe too.

'Then we put him in front of the UN, he cuts the balls off the French, and we give him a new identity and a new life. That's when we go and take over the Saudi oil, because no one can deal with France, and the Saudis can't do it without us.'

'Well,' said Admiral Doran. 'I'll tell you something, that Gamoudi character just became the most important man on this planet. And we got the added problem of the French trying to kill him.'

'If I were French, I'd be trying to kill him too,' said General Scannell. 'All I can say is we better get his wife real quick, and try to avoid breaking more than about a hundred international laws while we're about it.'

'You're right there,' said Arnold. 'We screw this up, we're in more trouble than France. Because without Gamoudi we can't prove a damn thing . . . anyone know what time John Bergstrom is due in?'

'1300,' said Frank Doran. 'He left San Diego at 0500 this morning.'

1330, Tuesday 6 April
The White House

Two armed, uniformed guards were waiting at the helicopter pad on the White House lawn, staring

508

into the skies way down across the eastern bank of the Potomac. They could see it now, the big US Marine guided-missile gunship, the Super Cobra, clattering in over the river.

On board was the Emperor SEAL, Admiral Bergstrom, Commander-in-Chief of SPECWAR-COM, the top Special Forces unit in the US military. The Marine guards watched the helicopter bank right and then settle gently on to the White House landing area.

The loadmaster was out before the brand new four-bladed rotor even slowed down. He opened the door for the admiral, who stepped down and returned the rigid salute of both guards.

'This way, sir,' said one of them. And beneath the steady gaze of a fully armed SWAT team, positioned with machine guns primed on the White House roof, the three of them headed up the short grassy slope to the West Wing entrance. Today's meeting, comprising just Admiral Arnold Morgan and Admiral John Bergstrom, would be, as ever, a strategic discussion, for 'action this day', between two of the toughest men who ever pulled on shoes.

They greeted each other like old friends and got down to business. Arnold outlined the situation, stressing the critical nature of the capture of Colonel Gamoudi and the even more critical nature of the kidnapping of his wife and two sons.

Admiral Bergstrom was thoughtful. 'I do see the problem,' he said. 'If we have his family, the Colonel will *want* to come over to us. If we don't, he will not want anything to do with us.'

'That's right,' said Arnold. 'And it's likely to be 10 times easier to find a man who is trying to find us than to find a guy who's essentially on the run.'

'And you are proposing to send a team of SEALs into Pau and snatch the family?' John Bergstrom looked highly doubtful.

'You see a problem there?' said Arnold.

'It's not a problem to grab them. And it's not a problem to get them away. It's the ramifications that bother me. First, it's plainly illegal; second, it's damn nearly a declaration of war, the US military going into action against innocent foreign civilians in full public view.'

'Well,' said Arnold, 'how about we put the SEALs in plain clothes?'

John Bergstrom was deeply unimpressed. 'Arnie,' he said, 'you can't hide or disguise SEALs.'

'Why not?'

'They're not the same as other people.'

'What do you mean?'

'They look different.'

'In what way?'

'They just stand out. Their powerful physiques . . . crewcuts. They just look too hard, too healthy . . . the way they carry themselves . . . the way they walk . . . straight backs, erect . . . fantastic bearing . . . they look like they're marching even when they're going for lunch. And they have this alert, wary look about

510

them, like wolves. Arnie, they can't help it. They're trained killers.

'And Mrs Gamoudi's going to be under escort, and those escorts will recognise my guys at a hundred paces. You want a nice quiet grab at three civilians, you gotta do it with civilians. My guys could cause uproar. Trust me. They're subtle but they're not trained in domestic niceties.'

Admiral Morgan nodded. For a few moments he paused, then said, 'I'm getting kinda used to making shaky judgements on this operation. Guess I must be getting old.'

'The best of us make shaky judgements,' said John Bergstrom. 'And it doesn't matter a damn. The only thing that matters is how quickly you recognise the problem, and how ready you are to make the change.'

'I'm ready,' said Arnie. 'What do you suggest?'

'Okay. We got a nice French lady and her two young sons. They're effectively under house arrest, right? By the French Secret Service, somewhere near the town of Pau in the Pyrenees. We have to hand this to the CIA and they have to locate her, and watch the house for a couple of days. When they pounce they do it quietly in the street. A diversion. The grab. Getaway car. Escape by helicopter. No problem. Very fast. No one knows what the hell has happened.'

Admiral Morgan visibly brightened. 'Gottit,' he said. 'You're right. But what about when we grab the Colonel himself?'

'That has to be in a seaport or on a beach. Then my guys can move in and complete the operation.

511

But if the French are trying to kill him, we may have to be pretty darned brutal in our execution of the mission.'

'The stakes are about as high as they can get, John,' said Arnold, quietly. 'We better get a full team of your guys on standby, probably in the Mediterranean. Because we're gonna find the ole *Chasseur* in there somewhere.'

'Who the hell's the *Chasseur*?' asked Admiral Bergstrom.

'Oh, that's Gamoudi's nickname. He's had it a long time. *Le Chasseur*. It's French for The Hunter.'

'That's not good,' replied the SEAL chief.

'How so?'

'Because guys don't get names like that unless they are damned dangerous. Was he ever in the Special Forces?'

'Sure was. First Marine Parachute Infantry. And the French Foreign Legion. And the French Secret Service on active duty in North Africa.'

'Jesus Christ,' said John Bergstrom. 'That's a trained professional fighter. You don't want to try and take him against his will. Otherwise someone's going to get killed. You have to get Mrs Gamoudi and the kids. And you have to get 'em real quick.'

Four days later
Saturday morning 10 April
Pau
Andy Campese and a CIA team of some 15 field operators, including his colleague Guy Roland, had

been tracking, watching and logging the movements of Giselle Gamoudi for several days. It had been a simple matter to trace her to her mother's house north along avenue Montpensier, to a tree-lined residential area near the Parc Lawrence.

But she was never out of the house for more than half an hour, and she was never without two obviously armed escorts, one of whom was, on more than one occasion, the same Secret Service officer Andy had met at her own home back in the village of Héas.

The boys were always with her, but Andy had seen no sign of them attending school. This was plainly an enforced break, courtesy of the French Government. He had expected it to be a mission packed with tension since the French Secret Service obviously wished to keep her away from any intruders.

But so far he had been mildly surprised at how relaxed his quarry and her minders seemed to be. Right now Andy and young Roland were sitting in a parked car watching the driveway of Mme Gamoudi's current residence. She was in the car with a driver, but the left rear passenger door of the car was open, awaiting, Andy guessed, the arrival of the two boys.

He was correct about that. The older one came running out first, followed by the yelling André. They both piled into the back seat and the car pulled out into the south-running avenue which led to the central area of Pau, almost a mile away. An identical car, parked in the street right outside the house, immediately fell in behind them.

Andy Campese hit the buttons on his mobile phone, making three short calls in the space of a minute. At the same time he ordered his driver to track Giselle's Peugeot and her escort car. All three vehicles moved out into the Saturday morning shopping traffic.

In the centre of town, at the junction of Place Clemenceau and rue Maréchal Foch, the lead Peugeot slowed to a stop and Giselle and the boys climbed out. Two men stepped out of the escort car and Andy Campese's man pulled into a no-parking zone of the adjacent rue Maréchal Joffre.

He and Guy Roland disembarked and moved quickly into Place Clemenceau from where they could clearly see Giselle and her sons walking slowly past the shops, with their two escorts strolling about 10 feet behind them.

Andy hit the buttons on his mobile again. This time he made two calls, and he finished only one of them. For the next hundred yards he walked with the phone held to his ear.

Giselle reached a large pharmacy and ushered the two boys inside. Her escorts did not follow her; they stayed outside, smoking, in front of the large window next to the main door.

It was a busy street and neither of them noticed three more CIA men disembark from a black Mercedes which was now double-parked 20 yards beyond the pharmacy. Nor did they notice two

514

more tough-looking characters wearing heavy dark-blue sweaters and Breton fishermen's caps, walking slowly along the street from rue Maréchal Foch.

Their attention was taken instead by a very pretty blonde in the passenger seat of another double-parked car on the other side of the street, who seemed to be smiling at them.

Minutes ticked by. Then five more. And, finally, Giselle Gamoudi emerged from the pharmacy with André, but not Jean-Pierre who showed up 15 seconds later. As the three of them stepped out into the street, Andy Campese raised his right arm.

The blonde stepped out of the car, showing legs up to her panties, and let out a piercing scream. It had taken Campese two hours to persuade Agent Annie Summers to wear a skirt that short and then scream her heart out in the middle of Place Clemenceau.

And now both of Giselle's escorts moved instinctively towards her, one of them falling over his feet to get to her. And as he did so, the first of the men in the Breton caps raced forward and intercepted him, kicking his legs from under him and slamming his boot into the back of the man's head, knocking him senseless.

His colleague did not have time to move. The second man in the Breton hat was on him, slamming his fist into his solar plexus, and driving his knee straight into his jaw as he fell forward. The men from the Mercedes rushed forward, dragged the inert figure out of the road and stood guard over both unconscious bodies.

A few passers-by noticed the commotion, and stopped to stare at the two fallen men. But Annie was still yelling and she managed to distract the entire area.

Simultaneously, Andy, Guy and the two 'fishermen' grabbed Giselle, and the boys, and carried all three of them, kicking and remonstrating, along the street to the black Mercedes. Powerful hands covered their mouths, but soothing voices were telling them in French – *take it easy . . . don't scream . . . you're safe with us . . . get in the car. We're here to rescue you.*

Only 20 seconds had passed since the CIA men had launched their attack, and now Guy Roland hit the gas pedal on the big automatic Mercedes. The car rocketed along rue Maréchal Foch and swung right down to Boulevard Barbanegre, hurtling along to the main entrance of the Parc Beaumont.

By now, Andy Campese had slipped handcuffs loosely on to all three of his prisoners. For their own sakes he did not want any of them to do anything reckless. The car slowed, turned right, and Guy drove into the Parc Beaumont.

With the doors and windows shut and locked they could not hear the helicopter heading into a wide clearing beyond the magnificent building of the Municipal Casino which dominated the park. Right now Andy Campese was talking to the pilot who was hovering 20 feet above the tree line.

Guy flashed his headlights and the helicopter came on in, touched down lightly, to the astonishment of

516

two groundsmen. The Mercedes ran right up close and Guy cut the engine. He and Andy Campese whipped open both passenger doors and hauled Giselle and the boys out.

While Guy hung on to André and Jean-Pierre, Andy ushered Giselle towards the open door of the eight-seater helicopter, which looked like a civilian aircraft, but contained two United States Navy lieutenants, and one chief petty officer.

Giselle felt strong arms lift her bodily into the cabin, and then Jean-Pierre came flying through the door as if on wings. He landed in the rear seat, followed by André who landed on top of him, laughing his head off. He, for one, appeared to be enjoying himself. The last man to board was Andy Campese who was needed because of his fluent French.

Then the door slammed, one of the lieutenants, Billy Fallon, removed the handcuffs and told them to fasten their seat belts.

The chopper was in the air and climbing less than half a minute after it had touched down. Young André looked out of the window and waved at Guy Roland, who had time to wave back, and then everyone was gone, the car moving back towards town to pick up two of its passengers, the helicopter beating its way up to a flight path 10,000 feet above the Pyrenees.

Lt. Fallon sat opposite Giselle and the boys and he spoke calmly but bluntly. 'Mrs Gamoudi, you were in the greatest danger. The French Secret Service has already made an unsuccessful attempt

517

on your husband's life; and if they should manage to assassinate him, you and the boys would . . . well, just disappear.

'We are United States naval officers and we are taking you to a place of safety. We are also desperately trying to save your husband, but we are uncertain where he is.'

Andy Campese translated swiftly, and Giselle Gamoudi's hand flew to her mouth, as if to stop herself crying out.

But Billy Fallon was not finished. 'You must try to be calm. Have you heard from your husband? No?' he said. 'Now, tell me, is your money safe – I imagine we're talking several hundred thousand? However much it is, we need to get it out of France, fast, because these guys might put a freeze on it. I need to know which bank it's with, the account number and any password.'

When Andy translated this for Mme Hooks, it was clear that she was taken aback. Still in something of a state after the shock tactics of that morning, she immediately clammed up. And when she spoke, it was to voice her considerable misgivings. 'Why should I trust you? You snatch me and my family off the streets in broad daylight. You tell me that you are United States Navy; you say that my husband is in danger of his life and that you are trying to save us all from an enemy that, until today, we never knew we had. You make assumptions that money has changed hands and then you make the preposterous suggestion that I give you details of my bank account . . .'

Andy gave his colleague a look which said 'I'll handle this', and then he spoke to Mme Gamoudi, swiftly and in French. No translation was needed for what he said to her but by the time he had finished her resolve had been broken.

With the information he wanted, Billy punched the buttons of his cell phone's direct line to the ship. He spoke briefly to the comms room, and relayed the banking details to the commanding officer, who would now call the private emergency number of the President of the Bank of Boston in the Champs-Elysée, Paris.

Back at the NSA headquarters in Maryland, Lt. Commander Ramshawe had put into motion the process which would release the Gamoudi money. And by special orders from the President of the United States, the bank was empowered to wire-transfer the entire account to the branch in State Street, Boston, Massachusetts.

Six minutes later, Billy Fallon's cell phone rang to inform him that $15 million had just crossed the Atlantic from Paris to the United States.

And now they were high above the Pyrénées-Atlantiques, and the great mountain range was rapidly flattening out to the west, into the Basque country which ran right to the shores of the Bay of Biscay.

It took only 45 minutes to reach the coastline which they crossed, still making 200 knots and flying at 10,000 feet, five miles north of Biarritz. Twenty minutes later they could see a tiny grey shape, in

519

the water way up ahead, and the pilot immediately began their descent.

They came clattering down through 2,000 feet, then 1,000, and now they could see clearly the outline of the 10,000-ton guided-missile ship USS *Shiloh*, a Ticonderoga Class cruiser, the world's most dangerous combat warship.

The sea was calm and she rode fair on her lines, making seven knots behind a light bow wave. On deck they could see the landing crew signalling them in. The pilot banked right around to the east and came in over her stern, hovering slowly over the Harpoon missile launchers, over the 5-inch guns, and then the SAM launchers, touching down on the flight deck, directly above the torpedo tubes.

'Sorry, guys. This is gonna be your home until we get Dad out of Saudi Arabia,' said Lt. Fallon.

Generally speaking, André Gamoudi considered this probably the best day of his entire life.

CHAPTER TWELVE

Gaston Savary could not believe what he was hearing. He leaned forward on his desk, resting on both elbows, the telephone pressed to his right ear. In a working lifetime in the Secret Service, he had never been quite so shocked, not even when he had first heard that the CIA was on to Jacques Gamoudi.

'What do you mean, they've gone? Gone where?'

They've just gone, sir. Several people attacked our men, who are both in hospital.

'But where the hell is Giselle Gamoudi, and the boys?'

They vanished, sir.

'What do you mean vanished?'

They left in a big Mercedes-Benz.

'Anyone get the number?'

No, sir.

'Well,' said Gaston, helplessly, 'Which way was it going?'

521

Sir, it was headed into the Parc Beaumont.

'Did we follow?'

No, sir. But someone saw the helicopter land.

'HELICOPTER?'

The one in the Parc Beaumont, sir.

'Is it still there?'

No, sir. It only stayed a few seconds, then it left. The chief groundsman was watching.

'But what about Mme Gamoudi and her sons?'

They left in the helicopter, sir.

'Holy Mary, Mother of God,' said Gaston, and gently replaced the telephone.

Two minutes later – two minutes of stunned silence in his empty office – Gaston Savary called back his Toulouse agent, the luckless Yves Zilber, who was now gloomily drinking a cup of coffee in the bar of the Hôtel Continental, on the avenue Maréchal Foch, just along the street from Place Clemenceau.

'Yves,' said Savary, 'may I presume you have told the appropriate authorities to try and track the helicopter?'

Yes, sir. I have. I told them the groundsman saw it flying very high, heading due west, towards the Basque region and the coast.

'I bet it was,' muttered Savary, replacing the receiver without a word for the second time in the last three minutes.

This was bad. No, worse. This was absolutely diabolical. If Colonel Gamoudi already knew that agents of the DGSE were trying to eliminate him, and he somehow now knew his wife and children were safely out of France . . . well, he'd never need to return to his home . . . maybe we should freeze his money.

Gaston Savary was flummoxed. He stood up and walked to his office window, staring out of the bleak 10-storey building at the depressing view of *La Piscine*, the indoor municipal swimming pool.

Was this really as bad he thought it was? Yes. Worse if anything. And was he, Gaston Savary, the only one of 60 million French citizens who understood the appalling consequences of the events in Place Clemenceau today? Probably.

The snatching of the Gamoudi family on the streets of Pau was a crisis which could bring about an enormous number of casualties, both in the government and the Secret Service. Worse yet, his head would almost certainly be the first to fall.

Standing there alone on that grey, rainy Parisian day, Gaston Savary had a fair idea how Louis XVI's Queen, the vilified Marie-Antoinette, must have felt in the hours before the guillotine in October 1793.

Wearily he picked up the telephone again and asked to be put through to the French Foreign Minister, M. Pierre St Martin. 'Don't hurry,' he muttered, too softly for the operator to hear.

Just then his other telephone rang angrily. At least it sounded angry to him. Yves Zilber again, still at the Hôtel Continental.

'Sir, I just heard from Biarritz Airport. An unannounced helicopter flying at more than 10,000 feet left France and flew straight out to sea over the Bay of Biscay. They alerted the Air Force Atlantic Region HQ but since the helicopter was transmitting nothing, they decided pursuit would be pointless.

'Ten minutes after that phone call, the helicopter was beyond French air space anyway, and heading west, out over the Atlantic. The Air Force said it was no business of ours, since the aircraft was not flying into France.'

Gaston thanked Agent Zilber and replaced the phone. 'They should have shot it down,' he muttered, unreasonably. 'Then we'd all be out of trouble – even though we'd be at war with the USA.'

One minute later his call to the French Foreign Office came through. Pierre St Martin listened silently as the Secret Service chief recounted the disastrous events in the main town square of Pau.

At the conclusion of the dismal tale of French mismanagement, he simply said, 'And where does the French Secret Service think the helicopter is headed? Washington?'

'Since its range is probably around 400 miles, I doubt it. More likely a US Navy warship, well beyond our reach.'

'So where, M. Savary, do you think that puts us?' asked M. St Martin.

'In as much trouble as it's possible to be,' he replied.

'Which means we have just one option,' stated M. St Martin flatly. 'And I am instructing you to

524

achieve that objective, no matter how much it costs in lives or money. You will find *Le Chasseur* and you will eliminate him. Because if you do not do so, the United States of America will destroy French credibility for the next 20 years.'

'But, sir . . . what about Mme Gamoudi?'

'Gaston. Get into the art of realpolitik. Stop chasing shadows. Mme Gamoudi has gone. There's nothing we can do about that. What she knows, she knows. What she tells, she tells. But anything she says is about 100 times less important than anything her husband has to say.

'He alone can sink us. Get after him, Gaston. And silence him permanently. You may assume that is an order from the President of France in person.

'And, Gaston, if I were in your shoes, I would bear in mind that it was your organisation that first leaked to the CIA the whereabouts of the Gamoudi family. It is now your organisation which has completely failed in its allotted task to keep Mme Gamoudi well out of the way of the CIA . . .'

'But, sir,' pleaded Gaston, 'I had eight armed men guarding her day and night . . .'

'Perhaps you should have had one hundred and eight,' said M. St Martin, none too gently. 'In matters of this importance, the cost is irrelevant. Only success or failure. And I say again. You will find Jacques Gamoudi. And you will have him executed. Is that clear?'

'Yes, sir. It is,' replied Gaston Savary. 'One last

thing: do you still want the Gamoudi family to have all that money, or shall I have the bank freeze it?'

'You may leave that to me,' replied the Foreign Minister, calmly.

But there, in the great building on the Quai d'Orsay, M. St Martin was trembling, both with anxiety and fright. He knew this was probably the end of the line. He knew this might spell the end of his own finely planned political career, and his hopes of attaining the Presidency of France.

He had, of course, listened intently to the speech made by the President of the United States a few days earlier. He had helped to draft his own Prime Minister's reply. But in his heart Pierre St Martin knew the Americans were on to them. It was obvious by the way Paul Bedford had spoken with such force and daring. He said he knew. And he did know.

Pierre St Martin had no doubt about that. And he also knew of the recall to the White House of Admiral Arnold Morgan. The newspapers and television stations had been full of it.

When he had first read it, every hackle he had had risen in alarm. And now his worst dreams were coming true: the United States knew precisely what France had done to help the Saudis.

Pierre St Martin stared out across the Seine from one of France's great offices of state. He realised that he might well be entering his final days in here. The final days of a lifelong dream.

'Damnation upon Arnold Morgan,' he said to the

deserted room. 'Damnation and blast the man to hell.'

110930APR10. 25.05N 58.30E
Course two-seven-zero. Depth 200. Speed 7
The brand new Virginia Class hunter killer *North Carolina* was running slowly west through the clear warm waters which led up to the Strait of Hormuz. Captain Bat Stimpson had just ordered the fastest possible satellite check, and the jutting ESM mast had split the surface waters for only seven seconds.

Now the great dark-grey hull was back where she belonged, running silently, as quiet as the US Navy's peerless Seawolf Class ships, betraying no wash on the blue waters of the Gulf of Oman.

In his hand, fresh from the comms room, Captain Stimpson held the critical satellite signal which would soon summon his ship to action stations. It read:

102300APR10. Washington. VLCC Voltaire, on charter to TRANSEURO cleared Abu Dhabi loading platforms 092200APR10. Assess current position 25.20N 57.00E. Speed 12. Voltaire 300,000 tons bound for Marseilles through Suez. Comply with last orders. Doran.

Bat Stimpson knew what his last orders were: *SINK HER.* And he gave an involuntary gulp. He had never actually sunk anything before, but he'd had a lot of practice in US Navy simulators. He knew, on this early morning, how to put a huge oil tanker at the bottom of the Gulf of Oman. He knew that as well as he knew how to eat his cornflakes.

He turned to his executive officer, the veteran

LA Class navigator Lt. Commander Dan Reilly, and said quietly, 'This is it, Danny. She'll be about 100 miles north-west of us right now. And they were serious. This is from Admiral Doran himself. How long we got?'

'Probably about five hours, sir. That tanker will speed up soon as she rounds the Musandam Peninsula and starts heading into open waters. She'll probably be making 17 knots when we locate her. I'm guessing she'll be in our preferred range around 1430, maybe a little earlier.'

'Under five miles, right?'

'Uh-huh,' replied the XO. 'But we'll need to go inside a half-mile to read the name on her hull. We can't risk hitting the wrong ship, and we won't see it much over 900 yards.'

'No,' said the CO. 'After that we better retreat 15 miles to our launch area. We don't want to be any closer. But we don't want the birds to miss.'

'You think a couple of those sub-Harpoons will do it, sir?'

'Oh, sure. Remember two French Exocets did for the Brits' *Atlantic Conveyor* during the Falklands War. She was just a very large freighter, but she burned for hours, glowed red hot in the water, and she wasn't full of oil.'

'She was full of bombs and missiles, wasn't she, sir.'

'Yes. But they didn't explode for a long time. The *Conveyor* just burned from the sheer heat of two big missiles crashing through her stern.'

'And these sub-Harpoons can't miss, can they?'

'No, they can't. Everything in this ship is damn nearly perfect.'

He referred to the flawless conduct of every working part in this sensational new submarine. The *North Carolina* was on her first operational voyage, after two years of sea trials and workup in the North Atlantic. If there'd ever been a better underwater ship, Captain Bat Stimpson had not heard of it.

They would pick up the *Voltaire* right after lunch, with a couple of radar sweeps. Only then would they close in and check her out at periscope depth. It was always slightly more awkward identifying a merchant ship, because she tended to transmit just regular navigational radar.

Merchant ships did not have a clear-cut 'signature' like a warship, which transmitted active sonar, pinging away, probably with her screw cavitating. And a modern nuclear submarine's ESM mast could intercept her radar and identify the pulse immediately.

'We'll head for her direct line of approach,' said the CO. '*Helmsman – Captain . . . make your course two-seven-six.*'

'*Aye, sir.*'

The President of France had been circumspect about the Gamoudis' money. He was plainly furious at the loss of the family to the CIA, but he recognised nothing could be done about that. His Foreign Minister was now quite rightly wondering about the $15 million paid to a man France was now obliged to eliminate.

'There is a moral issue here,' said the President, surprising himself. 'And I suppose it would be wrong to leave Mme Gamoudi absolutely destitute. After all, she did not ask to be kidnapped by these damn cowboys from Washington.'

'No, sir, she did not.'

'My suggestion is that we freeze the money, temporarily, and then retrieve $10 million of it, leaving Mme Gamoudi with $5 million. That might ease a little of the pain at losing her husband. We should also make it clear to her that she is welcome back to live among her own people in France. She is, after all, innocent.'

M. St Martin sounded doubtful. 'I agree it would be more comfortable to have her on our side,' he said. 'And when the Colonel is gone, we could take steps to bring her home.'

'Just so long as she doesn't know what happened to her husband,' the President reminded M. St Martin.

'Oh, she'll never know. An accident in a far-off land? Meantime, I should get to work on freezing that money. Ten million US dollars is rather a lot to waste on a dead man, *n'est-ce pas*?

For the next half-hour the Foreign Minister put 10 aides on to the task of opening up a bank on a Sunday afternoon. It took only a short while to locate the emergency number of the Bank President via the Paris gendarmes.

But when the call was finally made, the news was not good. 'I'm sorry, sir,' said the banker. 'But that account was removed from Paris and relocated in Boston, Massachusetts.'

'But when did that happen? And why were we not informed?'

'Sir, this account was set up deliberately fireproof. Only Colonel Gamoudi and his wife could issue instructions by means of a password. The money was removed about four hours ago, with a call from the United States Ambassador to France.

'The envoy had every necessary detail, and informed us that Mme Gamoudi was in the care of the US Government, and, if we cared to check, there was an edict from the President of the United States instructing the Bank of Boston to transfer the money to a different branch.

'Of course, sir, we made the checks. We even phoned back the embassy, and everything was in order . . . and, sir, it's not as if the money has disappeared. It's still in the Bank of Boston, still in the same account. It's just been moved to a different city.'

'A different planet, I am afraid,' replied M. St Martin, wishing the bank chief good afternoon and pondering the sheer futility of phoning a bank in the United States and asking for access to a $15 million account, controlled by two private customers.

'Hopeless,' he muttered. 'This operation is becoming more and more impossible, every hour.'

111330APR10. Gulf of Oman
The *North Carolina* was still steering very slightly north of due west. It was four hours since the satellite signal

had been received, and they came once more to periscope depth.

One sweep of the radar located a sizeable ship seven miles off their starboard bow. It was a hazy Sunday afternoon, and it was not possible to get a visual. So the submarine went deep again and continued to close, holding course two-seven-six, making seven knots through the water.

Ten minutes later the navigation officer put the oncoming ship at 24.40N 58.02E, and again the *North Carolina* came to periscope depth. And this time they could see the ship, a VLCC, a black-hulled tanker of at least 250,000 tons, riding low in the water, making around 17 knots.

From here they could see her bright scarlet upper-work through the periscope, but they would have to close in much nearer to read the name high on her port bow.

The captain ordered her deep again, and the *North Carolina* accelerated underwater on a direct course to the tanker's line of approach. They came in at over 20 knots for another nine minutes and the captain ordered them again to PD. And now they could really see her, less than a mile away, and every bit of 300,000 tons. But the name, in white lettering just below the massive sweep of her bow, was still not legible.

They slid back under the surface and ran forward for another half-mile before returning to PD. They were actually just astern of midships, which made it slightly more difficult to read the letters.

But now the name was unmistakable. This was the *Voltaire*, right on time, barrelling through the calm water off the coast of Oman, laden with Abu Dhabi's finest crude, and bound for Marseilles.

Captain Stimpson ordered the *North Carolina* deep again and a speed increase and a course change '. . . *make your depth 100, speed 22, come left to course zero-seven-zero.*'

The *North Carolina*, now running easterly for the first time, was moving much faster than the tanker, on a course which would take her slightly north of the oil ship. On this diverging course she would be 15 miles away inside 45 minutes, but she would still be directly off the port beam of the *Voltaire*.

'*Final missile check.*'

'*Captain – Missile Director . . . both weapons programmed . . . course one-eight-zero to target.*'

At precisely 1425, Captain Bat Stimpson, with his ship now 200 feet below the surface, ordered the missiles away. And one by one the sub-Harpoons ripped out of the underwater launchers, pre-programmed and unstoppable. At least they were by an oil tanker.

They swerved upwards towards the surface and burst clear of the water, cleaving their way into the clear skies, still swerving until they settled down on the course fed into the computer brain of each weapon.

These were not sea-skimmers, but they flew low over the water, coming in towards the *Voltaire* at over 1,300 mph. Flight time for their 15-mile journey: 41 seconds.

No one saw anything. The sea was deserted in that part of the Gulf, and the crew of the tanker was paying scant attention to anything out on the port side. Those who were on Watch were gazing steadily ahead when the big heat-seekers smashed into the hull 70 feet apart, 20 feet above the waterline.

The missiles exploded with sensational impact, sending two fireballs clean through the mighty ship. Each one of them blew the bulkheads separating the oil tanks, and the heat was so incinerating that it immediately ignited the gasses above the actual fuel, which exploded violently, blasting upwards two massive holes in the deck.

The deck pipelines were blown to smithereens, and in a split second the crude oil itself, unable to resist the terrifying heat of the missiles' warheads, burst into flames, the fire racing across the surface of the oil. It was a vicious, roaring fire.

Within 20 seconds the great tanker was doomed. She began to list to her port side and the fires were so intense that the entire upperworks quickly became too hot for human survival. The French captain ordered the ship's company to abandon, and lifeboats were lowered on the starboard side and over the stern.

Miraculously, no one had been killed, there being no one for'ard at the time. The crew were either on watch, sleeping or eating in the towering aft section. The nearest missile hit 100 yards for'ard of this. But the fire would not be quelled for three and a half days, and would melt the midships section of the deck and upper hull.

One minute after she had unleashed the missiles, the *North Carolina* turned away from the datum and ran south-east at 12 knots, leaving behind a puzzle which would confuse the world's tanker industry for several days. But in France, military leaders were highly suspicious of an involvement by the USA.

Indeed General Jobert, C-in-C of France's Special Forces, on that same Sunday evening convened a meeting with Admiral Marc Romanet, the Navy's Flag Officer Submarines. The general came in by helicopter to the dockyards in Brest and they talked through dinner.

There was one question on their minds: would the United States have dared to sink a French tanker?

Admiral Romanet was absolutely certain the all-powerful US Navy could have done it. '*I* could have done it,' he said, 'in a halfway decent attack submarine.'

'Leaving no trace and no clues?' asked the general.

'Not a problem,' replied Admiral Romanet. 'Mind you, with all the trouble for the US at the United Nations I think it extremely unlikely they would have done something like this. I mean . . . that censure motion was very serious last Thursday. But I expect you noticed the American representatives at the UN refused to attend any of the three Security Council meetings, nor indeed to recognise formally any censure by anyone.'

'I did notice that, of course,' replied the general. 'They are quiet, but defiant. It would still be very extravagant just to go out and blow apart a 300,000-ton tanker in the Strait of Hormuz, in complete disregard of world opinion.'

'Yes. It would,' said Admiral Romanet, slowly. 'But my fellow former submariner, Admiral Morgan, is in the White House at the President's side. And he is a very dangerous man to any enemy of the United States. And, whether we like it or not, at this moment he perceives us to be in that category.'

0530, Monday 12 April
The Red Sea, south end
Captain David Schnider, commanding officer of the US Navy's second brand-new Virginia Class SSN, the *Hawaii*, was waiting 200 feet below the surface, 36 miles north of the Bab al Mandab. His ship was making a quiet racetrack pattern, moving at only five knots in a surprisingly deep stretch of water, almost 700 feet, 25 miles off the remote desert seaport of Al Mukha on the Yemen coast.

This was where the Red Sea split into two buoyed channels, both of them with in and out lanes, one heading along the Yemen coast, the other swerving towards the Eritrea side. Captain Schnider did not know which lane his quarry would choose, which was why he was lurking quietly in deep water, positioned to hit in either direction. But his hit would be on a very special ship and there could be no mistakes.

Captain Schnider was one of the most able SSN commanding officers in the US Navy. At forty-four, he had already commanded the Los Angeles Class attack submarine USS *Toledo*, and there was a degree of envy among his contemporaries when SUBLANT appointed him to the USS *Hawaii*.

David Schnider was a short, swarthy man, with a crushing grip on facts and situations. He would have made one hell of a lawyer, but his father had served as a chief petty officer in a destroyer, and his grand-father, a gunnery chief, had died in the battleship *California* at Pearl Harbor.

Born within earshot of the old Brooklyn Navy Yards in New York, the Navy was in his blood. Despite a certain rough edge to his method of com-mand, and indeed his somewhat black humour, his men loved serving under him, and there were those who thought he might rise to the highest pinnacles of the US Navy.

Captain Schnider knew what he was looking for here at the south end of the Red Sea – an 80,000-ton red-hulled gas carrier, distinguished by four massive bronze-coloured holding domes, which rose 60 feet above the deck, with a long gantry crossing the length of the ship, 900 feet, above all four domes, and then descending to the foredeck.

David Schnider agreed with SUBLANT. She was damned hard to miss, so long as you were positioned in more or less the right place. His plan was to let her run by and then slam his missiles into the hull below two of the holding domes. The water here was plenty deep enough for a safe and efficient escape, but Captain Schnider had decided he did not wish to turn around

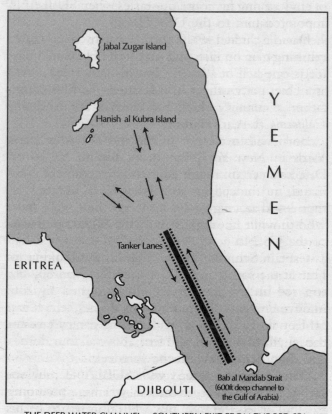

Jabal Zugar Island

Hanish al Kubra Island

Y E M E N

Tanker Lanes

ERITREA

DJIBOUTI

Bab al Mandab Strait
(600ft deep channel to
the Gulf of Arabia)

THE DEEP-WATER CHANNEL – SOUTHERN EXIT FROM THE RED SEA

and then run back past a burning ship that, so far as he could see, was not much short of an atomic bomb.

He had the details of these LPG carriers right in front of him. The TRANSEURO ship he awaited, the *Moselle*, carried 135,000 cubic metres – 3,645,000 cubic feet of liquified natural gas, frozen to *minus* 160 degrees. The liquid gas was compressed 600 times from normal gas, and formed, without doubt, the most deadly cargo on all the world's oceans.

'Jesus Christ,' murmured Captain Schnider. 'That sonofabitch could blow up Brooklyn.' And he made himself a promise: that no submarine in history would vanish from the datum faster than the USS *Hawaii*, in the split second after he had loosed off his sub-Harpoons.

Meanwhile, the *Moselle*, which had cleared Qatar's north gas field at the beginning of the week, had passed through the Strait of Hormuz the previous Thursday, three days in front of the *Voltaire*. Right now she had completed her crossing of the Gulf of Aden and was positioned to the left of the flashing light on Mayyun Island in the narrowest part of the Bab al Mandab, heading north.

Captain Schnider's orders were as succinct as Captain Bat Stimpson's in the *North Carolina* the previous day: SINK HER. And the only thing concerning the CO of the *Hawaii* was the temperature of his target.

'Since the Harpoons, in their final stages, are heat-seeking,' he told his missile director, 'how the hell are they going to find a target frozen to 160 degrees below zero? I mean, Jesus, that's as cold as a polar bear's ass. Like trying to find the heat in a goddamned iceberg.'

The missile director, Lt. Commander Mike Martinez, laughed. 'Sir,' he said, 'I promise you there's a ton of temperature in that ship. The refrigeration plants alone generate enormous heat, and the engines, situated towards the stern, generate 23,000 hp.

'Our missiles will go straight into the hull, probably at one of the refrigeration plants. We don't want to hit the domes, because they are seriously reinforced. But they won't be cool. The dome walls are too thick. The Harpoon explosions will be below the deck, right in the heart of the ship.

'And we don't need to slam one into the side of the dome; the sheer power of the TNT below decks will probably split at least one, maybe two, of them in half. And immediately, on contact with the hot air, the liquid gas will flash off into normal gas, the most volatile cargo on the ocean.

'One spark will turn the *Moselle* into something like Hiroshima. And I just hope to hell we're well underwater and moving away fast at that time.'

Captain Schnider smiled and said, 'Mike, we're firing from five miles off her starboard quarter, because she's going straight up the Red Sea to Suez, and most all fully-laden tankers moving straight through take the left-hand lane going north.

'We'll be so far away when that sucker goes off bang it'll be like we never existed.'

It was actually quite hard to believe they existed

now, while the *Hawaii* cruised 200 feet below the surface, making just five knots, and leaving no trace of a wake upon the surface. All through the night they had stayed on their deep, lonely station, listening to the roar of ships' propellers churning away overhead, travelling both north and south.

But not one of those ships, neither merchantman, tanker nor warship, had the slightest inkling that beneath their barnacled keels there lurked the most dangerous attack submarine on earth.

Two more hours went by after Captain Schnider had outlined his getaway plan to Lt. Commander Martinez. And then, at 0730, immediately they slid up to periscope depth, they spotted her. It was the *Moselle*, moving at a steady 17 knots north up the channel heading slightly towards her left, just as David Schnider had forecast.

At 80,000 tons she was small enough to make the transit through the Suez Canal, and from there it was a six-day run up to the huge underground terminal for liquid petroleum gas in Marseilles.

The USS *Hawaii* had spotted her on radar 90 minutes earlier, but there had been three other paints on the screen at that time. Only now, at 0730, with the sun climbing out of the desert to the east, was it possible to make a POSIDENT. The red hull of the *Moselle* was bright in the morning light, and the sun glinted off those huge bronze holding domes.

'We got her, sir,' called the XO, as he ordered, '*DOWN PERISCOPE*'. And then, '*We're about a mile*

541

off her starboard bow. Steer course two-seven-zero until we can read her name.'

The ESM mast slid down, and the comms room confirmed there were no further signals on the satellite. The orders were unchanged.

As the *North Carolina* had done on the previous day tracking the *Voltaire*, the *Hawaii* moved in closer, but only a few hundred yards, because the light here was much better. The periscope went up one final time and it was possible to see the huge white letters on her hull, *L N G*. Right below the safety rail on her starboard bow was the word *MOSELLE*.

Temporarily, the *Hawaii* turned away, back south at 20 knots. But only for six minutes. Then she returned to PD for her final visual check. And the *Moselle* was still on course.

'Missile Director final checks,' ordered Captain Schnider.

'*Both weapons primed, sir. Preprogrammed navigation data correct. Course three-three-zero. Launchers one and two ready.*'

'*FIRE ONE!*' snapped David Schnider. '*FIRE TWO.*'

Seconds later, the two Harpoons came hurtling out of the calm water, 100 yards apart, swerved as they hit the air and then settled on to their course, both making a direct line towards the *Moselle*, 100 feet above the surface.

Thirty-five seconds later they slammed into the starboard hull of the *Moselle*, around 20 feet above the waterline. The steel plates on this side of the double hull, both layers, were blasted apart and there was a firestorm of sparks and explosive inside the ship.

The reinforced aluminium of Number Two dome at first held, and then ruptured, and 20,000 tons of the most inflammatory gas in the world, packed with methane and propane, flooded out into the air – air which was 200 degrees Celsius warmer than its refrigerated environment.

Instantly it flashed off into vaporised gas and exploded with a deafening *W-H-O-O-O-O-M!!* Dome Three split asunder both from where the Harpoon had smashed into its shell and from the enormous explosion from Dome Two. This blew the for'ard dome and, before the captain of the tanker could even issue a command, the entire ship was an inferno, flames reaching 1,000 feet into the sky, the entire front end of the ship a tangled wreckage of ruptured, melting steel.

Again, as in the tanker, the crew was, to a man, in the aft section, in the control room, the engine room and the accommodation block. The captain issued the totally unnecessary order to abandon her, within one minute of the blast. He had not the slightest idea what had happened, and the crew who were able would have to leave in the two lifeboats on davits at the stern.

The whole length of the *Moselle*'s starboard side was a blowtorch of gas, rising up off the water and fed by thousands of tons of liquid petroleum cascading out of the hull from the aft dome, which had not yet exploded, but was somehow setting fire to the Red Sea.

The sheer size of the fire was already causing other ships to move in for a search and rescue operation, and a few men who failed to make the lifeboats were jumping off the stern, like a scene from *Titanic*. But the waters were clear, warm and deep, and the tide was carrying the gas on the surface to the north, away from them. Almost every one of the seamen who had crewed the *Moselle* would survive.

But the inquiries would be long and painstaking. She was the only LPG carrier ever to have a serious fire, except for one in the Persian Gulf a few years earlier which had hit a contact mine.

By the time the order to abandon ship was given, the *Hawaii* had gone deep, 400 feet below the surface, making 25 knots away from the staggering scene of maritime destruction. Captain Schnider had only two miles at this depth and this speed, after which he would slide into the regular south-running shipping lane, and make his secretive exit through the Strait, only 100 feet below the surface at six knots.

His satellite signal to SUBLANT in Norfolk, Virginia, would not be transmitted until they were safely in the much deeper water of the Gulf of Aden. It contained just one word . . . *GASLIGHT*.

0900 (local), Monday 12 April
The Foreign Office, Paris
There was an air of foreboding on the Quai d'Orsay. News of the *Moselle*'s demise was raging around

government corridors. The President was furious, the military was demanding orders and M. Pierre St Martin was trying to prevent himself doing something which might ultimately be judged as rash.

And, of course, the dark, satanic cloud of the United States of America hung heavily over the entire place. Had Uncle Sam just whacked out a couple of French oil tankers? Or had there just been two ghastly, coincidental accidents?

Pierre St Martin, as a lifelong career politician, knew it would be futile to ask the United States if their Navy had been responsible. And even if they answered, the Americans would certainly use the question to berate France . . . *not every nation is willing to use destructive firepower in the cause of its own interests . . . do not judge others by your own infamous conduct . . .*

No. M. St Martin could see no earthly reason to contact the United States, and he paced his elegant office, uncertain what to advise the President, uncertain what, if anything, he could do.

He was not helped by the simple fact that no one on board either the *Voltaire* or the *Moselle* had any idea what had taken place. So far as both commanding officers were concerned their ships had suddenly, for no discernible reason, exploded and burst into uncontrollable flames. Which did not help M. St Martin one iota.

His tenure as Foreign Minister had always been cushioned by the comfort and elegance of the job, and its many, many *accoutrements*; not to mention the priceless antiques and furnishings from bygone days of French glory, which perpetually surrounded him, as France's front-line executive in the global community.

But now the whole thing was turning sour. Everything possible was going wrong. He felt powerless, and vulnerable. And he turned to the portrait of Napoleon, with that smug expression on his round, complacent face. And M. St Martin understood, vaguely, how the Emperor must have felt as he prepared to depart for his final exile in St Helena.

The trouble was, at this level of government, there was nowhere to hide, worse yet, no one to whom he could turn. The President, at 7.30 that morning, had been incandescent with rage . . . '*All I have ever asked for is secrecy . . . and what do I get? Some jackass French officer from the Pyrenees having his photograph taken on the front of a tank! It's probably framed now in the US Embassy.*

'*I get incompetence, betrayal. I ask for my massive highly paid security forces to guard one slim French lady and two children, not a group of terrorists. And they can't even do that. And now I have America, which appears to know everything about us, blowing French ships out of the water and you tell me I cannot even remonstrate! Pierre, this is intolerable.*'

Pierre tried to calm himself. He picked up the telephone and asked to be connected to Gaston Savary over at *La Piscine*. And to him he repeated the words of the President: 'Gaston, this is intolerable.'

But he was preaching to a man on his way back

up the road from Tarsus. Gaston knew that everything about this mission had turned out to be intolerable. And, like the Foreign Minister and the President, he too believed that the US Navy was banging French tankers out of the water.

'Is it your opinion that we should cease all oil shipments from Gulf ports to France?' asked Pierre St Martin.

'Quite frankly, yes,' said Savary. 'Because if we were to lose another one, and a lot of people were to be killed, there would be a major uproar in France. The people would accuse the government of callous indifference to poor, hard-working sailors, who now leave widows and fatherless children, because of our own ambitions. Pierre, we cannot afford to lose another big ship. The risks are too great.'

'Can nothing stop a US Navy submarine doing its worst?'

'Not really. Those things can stay underwater for eight years, if necessary. At least their nuclear reactors can run for that long, supplying all the heat, light, fresh air, fresh water and power they need. They only come up for food when it runs out.'

'And what about sonar? We have zillions of euros worth of sonar on our ships. Can't we find the American submarine?'

'Not much chance. A nuclear boat can be anywhere, very quickly . . . you could be searching in the Atlantic and she's in the Indian Ocean. You could be searching in the Pacific and she's 6,000 miles away. Give it up, sir. They think we've smashed the

547

world's economy, and they're taking revenge. And there is not too much we can do about it, short of war with the United States, which we would swiftly lose.'

'So your advice is simply to stop all tankers travelling from the Arabian loading docks to France?'

'Yes, sir. That's my advice.'

'Then I shall have to seek further help from the Navy, Gaston. *Bonjour, mon ami.*'

Admiral Marc Romanet, at his office in Brest, besieged by government departments wondering what to do, or say, about the latest American outrage, was marginally more optimistic.

'Foreign Minister,' he said, 'the Navy could provide an escort to the tankers, as the British did for the Atlantic convoys against the U-boats in World War II.'

'You mean each tanker leaving the Gulf and bound for a French port would be accompanied by a battleship?'

'Sir, we don't have battleships as such. I was thinking of a destroyer.'

'*La même chose,*' said the slightly precious Foreign Minister, haughtily. 'Very large, very smelly, very noisy ships, loaded with guns and shells, and angry young men in badly pressed uniforms.'

Admiral Romanet was deeply unimpressed by M. St Martin's grasp of the French Navy.

'Not these days, sir,' he said, brusquely. 'Very large, pristinely clean, guided missile ships, fitted with state-of-the-art electronics, incomprehensible to a civilian, and crewed by very calm, very educated young men, in immaculately pressed uniforms.'

Comprehensively put in his place by one of the Navy's favourite sons and the head of the entire submarine service, Pierre St Martin beat a very fast retreat. 'Just joking, Admiral,' he said.

'I very much hope so, sir,' replied Admiral Romanet. 'Because in the final reckoning, should we ever come under attack, your life will very probably be in the hands of those young men in the pressed uniforms.'

'Of course,' replied the Foreign Minister. 'I was only teasing.'

'Naturally,' said the admiral. But he was not smiling. 'To continue,' he added, 'we have our newest Tourville Class destroyer, the *De Grasse*, exercising in the northern Arabian Sea at present. She's our specialist anti-submarine warfare ship. If anything can protect a tanker against attack, she can.'

'Against torpedoes? Which I believe is what the Americans used against the tankers?'

'To tell you the truth, sir, I don't think they did. The fires were too big, and too sudden, in both ships. My guess is they hit them with missiles. But the *De Grasse* is a specialist. She's loaded with her own missiles, but her torpedo capacity is formidable, 10 ECAN L5 anti-submarine active/passive, homing to six miles – with a 150kg warhead.

'She also carries two Lynx Mk 4 anti-submarine helicopters. She has towed-array torpedo warning, radar warnings, jammers and decoys. You want a ship

549

to protect a tanker from underwater attack, I'd request the *De Grasse*, if I were you.'

'Admiral, I thank you for this advice. Which I will pass on to the President. But I must ask you. Can you guarantee this destroyer will keep the tanker safe?'

'There's no guarantees in my business,' said the admiral. 'And, perhaps, unlike politicians, we do not like to say there are, when there are not. But I'd give the *De Grasse* a fighting chance against any enemy.'

'Thank you, Admiral,' said the Foreign Minister, who had not enjoyed sparring with a very senior officer in the French Navy. He had managed to make him feel faintly absurd.

Nonetheless, he called back the President, and, attempting a career-saving final throw of the dice, told him he could absolutely guarantee the safety of French tankers on the high seas, if they were accompanied by French Navy warships, particularly the Tourville Class destroyers, like the *De Grasse*.

'Perhaps organise them into half a dozen groups,' he said, ambitiously. 'Six of these Tourvilles would probably do the trick,' he added jauntily. 'Anti-submarine specialists, of course.'

The President did not know any more than M. St Martin that the French Navy owned only two Tourvilles, and that the other one was on sea trials in the North Atlantic.

Instead he trusted the word of his Foreign Minster, which would not do him much good. Meanwhile,

M. St Martin's tumbrel continued on its inexorable way towards the political gallows.

1430 (local), Wednesday 14 April
Strait of Hormuz
Captain Bat Stimpson had the *North Carolina* in the identical position he had occupied on the Sunday morning just before he sank the *Voltaire*. The Virginia Class hunter killer was steaming slowly up the Strait of Hormuz, 200 feet below the surface, awaiting the arrival of another tanker, chartered by TRANSEURO, this time a ULCC, the 400,000-ton *Victor Hugo*, fully laden with Abu Dhabi sweet crude, bound for Cherbourg.

The coded signal from SUBLANT had been retrieved from the satellite in the small hours of that Wednesday morning. It read: *140400APR10. ULCC Victor Hugo heading east along Trucia Coast from Abu Dhabi loading platforms. Escorted by French ASW DDG De Grasse. ETA your datum Strait of Hormuz 1600. Eliminate them both.*

Bat Stimpson showed no apprehension this time. The orders were succinct and perfectly straightforward. The *Victor Hugo* was already around the Musandam Peninsula, and past Oman's rocky headland of Ra's Qabr al Hindi.

The *North Carolina* ops room knew it was their approaching target, because the sonar room had picked up the sonar transmissions of the *De Grasse*, unmistakable on D–Band, Thompson Sintra DUBV 23. French warship.

At 1510, the operators picked up the *De Grasse*'s military Air/Surface Search radar transmissions, right at the end of its 16-mile range. Again unmistakable, beaming out from the top of the destroyer's mast, Thompson-CSF DRBV 51B on G-Band.

The torpedo director deep below the ops room in the *North Carolina* was already making his final checks. He had prepared two weapons in case of malfunction. But Captain Stimpson was confident they could sink the destroyer with a single wire-guided Gould Mark 48 ADCAP fired from 7,000 yards. They would take the destroyer before they hit the tanker, because, again, they would use submerge-launch Harpoons against the ULCC in order to burn the colossal amount of crude oil it carried.

Right now the ops room had the *Victor Hugo* and the *De Grasse* steaming on a south-south-east course, at 17 knots, 200 yards apart, the destroyer positioned off the tanker's portside bow.

And on they came, hard on their course, headed for the mouth of hell.

'*Ready number one and number two tubes, 48 ADCAP.*'

'*Aye, sir.*'

Fifteen minutes passed, and the sonar room called, '*Track 34 . . . Bearing one-seven-zero . . . Range six miles.*'

And now the guidance officer was murmuring into his microphone constantly, and the *North Carolina* seemed to hold her breath as the sonar team checked the approach of the French destroyer, calling out the details in that hyper-tense calm which grips a submarine in the moments before an attack.

The XO had the ship, and Bat Stimpson stared at the screen. Then he called . . . '*STAND BY ONE! Prepare to fire by sonar.*'

'*Bearing one-two-zero . . . range 7,000 yards . . . computer set.*'

'*FIRE!*' snapped the CO. And everyone felt the faintest shudder as the big ADCAP thundered out into the ocean, instantly making 45 knots through the water, straight towards the projected line of approach of the *Victor Hugo*.

'*WEAPON UNDER GUIDANCE, SIR.*'

Bat Stimpson ordered the torpedo armed, and, 5,000 yards away, still running fast through the water, it began to search passively for the warm hull of the destroyer.

Three minutes after firing, the Mark 48 switched to active homing sonar, pinging its way towards the destroyer. Now it could not miss, and it locked on to its target.

It was just 300 yards from the warship when the French sonar room, taken by surprise, caught the torpedo flashing in towards the stern, where the four huge turbines drove the twin shafts.

'*TORPEDO! . . . TORPEDO! . . . TORPEDO! . . . RED ONE SEVEN FIVE . . . ACTIVE TRANSMISSION . . . RANGE 300 YARDS.*'

Too late. Too close. The Mark 48 slammed into the stern of the *De Grasse*, detonated with barbaric force, blew the stern clean off the ship, split the shafts asunder and blasted the engine room to oblivion.

Eight men died instantly, and within moments the ship began to sink, stern first, as water cascaded through the open aft end of the warship. No one had been expecting anything like this and there were several bulkhead doors and hatches left open.

This might have been construed as short-sighted, since the destroyer's entire *raison d'être* was to protect, and perhaps fight, as she moved through a possible war zone.

However, 200 yards away on board the tanker, men stood at the rails on the high bridge and gazed in astonishment at their mighty escort, which had not only blown up, but appeared to be on fire at the aft end, and sinking as well.

And as they watched, incredulously, several of them saw the unthinkable, as two sub-Harpoon missiles came scything through the crystal clear skies and smashed straight into the hull of the *Victor Hugo*. They blew most of the 1,000-yard-long deck 100 feet into the air, straight out over the starboard rails like a can of sardines, opening sideways.

Again, the crew was largely saved by the great distance between the upperworks and the long front end of the ship which housed the oil.

However, four men who were working for'ard were killed instantly and the ensuing fires were unimaginable. From the bridge, it looked like a lake of pure flame, roaring up into the stratosphere. Crude oil is hard to ignite, but when it does, it is extremely difficult to extinguish.

As with the *Voltaire*, the master of the *Victor Hugo* had no option but to abandon her. There were two gigantic, 30-foot-long jagged holes in the tanker's portside close to the waterline, and oil was leaking out into the ocean and burning fiercely.

The fire was growing hotter by the second. If the captain and his crew did not get off this massive ship in the next 10 minutes, they would surely fry.

At that point, with the lives of everyone on board the two stricken ships hanging in the balance, Captain Stimpson elected to leave the area. He made one final visual observation of the havoc he had wrought and ordered the *North Carolina* deep again, instructing the helmsman to turn away, south.

'*Bow down 10 . . . depth 200 . . . make your speed 20 . . . course one-three-five . . .*'

In his seaman's heart he hoped that rescue would be prompt and thorough, using every possible ship and helicopter the Omani Navy possessed. For the catastrophe was closest to their shores.

But he could not afford to dwell upon the unfairness of the sailors' fate. France had trangressed the natural laws of survival on planet earth. And she deserved every last bit of vengeance the USA chose to inflict upon her.

The warship, and the men who sailed it, was the responsibility of the French Navy and the politicians in Paris. Captain Stimpson believed the survivors should be well compensated. Like him, they were only carrying out their orders.

*   *   *

1600 (local), same day
The Elysée Palace, Paris

The President of France had been this angry before. But not in recent memory. He twice brought his fist crashing down upon the Napoleonic sideboard, which made the Sèvres porcelain cups dance up and down in their saucers and the silver Napoleonic coffee pot bounce on the polished inlaid surface of the sideboard.

Much more of that and the burly little former communist mayor could have inflicted about a million dollars' worth of damage.

'*I AM NOT PUTTING UP WITH IT,*' he roared. '*THEY CAN'T . . . THEY . . . THEY . . . THEY CAN'T KEEP DOING THIS. IT'S . . . IT'S LUNACY . . . WHO THE HELL DO THEY THINK THEY ARE?*'

'That, of course, is the main trouble, sir,' replied M. Pierre St Martin. 'They *know* who they are.'

'Well, whoever they are, they cannot keep sinking ships and killing people.'

'Sir, they can. And I believe they will, until we stop trying to ship oil out of the Middle East. They have issued a very firm warning, and with that *bâtard* Morgan in the White House, they are going to continue.'

'Then you are saying we must stop trying to keep this country running?'

'No, sir. I am not. But we have to find other ways of importing oil than with tankers out of the Persian Gulf . . .'

'But, Pierre,' interrupted the French President, 'that's not acceptable. We cannot just lie down and give in, like a . . . like a . . . poodle.' The President was almost white with anger.

'Sir, we have to, because those submarines of theirs are impossible to deal with. You cannot even find them, far less destroy them. And even if we did, the Americans could probably produce 50 more.'

'FIFTY!' yelled the President. 'FIFTY! That's ridiculous.'

'Sir, I have told you already. The US Navy is invincible.'

At which point the President of France lost all semblance of control . . . *'YOU ALSO TOLD ME THAT DESTROYER WOULD PROTECT THE TANKER . . . YOU . . . YOU GUARANTEED IT . . . YOU SAID IT WAS A SPECIALIST ANTI-SUBMARINE WARSHIP . . . AND IT TOOK THE UNITED STATES ABOUT ONE MINUTE TO BLOW IT IN HALF . . . FUCK YOU, PIERRE! DO I MAKE MYSELF CLEAR? F-U-U-U-U-CK YOU!'*

'I was simply repeating naval advice . . .'

'Then your precious advice was WRONG. Can I rely on no one?' he bellowed. 'I am surrounded by lunatics. My friends and my enemies. Imbeciles and killers. And I am sick to death of it.'

At which point, the butler entered the room to announce the arrival of General Michel Jobert's staff car at the main door downstairs.

'Bring him straight up,' said the President, not even looking at the man.

And three minutes later the Commander-in-Chief of France's joint-service Commandement des Opérations Spéciales walked into the room. General Jobert had presented himself with the task of trying to prove what had happened in the Strait of Hormuz and in the Red Sea.

He instantly announced he was the bearer of important information, which was just as well, given the general atmosphere in that room – the President fit to be tied, his Foreign Minister cowering before the onslaught.

'Sir, as you know,' the general began, 'we were unable to discover anything about the *Voltaire* or the *Moselle*. However, today's atrocity is very different. Most of the *De Grasse*'s ship's company survived – that's 20 officers and 294 men.

'Their sonar room caught an incoming torpedo 300 metres out. They even had its bearing. They have the recording and the software, with someone calling out Torpedo! Torpedo! Torpedo!

'It's the first time we have had incontrovertible evidence that our ships were hit by an enemy. And, sir, this gets better. Four of the crew of the *Victor Hugo* were watching the destroyer burn when two guided missiles came in and smashed into the tanker's hull. They saw them in the air, aimed straight at the ship, sir. They were right there on the high portside rail.

'Mr President, we are in a position to go to the United Nations with irrefutable evidence that the United States has committed at least two most terrible crimes on the high seas.'

The President smiled for the first time that morning. 'Paul Bedford might have thought he had enough to accuse us publicly, but we *really* have enough to nail the Americans.'

'Except for one thing,' said M. St Martin. 'The Americans will deny it flatly. They'll just say it was the Japanese or someone.'

'Not quite,' interjected General Jobert. 'When a sonar search system acquires an incoming missile, or a torpedo, it instantly bangs it into a software program which identifies the type of sonar the enemy is using.'

He saw the puzzled look on the President's face and simplified his explanation. 'Sir,' he said, 'if I walked out of that door and shouted something from the other side, you would know it was me. You'd recognise my voice. Same with a sonar system . . . when it receives a radar or sonar beam its computer can identify the source of that beam.

'In this case, according to the *De Grasse*'s ops room, a Gould Mark 48 ADCAP, transmitting active. That's American. And, sir, the Omanis are just helping us to airlift the entire contents of the destroyer's operational computer system, before she sinks.'

Again, the President smiled. 'Then we have them, General?'

'We have, sir.'

'Then we shall humiliate the mighty USA publicly. I shall broadcast to the entire world, tonight, condemming their actions. I'll describe them as cold-blooded killers, cowboys, bandits. Irresponsible.

Reckless. I'll say the United Nations should not even be in New York. It should be in Paris. Centre of the world ... where people are ... well ... civilised, not madmen.'

'Steady, sir,' cautioned M. St Martin. 'The Americans would be glad to be rid of the UN. What do they call it ... ? Yes, the Chatterbox on the East River.'

'Hmmmm,' mused the President. 'We shall see, Pierre. We shall see.'

That night the roof fell in on international relations between France and the United States of America. The French President made his broadcast at 7 p.m. in Paris, in precisely the terms he had outlined in the Elysée Palace for M. St Martin and General Jobert. It was theatrical, accusatory, rude in the extreme, and political to the 10th degree.

The French President threw at the USA every insult every French President had longed to utter since World War II. Not even Charles de Gaulle, at his most insufferably imperious, had ever let fly at the world's policeman with quite so much venom.

And he ended it with a flourish: 'As from this moment, the envoys of the United States are no longer welcome in this country,' he thundered. 'I hereby expel them all. I hereby close down their embassy which pollutes the beauty of the avenue Gabriel, not 300 yards from where I am standing.

'I know that under international law that building and that land is officially designated property of the United States of America. As from this week, it is restored to its proper title deeds . . . avenue Gabriel, in its entirety, belongs to *LA FRANCE!*' And he raised both arms in the air and signed off with the joyous shout: *'VIVE LA FRANCE! . . . VIVE LA FRANCE!'*

And when he marched off the wide upper landing of the Elysée Palace, stepping between the television arc lights, he once more entered his private drawing room and clasped the hand of General Jobert, who had sat and watched the performance onscreen with the Foreign Minister.

'Well, General, how was that?' he demanded. 'Did your President do your country proud?'

'Oh, most definitely, sir,' replied the general. 'That was a speech which echoed the very . . . er . . . heartbeat of the French people. It needed to be said.'

M. St Martin once more sounded a word of caution. 'It was perfect, sir,' he murmured softly. 'Just so long as the Americans don't get to Colonel Jacques Gamoudi before we do.'

And that night the stakes were raised yet again. At 10 p.m. President Paul Bedford formally expelled every French diplomat from their embassy in Reservoir Road NW, Washington, DC. And while he was about it, he ordered the following French consulates to close down: New York, San Francisco, Atlanta, Boston, Chicago, Houston, Los Angeles, Miami and New Orleans.

It was the lowest point of relations between fellow permanent members of the UN Security Council

561

since the Russians shot down the United States Air Force U-2 spyplane almost half a century earlier.

And with the East Coast of America operating six hours behind Paris, the US newspapers and television stations had ample time to rearrange their front pages and the top story which they had been planning all morning.

That was the one about the state of the world economy, the one which had dominated the world's media ever since the fateful March night when the French Navy had blitzed the Saudi oil industry.

Every night things were globally bad, but tonight was especially dismal. There had been a complete electricity blackout in Tokyo, lasting from 11 p.m. to 6 a.m. Not one flicker of a neon light penetrated the blackness, and the government warned of the possibility of this being repeated every night until further notice. They urged the citizens of Tokyo to be patient. The lights had been off for three days in the cities of Osaka and Kobe, as the electrical power generators used the last of the fuel oil.

Hong Kong, another voracious consumer of oil-fired electrical power, was into its emergency supplies, and Rome, the Eternal City, was headed for eternal darkness. The north-west of France was running out of gasoline, and the great seaport of Rotterdam was virtually closed down.

There was a complete blackout in Calcutta. Traffic was grinding to a halt in Germany, and there was no power in Hamburg, with brownouts in Berlin and Bremen. In England the refineries in the Thames

Estuary were slowing right down, and the government banned all use of neon lighting in London. In the county of Kent, particularly south-east of Ashford, there was no electricity whatsoever.

On the East Coast of the United States the situation was becoming critical as the refineries along the New Jersey side of the Hudson River, opposite New York City, began to fail.

That should have been enough to keep the most insatiable news editor happy, but unsurprisingly the standoff between France and the United States knocked every other story off the front pages, and from the lead-off spots on television news.

Back in the National Security Agency, Lt. Commander Jimmy Ramshawe was trying to hold together a great web of agents all over the Middle East, all of them trying to find Jacques Gamoudi.

And the situation was not greatly assisted by a phone call every two hours from Admiral Morgan which always started with the words *Found him yet?* and always ended with *Well, where the hell is he?*

If they had but known it, the US operation was way behind the eight-ball in the battle with France to find the missing assault commander. Because France had inserted five top agents into Riyadh as assistants to Colonel Gamoudi in the run-up to the attack on the palaces.

Throughout his preparations, they had kept him informed of developments, and all five of them had enjoyed free and easy access to the ex-French Special

Forces commander. Three of them were still in Riyadh, just observing on behalf of the French Secret Service, and all three of them were regular visitors to the splendid white-painted house which King Nasir had made available to the colonel for as long as he needed it.

And suddenly, as both the USA and France stepped up the pace to locate Gamoudi, the game changed. Gaston Savary, the only man with access to these three French spies, called the senior officer, former Special Forces major Raul Foy, and instructed him, in the fewest possible words, to report to the French Ambassador in the Diplomatic Quarter.

Somewhat mystified, the major drove over to the embassy where the ambassador's secretary told him it would be necessary to wait for new orders, direct from Paris, which would be given to him by the ambassador in person. His Excellency would be free in 10 minutes.

In fact he was free in five, and Major Foy was ushered into the office. The two men shook hands, but the ambassador did not invite his guest to sit down. He said simply, 'Major, I do not wish you to remain here for one second longer than necessary. I have just been speaking for the second time this morning to Gaston Savary.

'I am instructed to tell you, in terms of the utmost secrecy, that you and your men are to assassinate Colonel Jacques Gamoudi this day, on the direct orders of the President of France.'

If the major had been given the courtesy of a cup

of coffee, he would have choked on it. 'But . . .' he stammered.

'No buts, Major. My own instructions are to call the Elysée Palace the moment you leave, to confirm I have passed on the orders . . . I don't need to tell you how serious this is. But I am asked to inform you, there will be an excellent financial reward for you upon your return to Paris. In the region of six figures.'

Major Foy, a man who had faced death more than once in the service of his country, stood and gawped.

'I'm sorry, Raul,' said the ambassador in a gentler tone. 'I know that you are certainly a very good colleague of the Colonel's, if not a friend. But I think I mentioned, this is supremely important. The blackest of black ops, you might say. *Au revoir.*'

The forty-one-year-old major turned away without a word and walked out of the building to his car parked outside the main door. He climbed into the driver's seat and sat there, still stunned. He was not the first soldier to bridle at an order, and perhaps not the first to tell himself *I did not join either the Army or the Secret Service to kill my fellow French officers.*

But he might have been the first to be told he had to assassinate his own boss. And all he could think of was Colonel Gamoudi's innate decency, professionalism and understanding of his own problems working under cover in the city. When he had first arrived from France, he had dined with Jacques Gamoudi on two or three occasions. The two men had spoken every day, always with immense dignity and mutual respect.

Like Colonel Gamoudi, Major Foy had served with distinction in Brazzaville at the height of the Congo revolution; and he was not at all sure about this, six figures or no six figures. But then, as men will, he thought of all it would mean for him, and for his wife and children.

He started the car and drove off, back towards his apartment in the centre of the city. He resolved for the moment to tell no one of his five minutes with the ambassador. He just needed some coffee and time to think. He glanced at his watch. It was almost eleven o'clock on that hot Thursday morning. Which gave him a lot of time to contemplate, since there was no way he was going to shoot down Colonel Gamoudi in cold blood in broad daylight.

10 p.m., Thursday 15 April
The Diplomatic Quarter, Riyadh
Major Foy parked his car approximately 200 yards from the grace and favour home awarded by King Nasir to Jacques Gamoudi. He had made up his mind now; he locked the car door and walked quietly up the deserted street, beneath the trees and the fading pink and white spring blossoms still hanging over the high walls of these impressive houses.

When he reached the wrought-iron gateway to the colonel's Riyadh home, he tapped on the window of the guardhouse outside and was pleased to see the men inside both knew him. They opened the electronic gates and waved him through.

At the front door, he faced two more Saudi armed guards whom he knew even better, and they too directed him inside. And there the duty officer greeted him, '*Bonsoir*, Major. I am afraid the Colonel has retired to bed for the night. I don't think he wants to be disturbed.'

'Ahmed,' said the major to a young man with whom he had been on friendly terms for more than four months, 'I have just come from the French Embassy. I have a message for the Colonel which is so secret they would not even commit it to paper. I have to tell him in person. I'd better go up. He's probably reading.'

'Okay, Major. If it's that important, I guess you'd better.'

Raul Foy walked up the wide staircase and along the left-hand corridor. At the double doors to the master bedroom he hesitated and then knocked softly. Jacques Gamoudi heard the knock and slipped out of bed, positioning himself behind the door with his knife in his right hand.

But he did not answer. The door opened quietly and Major Foy came into the room and closed it behind him. The colonel heard him whisper hoarsely, *Jacques, wake up.*

The colonel did not recognize that voice, and he leapt forward into the darkness, seizing the intruder by the hair and flattening the blade of his knife hard against the man's throat.

Raul Foy almost died of shock, for the second time that day. 'Jacques, Jacques,' he cried. 'Get off, it's me, Raul. I've come to talk to you – urgent. And get that fucking knife out of my neck.'

Colonel Gamoudi released him and switched on the light. 'Jesus, Raul, what the hell are you doing, creeping around in the middle of the night?'

'Jacques. Do not interrupt me. Just listen. This morning I was given personal instructions from the goddamned President of France to assassinate you, at all costs. I don't know why, but, Jacques, you are a marked man. They are determined to kill you. They even offered me money to do it.'

'Christ, you haven't come to shoot me, have you?' grinned the colonel.

'Not while you're holding that fucking knife,' he replied. 'No, Jacques. Seriously. I'm not even armed. I haven't even told my team. I'm here to warn you. You have to get out of here. Now. These guys are not joking. Go, Jacques. You've got to run.'

'And you, Raul? Now you have neglected to kill me, what will you tell them?'

'Jacques. You are going. Now. I'm going to tell them I came here to obey their orders, and you were gone. Do you want a lift to the airport or somewhere?'

'No,' replied Colonel Gamoudi. 'The King will arrange my transportation. I'll just round up General Rashood, who's in the billiards room, and we'll be on our way. And . . . thank you, Raul. I mean that. Because I just cost you a lot of money, in a way.'

The French Secret Serviceman smiled and told him, 'Earlier today I made a decision. I thought about some words written a long time ago by an Englishman. He was called Forster.'

And with that, Raul headed towards the door. But when he reached it, he turned back and embraced his former boss, saying, with genuine concern, 'Goodbye, Jacques. For Christ's sake be careful . . . and . . . and God go with you.'

'Well,' said Jacques, wryly, 'before you go, you might tell me the lines which saved my life . . .'

Raul Foy looked embarrassed, as if nervous about saying the words which would confirm his loyalties. 'Very well,' he said, and then picked out the words carefully. *'If I was asked to choose whether to betray my country, or my friend, I hope I'd have the courage to choose my country . . .'*

CHAPTER THIRTEEN

11 p.m., Thursday 15 April
The Arabian Desert

They prayed at sunset, out on the edge of the desert, south-west of Riyadh. King Nasir of Saudi Arabia, in company with all his most trusted council members, turned east towards Mecca and prostrated themselves before God in accordance with the strict teachings of the Koran.

That night would see the ancient ritual of the *mansaf*, and the prayers were as much a part of the rite as the dinner itself; the rice served on the flat wholewheat crust of the *shrak*, and the succulent boiled lamb poured upon it, with a sour-milk sauce.

Tonight the King would dine with his advisers, six of them, gathered in a circle around the great circular feast, eating with the fingers of their right hands, selecting pieces of lamb and rolling them expertly into rice balls with the dexterity of cardsharks.

These nights, in the opening days of the new King's reign, the prayers were particularly poignant because Nasir demanded that Islam and its teachings should reach every aspect of Bedouin life.

I witness there is no God but God, and Mohammed is the messenger of God — the murmured prayers of the most powerful men in the Kingdom were spoken with deliberation, and the words hung heavily on the warm night air.

The tall, bearded ruler of the Kingdom, now on his knees in the centre of the vast brightly patterned Persian rug, spread out on the sand, epitomised the strength which lay in the fellowship of faith. In all of their conferences since he had assumed power, King Nasir had made it abundantly clear that he was dedicated to a return to the ancient ways, and not merely in the creed of personal faith and piety.

King Nasir wanted to restore Muslim life, back to the correct code of ethics, the ones passed down through the wisdom of the Koran. He wanted a culture, a system of laws, an understanding of the function of the state — Islamic guidelines for life in all its dimensions.

And there was not a man among those seated on the great carpet in the desert who did not believe the King would achieve his aims. Nasir was a strong leader, unbending in his beliefs. He still refused to sleep in an ornate, lavishly decorated bedroom, preferring his plain, white, almost bare room, which was more like a cell.

And he preferred still to dine in the desert, sitting outside his tent, ensuring that everyone had enough to eat, including all the 15 servants who attended him. On this night, he had characteristically invited four perfect strangers, mere passers-by, to join the gathering.

And now the robed figures were preparing to sit up long into the night indulging in that most ancient of Arab rituals – sipping coffee, freshly roasted on an open fire while dinner was consumed, and served from a long-beaked, blue enamelled pot, with pale cardamon seeds.

It was an unchanging scene, out there beneath a rising desert moon – modern men upholding the traditions of their Bedouin past as if time had stood still down the centuries. Then at 22 minutes before eleven o'clock, the twenty-first century intruded: the King's cell phone rang loudly from somewhere in the folds of his robes. His expression changed from contented, to startled and then to irritation. It was as if someone had offered him a cup of instant coffee.

But he answered the call. Because it had to be critically important. No one could remember anyone having the temerity to interrupt Nasir al-Saud during the ceremony of the *mansaf*, not even when he had only been Saudi Arabia's Crown Prince.

The gathering was hushed as he spoke.

'Jacques? Are you safe?'

And then there was silence as Colonel Gamoudi explained there was about to be a second attempt on his life, telling the King how the French Secret Serviceman had arrived in his bedroom with the warning.

They all heard the King ask, 'And that saved

you? Those wonderful lines from *Two Cheers for Democracy*?' And they saw him smile, fleetingly, before adding, 'Yes. I do know them. I know them quite well.'

But the King's face was grave when he continued, 'Jacques, when you leave here I shall be losing a brother. I am deeply disappointed with the conduct of my allies in France, but I agree you must go, because no security is 100 per cent.

'I will have you collected from the house and taken to the airport where a private Boeing will take you anywhere you wish to go. I want you to keep it at your disposal for as long as it takes, until you are safe.'

He then asked quietly, 'Does this mean that General Rashood will leave as well?'

It was clear from the expression on Nasir's face that the HAMAS leader was also going to fly out of Saudi Arabia. 'You both go as my brothers, and my comrades in arms,' he said. 'Your names will not be forgotten here, and you have my support and my help until the end of my days.

'Jacques, go in peace, and may Allah go with you.'

Thirty minutes later, a cacophony of noise split the night air around the Diplomatic Quarter as a Royal Saudi Navy helicopter, an Aerospatiale SA 365 Dauphin 2, came in low over the houses and put down on the wide lawn outside Colonel Gamoudi's bedroom.

Jacques almost had a heart attack at the sight of the French-built Dauphin, assuming briefly it was Gaston Savary's hit squad coming to finish him off.

But when he looked more closely he could see the insignia of the Saudi Navy, and he could see too the crown painted near the stern which signified it was for the use of the King.

And the loadmaster who came to the front door was immediately admitted, as if the guards had been forewarned of his arrival. Both he and Ravi Rashood travelled light, each with a single duffel bag, a machine pistol, four magazines of 50 rounds and their combat knives.

Suits, shirts and uniforms were left behind for another time. The Dauphin took off instantly the moment they were aboard, and eight minutes later it put down at the head of the runway at King Khalid International Airport, right next to a fully fuelled Boeing 737, its engines running.

They raced up the stairway into the big private jet. The doors were slammed, and then the dignified second officer came through to inquire 'Where to, sir', as if the Boeing was a taxi.

General Rashood's mind raced. He considered Damascus to be a bad option, not on a direct flight from Riyadh. Jordan was not far enough away, neither was Baghdad. Tel Aviv was too dangerous. And so was Cairo.

'Beirut,' he said. 'Beirut International Airport.'

'No problem, sir,' replied the co-pilot.

And three minutes later they were hurtling down the runway and climbing above the sea of light which was Riyadh.

★   ★   ★

Gaston Savary hardly left his office these days. Mostly he just sat and fretted, unshaven, praying for the phone to ring, praying it was someone with the news that Colonel Jacques Gamoudi had been eliminated.

So far he had been out of luck. And that night was no different. Major Raul Foy was on the line from Riyadh, imparting precisely the opposite of what he wanted to hear.

'Sir, I gained entry to the house at 10.30 tonight. I entered his bedroom only to discover he had already left and was not expected to return. The guards there know and trust me. I understand the King himself organised his escape and one of the guards told me he believed the Colonel had left Saudi Arabia.'

The name of the major's target was, naturally, never mentioned, but Gaston Savary did not need reminding of it. '*Merde,*' he breathed. 'Do we have any clue where he's gone?'

'None, sir. All we know is that one of the King's private jets took off from King Khalid Airport shortly before midnight, and that our man may have been aboard.'

Major Foy, treading the treacherous line between traitor and efficient undercover agent, added, helpfully, 'It's damned hard to trace the King's aircraft, sir. They never file a flight plan from his own airport, and of course no one has any idea where it's heading.'

'*Merde*,' said Gaston again. 'What now?'

'Sir, that Boeing can fly more than 2,400 miles. But General Rashood may also be on board. He was staying at the Colonel's house. I suggest we place agents in the Middle Eastern airports where we think he might be going. I'd say Jordan, certainly Damascus, where it's possible the General lives, Cairo, which is a hell of good place to hide. Maybe Djibouti, because that's where General Rashood came in before the attack. Certainly Tripoli, because Rashood could get help there, and possibly Beirut, which is often beyond the rule of law.'

'How about Baghdad, Kuwait or Tehran?' suggested Gaston Savary.

'Not Baghdad, because the General might have enemies there. But perhaps Tehran. He is, after all, originally from Iran. And Kuwait . . . I don't think so . . . it's too close. It's like going next door.'

Gaston Savary scribbled the names on a pad in front of him. He told Major Foy to stay in touch, and he prepared to put at least two DGSE agents into the airports where it was conceivable the Boeing might land. That would be his first call. The second would be to M. Pierre St Martin. Gaston Savary was not looking forward to that one.

0030, Friday 16 April
25,000 feet above the An Nafud Desert
General Rashood had regained his composure. Relaxing in the comfort of his regal surroundings, he pulled out his state-of-the-art cell phone and for

the first time for almost four months dialled his wife's number in Damascus.

Shakira answered immediately, despite the lateness of the hour, and was overjoyed to hear from her husband. The tremor in her voice told him that she had been at her wits' end, fearful because she had not heard from him for so long.

And was it safe now? Could someone be listening in?

'Since I'm calling from a passenger jet, about five miles above the desert, it's unlikely,' he said.

'Are you coming home?' she asked. 'Please say yes.'

But Ravi's answer was stern. 'Shakira, I want you to write this down . . . meet me tomorrow afternoon in the city of Byblos, that's less than 30 miles up the coast road from Beirut.

'To get there, you'll drive 60 miles along the main Damascus highway, straight over the Lebanon Mountains. It's a good road and you should allow four hours from home to Byblos.

'When you arrive, you'll see signposts for some Roman ruins right at the edge of the town. You get into them through an old crusader castle. I'll meet you in there, in the castle, at 3 p.m.

'Before you start, please go to the bank and get money. A minimum of US$50,000, $100,000 if you can. We've got $5 million on deposit in the Commercial Bank of Syria. I'm guessing you'll be out of the bank and on the road by 10.30 in the morning.

'And, Shakira – bring an AK-47; conceal it in the

compartment I had built into the Range Rover. There are a few checkpoints on the Damascus highway, but they won't be thorough. Use your Syrian passport, and bring your Israeli one. I have three of my own.

'Shakira, repeat exactly what I have just told you and then ring off . . . I'll see you tomorrow.'

'Are we in trouble, Ravi?'

'Not yet.'

'Well, my beloved. Wait for me.'

1700 (local), Thursday 15 April
National Security Agency, Fort Meade, Maryland
The eight-hour time difference meant it was still late on Thursday afternoon in Washington when Colonel Gamoudi's Boeing roared up into the midnight skies above Riyadh.

Within minutes, there had been a check call from the CIA's duty officer at King Khalid Airport, informing the Riyadh embassy that one of the King's private aircraft had taken off with just two, unknown, passengers. As always with the Saudi royal family's personal transports, its destination was unknown.

The embassy in Riyadh was very quickly off the mark and on the phone to the CIA's busy Middle East Desk in Langley, Virginia. They already knew a Navy helicopter, transmitting military radar, had landed in a well-guarded private residence near the Diplomatic Quarter just before midnight, and had taken off again immediately.

578

Inside the NSA, Lt. Commander Ramshawe already had a report from the CIA's man at the airport who had photographed the chopper with night lenses as it arrived at King Khalid, and he had seen the Boeing take off. The assumption in Riyadh, Langley and Fort Meade was that *Le Chasseur* had been airlifted out of Saudi Arabia and that he was now somewhere above the desert in the Boeing.

The Americans knew the French had already tried to assassinate him once; it was now obvious the King was taking steps to protect him, in return for the enormous service he had done the Kingdom.

The question was, where was he going? The CIA did, more or less, what the French DGSE had done: they posted men at the likely Middle Eastern airports, watching and waiting for King Nasir's Boeing to touch down.

There was, however, one major problem. Beirut was last on the Americans' list and their man did not arrive there until 4 a.m., by which time General Rashood and Colonel Gamoudi had been whisked away to the new Saudi Embassy in Beirut, orders of the King.

It took the CIA agent an hour to ascertain the Boeing had indeed landed, which left him with little to do except sit and watch until it took off again.

The French agents were, however, on time. And while they never got anywhere near the two passengers, they were able to follow the diplomatic car to the embassy, so that at least they knew where the fugitives were. Whether or not they would be lucky enough to get a shot at them was another matter.

Nonetheless, the French were plainly winning the race. And when a different, smaller vehicle pulled out of the embassy the following morning, with a chauffeur at the wheel and darkened rear windows, the four French agents now involved in the chase elected to tail it. All the way up the coast road to the ancient city of Byblos.

12.30 p.m. (local), Friday 16 April
Outskirts of Beirut

Shakira Rashood had been an active member of HAMAS since the age of twelve. She was rarely more than an arm's length from an AK-47 and she had served on combat operations since she was seventeen.

She and Ravi had fled the battle in the Palestine Road in Hebron in the hours after they first met four years before. He saved her life, then she saved his. Their subsequent marriage was conducted inside the deepest councils of HAMAS, of which General Ravi swiftly became the commander-in-chief.

They had thus met and married in the harshest of environments, a place without sentimentality, only a brutal desire for victory. But theirs was a love match, and the beautiful Palestinian Shakira, stuck now in traffic five miles outside Beirut, was beside herself with worry.

She sensed danger. Why did Ravi want so much money? Why had he been so reluctant to talk after all these weeks apart? Why had he told her to be sure to come armed, when he knew she never did anything otherwise?

Every inch of her sensed something terrible was unfolding. And again she leaned on the horn of the Range Rover in exasperation, like everyone else.

As always seemed to be the case, the hold-up had been caused by a young man driving at a lunatic speed, zigzagging in and out of traffic and then managing to hit a construction truck head-on. The young man was the only driver no longer in a position to care one way or another whether his car started or stopped.

But about 300 other drivers were, especially Shakira who was held up for 40 minutes; it seemed more like eternity. There might have been a better way around the city, but, if so, she had missed it. She headed north towards the coast, straight down the rue Damas, and swung right on to avenue Charles Hevlou, a wide thoroughfare which jammed solid after half a mile.

The clock ticked on. It was almost two o'clock. And again they were dealing with an accident. Much of Beirut was still a building site, while contractors attempted to rebuild the shattered city in the long aftermath of the civil war.

By the time the road had been cleared, Shakira Rashood had 28 miles to cover in 45 minutes. And eventually she was compelled to start driving like a native, speeding up the coast road, with the blue Mediterranean to her left and the endless coastal plain in front of her.

The Range Rover raced along in the traffic, often reaching 80 mph. The last miles were endless. She sped into Byblos from the east at 3.05 p.m. and followed the tourist signs to the Roman ruins.

It was raining when she reached the parking area, and right next to the entrance was a stationary Peugeot, with a hefty, tough-looking character just heading into the main door of the castle.

Shakira's sixth sense, the one that had kept her alive in tougher spots than this, locked in. One hundred yards from the man, she began to run, her feet pounding through the puddles, her breath coming in short angry bursts. Her AK-47 was tucked under her right arm beneath her raincoat, and could not be seen, but she was sobbing as she ran inside the castle. Beside herself with fear, she bolted into the dark passageway. Ravi, she knew, was in desperate danger.

3.07 p.m., second floor
Crusader castle, Byblos

Ravi and Jacques were cornered, flattened against the stone wall on either side of the door. Their three armed French Secret Service pursuers were gathered outside, and had already decided that the best way to get this over with was for two of them to come in firing. There was no escape and, whatever happened, there was two-man backup outside.

There were no windows in the room but there was evidence that there had once been one in the bricked-up stone frame, five feet above the ground

582

to the left of the doorway looking out. Jammed inside the frame, his feet rammed into the lower corners, was Jacques Gamoudi, in position, on higher ground than his attackers.

The two French hitmen came in together and Jacques shouted, 'This way.' The man on the right, coming in, turned, and Jacques shot him clean between the eyes. The second man, on Ravi's side of the doorway, also swung around to his right in response to the person who had shouted.

That was not smart. Ravi blew away the back of his head with a sustained burst from his machine pistol. And both of them slumped down on to the stone floor. On the steps leading up to the corridor Shakira heard the shots and was gripped by a cold terror she had never before experienced. She kept repeating Ravi's name over and over, as if it would somehow keep him safe.

The trouble was, Ravi's cover was blown. Whoever else was outside in the passage now knew that both he and Jacques were in there, one on either side of the doorway. Secret Service combat officers have a way of dealing with such matters, the use of grenades being just one of them.

The third man who waited outside did not have any. The fourth man coming along the corridor had three. And very calmly he passed one over to his colleague and began to loosen the firing pin.

At this point the near-hysterical Shakira came racing around the corner, tears streaming down her face, but now with her AK-47 raised to hip height.

Both men spun around at the same time. The man she had followed dropped one of the grenades, mercifully with the pin still tight, and swung his rifle straight towards her. Too late: Shakira Rashood opened fire, pouring hot lead into both men, to neck and head, just as General Rashood had taught her.

'If you've killed him . . . I swear to God . . . if you've killed him . . .' The words spilled from her mouth as she stumbled over the two bodies and carelessly rushed into the stone room where her husband was still flattened against the wall and Jacques Gamoudi was still jammed into the granite window frame.

'I told you not to be late,' said the general, in that modulated Harrow School accent. 'You could have got us all killed.' Which proved, in a sense, that you can take the officer out of the British Army . . . but you can't take the British Army out of the officer.

Shakira did not care what he said, so long as he was still breathing, and she rushed across the floor and hurled herself into his arms, allowing her rifle to drop with a clatter, repeating again and again, 'Thank God . . . thank God.'

Meanwhile, Jacques Gamoudi, who was still positioned halfway up the wall, cleared his throat theatrically and suggested they get out of there very fast, before someone charged them with four murders.

He jumped down from the ledge and led the way out into the corridor and down the stone stairway. The place was deserted but for two groups of tourists. Beirut and its environs had retained its dangerous reputation over the years, and that coastline was still not especially popular among visitors; the fear of kidnapping was still present.

God alone knew what the first group to go inside would think when they stumbled on the four French hitmen lying dead on the second floor, covered in blood and surrounded by hand grenades and rifles.

Ravi Rashood mentioned that he was not anticipating a unanimous vote of thanks from the local tourist board. Then he told the embassy driver to head straight for the airport.

He used his cell phone to call two of his aides in Damascus and instructed them to drive to Byblos to pick up the Range Rover and take it back to the house on Bab Touma Street. Then he called the Saudi pilot and told him to file an immediate flight plan to Marrakesh, refuel the King's Boeing and be ready to take off quickly, in about one hour's time.

They had travelled six fast miles south before the HAMAS general found time to introduce Jacques Gamoudi to his wife. But Jacques was only human; since catching sight of Shakira he had scarcely taken his eyes off the neck-snapping, walnut-eyed, gazelle-legged Palestinian beauty; and when he muttered 'Mon plaisir', he really meant it.

But the situation in Beirut was now menacing: the three of them sat in tense but companionable silence most of the way to the airport.

'Does anyone know why we're going to Morocco?' asked Shakira finally.

'It's been a difficult decision,' said her husband. 'Jacques is probably in more danger than we are, because he has the entire French Secret Service trying to kill him. You and I are in no more danger than usual.

'But Colonel Gamoudi has to get out of the Middle East, find somewhere he can lie low for a few months, get his breath back. And his instinct is to fly back to Morocco to his home up in the Atlas Mountains. It will be less easy to find him there. He and his father were both guides.'

'Are we going too?'

'Uh-huh. We're staying with Jacques until I know he's safe.'

'Is that why you wanted all this money – for air fares?'

'No. We've got a plane.'

'Will it hold three?'

'It'll hold 200, plus crew.'

Shakira shook her head. 'Well, that's okay then,' she said. 'I was able to get US$100,000 from the bank.'

'Shakira,' said Ravi. 'Apart from being late, I'd have to say you have excelled this morning, as a wife, a financier and a marksman.'

'Thank you, General,' said Shakira, laughing. 'It's been my pleasure to work with you.'

It was amazing how thoroughly this Palestinian beauty had absorbed that British sense of irony from her husband. It's not a natural way of thinking for an Arab. But Ravi thought it definitely suited her.

He leaned back in his seat, having cheated the Grim Reaper once more, and told her, 'In the last 24 hours, I can say I owe my life to the former Shakira Sabah, and Jacques reckons he owes his to E. M. Forster.'

'Who's Eeyem Forster?' demanded Shakira. 'I never even heard that name Eeyem before?'

'He's not Eeyem,' said Ravi carefully. 'He's E. M.,' he enunciated carefully. 'Letters, the initials of his Christian names.'

Shakira thought about that for a moment, smiled, and said, 'You mean like G. A. Nasser, or O. B. Laden?' knowing full well it sounded ridiculous. 'Anyway, you still haven't told me. Who is he?'

'He's a very famous English novelist. My school insisted we read a couple of his books for A levels.'

'What books did he write?'

'Well, I suppose his best-known one was *A Passage to India*.'

'I've seen the movie,' cried Shakira in triumph. '*Mrs Moore! . . . Mrs Moore! . . . Mrs Moore!*'

'So you have,' replied her husband, smiling. 'Forster had a very sensitive touch with subjects like loyalty, treatment of those less fortunate, and, I suppose most of all, about friendship.'

'Yes, but . . .' said Shakira, employing her most reliable form of questioning when she was starting to dig deeply into a subject. 'How did he save Jacques's life? Does he live in Saudi Arabia?'

'No, he's been dead for more than 40 years,' said Ravi. 'But his words inspired a colleague of Jacques's to treat their friendship more seriously than he treated a government order.'

'Was he ordered to kill you, Jacques?'

'Yes, Shakira. Yes, he was.'

'And he didn't because he remembered the words of Eeyem?'

'Yes, that's what he said,' replied Jacques.

'Hmmmmm,' said Shakira. 'You too have read his books?'

'No. I have never read them. But I think I will now.'

'Then I think you better get started,' said Shakira, gravely. 'This Eeyem, he's a very influential man.'

By this time they were within a couple of miles of Beirut International Airport, the traffic was terrible and General Rashood again called the pilot on his cell phone and told him to be ready.

The embassy driver turned in through the cargo area and made straight for the runway where private aircraft were parked alongside. The car pulled right up to the waiting Saudi Boeing 737 and the three of them hurried up the stairway.

The flight attendants, who had been hanging around all night in the aircraft, greeted them cheerfully. 'Marrakesh, non-stop?' one of them smiled.

'If you would,' replied General Rashood.

'It's almost 2,300 miles,' the attendant replied. 'And that'll take us almost five hours. But we pick up three hours on the time difference. We should be there around 7.30 in the evening.'

By now the aircraft was rolling, thundering down

the runway. The flight attendant, a young Arabian pilot in the making, hastily sat down and clipped on a safety belt; he took his pick of the 200 or so empty seats.

The Boeing screamed up into the blue skies above the eastern Mediterranean and set a westerly course. And as it did so, the CIA agent in the airport, the one who had arrived too late in the small hours of the morning, reached for his cell phone and hit the buttons to Beirut flight control.

He spoke to his airport contact. Twenty seconds later he knew the Saudi King's aircraft was heading to Marrakesh, with three passengers who had arrived in a Saudi Embassy car.

There was one difference between the two latest departures of the Boeing. At King Khalid International Airport, Riyadh, the captain had not been obliged to file a flight plan. Here, in Beirut, he was. And that put the Americans ahead of the game, because the six French agents in the Lebanon were temporarily stymied. Four of them were dead inside the crusader castle. The other two were still parked outside the Saudi Embassy.

The US field agent dialled Langley direct and reported that the King's Boeing had just taken off, heading directly to Marrakesh, no stops. Langley moved swiftly. They immediately contacted Lt. Commander Ramshawe and asked him for a degree of certainty on his report that Colonel Jack Gamoudi had been born in the tiny village of Asni.

Lt. Commander Ramshawe, who had spent days

searching through computerised French military data, had eventually filed away a copy of Jacques Gamoudi's birth certificate, courtesy of Andy Campese in Toulouse and a Foreign Legion filing clerk in Aubagne who had reacted positively to Campese's $500 bribe.

Jimmy Ramshawe pulled up the photocopy of Colonel Gamoudi's birth certificate, and read off: *born Asni, Morocco, 12 June 1964 . . . father Abdul Gamoudi, mountain guide . . .*

'Beautiful,' said the voice from Langley.

'You guys got a lead?' asked the lieutenant commander.

'Sure have. The Colonel's right now in a Boeing 737 owned by the King of Saudi Arabia, and he's heading for Marrakesh, non-stop.'

'My boss will want to alert the Navy about that . . . but, wait just a minute, I have some extra data on Asni which may help.'

Jimmy Ramshawe's fingers hit the computer keyboard like shafts of light, until Jacques Gamoudi's early military record came up . . . *he worked as a mountain guide with his father in the High Atlas range around his home village . . . he also worked in the local hotel . . . and . . . this is interesting . . . the owner of that hotel . . . a former major in the French Parachute Regiment named Laforge sponsored him in his application to join the Foreign Legion . . .*

'Hey, that's great, Lt. Commander.'

'Guess you guys think Jacques Gamoudi's going home, right?'

'We're thinking if the French Secret Service are

trying to kill him, the Atlas Mountains are not a bad place to take cover. Christ, you'd never find him up there, not in those high peaks where he knows the territory backwards, and where he probably still has friends.'

'That'd be a tough one,' replied Jimmy. 'But we're not trying to kill him, and we got two damn good leads in Asni – his father and his old boss at the hotel. If one of them's still there, we might be in good shape.'

He rang off and headed immediately to brief Admiral Morris, who listened to the latest twist in the saga of *Le Chasseur*. When Jimmy was through, Admiral Morris pulled up Morocco on a computerised wall map.

'Let me just get my bearings, Jimmy,' he said. 'Right, now here's Marrakesh . . . where the hell's Asni? Is it close?'

'Right here, sir.'

'Ah, yes. Right astride the old mountain road between Marrakesh and Agadir on the Atlantic coast . . . see this place here . . . where it says Toubkal . . . ? That's one of the highest mountains in Africa. Guess that's why Asni became a major mountaineering village. That's where Jacques Gamoudi's dad made his living.'

'So did Jacques, for a while.'

'Hell, those French killers have their work cut out. Can you imagine chasing a professional mountain guide through that range? You'd never find him.'

'You been there, sir?'

'I've been to Agadir. That's how I remember Mount Toubkal. A bunch of our guys had shore leave for a week and they were going to climb it. It's damned high, and extremely steep – something like 13,000 feet.'

'You didn't go yourself, sir?'

'Jimmy,' said George Morris. 'I might look kinda stupid. But I've never been crazy.'

Jimmy laughed. 'So what do we tell the Big Man?'

'We tell him both the CIA and the NSA consider *Le Chasseur* is going home to the Atlas Mountains, to hide out from the French assassins. And we tell him it's going to happen fast, and it looks like our best bet to grab him might be off the dock in Agadir.'

'We're assuming he wants to be grabbed.'

'Jimmy, we've rescued his wife and family. His money's safe in the USA. And the French are trying to kill him. He'll come, and he'll do as we ask. He has no choice. Because if we don't get him, the French will eventually take him out.'

'But how are we going to find him?' asked Jimmy.

'Why don't you call Admiral Morgan and see what he says?'

'Okay, sir. I'll do it right away.'

He marched back down to his office and got through on the direct line to the White House at a particularly bad time. Admiral Morgan was wrestling with a statement from the United Nations condemning the action of the United States of America in sinking at least two, maybe three and possibly four French ships.

The statement was withering, for the UN, which spent a certain amount of time each year expressing '*dismay*', a small amount of time being '*disappointed*' and considerable time finding things '*incomprehensible*'.

But, essentially, the UN did not *condemn*. As a word, it was too inflammatory, too likely to make a bad situation worse, and too difficult a word from which to retreat.

That day, however, the United Nations not only condemned, it issued a paralysing anti-American statement which read, '*The probable actions of the US Navy in the Strait of Hormuz represented bullying on a scale totally unacceptable to the rest of the world.*'

It added that the Security Council intended to summon the United States representatives to appear before the General Assembly, the main debating chamber of the UN. And there, every member state, all 191 of them, would be invited to cast a vote in favour of the severest censure the UN had issued in a quarter of a century.

'*There was no state of war existing between France and the United States,*' the statement said. '*Therefore the action of the US Navy must fall under the heading of, at best, a reckless and careless attack, or at worst, cold-blooded murder of innocent seamen.*'

Either way the UN could not condone the actions of the USA, and the General Assembly would also be asked to decide whether substantial damages, possibly a billion US dollars, ought now to be paid in reparations to the French Government.

When he read it, President Bedford shuddered at

the enormity of the ramifications. Not many US Presidents have been accused of 'murder' by the UN. And Paul Bedford was not much enjoying his place in that particular spotlight.

Since Admiral Morgan had masterminded the entire exercise, he asked him to come into the Oval Office. And that's exactly where they were when the phone rang and Lt. Commander Ramshawe came on the line from Fort Meade.

Arnold Morgan growled, 'We got him yet?'

'No, sir. But we're in better shape than we were yesterday. We know where he is, and we think we know where he's going.'

He outlined to the admiral the developments of the day, the new significance of Morocco, and then posed the question he had asked Admiral Morris.

'If we want to pick him up in Agadir, sir, how the hell do we find him?'

'Jimmy,' rasped the admiral, 'we got to get him a cell phone, one of those little bastards with a GPS system attached. That way we can hook him up with his wife on board the *Shiloh*, and he can show us where he is.

'Do the guys at Langley think the French are in hot pursuit?'

'They don't know whether Paris understands yet Gamoudi is on his way to Marrakesh. But I guess we'll find out soon enough.'

'Right. Meanwhile you better get Langley to deliver one of those phones to *Le Chasseur*.'

'How and where, sir?'

'If the CIA can't get a telephone to a guy who's trying his damnedest to get into the USA, they might as well close the place down,' snapped Arnold, slamming down the phone.

President Bedford was extremely relieved to see that his main man had not lost his nerve in the face of a frontal assault by the UN.

'This is very serious, Arnie,' he said.

'Serious!' growled Arnie. 'You think we ought to be nervous about some half-assed, know-nothing Security Council which contains among its 15 members the Philippines, Romania, Angola, Benin and Algeria? Jesus! These guys are not major league. They have trouble enough looking after themselves, never mind solving the problems of other countries.'

President Bedford had to agree.

'And I don't want you to lose your nerve, Mr President,' added Admiral Morgan. 'Remember what we know has happened. The French, in partnership with some kind of an oil-rich nutcase, have forced the world into its worst economic crisis since World War II.

'With reckless disregard for any other nation's plight, they cold-bloodedly smashed the Saudi oil industry with naval explosive, and then provided two supreme commanders to force the surrender of the Saudi armed forces, and then assaulted the royal government in Riyadh.

'Now half the world's without oil, and not everyone realises – yet – that the French did it, for some sleazy financial deal with this Nasir character . . .

'And *we* have to get the industrial world out of this. And if that means sinking a handful of French ships, that's the way it's gotta be. They're goddamned lucky we haven't sunk 'em all.'

'But, Arnie, what about this United Nations censure?'

'Sir, this is a momentous chain of events. It's something history will judge in the fullness of time. Ignore the short-term rantings of a few nitwits who only know about a tenth of the facts. Sit tight, don't crack, and we'll win this. Probably in the next week.'

'You mean if we can get this Colonel Gamoudi to testify at the General Assembly, for us?'

'Absolutely. And he will, because his own country has turned against him, he's been betrayed, and he only has one set of friends in the world. That's us. We've rescued his family, and his money, and we'll save him. And when we've done it, he'll sing – that guy will sing like Frank Sinatra.'

The President stared at him with doubt in his eyes.

'I'll tell you what,' Admiral Morgan continued, 'I'll just call Alan Dickson, we'll have a couple of cups of coffee, and we'll hear more. This is hotting up, and I'm darned sure we're out in front.'

1730 (local), Friday 16 April
Royal Navy Dockyard, Gibraltar
The eight-man US Navy SEAL team which had been airlifted from a joint exercise with 22 SAS in Hereford, England, arrived in a red-painted Royal

Navy Dauphin 2 helicopter in the great sprawling British base which stood guard at the gateway to the Mediterranean.

Moored alongside on the North Mole, the great breakwater which protected the strategically important harbour, was the 10,000-ton Ticonderoga Class cruiser the USS *Shiloh*, fresh from a 900-mile run down the Portuguese coast from the outer reaches of the Bay of Biscay.

Back in Norfolk, Virginia, Admiral Frank Doran had reasoned that, if they were going to haul *Le Chasseur* out of some Middle Eastern bolt hole, they would need a big US warship on hand to deal with the problems. The middle of the Mediterranean, somewhere east of the heel of Italy, seemed as good a place as any to set up shop.

However, the way things were now moving, there was a major change of direction. The *Shiloh*, complete with the Gamoudi family and the SEAL team, would leave the Med within two hours, heading 428 miles south down the Atlantic along the long sand-swept coast of Morocco. Latest orders, direct from the Pentagon, recommended the SEAL team go in and grab the French colonel sometime in the next three or four days.

Captain Tony Pickard had been ordered to make all speed from Gibraltar to an ops area 100 miles off the Moroccan port of Agadir. When SEAL Team Number Four, home base Little Creek, Virginia, was safely aboard, the USS *Shiloh* would cast her lines and leave immediately.

The SEAL's team leader was Lt. Commander Brad Taylor, the Virginia garrison's resident iron man, one of those SEALs who pinned the Trident on his pyjamas before he went to bed. A veteran of the Iraq war, thirty-one-year-old Brad Taylor was a graduate of the US Naval Academy, Annapolis, and leading classman in the SEALs' brutal indoctrination course BUD/S, known in the trade as The Grinder.

His father was a US naval captain from Seattle, Washington, and his mother a former actress who had spent much of her life wondering how she could possibly have given birth to this miniature King Kong.

Brad was 6 foot 2 inches tall, but with every stride he took he looked as if he were just out of the gym and on his way to a world heavyweight title fight. To complement that natural-born swagger, he had wide shoulders, massive forearms and wrists, and thighs like mature oaks. He seemed shorter, but he looked like a young John Wayne, with slightly floppy brown hair worn longer than the standard SEAL hard-trimmed buzz cut.

Brad Taylor had won collegiate swimming championships, over 100 yards, a half-mile and one mile. He had also won a US Navy cruiserweight boxing championship, flattening all three of his opponents in the quarter-final, semi-final and final. Only injury had prevented him playing free-safety for the cadets in the Army–Navy game.

Brad Taylor was one of those people born to

service in the US Navy, born to lead a combat SEAL team, born to carry out SPECWARCOM's orders, no matter how difficult. And today his orders were short and succinct, straight from the White House, via the Pentagon . . . *Get the French Army colonel Jacques Gamoudi out of Morocco.*

The US guided-missile warship cleared Gibraltar at 1930 (local) and made all speed through the Strait and into the Atlantic, turning south on a course which would keep her 100 miles off the Moroccan coast, steaming past Tangier, Rabat and Casablanca.

At 30 knots it took the *Shiloh* five and a half hours to cover the 165 miles to a position off the capital city of Rabat, which was where the first activity of the night took place. At midnight (local) one of the two boarded helicopters, the SH-60B Seahawk LAMPS III, took off into the night and headed directly into Rabat.

Clasped in the first officer's hand was a cardboard box containing the cell phone Admiral Morgan had ordered. It was satellite-programmed to connect with the comms room of the USS *Shiloh* from any point on the globe. It also had a built-in GPS system, operational via satellite, which would pinpoint its user's position accurate to 30 yards.

Furthermore, that position could be relayed to the *Shiloh* without even speaking. With the phone held in the open, one touch on one button would automatically inform the warship's ops room precisely where the caller was standing.

The LAMPS III took 25 minutes to reach the city.

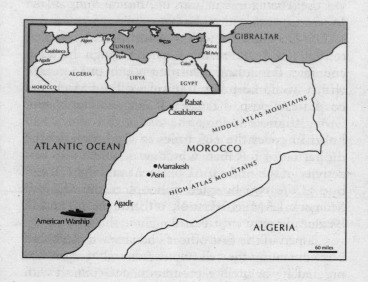

It made a long sweep to the north and, following the lights, came clattering up the river before banking right and putting down in the expansive grounds of the US Embassy on Marrakesh Avenue.

On the strict instructions of Admiral Morgan, the Moroccan authorities had been fully informed that a US military aircraft would make this night delivery to the embassy; it was the normal courtesy between countries. Right now Admiral Morgan had a golden chance to humiliate and embarrass the French and he did not wish the United States to put a foot wrong, diplomatically.

Which was the principal reason why he had insisted the rescue of the French colonel should be a clandestine grab by the SEALs, rather than a winch-out by a US Navy helicopter, operating illegally deep in Moroccan sovereign territory. As the admiral had stated: 'When you want to play the knight in shining armour, you don't walk around with a goddammed blackjack.'

And now, awaiting the helicopter, next to the flashing landing light on the embassy lawn, was the US Ambassador to Morocco, and one of the CIA's top North African field officers, Jack Mitchell, a native of Omaha, Nebraska, who kept a careful eye on Algiers and Tunisia from his Rabat base.

The helicopter never even opened its door. The cell phone was tossed out into the waiting hands of Agent Mitchell and the pilot took off instantly, not even bothering with his northern detour, just ripping fast above the city and out into the black skies above the Atlantic.

No one beyond the air crew, the ambassador and the CIA knew of this swift insertion. Which was precisely as planned. Because Morocco leaked. And Morocco had deep French connections. It was, after all, a French protectorate for half of the twentieth century, and, at this critical time, the Americans understood full well the French Secret Service were bound and determined to end the life of *Le Chasseur*.

Jack Mitchell, watching the departing Navy chopper climb away to the west, was now awaiting a flight of his own, due on the embassy lawn in twenty minutes. This would be a non-stop 145-mile flight to Marrakesh, where Jack, a divorced former Nebraska State Trooper, would pick up his Cherokee Jeep and head into the Atlas Mountains in search of either Abdul Gamoudi or the proprietor of the only hotel in the village.

So far, he knew that King Nasir's Boeing had landed at a crowded Menara Airport, four miles south-west of Marrakesh, just before 7 p.m. But the young CIA man there had not been able to see anyone disembark, and it was impossible to find a man who might or might not have been travelling alone, and who might have been in Arab or Western dress. Right now the CIA had no idea where Colonel Gamoudi was.

The only lead was Asni, the tiny mountain village of his birth and boyhood, which lay 30 miles south of the airport. There was a chance his family still lived there, and that Major Laforge still ran the hotel.

But the trail was very dead. Jack Mitchell's man at the airport had conducted an airport search as best he could, questioning, and tipping, the sales clerks at the car-hire desks. But nothing had been signed by any Gamoudi, or indeed, any Jacques Hooks.

For all Jack Mitchell knew, the colonel could have decided to hide out in Marrakesh, although he doubted that because of the strong French presence in the city. There was no doubt, Asni was the key. That's where Agent Mitchell would have headed if he had been on the run, and there was a lot on his mind as his helicopter took off from the embassy grounds. He was clutching the little super-cell phone which would be, ultimately, the lifeline of *Le Chasseur*, if Jack could deliver it.

Same Friday night 16 April
Marrakesh Airport
As soon as they disembarked from the Boeing, Ravi, Shakira and Jacques Gamoudi split up. They had no luggage except duffel bags, and they made for the Europcar desk in the arrivals hall.

Their car was in the Europcar parking lot. They threw their stuff into the boot of a small red Ford. It was 10 p.m. before they were ready to go, and Jacques took the wheel, heading south up the old mountain road to Asni, where he knew his father would be, even though they had not been in contact for several months.

Jacques had no intention of going into the village, where the French might be waiting. But he intended to contact his father by phone, and the old man would arrange for all three of them to get kitted out the next day with good mountain gear, for their journey into the still snow-covered peaks of his boyhood.

This was certainly the one place on earth where the odds favoured them against a determined military pursuer. All three fugitives knew the French Secret Service could not be far behind.

Jacques knew that he was putting Ravi and Shakira into considerable danger by allowing them to accompany him. He had argued the point with Ravi exhaustively the evening before. Ravi had ended the matter by placing his hands on his friend's shoulders and looking him straight in the eyes. 'Look,' Ravi had said, 'neither one of us got where we are today without being stubborn bastards. But you saved my life, as I saved yours, and it would be remiss of me to let you go off alone to face whatever the French are going to throw at you. But more than that, you are my friend, and I could not live with myself if I wasn't there when the time came.'

Gamoudi had conceded. He had come to trust Ravi and to think of him as more than a friend, as a brother. There was still one thing worrying him. 'I don't want to put Shakira at risk . . .'

Ravi had chuckled. 'Just try stopping her,' he had said. 'If she hasn't proven to you already that she can take care of herself, I don't think she ever will.'

As yet they had no knowledge of the intention of the Americans, and Jacques was still unaware that his family had been snatched in the main square of the Pyrenean town of Pau.

Jacques had decided they should head up into the mountains, call his father and then wait for the dawn. Banging on the door of his father's house in the small hours of the morning was out of the question. In a place like Asni, that would most certainly attract the attention of someone, somewhere, whose suspicion might be aroused.

As it happened, Jack Mitchell got there first. He slipped into the Moroccan tunic and hat he always kept in the back of his car and inquired at the local bar where he might find Abdul Gamoudi. It was only 50 yards away, and Jack tapped sharply on the front door.

The man who faced him was lean and tanned, a true Moroccan Berber of the mountains. He was in his mid-sixties and he was wearing jeans and no shirt. He confirmed readily that he was indeed the father of Jacques Gamoudi.

Jack explained rapidly that he was expecting the colonel either to arrive at the village within the next few hours, or, somehow, to make contact. Either way, the CIA man said, Jacques was in great danger.

Jacques's father nodded, almost as if such a scenario was not entirely a surprise to him. 'Ah, Jacques,' he said slowly, in French. '*Mon fou, mon fils fou.*' My crazy son. '*Malheureusement, vous êtes en retard.*' Unfortunately, you are late.

Abdul Gamoudi admitted Jacques had been in

contact during the past hour, but he was not coming to the house.

'*Est-ce qu'il vous téléphone encore?*' – Will he call you again? Jack Mitchell's French was passable, but certainly not fluent.

'*Bien sûr, demain.*' – Of course, tomorrow.

This was no time for idle chatter. Jack kept speaking in French and told Abdul there was a hit squad somewhere behind him, searching for Jacques, determined to assassinate him.

He told him the Americans had the Gamoudi family, and their money, safe. Jacques was to use this cell phone which would connect him direct to the US warship, where Giselle and the boys were waiting to speak to him.

The Americans would get Jacques out of Morocco, with the help of this cell phone. Jack Mitchell struggled through the French verbs, informing the old man about the phone's GPS, which would beam its position to the ship's communication room.

'*Les Américains sont les amis,* Abdul,' said Jack, with much gesticulation, trying to make it clear that everything would be fine if the colonel could reach them. He hoped his final, dark warning was understood by M. Gamoudi . . . *if the French find him first they will kill him.*

Abdul Gamoudi nodded gravely. '*Je comprend. Je lui donnerai le téléphone et votre message.*'

Jack Mitchell handed over the phone and hoped to hell old Abdul would remember everything.

In fact the French were some way behind. They

did not even discover the Saudi Boeing had left Beirut until after 10 p.m. when the local radio station announced that four dead bodies had been discovered in the crusader castle at Byblos. The two men still on duty outside the Saudi Embassy heard it and tried to contact Paris.

That took longer than usual, and it took four more hours to establish the Saudi Boeing had left, probably carrying the passenger who had fled Riyadh.

The flight control office was closed and it was not until seven o'clock on Friday morning that the French Secret Service established the Boeing had gone to Marrakesh, almost certainly with Colonel Jacques Gamoudi, a native Moroccan, on board.

Back in Paris, Gaston Savary was furious. He had felt 'out of the information loop' on this case ever since the operation had begun, as if he were always trying to catch up. But now in his military/policeman's mind, he knew a few things for certain:

1) His men had failed to eliminate Gamoudi in the car 'accident' in Riyadh. 2) His men had not been in time to catch him at his residence in Riyadh. 3) Having successfully tailed him to a city north of Beirut, all four of his agents had got themselves killed. 4) His men had failed to detain Mme Gamoudi in the town square of Pau. 5) His Beirut team had somehow failed to track the Boeing without a delay of almost 12 hours. 6) The CIA wanted Colonel Gamoudi as badly as he did. 7) M. Pierre St Martin was going to have a blue fit when he found out that, right now, no one knew where the hell Gamoudi was.

He picked up his phone and went through on the direct line to General Michel Jobert at the Special Forces headquarters in Taverny. It was the middle of the night, a fact not even noticed by either of the two men. General Jobert needed to move from his bedroom, and his sleeping wife, into his study next door. But that was the only delay, 20 seconds.

At which point Gaston Savary recounted the entire sorry tale of the failure of the French Secret Service to put the matter to rest.

'And now, Michel,' he said, 'we have this armed, highly dangerous military officer, loose in the High Atlas Mountains, in an area in which he grew up, giving him every territorial advantage, and I'm supposed to catch him.'

Gaston paused and then said, 'Michel, this is no longer a Secret Service operation. The President of France wants this man eliminated, and my organisation is not equipped to stage a manhunt in the mountains. This has suddenly become military, people can get killed: we need helicopters, gunships, search radar, maybe even rockets, if we are to catch him.

'Michel, I am proposing to hand the entire operation over to the 1st Marine Parachute Infantry Regiment . . . quite frankly, I hope you'll agree, but anyway I am proposing to recommend to M. St Martin that the Special Forces take over from here. You do, after all, have two helicopter squadrons under your permanent command . . .'

'Gaston,' said the general, 'I am in agreement with you. If they want Gamoudi killed, it will have to be Special Forces . . . I imagine that will also mean getting rid of the body . . . ?'

'Most certainly. They want Gamoudi to vanish off the face of the earth and to stay vanished.'

'Well, I have no doubt that can be arranged, Gaston,' said the general. 'What's our focus point for the operation?'

'Little village called Asni, 30 miles south of Marrakesh. It's way up in the Atlas Mountains, and that's where we think Gamoudi is, hiding out, until we tire of trying to track him down.'

'You know, Gaston, it's over 1,000 miles from Marseilles . . . we'll make the journey overland across Spain, with a refuel before we cross to North Africa. We have three of those long AS532 Cougar Mk 1s, ready to deploy instantly, they hold 25 commandoes each, and they're well armed — machine guns, cannons and rockets. Plus tons of surveillance. I can have them in Marrakesh tomorrow morning. Do I speak to St Martin, or do you?'

'I will, now. I'll tell him you're on the case. And I'll send detailed briefing papers by e-mail in ten.'

'Okay, Gaston. Let's go and silence this troublesome little bastard, once and for all.'

1100, Saturday 17 April
The High Atlas Mountains
Abdul Gamoudi had made an excellent delivery. His closest friend owned the main ski shop in the area, and he met his son at the foot of a high escarpment, 500 feet below the ice line. Jacques's father arrived

cross-country in a pickup truck full of equipment, boots, socks, climbing trousers, sweaters, weatherproof jackets, and, as requested by Jacques, none of it in bright modern colours, all of it in drab almost camouflage colouring.

There were sleeping bags, gloves, rucksack bergens, ice axes, crampons, hammers, nylon climbing ropes and a small primus stove to heat food and water.

Abdul had followed Jacques's instructions to bring everything three people would require to stay alive up there for a week. He had also brought the 'magic' cell phone.

Abandoning the hired Ford, Ravi, Shakira and Jacques climbed aboard the pickup. Ravi, sitting on the sleeping bags in the back, handed over $100 to Abdul, who now drove them even higher into the mountains to a point east of the ski centre village of Imlit.

This was their last stop-off. They unloaded the truck and gladly put on warmer clothes. They shared out the climbing equipment, while Abdul drove into Imlit to collect food and water. When he returned, they dumped their old clothes and bags into the pickup, and they made their farewells.

Abdul smiled and shook hands with Ravi and Shakira, and he hugged Jacques. Tears streamed down his tough, weatherbeaten face as he stood alone on the mountain and watched them trudge off to the north-east, uncertain whether he would ever see his only son again.

Jacques had selected a familiar but lonely route

which would swiftly bring them into a rugged stretch of hillside with deep escarpments and plenty of cover. After two miles they stopped, and Jacques sat on a low rock and fired up the cell phone.

He pressed the 'power' switch and then hit the single button which would relay him and his satellite position to the comms room in the USS *Shiloh*. He felt an instant tremor of excitement when the call went through immediately, and a voice responded, '*Comms.*'

However, Jacques's excitement hardly registered in comparison to the exhilaration on board the *Shiloh*.

We got him! 33.08N 08.06W. He's on the line. Captain – Comms . . . we got him right here . . . get Mrs Gamoudi . . . it's Colonel Gamoudi, and he's damn close.

The words '*We got him*' were repeated about 200 times in the next half-minute – comms to Captain Pickard, comms to the XO, Giselle, the ops room, navigation room, the SEAL boss Lt. Commander Brad Taylor. Sometimes you don't even need a telephone in a warship – everyone just finds out, from the engine room to the foredeck, from the galley to the missile director. It's a bush telegraph on the high seas, perfectly reliable and very fast.

Captain Pickard spoke carefully. 'Colonel Gamoudi, my ship is about 80 miles off the coast of Morocco, the port of Agadir. How far are you from the port?'

'I'm in the mountains, around 100 miles east of Agadir.'

'Are you in significant danger?'

'Negative right now. But the French Secret Service has made three attempts on my life, and I have reason to believe there will be others.'

'Are you alone?'

'No. Two friends.'

'Can you make Agadir?'

'I think so.'

'How long?'

'Maybe five days trekking.'

'Can you remain in communication?'

'Affirmative. Say every 12 hours?'

'From now. Let me connect you with your wife . . . but don't waste your battery.'

Jacques Gamoudi gave himself one minute on the line to his wife, who had recovered fully from being kidnapped in Pau and now wanted to know only that he was alive. There was no time for details, no time for explanations. Just the overpowering sense of relief that they were both safe, in his case temporarily perhaps, but for the moment safe.

The colonel shoved the phone into his pocket, climbed to his feet and led his little group up the steep slopes of what resembled a craggy, barren moonscape. It was now clear that Agadir was their destination, and Jacques selected a route which would take them off the beaten track, away from other trekkers and the mountain guides.

Over the next four hours, they climbed almost 1,800 feet in six miles. Here they took a rest and drank some water, and, very slowly, Jacques Gamoudi turned to

Ravi and said, 'You don't have to come any further with me. I can find my way to the seaport. You have both done enough.'

At this the HAMAS general grinned and said, 'If it hadn't been for you, old friend, I'd be in a grave in Marseilles. I'm not leaving you until we reach the dockyard. Besides, you never know when the French hitmen are going to arrive.'

'They'll never find me,' replied Jacques.

'Maybe not. But I'll bet they try. And they might get lucky.'

Down below them they could see other climbers and walkers on the regular trail, almost all of them with guides, and some of them with mules carrying the baggage.

'We just need to avoid being seen by any of them,' said Jacques. 'The country's steep and rough, but we must avoid the villages of Ouaneskra and Tacheddirt – that's where everyone is headed. We'll stop at a summer settlement called Azib Likempt. It won't be open yet but we'll find shelter in some old stone huts.'

They camped there for the freezing cold night, cooked some sausages and thanked God for the quality of the sleeping bags Abdul had purchased. By mid-morning on the Saturday they were up beyond the snow line, through the windy mountain pass at Tizi-Likempt and on their way to the flat pastures high above the Azib.

Right then, Ravi Rashood heard the first sound of a huge military helicopter, its massive rotor lashing noisily through the mountain air. The high peaks completely obscured the view, but the sound was so intense that General Rashood guessed there had to be more than one.

'Jesus,' he said. 'Jacques, we have to find cover. Which way?'

'That way,' snapped *Le Chasseur*, pointing south-west. '*Come on . . . run . . . run . . . run.*'

And, carrying their heavy burdens, all three of them set off down the escarpment, heading for a great rocky overhang, which they could dive behind. Jacques kept urging them forward, and they reached the rock just as two AS532 Cougar Mk 1s came rocketing around the high southern slope of the mountain.

The noise was ferocious, but the pilots were going slowly, making short low-level circles above the terrain, obviously in search mode.

'Holy shit,' said Ravi, looking up. 'Those fucking things have search radar, infrared heat-seeking, and Christ knows what.'

'I'm too cold to register,' volunteered Shakira.

'*Quick, get under there!*' yelled Jacques. 'And you, Ravi. They're headed straight towards us.'

All three of them dived for cover; Jacques Gamoudi was the last to follow. But it was immediately obvious that the helicopter surveillance crew had picked up something. They circled around at low speed, one after the other, flying back only 50 feet above the ground, above the enormous rock which sheltered the three fugitives.

Ravi, Shakira and Jacques flattened themselves into the ground, praying the helicopters would not land and begin a ground search. There was no doubt in Colonel Gamoudi's mind: the French could operate with impunity in Morocco, which was a privilege the United States did not have. *Great for Ravi, not so hot for me*, he thought.

The helicopters circled for a further 20 minutes before clattering off, dead slow, almost reluctantly, to the west. 'We have to get the hell out of here,' said Ravi. 'Didn't you get the feeling they thought they'd spotted something?'

'I did,' said the colonel. 'And in my view they've gone to get permission to stage a military search up here.'

'From the Morrocans?' asked Ravi.

'No. No. Just from their superiors. But they might want to touch base with the Moroccan military before they go ahead. It's a serious matter to start operations in a foreign country, especially if people are going to get shot.'

'You're not referring to us, are you, Jacques?' asked Shakira.

'I hope to hell I'm not.'

'Well, where do we go?' said Ravi.

'I know somewhere, two miles west. The country's pretty flat getting there, so we'll have to be fast across the ground.'

'How about those wild men in the helicopters come back and start searching?' said Shakira.

'That's what bothers me,' said the colonel. 'If we

stay here and they come back and land, we're dead. We have to run, and we have to run now, while the coast is relatively clear.'

'That's my view also,' said Ravi. 'Come on, let's go . . . Jacques, lead the way.'

Running fast with the big packs was out of the question. Shakira carried less weight and could manage a decent jog, but it was very tough for the two men, who kept going at a steady military pace which would not break any records but would probably have caused a person of normal fitness to drop dead.

They made the shelter of a big shadowy rock face to the north-west, and fought their way along a mountain trail which was really not much more than a ledge. All the way along the stones and dust beneath their feet shifted and crumbled. And all three of them tried not to look to the right, to the almost sheer drop of 2,000 feet to the floor of the valley.

The helicopters returned when they were at least a slow 200 yards from the destination Jacques Gamoudi had planned. Out of breath, and holding on to any foliage which occasionally sprung out of the face of the mountain, they were now inching their way forward, grabbing with their left hands, trying not to slide over the edge.

The mountain shielded them from direct sight of the pilots, unless they suddenly swerved westwards and began searching the granite wall of the escarpment, which they very well might, at any moment. The fact was, there was no cover, and the only hope was for the French pilots to continue searching the reasonable side of Mount Aksoul, rather than bother with the sheer rock face on the west side, just below the summit; the side upon which only a lunatic would venture.

The racket from the rotors was still echoing in the mountain air when the three of them reached a point where Jacques Gamoudi told them to unclip their packs and haul out the mountaineering gear.

He swiftly uncoiled the ropes, hammered in the securing crampons and made the lines fast. He then looped the harness expertly around Ravi's chest, clipped on the climbing ropes, handed over the gloves, and told him to assay over the edge, and down the rock face for exactly 47 feet and then swing into a cave.

'Who, me?' said Ravi. 'What if there isn't a cave?'

'There is,' replied Jacques. 'I've been in it dozens of times. Go now, feet first . . . and hang on tight to both lines.'

Ravi slithered over the edge, leaned back and began effectively to walk backwards down the sheer cliff face.

'You're secure up here . . . this'll hold you, even if you fall.'

'I'm not going to fall,' called back Ravi. 'I'm going straight into that bloody cave when I find it.'

Colonel Gamoudi smiled and watched for the piece of black sticky tape he had attached to the line to reach the edge. When it did so, he called, 'Right there, Ravi, right in front of you.'

'Gottit,' yelled the general. 'I'm in.'

'Great work,' called Jacques. 'Now, unclip and send the line back . . . okay, Shakira. You're next . . . and I want you to understand, I have the spare line attached to your belt, and it's playing out throught this fitting. You *CANNOT* fall. Even if the rope broke, which it wouldn't because you weigh less than a ton, you still could not fall.'

Shakira was terrified. She watched Gamoudi clip on the harness, then the lines. She pulled on the gloves and slithered backwards to the edge. However, the thought of leaning back was too much and she just kept scrabbling at the rock face with her feet, until she felt her husband's hands grab her and haul her into the cave. She was trembling like a songbird's heart.

Jacques checked the lines were set for the climb back and then he went over the edge himself, hot-roping it down in five long strides, landing dexterously on the front ridge of the cave.

'You've done that before, haven't you?' asked Ravi.

'Just a couple of times,' grinned his companion. 'I could do that when I was nine years old.'

Ten minutes later the first of the Cougars came rattling around the mountain, about 400 yards from where they sat at the back of the cave, 30 feet from the entrance. It was impossible for anyone to see into the cold gloom of the place, and the dark brown colour of the lines outside made their climbing equipment invisible. Even the crampons were black.

But Ravi feared the heat-seeking radar and they

flattened themselves against the floor of the cave as far back as possible. The lead helicopter came past twice more, and intermittently, throughout the afternoon, they could hear the search continuing.

Just before dusk both Cougars flew slowly across the west face of the mountain once more, and Ravi was relieved they did not fire a couple of rockets straight into the cave, as he himself would most certainly have done if he'd had the faintest inkling his quarry was inside.

But perhaps they didn't. And, as night fell, Jacques Gamoudi hammered one of the crampons into the hard rock of the wall and made the climbing rope fast. He clipped on, and with a bag of crampons attached to his belt, moved out on to the rock face, left of the entrance. Secured now by two ropes, he began the climb up, hammering in a stairway of steel crampons for Ravi and Shakira to follow him.

At the top he dropped the rope down for Shakira and called for her to clip it to the harness. He half-pulled, and Shakira half-climbed her way to the top, following the zigzagging line of crampons expertly smacked into the mountain by Jacques Gamoudi.

Ravi brought up the rear, faster than Shakira but not like a true mountaineer. In fact the HAMAS C-in-C looked mightily relieved to be standing on firm ground rather than in an eagle's nest, 2,000 feet above terra firma.

The next leg of the journey was a long four-day haul through the wildest lands, over the Ouimeksane

619

mountain range and down to the deep blue waters of the d'Ifni Lake. But they were now no longer being pursued, and the days passed easily. They hit the tiny village of Taliouine on the morning of 23 April and bought a hot meal of spiced lamb and rice in the only restaurant as well as the proprietor's car for a further 30,000 dirhams.

Three hours later, after a fast run down the P32 highway, they reached the outskirts of Agadir. It was now 3 p.m. and Jacques touched base with the *Shiloh*, suggesting they send in the boat to meet him on the dock in five hours, after dark.

The comms room informed him the phone would now be connected to that of the SEAL team leader, Lt. Commander Brad Taylor, a fluent French speaker, who was bringing in an eight-man squad for the getaway. 'Just keep hitting the GPS beam so we know exactly where you are, every few minutes after 1930.'

Colonel Gamoudi thanked the American communications officer and spoke briefly to Lt. Commander Taylor.

'Try to get down there and get your bearings before we arrive,' he was told. 'But don't risk anything.'

'I'm afraid I have no idea what the place looks like, and I have no chart or even a map,' replied the colonel. 'How about I touch base in three hours? I'll know more by then.'

'Perfect,' replied the SEAL boss. 'And remember, they've got a couple of Moroccan Navy warships at one end of the harbour. We'll be staying well away from them. Check out the other end, to the north. We'll talk in three.'

Out here on the edge of the town, Jacques could see no sign of his French pursuers, but that did not of course mean they weren't there. They filled up the car and parked it in a deserted, out-of-the-way square above the town. Then they all changed out of their mountain gear, wearing only the light under-trousers, sneakers and shirts.

It was much warmer on the coast and they strolled down to the port where they were shocked to see 20, perhaps 30 French commandoes standing around in small groups all along the docks.

They instantly turned back up the narrow, busy street, comforted by the knowledge that no one knew them, no one would recognise them and no one had any idea they were travelling as a group of three. Nonetheless, it might not be easy to make a break that night and board a boat in the harbour, even with the help of the fabled US Navy SEALs.

And so they waited, out on the edge of town. At 7.30 Colonel Gamoudi beamed up his GPS position, and told Lt. Commander Taylor he was about to walk down to the dock and would meet the SEALs, as agreed, on the south side of the north harbour, the one filled with 22 little blue fishing boats and surrounded by a rocky sea wall. Jacques had seen a tall yellow crane on the shore side and they would use that as a beacon.

'We're less than a half-mile offshore,' said the

lieutenant commander. 'We're gonna cut the engine and row in.'

'Copy,' said the colonel.

He walked on down towards the water with Ravi and Shakira. And out in the offshore waters, Brad Taylor, in company with four other SEALs, went over the side, complete with wet suits, Draeger breathing apparatus, flippers and sealed waterproof automatic rifles.

There were 400 yards left to swim and they headed straight for the crane, all five of them, staying 12 feet below the surface. Brad Taylor wanted an armed guard on that dock, and he was not going to get one by driving the big inflatable up to the jetty and tying up beneath the lights, in full view of anyone who might be watching.

They landed on the pitch-black beach, around the corner from the sea wall, and removed their flippers, clipping them to their belts. Each man kept his black rubber hood on, which was damned uncomfortable but at least rendered them all but invisible.

And they hovered in the darkness, taking up positions in the construction areas which seemed to surround the entire place. Brad checked the GPS. So far as he could see, Colonel Gamoudi was walking within 200 yards, straight towards him.

He hit the button of his phone and Jacques answered. 'How many of you?' asked Brad.

'Still three, my two friends,' replied Jacques.

Suddenly the SEAL boss could see them, walking

through a narrow shadowy gap between two buildings. And as he watched, an armed patrol of three uniformed men stepped from the shadows and challenged them.

'Shit,' muttered Brad and signalled for two of his team to follow him along the other side of the alleyway. He watched from the darkness as Jacques and his companions appeared to answer questions.

But he knew these soldiers were French and his orders were to take no chances. He hissed to his team to open fire. No mistakes. The chatter of the sub-machine guns was instant, and the three French commandoes went down like three sacks of laundry.

Lt. Commander Taylor burst out of his cover and crossed the rough ground. 'JACQUES!' he snapped, 'WHICH ONE?'

'Right here,' replied the colonel.

'LET'S GO, BUDDY!' And, with that, all four of them took off towards the water, leaving an astounded Ravi and Shakira gawping at the disappearing figures, three of them with scuba kit on their backs.

Out of sheer habit, General Rashood leaned down, picked up one of the rifles lying on the ground and then led Shakira back into the construction sites and towards the town. Their waiting car, up in the square above town, would take them back down the main highway to Marrakesh Airport. For them it was over.

It was not, however, over for Jacques Gamoudi. Two more French commandoes came racing along the dock following the sound of the gunfire. One of them kept going straight into the rough ground, towards his dead comrades. The other drew his pistol and came straight at the US SEALs. It was like charging a full-grown Bengal tiger, and they cut him down in his tracks.

The SEALs reached the edge of the sea wall. *'JUMP, JACQUES, JUMP!'* yelled Brad Taylor. And all six of them leapt over the side into the harbour, bobbing up in the middle of the front row of fishing boats. Jacques, gasping for air, was not as good a swimmer, but the other were born to it.

Behind one of the boats, they clipped on their flippers, and rifles, which were stowed in waterproof back holsters, and began to swim, kicking fast for the harbour mouth, each of them with one hand on Jacques Gamoudi. The colonel was lying motionless on his back, being dragged through the water faster than an Olympic 100-metre freestyler.

There were only 300 yards to go – 30 powerful kicks from the Navy SEALs. And at the end of that, Jacques Gamoudi was dragged aboard the 24-foot-long inflatable.

They kicked the twin Yamaha outboards into life and the boat surged to the west, making almost 40 knots across the calm water as the lights of Agadir began to fade behind them.

Brad took the cell phone off the dashboard and hit one button. And for the second time in a week there was a loud burst of applause in the comms room of the USS *Shiloh*, for the same three identical words . . . *We got him.*

EPILOGUE

11 a.m., Thursday 20 May
The United Nations
New York City

Colonel Jacques Gamoudi stood before the General Assembly in one of the most extraordinary sessions ever to take place inside the great round hall of delegates. He was surrounded by bullet-proof glass on all four sides and there were 74 different interpreters in the UN's operations room.

The glass was the idea of Admiral Arnold Morgan, as part of the round-the-clock protection of Gamoudi against the lawlessness of France, whose representatives were not present. The admiral had also framed the questions which would be directed to Colonel Gamoudi by the soft-spoken North African diplomat who now served as Secretary General.

The interrogation lasted for two hours, and, by the end of it, the international reputation of the Republic of France lay in shreds. Among the exchanges, which were heard around the world, were the following:

Q: And did you personally command that large assault force in Riyadh which overthrew the Saudi King?

A: Yes, sir, I did.

Q: And who hired you to do so?

A: The French Government, sir.

Q: And how much were you paid by the French Government?

A: $15 million, sir.

Q: And could you prove that beyond any doubt whatsoever?

A: I could.

Q: And who was responsible for the destruction of the Saudi oilfields and the loading docks?

A: The French Navy, sir. Two submarines, the Améthyste and the Perle. Frogmen and submerged-launch cruise missiles.

Q: And the destruction of the King Khalid Air Base?

A: French Special Forces, sir. Ferried in from Djibouti. Specialists. Trained in France, blew the aircraft to pieces.

Q: And could you name the French commanders?

A: Yes sir, if you wish.

Q: And why have you decided to speak as a witness against your country?

A: Because they have tried six times to assassinate me, after I carried out my orders, direct from the President, to the letter.

Q: And how were you saved from the assassins?

A: By the United States Navy, sir. I owe them my life.

Q: And do you know why they saved you?

A: Yes sir. In order that the world should know the truth of France's actions.

Q: And will you ever be returning to France.
A: No, sir.

At 3.25 that afternoon, on behalf of the General Assembly, the United Nations Secretary General apologised unconditionally to the President of the United States for the previous directive condemning the actions of the US in the Strait of Hormuz and the Red Sea. This was formally accepted by the US Ambassador to the UN.

The following morning, Admiral Morgan himself opened negotiations with King Nasir for the USA to take future charge of the Saudi oil industry. The Saudis would still receive the same money but the USA would be responsible for security and the marketing of the product worldwide.

Admiral Morgan was, in fact, surprised by the ease with which negotiations proceeded, the relaxed way the King cut the French right out of the equation, confirming, for the moment at least, that he wanted nothing more to do with the Republic of France.

Arnold Morgan privately considered that the King's attitude bordered on treachery towards his former partners in crime, in the overthrow of the free-spending former Saudi royal household.

But then, he had not been party to a conversation between the King and the French President, which unhappily ended thus:

'I am afraid, Mr President, your conduct towards a very close friend of mine is entirely unacceptable to me. As a Bedouin, I cannot condone such betrayal of a good and loyal soldier, and, I believe, a friend to us both.

'If it helps you, I should remind you I was a student of the works of E. M. Forster. I wrote my English Literature thesis on him at Harvard. That, perhaps, is all you need to know.'

But the French President did not know. And probably never would.

Two years later
Boise, Idaho
The two Royal Saudi Air Force Boeings touched down lightly, one after the other, on the runway at the little airport south of the state capital of Idaho. Here, in one of the great mountainous regions of the American Midwest, was the new home of Mr and Mrs Jack McCaffrey.

Jack and Giselle stood at the doorway to the tiny arrivals lounge awaiting their guest, who was, as usual, accompanied by an entourage of 47 family and staff members . . . kid's stuff compared with the retinue of 3,000 which had often travelled with his predecessor on the Saudi throne.

They'd filled the biggest of the local hotels, but the King himself insisted on staying at the McCaffreys' home for three days – *we fought a great battle together, I stay under your roof.*

And, if he did but know it, it was a pretty reasonable roof under which the King pitched his tent: a beautiful white-columned colonial-style building on the edge of the small city, with the snow-capped Sawtooth Mountains rising spectacularly to 6,000 feet to the east, and then, beyond, to 11,000 feet.

The family had come to Idaho with their two boys as soon as the United Nations hearings were concluded. Jack, in different, but soon to become beloved, mountains, had never been happier.

With his great fortune, he had bought the big house, and another large ski chalet over in Sun Valley, and set up a chain of ski shops and mountain guide centres – three so far – which immediately prospered.

The boys, now known as Andy and John, had settled swiftly into American schools, and Jack spent many cheerful hours with them and Giselle, exploring the great Idaho Peaks above the hundreds of cold blue lakes.

Jack and Giselle had found a special place in the south-west of the state where so many Basque immigrants had once arrived from the Pyrenees in search of cheap land to farm sheep on the mountainsides.

There was evidence of Basque culture everywhere in Idaho, in the food, restaurants and timeless stories handed down among the local farmers. You could even buy the famous spicy Basque *chorizo*, the sausage specially made by fourth-generation immigrants, in nearby Payette County.

The McCaffreys had found an earthly paradise among people of a distant but often shared culture. Even the towering mountains, in a certain light, looked much the same as the Pyrenees. They had agreed to change their names, not because they were scared of repercussions, from the French, where the new government had apologised unreservedly to Jacques, but because they wanted to start afresh.

And, suddenly, here was the King of Saudi Arabia, dressed in Western clothes but waving the distinctive greeting of the Bedouin as he walked down the aircraft steps. He wore the smile of a man whose oil economy had been rebuilt and was back on track, and he walked on to American soil with all the confidence of the political partner of the US President that he was.

A few local photographers took pictures but the King walked straight up to his former tank commander in Riyadh and hugged him. '*JACQUES,*' he exclaimed, beaming, '*COLONEL JACQUES GAMOUDI!*'

In his left hand the King carried a gift, a gilt-edged, leather-bound first edition of E. M. Forster's *Two Cheers for Democracy*. Inside he had inscribed the words: *For Le Chasseur, my friend . . . as salaam alaykum, upon you be peace, Nasir.*

AUTHOR'S NOTE

Because my principal publishers are in New York and London, I have chosen to work, essentially, in miles, yards and feet. In terms of weight I have stuck with pounds and tons, except where military and naval protocol requires something different in the area of missile warheads.

However, in instances where serving French naval officers and Special Forces are quoted directly, I use the correct metric measurements of their native language, the actual words they would have spoken.

Anyone mildly confused by all of this needs only to know a metre is roughly a yard – the Olympic metric mile, the 1,500 metres, is about 130 yards short of a proper mile. And a kilometre is roughly two-thirds of a mile.

I would also like to point out I had no wish to portray the French nation as cunning and unscrupulous. I was merely selecting an individual nation to suit the purposes of this fictional work, in the year 2010, five years into the future from the date of publication.

I could have chosen Great Britain, but they are too close and loyal to the United States. I suppose

I could have chosen Germany or Spain, or even Ireland. But none of them has quite the naval muscle and know-how of France.

I hope I have treated the French fairly and reasonably, despite casting them sometimes as heroes and sometimes as villains. It's one of the hazards of writing 'techno-thrillers' – the villains are all fictional, but I write on a pretty broad canvas and occasionally entire nations are scorched by the white-hot lance of my keyboard! No hard feelings (I hope).